ANNA FITZALAN

BY MARGUERITE STEEN

Novels
in chronological order

THE GILT CAGE
DUEL IN THE DARK
THE RELUCTANT MADONNA
THEY THAT GO DOWN
WHERE THE WIND BLOWS
UNICORN
THE WISE & THE FOOLISH VIRGINS
STALLION
SPIDER
MATADOR ⎫
THE TAVERN ⎬ Spanish Trilogy
THE ONE-EYED MOON ⎭
RETURN OF A HEROINE
THE MARRIAGE WILL NOT TAKE PLACE
WHO WOULD HAVE DAUGHTERS?
FAMILY TIES
THE SUN IS MY UNDOING
BELL TIMSON
TWILIGHT ON THE FLOODS
THE SWAN
JEHOVAH BLUES
ANNA FITZALAN

Short Stories

A KIND OF INSOLENCE

Biography

THE LOST ONE (Mrs. Perdita Robinson)
HUGH WALPOLE (critical and biographical study)
WILLIAM NICHOLSON

Belles lettres

GRANADA WINDOW

Plays

MATADOR (with Matheson Lang)
FRENCH FOR LOVE (with Derek Patmore)
etc., etc.

MARGUERITE STEEN

ANNA

FITZALAN

DOUBLEDAY & COMPANY, INC., GARDEN CITY, NEW YORK
1953

LIBRARY OF CONGRESS CATALOG CARD NUMBER 53-7986

For
NATALIE HAYS HAMMOND

Love is the child of illusion and the parent of disillusion; love is consolation in desolation; it is the sole medicine against death, for it is death's brother.

Unamuno, The Tragic Sense of Life

ANNA FITZALAN

CHAPTER I

*T*he railhead commanding the single track that stood for communications with the mining districts presented, in 1910, no inspiring appearance. The track itself—a rusty narrow-gauge affair laid down primarily for the conveyance of ore and mining plant—broke abruptly into nothing, like a child's abandoned railway, in the middle of a featureless space vaguely sprinkled with huts, jack crows, pigs, goats and sheep. There were also the carriers, whose principal occupation was to wait, doubled up on their haunches, in varying stages of catalepsy, for the arrival of the train. The train came, nominally, once a day, at an unspecified hour; actually, and for a variety of reasons, which might include the weather, damage to rolling stock or alcoholic aberration on the part of the driver, a couple of days might elapse before the line of trucks, pushed from behind by a small and decrepit engine, lurched squealing round the bend where, as a matter of course, two or three toppled over— to the never-failing amusement of the tee-tees and little boys summoned from the huts by the sound of the whistle.

But today no one cared about the train. A totally new sensation was provided by the presence of the stranger who, for the last couple of hours, had been sitting on the pile of baggage dropped by the boys at the foot of one of the straggling palms that had survived the construction of the railhead.

The spectacle of a young man in the Savile Row interpretation of tropical suiting was a novelty to the locals; faintly alarming to begin with, its fascination had grown on them to a degree embarrassing and, eventually, irritating to the object of their interest. He had started by grinning at the circle of black forms and faces that slowly thickened around him; not having a syllable of the language, he had no other means of showing goodwill. He pulled a few faces at the children, but this form of humour did not appear to register. At the end of half an hour he was bored, tired of the heat and the flies and the colourless yet burning sky; no one appeared to know when the train would be in. He pulled out his tobacco pouch and looked at its contents with misgiving; it would not do, to run out before he could get at his baggage. But the stink from the huts was intolerable, and smoking helped to keep the flies off. He refilled and lit his pipe, pulling angrily on the stem clamped between a set of singularly white and even teeth.

His teeth were an incident in Evan Crewe's good looks—of which, not being a fool, he was aware, and which were (he recognized it ironically) partly responsible for his present situation. To judge by the specimens that presented themselves now to his eye, he was not likely to be involved in woman trouble here. Slapping a horsefly off his chin, he felt the stubble thrusting its way through the soft, moist flesh. It was only an hour or two since he shaved. At this rate one would have to grow a beard—or scrape oneself raw three or four times a day. Supposing he were to return to Laura with a beard! The prospect jerked an involuntary laugh out of him —and one of the more venturesome children, who had edged up near his leg, let out a yell and scuttered squealing under its mother's cloth.

Not that there was the least question of returning to Laura. A guilty sense of relief added to Evan's discomfort as he smote another of the bloodsucking flies off his ear. He had been an idiot— but it isn't so easy, when you go up to the 'Varsity with a handsome allowance, with horses, a groom and everything calculated to enhance the prestige of a youth of twenty, already extravagantly endowed with personal gifts and charm, not to make a fool of yourself.

He had gone up in the Hilary term, and by the end of Michaelmas was embroiled with the young, discontented and indiscreet wife of a don, who, far from being the vague and complaisant character his wife had painted him, gave the pair of them enough rope to hang themselves and then communicated with Evan's uncle, who was also his guardian and, incidentally, had made Evan his heir.

There had already been enough trouble about the 'Varsity project. Everett Crewe had ironically requested to be informed what use an Arts degree was likely to be to the business, and Evan, with charming candour, announced that he had not the remotest intention of taking a degree, and had the impudence to add that, if it came to that, he would much rather go to Rome or Paris and study art.

"Don't get excited"—he anticipated, with a grin, his uncle's bellow—"There's nothing in painting; no money, I mean. I'm coming into the business; make no mistake about that!" The young, thin face, structurally handsome, keen as a knife, with a faintly mocking twist to the mouth, had some of the ruthlessness of the elder man's. "But it's a new century, Uncle Everett, and the pace is changing. Not only the pace, but the pattern. Society isn't going to be neatly boxed off, much longer, into separate compartments for aristocracy, and industry, and wholesale and retail——"

"And what, may one ask, have you to do with 'society'?" Everett spat the word out with the fine contempt of his class. "I suppose you want to make yourself into a swell!"

In no way discomposed, Evan nodded his head slowly.

"People like us are going to take the lead, and, to do that, we've got to be right 'inside': not only industrially and politically, but socially. We've got to know people—not just across a board-room table, but in their clubs and at home. That's the idea of going to

Cambridge. The fellows I meet there will be useful later on. A firm like ours has always got to be one jump ahead of the crowd—especially," ended Evan, "when the next war comes along."

"What are you talking about? We ain't armament makers; we're civil engineers—railways, wells and mines."

"All part of the future war picture," said Evan, with the coolness of youth.

"We're taking no part in mass murder," said Everett stubbornly.

"Doesn't that sound a bit like—pacificism?"

"There's no need to be a pacifist, to refuse to connive at the slaughter of human beings."

"But Lord Roberts says——"

" 'To prevent wars, prepare for war.' When you're my age you'll pay less attention to claptrap."

"The more prosperous a nation is, the more it invites attack from foreign powers," persisted Evan.

"When are you going to take your engineering exams?" roared his uncle.

"Any time you like," said Evan, with provocative calmness. "You know I've spent practically every minute of my holidays, so far, in the shops. In between the 'Varsity terms—well, I suppose you won't mind paying for me to have a coach? If I squander away the term in 'riotous living,' I'll expect to make up for it in the vacation!"

"You'll do that, all right," muttered Everett, and, partly from softness, partly because the lad's ideas might be right—young eyes see farther than old ones—gave in.

With threats of a divorce burning his evangelical ears, Everett Crewe descended on his nephew like an avalanche.

When Evan got over his fright (which was considerable; it was no joke to forfeit one's inheritance, and this, among other things, was threatened, in the flaming row that took place behind locked doors), he showed an obliging readiness to accept his uncle's disposal of his immediate future.

"You'll go out to Kwakwan! You'll find out what it means to be a mining engineer, with every mortal factor against you. You'll go out—not as a swell, with the name of Crewe behind you. You'll be a bottle washer for anybody that's got time to make use of you."

"For how long?" asked Evan, between his teeth.

"That depends. A year. Two—however long it takes to teach you a lesson."

Evan shrugged his shoulders.

"All right. It just seems—a frightful waste of time."

"That's your lookout!"

Dismay was oddly mixed with satisfaction: the satisfaction of departing prematurely in an aura of scandal and drama which increased his prestige in the wide and eclectic circle of friends he had already established. The one person he minded saying farewell to was Edward Fitzalan, who, in the casual way such things happen, had become his *fidus Achates*. Too proud to admit it, he had nevertheless learned from Edward the outlook and standards of a class with which, formerly, he had had no contact: a class that cared nothing about money, and laid all its emphasis on principle and breeding. Edward had maintained an aristocratic aloofness from the affair with Laura. . . .

As for Laura—he supposed it was caddish. But, brought up sharp —as he now was—it wasn't much fun, at the age of twenty-one, to be cited for divorce in connection with a woman a good deal older than oneself! Laura was pretty and charming, but she cried too much. Already he had learned to dread her tears. She was wonderful in bed. But he had had, for some time, the suspicion that it would be rather awful—to spend unlimited time with Laura.

ii

An ear-splitting whistle tore the heavy air, and, pushing himself to his feet, Evan was conscious, with relief, of the diversion of his companions and of the arrival of the train. A moment later, his heart sank. Down the line, rocking and lurching, appeared an obsolete little engine, a museum piece, belching a black cloud of smoke. As it came to a standstill, he went doubtfully towards it.

"Hallo. You're Crewe, aren't you?"

It had taken him several seconds to realize that the person addressing him, although black from head to foot, was a white man.

"Why, yes; I'm Evan Crewe. You're——?"

"Johnson. Your telegram only got through last night." Teeth gleamed murkily through a black mask.

"Last night? I sent it off from Sekondi, forty-eight hours ago!"

"Here's Sephton," grinned Johnson.

He found himself gripping another grimy hand. Sephton? Of course, the chief engineer at the Kwakwan mines. And Johnson was the manager; he was to live with Johnson, but Sephton was supposed to be his boss. Pretty nice of them, to come down and meet him; but, presumptively, that was due—to the nephew of Everett Crewe. The nephew of Everett Crewe—in a tussore suit tailored in Savile Row; in an expensive topee; dolled up as for a garden party at one of the Residencies! He felt his face burn. How did one live this sort of thing down? Everett could have warned him—and hadn't.

He wished he could see their faces, see what they were thinking; but both were black as niggers, their bare chests, beards and arms streaming with coal dust and oil. Johnson was a long, gangling type, and Sephton a stringy little man whose head barely reached Evan's shoulder.

"These your traps?"

He was obliged sheepishly to acknowledge ownership of the far too numerous and (despite local porterage) too immaculate collection of bags, cases and trunks at which they were staring. It was like turning up on the first day of term, a new boy, with all the wrong kit. Johnson, the more genial of the pair, was chuckling and wiping the grease off his hands and arms with a wad of cotton waste.

"They'll load 'em on the bunker while she cools down. Pretty near red-hot—ain't you, old gal?" He patted the side of the grotesque little engine, with the long, obsolete funnel, affectionately. "She's a great girl, though she ain't exactly a flyer. Victoria Regina!" Johnson pointed with a grin to the scroll on her belly. "She's a bit of a tomboy, is Vicky; you won't look so dandy, by the time she's done with you. Come on; let's get a drink."

Over lukewarm gin and lime, in one of the huts that turned out to be the local store, Johnson observed, with a wink at Sephton,

"Pity the ladies wasn't with us. They missed a treat!"

It seemed politic to ignore the jibe. Evan drained his glass before replying.

"Ladies? I didn't know—that's to say, I thought——"

"Nachrally, you wouldn't know you was arriving at the height of the season! I got my missis out for a couple o' months, and Seph's wife's coming up from Accra to keep her company. And there's Miss Armstrong—that's the missionary's sister. It's a shame," said Johnson, wagging his head, "you can't keep them fancy togs clean for a tea party. Now nobody's likely to get the benefit of them but Vicky."

Four hours of lurching and clonking along the perilous little track, his eyes filled with smoke and cinders and his clothes with the oil there was no means of avoiding in Vicky's narrow cabin, had at least preserved him from the ignominy of making his début on the Kwakwan scene like the juvenile lead in a musical comedy, thought Evan, as he climbed stiffly down upon a scene of desolation that went far to reduce his enthusiasm for the new adventure. He was as filthy as his companions; he blinked, through eyelids crusted with dirt, upon a clutter of corrugated iron that masked the entrances to the shallow mines, a squalor of native huts, a blind and scarred confusion of abandoned workings—for even in 1910 the Kwakwan gold workings had started to peter out, and a few years later were closed for want of labour and operative facilities. What was he supposed to learn—to gain—from all this? Not a thing, decided Evan, in that first glance. This is the old brute's notion of discipline.

A few miners crawled languidly after trucks half loaded with the precious ore. At the mouth of one of the shafts, a big man, nude to the waist, turned round to stare at the advancing three, but made no movement of acknowledgment or welcome. His flaccid breasts and belly were burned purple, a pair of bright blue eyes were ambushed in a tangle of beard and brows.

On the way up, Evan had learned a few things.

"Apart from Armstrong—that's the missionary—there's no resident whites, bar ourselves."

"And Cotter."

"Uh—Cotter."

It was a shock—having been introduced—to take the big, soft hand, and to hear, in a high-piping voice at odds with its owner's appearance——

"Dr. Livingston, I presume?" followed by a titter.

Yet, in these mephitic surroundings, which Evan had already sensed—and also the antagonism of Johnson and Sephton to the man introduced as Cotter—the bright blue eyes and ironic grin offered something that relieved the depression which had descended upon him with his first glimpse of the scene to which he was committed for at least twelve months. Everett—that old fox!—was having his revenge. This much was apparent during the first hour of his introduction into the Johnson household.

iii

"The girls'll be glad to see a visitor. Not met 'em, have you? Maggie's had a go of fever and Jo's been nursing her."

("The Cotter 'girls'?" The acidulated cockney accents of Mrs. Johnson revived in Evan's memory. "You don't want to have anything to do with *them*! Daughters of our local drunk—oh, well, you've met Cotter. Came out as undermanager donkeys' years ago and got the sack. Wouldn't go home—or couldn't. Remittance man. Even the Armstrongs don't have much to do with him! And the girls don't mix. They say Josephine's a bit dotty.")

"Ought to send them home," Cotter was saying, in his absurd, high-piping voice. "But it's damned expensive. Nuisance having 'em here. A man gets on better by himself——"

Evan murmured something about housekeeping, and Cotter made a rude noise.

"Give me blacks; less fuss and more comfort."

He could be right, thought Evan, at his first meeting with Cotter's daughters.

"My name is Josephine." The elder of the two women stuck her hand out stiffly. "And this is my sister Margaret."

They shook hands: Josephine reluctantly, immediately snatching her own away; Margaret, with a schoolgirl's wriggle, allowing a soft, plump palm to linger in that of the embarrassed young man to whom they had been introduced as "Jo" and "Maggie."

Cotter chuckled, rubbed his unshaven jaw, hitched the belt over his hanging belly and winked at the guest.

"Get him a drink, Joey." Then he left them, swearing and stumbling his way round the rotten porch.

Face to face with the Cotter "girls," Evan found it impossible to guess their ages. Their yoked blouses, trimmed with tattered flounces, and shapeless skirts pulled into belts of tarnished metal, successfully disguised such charms as each might have possessed. Their dried-up hair, puffed out by combs which might once have been studded with brilliants, clumsily framed faces superficially alike: dark-eyed and sallow-skinned. He would have suspected colour, but even the vicious tongues of local gossip had no worse to say of the late Mrs. Cotter than that she was a Lancashire girl who made a runaway marriage and put herself outside decent society by "going native": probably from despair at her husband's misdemeanours.

Miss Josephine's face was long and bony, Miss Margaret's oval, soft and, in comparison with her sister's, without character. He found it so uncomfortable to look at their faces that he dropped his eyes to their hands.

Margaret's were short-fingered, rather pretty in a dimpled fashion, sensual and impractical; they lay flaccidly in her lap, like a forgotten pair of gloves. Josephine's were posed on her knee; the raised wrists shot out the fingers in a graceless posture, as though to call attention to their ugliness. Eccentrics of all kinds, repressed natures, characters that took violently to cults, or religions, or polemics, had hands like that.

If not ladies within the strict sense of the term, they were women of some refinement; Miss Josephine, of the two, showed the haughtier consciousness of it. There was a faint commonness in Margaret's accent, in the coy tilt of her head and her little, coquettish movements. Josephine's scowl of admonition, when Margaret giggled, or pointed her toe, or twitched up the hem of her skirt to display an ankle, suggested, not only that she regarded herself as her sister's keeper, but a fierce, almost savage devotion to the younger woman that suffered vicariously from a stranger's criticism.

"Josey hasn't given you a drink? That's her, all over!" Cotter had returned, a bottle under each arm. "Now, you two! Get chop. I'm going to show Evan my pictures."

A purple flush suffused the dark face of Josephine. She rose with dignity. In proportion to the length of her head, her body was short, the shortness emphasized by the tightness of her belting. She had no breasts. But she carried herself like a queen.

"Come, Margaret."

"I'm going to stay. Tell Tin-Lid or one of the other boys to fetch in dinner!" Margaret tossed her head and flirted her lashes at Evan, who looked hurriedly aside. "Did you know Papa was an artist, Mr. Crewe? I'm sure you didn't. Well, he's always daubing away, and he never shows us his pictures. So now I'm going to make the most of my opportunity!—Oh!" Her coquettish defiance ended in a small shriek, as Cotter bellowed at her. She skipped hurriedly after her sister.

Cotter swung the gin with a practised movement into a couple of tumblers.

"Nothin' like a drink, for encouraging appreciation of the arts!" He sniggered, and lifted some boards away from the walls. It occurred to Evan that, if his daughters were interested in Cotter's paintings, there was nothing to prevent their indulging their tastes.

The works themselves were sufficient explanation of Miss Josephine's burning blush; no question of her not having seen them! A nude of the D.C.'s lady did full justice to the fertility of a grisly imagination—as did the study of Miss Armstrong in the embrace of a baboon: which suggested no reluctance on the part of the lady.

"I say, they're infernally clever!" He wondered guiltily whether the honk of laughter he had been unable to repress had reached the ears of Miss Josephine. "Where do you get your paints?"

"Lembarene. Lebanquier gets them for me, from Paris. I studied at Julien's," said Cotter casually.

"Did you, by Jove." So this was the thing that did not fit into the local picture of the drunken ex-undermanager, hanging on to whatever supplied him with his chief necessity for living. This was the moment—Evan recognized it later—when his vision of the whole Cotter setup altered its focus; when the dangerous driftover to the Cotter "side" began.

He had his first passage of arms on the following day, with Mrs. Sephton. Sephton, after a spell in hospital at Accra, had married his nurse. Of the three women—Miss Armstrong, Mrs. Johnson and Mrs. Sephton—he had met, up to the time of his introduction to the Cotters, Evan disliked her the most, notwithstanding the fact that she had been particularly—not to say embarrassingly—agreeable to him.

"That hard-faced old camel!" she said of Josephine: drawing, in an unguarded moment, an expostulation from Evan.

. "I don't know why you're all so down on the Miss Cotters. They have a pretty rotten time, and it isn't their fault that their father doesn't happen to measure up to standard."

She let out a shriek of laughter. She was a buxom, high-coloured woman with a fine figure, of which she took care her companion should be conscious.

"It's easy to see they've been getting on your soft side!"

"I don't know any more of them than you do!" He felt like hitting her. "But, considering they're white and a pair of decent women, I don't understand——"

"Decent. Decent!" She repeated it like a parrot, letting her breasts and her hips shake with her peals of ironic mirth. "Excuse me!—but you're a simple specimen, aren't you?"

At twenty-one, with an illicit love affair behind one, to be called "a simple specimen" is the final insult. Evan swung on his heel. At the next moment, she had hold of his arm, was pressing her bosom against it.

"Mad with me, aren't you? Never mind; I know. It's lonely up here, isn't it? You'll have to take a trip to Accra, one of these days. We'll find you something better than Jo Cotter down there!"

Revolted by the touch and smell of her, he tried vainly to break away.

"Listen, little boy; don't talk baby talk about 'decent women.' You'll only get yourself laughed at. As if any decent woman would stop on here, year after year, the way those two have done since their mother died—sleeping in that shack, and Cotter having his nigger women in the next room! Like me to tell you something? They say it doesn't stop at niggers. They say Jo Cotter's taken her mother's place in more ways than one——"

iv

He saw, in the brief twilight, the gaunt figure of Miss Josephine bearing down on him. She barely acknowledged his greeting.

"I must find some way of getting my sister back to England."

"Does she want to go?" asked Evan surprisedly.

"That is the difficulty." Her air of stiff yet helpless perplexity touched him.

"Of course, if she's unwilling, it creates a problem." He felt ashamed of minding that people were looking at them; that the news would have reached the Johnsons before he got in.

"I think you might help—by influencing her."

"But—it's no business of mine, is it?" He was youthfully aghast.

"You mean, you don't wish to accept responsibility. Why," she said bitterly, "should you? Who, in these days, is his brother's keeper?"

"That wasn't what I meant——"

"Do you really believe we live to ourselves?—that no human being owes anything to another? Yes, I see you do," she concluded with scorn. For some reason, her anger did not rouse him to antagonism. He said, after a pause,

"What's brought you to this conclusion about Miss Margaret—after so long a time?"

"Various things. You've seen how we live," she muttered. "Everybody knows what goes on in our house. It doesn't matter to me, but Margaret's five years younger than I, and there must be a life for her—somewhere!" She threw it out as a challenge. "All she needs is to get away. We have relatives in Lancashire; they're childless, and the last of my mother's family. They'd treat Margaret as a daughter——"

"Have you contacted them?"

"Yes. It was a long while before they wrote, and I wondered if they were dead, but they'd moved to another address, and it took time for the letter to reach them."

"And what does Miss Margaret say?"

"She refuses to go, absolutely. She is very childish, in some ways," said Josephine. "I think she's afraid of the kind of life she would be obliged to live, with strangers. I've done my best," she said pitifully, "to bring her up according to the little we know about conventional living! I was born in Manchester, and I just remember Paris; then we came out here. We had a couple of years in England when Margaret was about six, and I went to school. Later on, I had some lessons at the mission, but Margaret wouldn't go, so I taught her as much as I could at home." He was conscious of vast lacunae in the record. "She's unused, of course, to any kind of routine; time, to her"—she gave a wintry smile—"is the rising and setting of the sun. It's reasonable, isn't it, that she should shrink from a life governed by factors which, up to now, have played no part in her existence?"

"You wouldn't go with her?"

"How," said Josephine with simplicity, "can I leave my father?"

It was the first time he had come face to face with the sacrificial spirit in its purest, least adulterated form. Somewhat surprisingly, for a youth of his age and upbringing, he recognized it. Although he had much, thereafter, to forgive Josephine Cotter, his judgment, to the end, was affected by that moment of revelation. He muttered,

"What do you expect me to do?"

For the only time, he saw beauty in the long, sallow face: in the mouth which squared itself from its habitual, hypochondriacal droop into a smile of penetrating sweetness.

"Expect, Mr. Crewe? Nothing! Yet—there is such a thing as humanity. And, if anyone could help to change my sister's mind, I think it might be you."

"Wouldn't she be more likely to think I had a—a great cheek, for intruding on her affairs?" he stammered.

"Try her," urged Josephine.

He felt himself shrinking from the compulsion of her eyes—small, short-lashed, shaped like almonds, empty of all but a formidable will. But he was at the age when romanticism lays easy hands on a man; when pity lights the heroic which, in its turn, is fed by female admiration. Josephine Cotter was an eccentric, and possibly crazy, old maid, but he could not help respecting her effort to maintain a personal dignity for herself and her sister, in despite of the scandal surrounding their father's name. Respect craves its return, in kind.

Margaret confided to him that she was twenty-five—four years older than he—and he was sufficiently sophisticated to suspect she had subtracted from her age. She looked fully as old as Laura—who admitted to twenty-eight. Actually, he found her childish; but she was sweet and gentle, appeared to like him and showed evident interest when he painted for her the pleasures and advantages of living in England.

She was either better-looking than she had originally appeared, or he had grown used to her appearance. She had masses of thick, charcoal-coloured hair, and her skin, though sallow, had a soft, moist, delicate texture, like a tropical flower. As she grew used to his company, she shed the small affectations that jarred on him, to begin with. Sweet-tempered, if brainless, she showed herself responsive to all the efforts he made to please her.

He brought over a set of dominoes, and taught her and Josephine to play; and some old copies of the *Play Pictorial*, whose photographs and letterpress were of less interest to her, who had never been inside a theatre, than the illustrated advertisements of hair tonics and the new "Directoire" corset. "Is that the shape women are supposed to be nowadays? How very odd we must look!" And Rowland's Kalydor. "Would it take off our sunburn? I go nearly black in the dry season!"

He borrowed—without permission—the Johnsons' Pathéphone, and the voices of Florrie Ford and Hayden Coffin rolled out into the bush, scaring the houseboys and drawing crawling things from the thatch overhead. He knew the Johnsons and the Sephtons were highly resentful of the hours he spent at the Cotters' bungalow, and cared nothing about it, for he was young enough to take a malicious pleasure in shocking the bourgeoisie and vain enough to be flattered by the appeal to his "influence" over Margaret.

The first time he doubted the latter's innocence was on an afternoon when, Josephine being briefly absent from the room, Margaret flung herself suddenly against him and set her teeth into his lip.

Up to that moment, he had never been aware of her, physically. To put it in the lowest level—the snobism of a youth who had already proved himself would have rejected a woman like Margaret Cotter. But, young, quick and starved, his response was automatic. Even in returning the kiss, distaste overcame him; he flung her angrily away and fled. Stumbling back to the Johnson hut, he tried to pin her down, in his mind, to his original impression of a rather grotesque, young-old maid; but the brief contact of her flesh with his had touched off a spark he recognized as dangerous. If he had to get caught again, it should not be in this ludicrous way!

To return without Everett's sanction was asking for trouble; he was sufficiently in disgrace to make no claims on his uncle's solicitude. And if Everett caught so much as a breath of this present entanglement—well!

During the weeks that followed, Evan spent considerable time in drafting a letter to his uncle, that should impress on the latter his anxiety to get back to work; the unprofitableness of his present occupation—the plant was obsolete: apart from a few trivial technicalities, there was nothing to learn from the setup at Kwakwan; his earnest desire to get on with the career which—owing to the caprice of an implacable old man—was at a standstill. It was painful to eat humble pie, and sheer agony to set contrition down on paper, to be filed among the records at Head Office! But the only thing that mattered was escape: escape from the death thought that lay on the workings, and was reflected in the languor of executive and labourers—and from the peril of Margaret Cotter. He posted it at last and hoped for the best. That was the day he came face to face with Cotter, who had been absent, on one of his periodical jags. Cotter's face was broken up, his eyes muddled—but not so much as not to direct a glance of fuddled resentment at Evan.

"You not been to see the girls lately."

"No—I've been doing a lot of clerking for Johnson," stammered Evan.

"The girls—been pretty nice to you. Josey"—he belched—"don't take a fancy to many fellows."

Evan mumbled some apology, which appeared to soften his companion. Cotter's unsteady hand fastened on his sleeve.

"Don't feel like taking her off my hands, do you, ole boy?" He brushed aside Evan's involuntary gasp with a gesture of tipsy understanding. "Nachrally not. She's a bit long in the tooth—poor ole Jo. Bad luck—ain't it?—being stuck in hole—like this—with—couple ole virgins!"

Evan's effort to escape was thwarted by a more ruthless grip on his arm.

"They are virgins, ole boy"—Cotter was deadly serious—"on my word 'v honour!—Jo by inclination and Maggie because Jo never give her the chance; she'd disembowel anybody that laid a finger on Maggie. She'd kind of adopted Maggie as her baby; never lets her out of her sight. . . ."

Evan, who could have supplied at least one occasion when Margaret was out of Josephine's sight, cut short the conversation. For the first time, he wondered if he had been impossibly naïf; whether Josephine's leaving them alone, and Margaret's assault, were part of some deep-laid plot—possibly involving Cotter himself—to compromise him. Disgusted by the suspicion—as dishonouring to Josephine's probity as to the simplicity of the younger woman—he thrust it aside.

v

The Johnsons had taken a dislike to him. He could find no reason for it, excepting the state of nervous tension that arises from the sharing, by uncongenial individuals, of close quarters. Johnson, to whom Evan had imparted, in confidence, his intention of returning as soon as possible to England, received the information sulkily: why, Evan could not imagine. It should have been a relief. Through the thin wall of the hut he received enlightenment, in the embittered accents of Mrs. Johnson: "I suppose we aren't class enough!" He heard her titter. "Or p'raps he'd be more at home with Maggie Cotter!"

This hardened his resolution to have nothing further to do with the Cotters. It was unpleasant, to show discourtesy to people who had been nothing but kind to him, but any continuation of friendliness on his part could only increase the viciousness of the other women towards them. Meanwhile, he was conscious of his growing unpopularity, not only with Cotter and the Johnsons, but with the Sephtons. Mrs. Sephton could lose no opportunity to jibe at him—in front of the Johnsons and whoever, white or coloured, happened to be there; if she happened to get him alone, her derision took on a more personal note, reflecting—by no means obscurely—on his manhood. Evan was no fool; he knew how he could have shut her jeering lips, for good. Instead, he allowed her to see his contempt and, in doing so, added fuel to her hatred. He was surprised to come on her, one day, in conversation with Josephine Cotter. The two women turned their backs—Josephine with slow dignity, Mrs. Sephton flouncingly. He would have liked to apologize to Josephine.

Waiting for Everett's reply to his letter, the days seemed endless. The heat, the squalor, the want of useful occupation played havoc with human nature. There was literally nothing to do, save brood over textbooks he already knew by heart, make drawings there were no means of translating into models and—common recourse of the exile—drink. He had given up sharing the living room with the Johnsons; made aware that, although tolerated, he was not welcome, he withdrew to his camp bed and oil lamp, which he shared with the million buzzing, hissing inhabitants of West African night; he sweated his soul out under a roof of corrugated tin; he stupefied himself with quinine and managed to hold fever at bay. Sephton went sick, and Evan dragged himself down to the mines, for a perfunctory examination of plant that was fit only for the scrap heap; to the railhead, to make sure the new stretch of track offered no more menace to human survival than the old one had done, and staggered back to his bed. It was like living in a dull nightmare.

At the end of a month, he could endure it no longer. The Johnsons were out—at any rate, the living room was empty—when he dragged himself out on the porch. There was no moon, but the light of the immense stars blotted out the squalor of the scene.

The Cotter bungalow was rather more than a mile away, close to the old workings which, in common with most local ventures in mining, had run out and been abandoned years ago. Reclaimed by the bush, it was a risky trail to follow—especially in the wet season, when a false step might plunge one into twenty feet of water and vegetation, in which it was impossible to swim and equally impossible to find support for one's trammelled limbs. But in dry weather the water holes were shallow and there was no danger beyond a ricked ankle, a possible sousing—and Josephine Cotter's frozen astonishment.

He could not stand this morbid isolation any longer; the jar of the Pathéphone, Mrs. Johnson's endless gossip of a Liverpool suburb, Johnson's growling of the evening prayers—in which Evan had found, to his embarrassment, he was expected to take part—and the endless, malicious small talk that went on when the women were together. Better risk Josephine's snubbing and Margaret's recriminations than this! He turned back, to pour himself another drink, and stumbled from the porch onto the trodden earth.

He turned sharply, thinking he had heard a whisper, but there was no movement in the shadowless night. The blotches of black that the moon would have cast were resolved in an all-pervasive indistinctness. One of the boys, he thought, under the porch with a woman. Stumbling through half-grown bush, repeatedly tearing himself free from tie-tie—he came at last within sight of the hut that had housed the Cotters—according to local history—for twenty years: dropping to pieces, patched up from time to time with bits of other huts that had fallen into dereliction around it, and overgrown by the greedy vegetation that swarmed indifferently over wood, metal and water.

"Hallo. Anybody in?"

There was no light in the main room. Early though it was, thought Evan, the girls might be in bed and Cotter out on one of his sprees. He hesitated before shouting again, but, almost before the echo of his voice died on the starlight, he heard his name called faintly.

An inner screen was pushed aside and an oil lamp sent its hazy bar of yellow across the threshold where he stood. He saw, incredulously, Margaret, in a cotton wrapper, her hair streaming on her shoulders. The lamp in her hand revealed her open mouth, her frightened eyes.

"Oh, mercy—how you scared me!"

"I'm terribly sorry," he muttered. The spectacle of Margaret, so evidently undressed, just risen from her bed, sent a shaft of warning into his brain. His immediate instinct was to bolt, and he knew he was only partly sober. He stammered.

"Where's Josephine? Where's your father?"

"Papa?" She had the air of a somnambulist, as she advanced slowly towards him; still keeping her eyes upon him, she set the lamp down on the table. "How should anybody know where Papa is?" She tittered; he could feel her eyes holding him, as though resolved to prevent his escape. "Josephine—she—she went to the store—with Mrs. Sephton——"

With a rush she was on him, clutching his arm in both hands, gazing upwards, the breath panting through her open lips.

"Fancy not coming to see me, all this time! Oh, how cruel—how unkind!"

"Please let go"—he strove in vain to free himself; there was a formidable strength in those small, weak-looking hands. "I didn't know you were alone—of course I wouldn't—I'll come in some time tomorrow——"

"No, no; you must stop, and see Josephine. She'll be so pleased—she was as hurt as I was! Oh Evan, if you knew how I've missed you——!"

She was about to throw herself on his bosom when Evan's movement of repulsion, much more brusque than he intended, flung her back against the table. Throwing out her hands to prevent herself from falling, the wrapper slid open and dropped to her elbows over her naked body.

As Josephine Cotter and Mrs. Sephton walked into the room, he knew it was a trap. Margaret was sobbing and clutching at the garment, on whose hem she had by some means planted her foot, so that, for all her frenzied efforts, it failed to cover her. Josephine flung the cape she was wearing round her sister and, covering Margaret with her body, turned to face Evan. The double row of her teeth showed, and her eyes were like two bullet holes in a sheet of cardboard.

"So this is your repayment for hospitality, Mr. Crewe!"

In the scene which followed, when, for all his confusion, Evan recognized Mrs. Sephton's enmity as the more vicious and triumphant of the two—Margaret was shriller than either in her disclaimers of ill intent. She showed more sense and strength than he had ever suspected, in her reiterations that Evan had never, never, never!

He absolved her, then and for ever, of complicity in the plot. Later on, when sober, he would have taken his oath before any court in the country that Margaret had nothing to do with the deadly outcome of the scene.

"Well, you've ruined the girl."

"What absolute rot!" He tried to clear his mind. "As Margaret has told you, I haven't laid a finger on her."

The elder women exchanged glances; Mrs. Sephton's lips were glittering, she let out a high-pitched snigger.

"You'd better try telling that to Kwakwan—I suppose you don't think you've had your fun all to yourselves?" she cried. Josephine

Cotter turned perfectly white and her eyes rolled back, as though she were about to faint; she shot out her ugly hand to prop herself against the wall. "Won't the houseboys have enjoyed themselves, and won't they have something to talk about in the huts tonight! Won't the mission girls get a laugh, and that uppity half-breed youth in the office! News travels fast in these parts, you know; I bet I'll hear all about this when I get back to Accra."

"Will you hold your filthy tongue?" shouted Evan.

"I'm not the sort that starts gossip." She tossed her head. "But everybody round here knows the Cotters. I suppose you'll marry her?"

The sincerity of Margaret's shriek might well have convinced a more sophisticated person than Evan Crewe.

"Oh, no, no, no! For pity's sake—not like this! Oh, Evan, forgive me—forgive me!" She held her hands out towards him with a gesture so full of humility and shame that, touched, Evan took one of the trembling hands and held it in his own. He heard his own voice say, in a daze,

"If Margaret wishes me to marry her, I will."

Again she cried "No!" but Josephine, with a terrible smile on her bitter mouth, interrupted.

"My sister's wishes have nothing to do with it. Margaret was a pure and innocent girl before she met you, Mr. Crewe, and everyone knew it. Whatever you intended, by your visit tonight—whatever"—her mouth twisted itself with disgust—"has happened—you have robbed her of the only precious thing she had in the world: her good name. My father will make you marry her!"

. . . Out of the confusion of his brain emerged only his complete helplessness, his isolation from all who could have advised or assisted him, the fact that each member of the community was against him and—his hateful duty to Margaret Cotter. Had he been older, had he not had the guilt of his Cambridge affair on his mind—this last might have weighed less heavily. Had word come from Everett, he would not have felt so derelict. He even meditated cabling to Everett and risking departure by the first ship that would give him a passage. This, however, was not going to be easy; knowing nothing of the country or its languages, his only means of escape from Kwakwan was by rail, and that, for obvious reasons, might be dismissed.

The missionary, Armstrong, was away. Johnson, he suspected, was responsible for the Belgian missionary, who turned up from somewhere and married them. Evan had been barely sober for forty-eight hours. He had to restrain an indecent shout of laughter when Margaret stumbled into the room, her poor face swollen with weeping, her head decked with a frightful wreath of white flowers —for which he guessed Josephine was responsible: Josephine, whose grim face wore the ecstatic look of a bride! She gave him one smile of triumph and went to stand beside her father. Cotter did not even glance in Evan's direction; too drunk to perform his duty, it was Josephine who gave the bride away. Evan thought, I wonder how long a divorce takes—and was ashamed. Someone produced a ring, and he pushed it on a finger that felt like sweaty dough.

Josephine went to the missionary's for the night, and Evan and Margaret to the bungalow. She cried all night long. Each time he woke, he heard her crying, but it was as though he had become ossified. He could speak no word, make no sign of comfort.

On the following morning came Everett's letter, bidding him home.

vi

She was so pitiful, during the first days of the voyage, that he grew almost fond of her. Then, with disconcerting celerity, she recovered her spirits and all the tricks that grated on him at their first meeting.

She had bought herself—with what money he never discovered— what she called her trousseau, in Accra. Making all allowance for unsophistication, he could not bring himself even to pretend admiration of her taste. Long before the ship reached Liverpool, he knew that in mind, speech and deportment she could never take her place in the society to which, naturally, he would have introduced his wife.

A telegraph boy met him on the dock. Half-dazed, Evan read the announcement of his uncle's death. Torn between sorrow—for he had been very fond of old Everett—and relief, he wondered what good angel had prevented his cabling the news of his marriage, as he had first intended, from Accra? He would have blamed himself for bringing on the stroke which carried Everett away.

Installing Margaret in a hotel, the first weeks of his return were taken up with lawyers' conferences and with appearances before the Board of Directors. He learned, to his amazement, that he held controlling shares in Crewe & Company. He was elected, as a matter of course, to the Board, and had the somewhat surprising humility to decline, for the present. A directorship held out no particular allure to a young and ambitious man, whose interest lay rather in the executive than the administration. "I want to get into the shops; I want to learn my job properly," was his stubborn reply to those who indicated that, for the nephew of Everett Crewe, there was a royal road to advancement.

He was wealthy enough to have set up an imposing establishment, but they lived, like small-town people, in a suburban villa. He entertained his friends, and those who, in the way of business, he needed to impress, in hotels and restaurants. On none of these occasions was Margaret required to function as his hostess.

Inevitably, he was unfaithful to her, but took care she should not know of it, because he did not want, yet, to hurt her or to oblige her to divorce him before he was in a position to make the provision for her that his conscience demanded. Nor, among the many he made his mistresses, had he met the woman he wished permanently to link into his life.

A year after their marriage, she bore him a dead son. Her behaviour on this occasion was the first thing that gave him seriously to question her normality. He came to her, prepared to be kind, to comfort, and she looked up at him with a bright almost impudent smile, and spoke with a titter.

"All that trouble for nothing! Never mind; we know the old saying—don't we, nursie?" She ducked her head under his arm to call to the nurse, who was tactfully leaving them alone. " 'If at first you don't succeed, try, try again!' "

Her levity so took him aback, so disgusted him that he felt he could never again go near her; but towards the end of 1913 she was pregnant, and, having taken her first experience with calm, was frantic. Or pretended to be. Actually, she had become conscious of his slipping attention—although she had not started to connect it with another woman—and was determined to play up her condition to the last degree, to force his sympathy. She meant him to share every inaesthetic detail of her discomfort, and her terror of the delivery, and, while forcing himself to pity, he was horrified to find himself hating her for every affront she offered to his male fastidiousness. Nothing, to a man of Evan's calibre, is so repellent as want of modesty in a wife, and some obscure defiance—the defiance of one who senses she is playing a losing game—made her fling away the solitary line of appeal she could have made to him.

One morning the high heels she insisted on wearing, in despite of the doctor's advice, precipitated her down the stairs, almost at Evan's feet. Lifting her up and finding her, apparently, unharmed, rage burst from him in an unforgivable phrase: "I suppose you want to give me another dead child!"

She wept, accused him of cruelty and neglect and declared hysterically that no one had ever loved her but Josephine. Compunction prompted him to ask if she would like him to send for her sister. Oh yes! If she could have Jo, she would be of no more trouble to anyone.

While the ship bringing Josephine waited off the bar, excitement brought on a *fausse couche*. For some days she did not know her sister; recognition, hysteria and collapse succeeded each other—and were followed, eventually, by a faint improvement. But she was now Josephine's "baby": demanding her full attention, talking baby language, depending, not only physically, but mentally and morally, on the grim woman by her side; pretending to be frightened of Evan—"Naughty Evan! You don't know how cruel he's been to poor little Maggie!'"

One day she was found nursing a pillow, calling it "baby" and insisting on its "likeness" to Evan. They snatched from her hand the knife she used to disembowel it. Sitting there, in a welter of feathers and blood—she had cut herself in the performance—she giggled at them. Well, Evan had wanted another dead baby, so she had given it to him!

This was 1914. In October, Evan took a commission. He served two years, and was wounded out in 1917. Some of his friends, who had not seen him since he went to West Africa, did not even know he was married; others took it for granted that the marriage had come to grief—there was plenty of that kind of thing in wartime.

vii

Margaret's insanity, which fluctuated, did not justify her immediate consignment to a mental home; nor, indeed, would her sister have heard of it. He made, through his solicitors, an arrangement whereby Josephine, in return for taking full responsibility and charge of her, should receive an adequate income, on condition she made no personal approach to him, on her own or Margaret's behalf. He was assured by the doctors that certification was only a matter of time.

It was during this bitter period that he again made contact with Edward Fitzalan, his *fidus Achates* of the brief 'Varsity interlude: Edward, the "pocket soldier," who, in spite of his unusually small and slight stature—his head reached barely to Evan's shoulder—had achieved brevet rank, together with the V.C. and the D.S.O.

Edward, stiff as a very small ramrod, flung back his head to look Evan in the eyes, and the old confidence revived between them. To tell someone seemed the best way of getting rid of the poison, and Edward was secret as the grave.

"Why," said Edward casually, when, later, they sat over their wine in his rooms in Albany, "don't you go and see Anna? You know she married Hugh Sturges? They're in Eaton Square; they'd love to see you. You know what a favourite you were with Anna!"

He wrote the address into his notebook. For the present he was not much inclined for social life; apart from that, Crewe & Company was absorbing all of his time and energy. But a few weeks later, in an unexpectedly free and lonely moment, he recalled Edward Fitzalan's proposal, looked in the telephone directory and picked up the receiver.

The voice that answered shocked him with its reminder of all kinds of forgotten things: of a summer vacation when, sponsored by Edward, he was introduced into a world of culture and tradition foreign to the son of industrialism. At Edward's home, Camelhurst, he made his first acquaintance—apart from that of the sightseer—with the arts of the Regency and the glories of the English landscape garden; he learned to recognize an exedra by Kent, the careless genius of Nash, the serene and spacious formulae of Capability Brown; he had time to meditate upon the outlook of those who, brought up, like Edward, in these surroundings, absorbed into their souls and minds an aristocracy as much of environment as of breeding. It was all very impressive to a youth from a wealthy but tasteless home, and, snobbery apart (few young men in Evan's position are guiltless of a degree of snobbery), increased his understanding as well as his respect for Edward.

He remembered a pavilion (by Vanbrugh, he learned) set in a maze at the end of a green alley, where sometimes their reading was interrupted by a serious little girl with long, fawn-coloured plaits and thin summer frocks that fell without waistbelts from a bunch of smocking. Her delicate chin was lifted on a thing called, he believed, a "tucker"—he found himself smiling; what an absurd thing to remember! She never stayed long—was probably too shy—but came and went softly, like a shadow, like the ghost of one of her little ancestresses painted by Reynolds or Lawrence for the Long Gallery; she had their fragile colouring and their unconscious childish grace.

He had never met a child like Anna Fitzalan. Secretly and shamefacedly—for Laura, by then, was well on the *tapis!*—he fell a little in love with her, though their intercourse was limited by a governess to the barest formalities. Once—it was a birthday or something—Edward and he were invited to tea in the schoolroom. He, a dashing young man already embarked on a love affair with a married woman, was horribly shy of the sweetly solemn child presiding at the tea table, and horribly put-out by Edward's unceremonious teasing of his little sister. By sheer innocence, she in some way vulgarized his morbid little affair with Laura—just for a week or two.

"Evan?—Evan *Crewe?*" the voice was saying; it sounded incredulous. "But of course I remember; it's wonderful. Come to dinner! Yes, I mean now. I'll tell them to hold it back for half an hour." (What kind of woman was it, who had preserved that spontaneity through a reputedly successful marriage and the demands of society on a fashionable hostess?) "Don't dress; Hugh's just back from Newmarket; we're sitting down as we are."

When he saw her, he could not imagine how he had come to forget the deep eyes, the lids that were thin flakes of jade, the sweet sculpture of a face that time had thinned and sharpened without sacrificing its gentleness; or the softly falling hair—no longer in the plaits of little Anna Fitzalan, but gathered in a small, gleaming knot on the nape of the long neck. How, in a postwar world of hard-faced, sharp-tongued women, of the "Bright Young Things," the "Treasure Hunt," the bobbed head and the night club, had this one managed to preserve her air of floating perpetually through a green grove, under the shadow and light of leaves whose delicate rhythm was reproduced in her own movements?

He looked at the husband. No, the answer was not there.

Evan said to himself, this is my woman.

But he did not say it to Anna's brother. Nor, for fifteen years, did he say it to Anna herself.

CHAPTER II

*I*n spite of the warnings of her contemporaries—prompted for the most part by envy ("You won't get anybody of importance to dance with you"—"Your hair will come down!"—"Suppose you aren't asked for the supper dance?"—"If you have to sit out, what *will* you find to talk about?")—Anna's first ball was sheer bliss.

She must have been a very simple, not to say foolish, little girl, for those were terrible years for the débutante—hurled straight from the schoolroom into a society conditioned by Diaghilev, Camondo and Astruc. The second decade of the twentieth century, breaking in a wave of pseudo-Orientalism, all but submerged a luckless generation doing its painful best to look as though it had strayed from the pages of Pierre Loti. Outraged mammas, bidding their offspring wash their faces, were cruelly blind to the truth: that the modest bloom of *papier poudré* simply would not stand up to Bakst. There were many tears and some small, nervous rebellions, but the 1914–18 war had not yet liberated the débutante from parental control.

Little Anna Fitzalan neither wept nor rebelled; serenely content in oyster-pink mousseline, she must have looked like a ghost—but gave no thought to it. An air of breathless rapture, of radiant expectancy, lighting her large, pale eyes and enhaloing her innocent head of a small, blond mouse, bore her like foam on the crests of those breakers of flame, gold, purple and peacock, deriving from the Ballet Russe, which were apt to convert any evening party into an amateur revival of a scene from *Scheherazade*. In spite of her unfortunate gown (a product of the village dressmaker; there was no point in dressing a girl who was not, technically, "out," and owed her presence at the ball only to the partiality of an elder brother), many eyes, apparently, were drawn to Lady Fitzalan's little daughter, and, within less than an hour of her arrival, Anna's card was full.

It was the era of the "hobble" skirt. Encased in a dreadful tube of pink satin (the mousseline had, for modesty's sake, to have a foundation), Anna hopped and skipped beneath the fountains and garlands of her bewitched imagination. She had forgotten the croakings of her friends. Each one of her partners seemed more charming than the last. To the tune of violins (jazz had not yet thrust its way into the better country houses), she tripped, unconsciously, straight into the arms of the handsome young man who was waiting, of course (a Present for a Good Girl), at the end of the magic grove.

She was engaged before midnight, when, obedient to her mother's command, she retired to her bedroom. Overwhelmed by the envious compliments of her contemporaries, a little transported by her success, she had neglected, in her excitement, closely to examine her prize. If, in the afterglow, she was conscious of a shade of disappointment, she was too shy and too polite to give expression to it. Mamma was so pleased! And Hugh was so good-looking, and so very, very attractive and charming!

And so the whole of the season—"*le tableau se déroule à mes pieds!*"—proceeded to dérouler itself, by way of red carpets, pink lights, orchestras (not yet spoken of as "dance bands") and innumerable invitations, at the feet of a little girl who, a month before, had been inking her fingers at a schoolroom desk; who, on a frosty November morning, was the much-photographed bride at a country wedding (with one of her rare touches of obstinacy,

Anna had firmly refused to be married anywhere but at Camelhurst), and who returned, rather pale and grave, but as serene as
ever, from her honeymoon, to make the most of her new importance as the wife of that popular man about town, Hugh Sturges.

ii

I'll never walk on pink carpets, under pink lights, with music
in the distance, without expecting something wonderful to happen! thought Anna Sturges, in 1933.

"To your left, madam."

She looked up quickly, from smoothing the fingers of her gloves
—and smiled. Of course; it was a new lift boy. The old one would
have known. . . .

Stepping out of the lift, her cape rustled after her, with a noise
of dry leaves on a gusty evening. She had an amused sense of being
lifted out of a box, out of tissue paper, as her own scent lost itself
in a dozen others. Immediately opposite, in a sheet of pinkish
mirror glass, a woman in a wide gown of grey net, scattered with
petals of black velvet, paused, for a glance of polite approval. Why,
it's me! thought Anna. She had forgotten how well it became her—
that old net gown, dating back twelve months or more; at any
rate, before she went into mourning. Helen had looked at it rather
oddly.

"I didn't know what to put on; it has turned so suddenly warm!"
There was no reason to produce an apology, or a justification; it
was only that, in her mood of contentment, she felt she could not
bear to draw the shadow of Helen's unspoken criticism across an
anticipated pleasure, or to provoke the attitude of unnecessary
defensiveness Helen was apt to assume towards anything she chose
to interpret as a slight on her father's memory. There was, perhaps,
something a little incongruous in a widow's casting her weeds,
while a young bride continued to wear mourning. Anna had an
impulse to say, "Don't manufacture grievances, dear; please don't!

Hugh and I understood each other—truly we did—in a fashion of our own. Surely you can imagine that—now you are married?"

Helen's short, stocky figure derived sudden pathos in her mother's eyes. She was wearing a black tailor-made "off the peg" ("I can't be bothered with fittings," she had muttered; but Anna suspected the truth—that she could not trust herself, when getting her mourning, not to burst into the tears which, for some-one as impassive as Helen, were always surprisingly near at hand) and an expensively dull black hat, mounted on a too recent wave. Anna made one of her quick capitulations—inexplicable alike to her husband and her children.

"Would you rather I put something else on?"

"Me? I don't care—why should I?" Helen's voice, quick, but flat, without timbre or inflection, exactly matched her convention-ally pretty face, too nondescript, in spite of its charming colouring, to attract attention. She concluded, in an offhand manner, "It was one of Daddy's favourites, wasn't it?"

"Was it?" As long as Anna could remember, Hugh, far from expressing a preference, had never known what she was wearing. That was implicit in his interpretation of British manhood: an intrinsic principle of which is not to pander to feminine vanity; not, at any rate, in the case of a wife. She seemed to remember a time while they were engaged, when he had told her she was wearing "a ripping hat" or "a jolly good gown!" But when, shily, she had invited his approval of some of her honeymoon dresses, she was given to understand, by inference, that mention of such matters became slightly indecent with the slipping on of the wed-ding ring. It was therefore a little disconcerting, now, to hear of Hugh expressing his preferences, not to her, but to their daughter.

A memory slid into her mind, of a stout little girl in jersey and kilt, stolidly resisting efforts to make her put "expression" into her recitation of The Gillyflower of Gold; and another—of Helen's and Roger's unconcealed disgust at her rather emotional rendering, on the schoolroom piano, of a Chopin ballade. "Oh Mummy!" Both their heads were turned away, their faces red. Both children shared their father's distaste for the betrayal of feeling; each inherited his gift for converting a sentiment into a flat statement that successfully destroyed the mood that inspired it. Helen, at twenty-one, and Roger, at nineteen, still had her guessing at the depth, or otherwise, of emotion that lay behind their dispassionate utterances.

"I'll change it!" said Anna impulsively, and plucked at the hooks under her left arm. Helen's hand checked her.

"Don't be so silly, Mother!" She looked Anna up and down. "You certainly look very nice——"

—as though, thought Anna, having made me feel guilty, she could afford a compliment. She thrust back the uncharitable thought as she twisted the thick string of cut jet round her throat and pinned the dark pearls in her ears.

"Have you anyone dining tonight?"

"I wouldn't be here if we had, would I?" said Helen, not rudely, but reasonably. "Come on; here's your cape—and I don't suppose Evan will be mad with you for keeping him waiting! Norman goes up in flames if I'm even five minutes late, but that old school seems to think unpunctuality's just part of female charm!"

Anna laughed and glanced at the clock.

"You dine at eight, don't you? I'd better drop you on my way to the Savoy; you've not left yourself much time for dressing."

"We don't dress unless it's a party. Norman goes to his study after we've had coffee, and I don't see any point in stripping to play Patience while he's working on his briefs."

"Oh, darling——" It's Helen's choice, Helen's life, she reminded herself quickly. An impulse of tenderness made her lean over to kiss Helen—who, within the limits of her inexpressiveness, looked surprised, but took the kiss with equanimity on a fresh pink cheek glowing with health. She used powder and lipstick—the former unscented, the latter collected at random from a tray at the stores— and neither made any difference to her essential wholesomeness of an English schoolgirl, who believes in hot water, exercise and internal hygiene, rather than in the enhancement of her charms by artificial means. But since, in 1933, everyone was putting stuff on their mouths and nails, Helen subscribed to the current practise: the one unforgivable thing, in her code, being to appear different from anyone else.

"I suppose," she said in her offhand way, "I'll have to start shopping soon. The baby'll be born about the middle of September."

. . . In September, thought Anna, looking at her face in the pink looking glass, I shall be a grandmother.

The reminder was inopportune and a little absurd. She continued to look wonderingly at her reflection: at the wide, pale-grey eyes, deep-set in the fine, indestructible architecture of broad brow and cheekbones and small pointed chin. Like the majority of beautiful women, she had never given much thought to the design; only latterly she had begun to be aware of it, as a useful foundation for the arts she had learned to expend on it. Working on it conscientiously, like a good child filling in the outlines of a painting book, she was surprised to discover the possibilities of her face: the eyelids which became exotic when delicately brushed with iridescent green, the eyes which a fine fringe of black rendered more palely luminous, the curve of the mouth made sharper and sweeter with a light coral. These things had helped to preserve the face of little Anna Fitzalan—which a number of people had considered beautiful. Women were fortunate, nowadays, when convention no longer required them to surrender the charms of their youth before reaching their thirtieth birthdays! How lovely Mamma might have been. . . .

It was enjoyable, lingering there, putting off the pleasure to come. As she went leisurely down the corridor, Anna amused herself by visualizing it.

The door would be ajar, and Evan would lift his narrow, handsome head from the evening paper, or from his newest purchase (he had become an extravagant patron of the St. James's dealers): with his usual air of limitless leisure at variance with the legend of high pressure surrounding one in perpetual conference with principalities and powers. She always felt that that side of his life had nothing to do with her; that her only concern was with a thin, polite undergraduate introduced by Edward to Camelhurst twenty-five years ago—with whom a shy child fell instantly in love.

"Come and look at this," he would say. Or, "I've come to the conclusion you were right about——" referring to some matter they had discussed days, or weeks, or even months ago. Sometimes her memory failed her; she would see the twinkle in his eye; presently he would begin to count—"One! Two! Three!"—and if she had not reached the context before he said "Six!" she was lost. It rarely happened. Triumphantly she would pick up her cue, and the illusion of continuity established itself once more.

"Do you know," it amused her, one day, to tease him, "you never wish me 'Good evening,' or even 'Hello'? Don't I rate the courtesy you show to other people?"

"Courtesy? I never remember we aren't together all the time," he answered, with such candid surprise that she burst out laughing. "Well; how are you?—how's Hugh?"

Hugh. For no reason—she was within a few yards of the door—the thought of Hugh struck at her sharply. Her eyes fell to the net gown; would Evan, like Helen, feel she should still be wearing black? He most certainly would not; yet the faint sense of guilt, evoked by Helen, revived. Her silk cape was black, and instinctively she folded it round her. *Forgive me; I owe you so much gratitude.* Gratitude, above all, for this: that you never interfered with my friendships.

It was "good old Evan," or "poor old Evan": because, to Hugh, any person who was obliged, or chose, to work for his living was an object of genuine commiseration. If sufficiently distinguished, he might command a lazy tolerance; but Hugh jibbed instinctively from any kind of intimacy which would betray, not only his indifference, but his ignorance. "Oh, come, old boy—let's not be strenuous!" Any conversation was "strenuous" which went beyond anecdote, reminiscences of school or 'Varsity days or—Hugh's sole serious preoccupation—racing.

Yes, it was kind and generous of Hugh, to lay no embargo on her friendships with people who cared for none of these things, to sit patiently through dinner parties at which he was as much out of his element as a fish out of water; to accept—albeit reluctantly—occasional invitations to Evan's private suite at the Savoy; although it meant his sitting mum, and looking offended, when Evan's "frog" or "dago" guests spoke in languages he did not understand and was too indolent to learn. He detested anyone who did not speak in the clipped or snuffling drawl he called "the King's English." People who occupied themselves with the arts were "cads": painter cads, or writin' cads, or actor cads—the last, however, to be tolerated if they appeared frequently in West End comedy, were knowledgeable about stables and knew how to conduct themselves in conformance with the formulae of (Hugh's) society. Poor Hugh . . . She checked herself. One has no right to insult with pity one who lived with perfect content within the small, dull pattern laid down by his forebears, and who died, with a look of mild surprise on his face, before he had time to exhaust its resources.

Small wonder that he formed the habit of going to the club on nights when they were neither entertaining nor being entertained. "You cut along and have a bite with Evan, old girl. He'd love to have you. Still got that house of his in Queen's Terrace, hasn't he? Why the deuce doesn't he get rid of it, now he's dug himself in at the Savoy?"

"I suppose he might go back there, some day. Travelling so much, he probably doesn't want the trouble of housekeeping."

"Then why doesn't he let it?" demanded Hugh, with the irrational petulance he frequently brought to bear on matters which were no concern of his. "I know two or three people who'd be jolly glad to rent it for the season. Why don't you drop him a hint?"

"I hardly think it's my place to do that; do you?" said Anna, after a hesitation.

"I thought you two were as thick as thieves!"

"When thieves get together, what do they talk about? Shop, I imagine. I shouldn't think they go in much for domestic matters."

He gave her his sullen, sly look.

"You aren't 'in love,' are you?" He made a sneer of it. Anna was confounded. Realizing he had gone too far, Hugh said blunderingly, "All right; don't shoot. I just—wondered. Evan's not the sort to cut an' run with the wife of a friend."

"Thank you for that," she said in a low voice. "And what about me?"

"Oh—you . . ." His eyes and voice slid away from her.

"I'd like you to answer that," she said, even more quietly.

"Now you're jumpin' down my throat. I trust you," muttered Hugh, gruffly public-school, "exactly as I trust Evan."

"You are right to do so," she told him.

'Of course"—he cleared his throat—"I know I'm a dud, from your point of view——"

"Must you say these things?" She was almost laughing.

"—but I'd hate it, if you bolted."

She was moved by an inexplicable pity to lay her hand on his shoulder.

"You know I don't lie. It's never even entered my mind to bolt—as you call it. You're terribly good to me——"

"Oh, for God's sake, don't let's be strenuous!" Edging away from her touch, he reacted in his habitual fashion.

"But"—before she had time to think what she was saying, the words slipped past her lips—"you think Evan and I go to bed together."

The look of horrified disgust that slid over his face brought the blood to hers. She had committed the unforgivable sin: of putting into words what one might think, but never, never utter. And, in doing so, she had outraged one of the strongest tenets of conduct of people like Hugh. It was no use trying to explain that loyalty, to him and to Evan, had driven her to it: to shattering, in a phrase, all the flimsy and unreal house that contained her life and Hugh's. Too late, with the fragments about her feet, she knew there was no hope of rebuilding from the shards that stronger house which, in a moment of insensate dream, she had envisaged.

He said in a whisper,

"For God's sake, don't speak like that. It *dirties* you."

She burst into tears. When she recovered herself, Hugh had gone. Not only Hugh, but the whole structure—such as it was—of their married life.

It only occurred to her later that she and Evan might, in actual fact, have been lovers, and that the animal sense which, in Hugh, took the place of sensitivity, might have informed him that they were lovers: and that he would not have cared—much—so long as the fact was not thrust upon him in some fashion that obliged him to admit it.

If there is anything, Anna was thinking, as she reached the threshold of the suite, in the theory that those who pass on keep watch over the ones they have loved (yes, you did love me, in your fashion), you know, by now, we were innocent.

An absurd vision came to her, of Hugh, standing up there, on some celestial racecourse—unaltered, even on that planet—standing there stiffly, in his loose, immaculate clothes, with field glasses slung over his shoulder and a race card in his hand and a look of sheepish vexation on his handsome face.

"I'm sorry I mucked it, old girl."

"It's all right; just a misunderstanding." The main thing was not to detain him, to put him at his ease, so that he could get away to where his jockey waited in the paddock, and place his bets before they were under starter's orders.

iii

The doors, into the suite itself and beyond, into the sitting room, stood ajar, as she had learned to expect, but, for once, Evan was not in sight. She stood for a moment, to admire the burst of lemon-yellow gladioli lighting up the Poussin that was his latest purchase, and to sniff the bowl of violets placed there—she guessed—for her special welcome. With the instinctive coquetry of a beautiful woman, she made her silk cape rustle a little; when the sound did not bring him immediately to the inner door, she wondered if he had company: which meant they would be dining, not in the restaurant, but here, in the apartment.

It was, she supposed, old-fashioned convention that prevented his dining her *tête-à-tête* in his own quarters—although, after dinner, they invariably returned for the coffee his man Chadwick served from the pot that stood constantly, over its blue bubble, on Evan's writing table. Chadwick was always within call during the hour while they listened to the latest record, or looked at the latest picture, or, simply, talked. How few men pay women the compliment of intelligent conversation. A cleverer woman than I, thought Anna, would make more of the things he gives me: the sidelights on European politics, the intimate angles on his vast and complicated world, which interests me only because it makes up his background.

She knew, on reliable hearsay, that there were many women in Evan's life. Some of them dined up here; he made no secret of it. "Clarissa" (or Edith, or Patricia) "had dinner with me last night." There was a tone in his voice that invoked Anna's rarely roused resentment on behalf of her own sex. At least, he could never say, "Anna dined with me last night," on that note of subtle disparagement. She accused him once—only half playfully—of being "caddish." He lifted his eyebrows, and she saw, with a sharp sense of shock, that Evan's face could be both cruel and ironical. He did not even trouble to answer her observation, but changed the subject. For the first time, she was not wholly at ease with him. It was not until their next meeting that she felt they had recaptured their former relationship. Well, she had had her lesson. . . .

"Here I am; late—I'm afraid—as usual!"

She had pushed the door open—on what seemed, to her surprise, to be an empty room. Then she saw him, doubled up in the corner of a couch.

"Who is it?"

"Evan!" She rushed to him. "What's the matter?"

"Oh—it's you—Anna. I'm sorry. I meant to ring——"

Before she could say any more, he had dragged himself to his feet, and, thrusting her aside, lunged past her. The noise of a slamming door cut her off from him, but did not shut off the sounds of vomiting. She waited, for what felt like eternity, and when he reappeared, went quickly to support him, but he motioned her aside, collapsed again on the couch and pressed a handkerchief soaked in cologne to his face. Little as Anna knew about illness, she recognized this as something to be taken seriously: the hand pressed over his abdomen, the long shudders that drove him back against the cushions.

"Where's Chadwick?" she asked distractedly.

"His free afternoon. Be back—any minute."

"When did this start?"

"An hour ago. Might be more." His teeth snapped audibly. He was locked in another rigor. "Sorry. Some sort of chill. Chadwick will——" She felt him resenting her presence.

"You must go to bed. Please go to bed at once."

After a pause—to her surprise—he obeyed. As the door closed after his wavering figure, she picked up the telephone and dialled a Harley Street number.

"Dr. Maxwell? . . . It's Mrs. Sturges speaking. Can you come at once, please, to the Savoy? It's Mr. Crewe; I think he's very ill." She gave the number of Evan's suite and replaced the receiver.

She had waited, she thought, long enough for him to be in bed, when she went to the communicating door and said hesitantly, "Evan?" When there was no reply, she pushed the door open. Partly undressed, he had fallen across the bed; he did not appear to hear her speaking to him.

She had never undressed a man, but she did the best she could. Her nails broke on the hard stuff, but she managed to pull the pyjama jacket round his shoulders and to drag off the trousers. It took all her strength to tug the bedclothes from under him and lift his legs, swivelling them round, so she could straighten and cover them. The rigors started again. She looked wildly round, for brandy, for anything. Like all people unused to illness, she was terrified.

. . . They operated at midnight. She had insisted on travelling in the ambulance. The injection had taken effect. Somewhere, held up by traffic lights, they stopped. Evan opened his eyes.

"Anna. What the devil are you doing here?"

"What the devil do you mean by giving us such a scare?"

"What's it all about?" He sounded petulant.

"Peritonitis. That's what you get for neglecting a grumbling appendix."

"Ah. I suppose they're going to operate. Damn. Where's Chadwick?"

"Packing your things. Is there anything I can do? Can I ring anyone up?"

"Chadwick will see to that—and Miss Ryder." His closed eyes dismissed her.

She saw him carried out on a stretcher, placed on a trolley, wheeled out of sight down a long passage. There was just time to touch his hand, and for Evan to say with a smile,

"Thanks for being here. Don't look so scared. See you—soon."

In the waiting room, she had time to face the future: *the total emptiness*—if anything went wrong.

She was alone. The silence was like lead. A few cars hummed down Welbeck Street. Somewhere, beyond these walls, were beds, with silent people in them; the quiet night activity of a nursing home; temperatures, charts, bedpans, renewal of hot-water bottles, nurses in rubber-heeled shoes, answering the flash of a red bulb, preparing an injection. She had never seen an operating theatre; her mind made a picture of it. Concentrated white light; whiteness, and steel, and blood.

Her head began to swim, and she felt moisture collecting in the icy palms of her hands. The swimming increased, and she looked down at the spread of grey net about the chair on which she was sitting. If you feel faint, put your head between your knees: that was what Mamma said, when Anna went through that phase of fainting at early Communion. She bent over obediently, felt her balance go—and someone was raising her. A glass was tapping against her teeth. She smelt brandy.

"Swallow it, Mrs. Sturges."

She did so and gave a long shudder. The person looking down at her must be the surgeon. There was an edge of impatience on his voice—the impatience of someone called away from Crockford's to perform a routine operation.

"Is he—all right?"

"Naturally he'll be under the anaesthetic for some time. But the heart's in fairly good order."

"Thank you. Thank you very much. Could—could I see him?"

"I wouldn't recommend it. There's not much point in seeing a person under ether!"

She insisted, against a feeling of foolishness,

"Then—tomorrow?"

"If things go normally, no reason why not."

"I don't know anything about operations," she said humbly.

"It's not very professional"—he gave a reluctant smile—"but I congratulate you, Mrs. Sturges."

"What does 'normally' mean?" She reverted to his previous remark.

"There's always the possibility of a rise in temperature. There's also a variety of postoperative conditions that may hold up progress for a few days."

His evident impatience stiffened Anna's determination to know at least as much as he could be induced to tell her.

"But the operation itself was successful?"

"Perfectly. Mr. Crewe may consider himself lucky; that appendix should have been whipped out months ago."

. . . Roger was in the hall when she got back to Eaton Square; with a white scarf slung from one shoulder and ruffled hair, he looked very much like Hugh, after a convivial evening. He gaped at his mother.

"Good Lord; I didn't know you were out on the batter!"

"They've just operated on Evan for peritonitis."

"Crikey. Well, you'd better go to bed," he mumbled. She allowed him to precede her, turning aside into the breakfast room, so as not to embarrass him by her observation of his stumbling progress.

"How is he?" she asked, in the morning, at Welbeck Street.

"Rather weak. He was asking for his secretary, but we were obliged to refuse. Not more than five minutes, please, Mrs. Sturges."

The narrow, white bed seemed at first to be empty; she looked down on him, realizing that she had never visualized him like this: drained, speechless, helpless. When his eyes opened for a moment, she had a sense of looking down into a waterlogged pit, in the heart of forsaken land.

"He's very, very ill," she said, outside the door, to the nurse, who gave her a reflective look, as though deciding the degree to which she was to be trusted.

"He won't be out of the wood yet awhile. He must have been overworking for a very long time?—Of course, it's not as though he were a young man——"

Anna looked at her coldly, then remembered, and her glance softened. Of course, to this cool, blue-eyed girl anyone out of his thirties was virtually elderly!

"You mean, overwork is the cause of it?"

The nurse gave her a smile of professional superiority.

"Hardly—of peritonitis! But it reduces his recuperative chances, doesn't it? When everything's run down, almost to stopping point, it means a long convalescence."

A month went by, before he was fit to sit up and discuss the immediate future with her. His shoulder blades and collarbones peaked the silk pyjamas into ridges, and his wrists were like ossified twigs, but the old devilment glittered in his eye. The room reeked of flowers: vases, bowls, baskets. To Anna's amusement, the secretary, Miss Ryder, in departure, had discreetly removed a pile of cards and notes. Was she—Anna—supposed to be curious, or jealous, about Evan's "hidden life"?

"I'm to have two months' holiday; did you ever hear of such rot?"

"Admirable rot. What are they suggesting?"

"Among other idiocies—a cruise!"

Anna laughed outright.

"Come, a cruise at this time of year will be very pleasant, and you know you are fond of sailing."

"In company with a boatload of overdressed—or underdressed!—provincials, playing shuffleboard and deck tennis? Gala nights with fancy dress? Dance bands—and that poisonous game with wooden horses——?"

"You won't be well enough for any of those. But it might be a little noisy," Anna conceded. "You might be able to borrow someone's yacht—or even hire one: although I imagine that would be very expensive——"

"When I spend money, I like to do it in my own way: not to the order of some Harley Street quack," he snarled at her.

Where, if he had his choice, would he care to go? He mumbled that he wished to go nowhere, but she persevered with suggestions. Bermuda?—or, if that seemed too far, Sicily; or even Madeira. Each suggestion raised the scale of petulance. She left him flatly reiterating his intention of going straight back from the nursing home to his suite at the Savoy.

Even Miss Ryder, his secretary, was driven at last to confide in one towards whom, so far, she had preserved a polite neutrality.

"It's not just convalescent contrariness! Nobody can make any headway, if Mr. Crewe just makes up his mind. I did think of something last night, but I didn't care to suggest it myself. I hope you won't think it's impertinence," she went on, encouraged by Anna's nod, "but do you think your brother, General Fitzalan, would have him at Camelhurst for a few weeks? Mr. Crewe's very attached to the General, and I think he might be—well, sensible, and not fight too hard against doctors' orders, if he was with somebody he was fond of——"

"It's an excellent suggestion," said Anna regretfully, "but my brother, unfortunately, is in South Africa. And my sister-in-law——" No, indeed; poor Griselda, drooling on about her local committees and the iniquities of the parish council, would never do for Evan.

The solution came from—of all unlikely people—Roger. Anna had been pestered for weeks about flight reservations, lightweight baggage and all the less amusing details of travel, while parcels arrived on every delivery from tailors, shoemakers and dealers in sports equipment, cluttering her son's room and overflowing on halls and landings.

Roger now announced, suddenly and sullenly, that his projected trip to the South of France was "off."

"Oh, my dear, I'm so sorry." She pitied his angry disappointment, so like Hugh's, when any project went awry. "What has happened?"

"If you ever read anything but the Court Circular and the women's pages," snarled her son, "you'd know about the Hattersley-Bondfield crash."

"But——"

"Oh God," groaned Roger, "Maurice's father is Hattersley-Bondfield! I mean, there's no Hattersley and there's no Bondfield—Maurice's old man's the whole thing—and they're broke, flat, stony—oh blast, oh hell."

"How very sad for them, poor things."

"Poor nothing! Maurice himself says that if his parents had got the brains of lice they'd all clear out and *live* in the villa; I presume they've got to live somewhere!—and living's dirt-cheap in France. Instead of which, they've got to muck up *all* our plans and *ruin* the vacation"—Hugh again: infuriated by anything that interfered with his personal pleasure, indifferent to anyone's comfort but his own.

"I suppose"—The thought came to her later, as they sat gloomily over a table at Quaglino's. Roger, something to her surprise, had no engagement for the evening and moodily fell in with her suggestion they should dine out. "If your friends aren't going to use the villa this summer, do you think they'd be likely to let it for a few weeks?"

"How in blazes should I know?"

"Then find out," said Anna, with unusual sharpness. "Get on the telephone now, and find out. They might be glad to have it taken off their hands——"

"I say!" Light broke on Roger's face. "That's a whale of a notion! And Maurice could come and stay with us, instead of me with them!" He was out of his chair; nearly as tall, already, as his father, the boy glittered with handsomeness. With a little stab in the heart, Anna recognized the charm that swept her into Hugh's arms, twenty-two years ago.

"My darling boy." She was obliged to smile, at this characteristic sample of wishful thinking. "I'm not exactly short of cash, but my jointure doesn't take into account the renting of Riviera villas. I was thinking of Evan."

"But"—his face, which had clouded, cleared into even greater brilliance—"that's positively *wizard!* Good old Evan—he can invite us *all* out! According to Maurice, it's a thundering great place——"

"Give me the number," said Anna, "and I'll speak myself." Her handling of the matter was likely to be more tactful than Roger's.

When she came back, the matter, subject to Evan's approval, was arranged.

"Darling, don't be foolish." She was obliged to quash her son's raptures. "Evan's an invalid; there can't be any question of house parties until he's stronger."

"He'll be as fit as a fiddle down there in a couple of weeks," asserted Roger with confidence. (Were the other diners conscious of the light dancing round their table? As always, when his wishes were gratified, the boy radiated charm. He summoned the waiter, ordered *café diablé* for himself and his mother, was serious over the choice of a brandy.)

"I'll go, if you'll come too," was Evan's reception of the proposition, when she laid it before him. Anna laughed. "I'm serious. What do you suppose I'd do, alone in a villa in the South of France?"

"Chadwick?—and I suppose you'd take Miss Ryder?"

"Kindly leave off supposing! Miss Ryder's an excellent person who doesn't happen to fit into the picture of my immediate future. Do you see me listening to her and the nurse, clacking, at every hour of the day?"

"Ah, I'd forgotten the nurse," said Anna peaceably.

He looked at her for a moment in silence.

"You're a lovely, forgetful creature. Well; it's a bargain. If you'll come out with me to Les Sablons, we can have done with these arguments."

"But—you've forgotten." She seized on the first excuse that came to her mind. "I'm going to be a grandmother, in September! I can't possibly be away, for that."

"It's the most excellent reason for being away. For a woman of your age to become a grandmother is sufficiently indecent, without doing it in public!"

"For a woman of my age to share a villa with a man of yours," she retorted, "invites some curious comments!"

"Good . . . God. Anna! I'd no idea you were a puritan."

"That's not fair. I have a girl in her twenties and a son at the 'Varsity. We've got no right to involve them in scandal."

"Very well; I'll arrange a chaperone, if you're so squeamish."

Something to her surprise, neither Helen nor Roger saw anything strange in her going to the South of France with Evan. Roger, in particular, was in a tolerant mood; it appeared that his prospects had improved since their former conversation.

"That's fine! We'll be seeing you. An American friend of Maurice's has turned up with a car, and we're going to tour: much more fun than sticking in one place! You may have to put all three of us up for a few days. After all, it's Maurice's villa."

"For which Evan is paying a swinging rent! I think, with that and his illness, it would be nice to wait until you're invited. I expect we'll be very quiet."

It was, naturally, Helen, who produced the question for which Anna was prepared.

"Who's going with you?"

"Well, of course, there's the nurse——"

"Oh, then that's all right."

That Helen, stern for the proprieties, considered the chaperonage of a nurse adequate did something to relieve Anna's mind, since the matter of a fourth party was proving more difficult than they had expected. The elderly Fitzalan connection on whom they had been depending wrote—almost at the last moment—that her doctor advised her against the climate at that time of the year. Anna and Evan looked at each other blankly.

"I'm sorry." He obviously meant it. "Well, Anna, it's up to you. If you are unhappy about anything, the whole thing is 'off.'"

"You mean"—she trembled—"you won't go?" It had been impressed on her that he must have these weeks of complete rest. He smiled a little.

"When have I held a pistol to your head? I'll go. I'll hate every minute of it—and I'll be back in a month, instead of two."

"Isn't that holding a pistol? You promised——"

"To stay until I was 'well.' Have no fear; I'll keep my word. But will power can accomplish a great deal, and I'll use all I have, to be back at the end of next month. Speaking objectively"—he tapped his pen on the edge of the writing board propped across the arms of his chair; he was dressed, frail, but formidably like the old Evan— "I should have called Nurse Whitney—who, not to be ungallant, must be every day of sixty—equal to the situation."

"Oh, don't. You make me feel—what is the horrid word?—coy!" burst out Anna.

For better or worse, this is it, was in her mind, when she walked down the platform beside the chair that wheeled Evan to their reserved compartment on the Blue Train.

iv

A broad terrace, swarming with morning-glory, overhung the dancing sea. At the end of a fortnight, Evan was walking up and down it as impatiently as though on the deck of a ship. The sun had coloured his fine, thin skin into an illusion of health. Nurse Whitney shook her head.

"Don't try to run before you can walk, Mr. Crewe. You've been a very sick man, and, while I'm here, you shan't forget it!"

Anna, coming along the terrace, her slender limbs shadowed through the translucent skirt, the wide, rose-coloured brim of her hat flinging colour into her face, her arms piled with books from the Toulon librairie—everything about her light and sparkling, like water—rejoiced at the sight of him.

"Don't you want to go swimming?" he smiled at her.

"Not till you're ready to come in; it's no fun alone. Toulon's heaven! I can't wait to show you the flower market, and the rade, and the little eating places. I've got a marvellous recipe for brandade de morue—we must have it for dinner."

Presently he was strong enough to take drives: short, to begin with, but penetrating slowly farther and farther into the Mauresque, into the deep country between the coast and Avignon. At first, Nurse Whitney accompanied them; presently she excused herself— whether from inclination or because she sensed herself superfluous Anna was not sure. One afternoon she came to Anna's room.

"It's my duty to say I'm not necessary, Mrs. Sturges; and there's such a shortage of nurses, I feel I ought to be getting back."

"Yes, I understand. Have you said so to Mr. Crewe?"

"I wondered if you'd wish to make other arrangements, before we settle the date."

She felt her cheeks burning at the implication that Nurse Whitney was fully aware that her services were not wholly professional.

"You had better speak to Mr. Crewe this evening."

"The twenty-third?" Evan made a show of consulting his diary. "That will suit us very well; that's the day Madame Lemonnier arrives."

Madame Lemonnier? From the look on Nurse Whitney's face it was the first she, as well as Anna, had heard of Madame Lemonnier.

"A very old friend of ours," Evan was saying blandly. "She's taking us on to her château in Haute Savoie."

(Had Evan gone crazy?)

"Oh—I thought you'd taken the villa on till the end of the month." Surprise broke through a veneer of discretion.

"It's getting rather hot, don't you think? Madame will spend a few days here, then we'll make for the mountains. We'll miss you," said Evan with gravity, "when you go!"

"Who in the world," asked Anna, when they were alone, "is Madame Lemonnier?"

"Don't you know?"

"Only—hats!"

He affected to sigh.

"I know; very unimaginative. It was positively the only name that came into my head."

"Evan; what are you doing?"

"Saving your reputation." He grinned wickedly. "It's what you wanted, isn't it?"

"You needn't rub it in. What, actually, do we do, when Whitney goes?"

"Chadwick is—a tolerable chauffeur." He reached for her hand. "Anna. Don't you trust me?" He held her hand, which struggled to escape, tightly in his own. "In Georgian diaries there is a great deal about the confidential maid; the species seems to have died out, but the male equivalent survives." He felt her shrinking. "If he embarrasses you, Chadwick can go back to England; he's used to—doing as he's told."

She found herself wondering how much Chadwick knew of his master's private life; and—painfully—whether she was only one in a progression.

"Tell me what you are thinking."

"I was wondering," she stammered, "how you would manage without Chadwick. . . . No; it's impossible!"

When he answered, "Nothing is impossible," she recognized, with a shock, it was true. To Evan, nothing was impossible; like a surf rider, he rode with arrogance over waves that would have submerged less experienced athletes.

That was the night he came to her room.

On the following morning, they sat on the rocks, hand in hand, facing a dazzling sea. Evan's hand, gripping hers, was no longer that of a sick man; the sun tan no longer covered a faint mask, reminiscent of the face she had known intimately for—how long?— for nearly thirty years? They sat there, looking into a harbour each had hoped for, towards which they had been drifting, for nearly thirty years; seeing the reefs ahead; wondering what seamanship would carry them into quiet waters.

"There's no going back now, Anna." Her fingers tightened in his hard palm. "But I'll find the answer. So long as you trust me."

A vision of the future—the so terribly obvious future—for a

woman in her position, glazed her eyes with tears. But she was prepared to trust him with her soul.

She should have known him better, she thought, on their first night in Avignon. The folly of imagining him capable of accepting the cheap and easy solution of their problem was borne in on her as they lifted their two faces to the soaring buttresses of the Palace of the Popes. She stared at him, doubting her hearing. She felt as she used to feel in the night nursery, when they took away the lamp.

"Are you—mad, Evan?" she asked unsteadily.

"It all rests with ourselves."

"Now you are talking like a child, like Roger. You know he never admits any barrier to something he wants."

"That will take him a long way." His smile was full of tolerance. "How you underestimate the snobism of success!"

"And how your common sense has been undermined by—all this!" She tried, with a gesture, to convey her meaning: the magic in the air, the bat-haunted twilight, the immemorial stones at whose foot they were standing. Who—above all, what lovers—could not be forgiven for going mad in Avignon?

He took her to Les Baux—from which she shuddered away, feeling evil in each cave mouth, in the diabolical valley.

And to the Roman cities. In Orange they had the amphitheatre to themselves, because it was the hour when tourists were eating. He deserted her, to appear suddenly from one of the hidden galleries that break from the bowels of the earth upon a rocky platform. Anna caught her breath at the beauty of the figure, reduced by distance to a figurine, but dominating its surroundings, that lifted its bronze face to a sky of brazen blue: at the strength of the torso flung back from the forked column of the legs; at the arms thrown up in a mock-heroic gesture—an attitude of unconscious, savage nobility. Reflected light from the tawny rock coloured his hair.

"Sive ad felices radem post funera campos
Seu ferat ardentum rapidi Phlegethontis ad undam,
Nec sine te felix era, nec tecum miser nunquam."

He ended with a flourish, took a flying leap from the rostrum and bounded across the broken stonework to her side.

"Oh, do, do take care!"

"Do you know any Latin? I bet you don't! *'Qui in amore praecipitavit, pejus perit quam si saxe saliat!'* That means, Who falls in love meets a worse fate than he who leaps from a rock."

She laughed.

"And the piece you were reciting?"

" 'Heaven would not be Heaven were thy soul not with mine, nor Hell be Hell were our souls together!'—a very pretty sentiment. Who says I'm no good at declamation? If all else fails I might succeed as a Shakespearean actor. I don't see you, somehow, as the mummer's wife. You would look divine as Perdita, or Ophelia or anything lost and lovely, but I never met a woman with a less capacity for acting. You're as transparent as water!"

"I believe," said Anna, after a pause, "I've been insulted."

He burst into a roar of laughter and clasped her in his arms.

They came to an aqueduct, and he forced her to walk with him across the narrow and dizzy parapet. Her head swam with light, air and wind; as she reeled a little, he pressed it against his shoulder.

"Shall we leap over?"

When she did not answer, he took her chin roughly and jerked it up, so that he could look into her eyes.

"Anna! You weren't supposing I was serious?"

"I was only thinking," she told him, with the simplicity that he found the most unbearably touching thing about her, "that if you had been—I'd have done it."

They stopped by a millstream, and a deep pond of brown water, patched with green—like a Cézanne. He showed her the square brush strokes on the quiet surface, brown on brown, green on green. They told Chadwick to drive on, and slid into the cold water—she in brassière and panties, he in his linen shorts. What would Helen and Roger have said? A divine freedom and folly possessed her. She had never, with Hugh, done these foolish things. Hugh, for whom "mixed bathing" carried its own convention of clothing and deportment, would have been shocked. After the swim they lay out in the sun, to dry. An hour burned up Anna's fragile garments. Chadwick unstrapped a trunk, to get another pair of slacks for Evan.

Each day brought her closer to the moment of decision; but the verdict—she told herself—would have gone against Evan but for the sunstroke which, for all her warnings, her efforts at precaution, undid in twenty-four hours most of the good of their weeks of vagabondage. It did not seem possible that anyone could, in a few short hours, be knocked back to utter helplessness and take so long to recover some small part of the strength they had laboriously built up.

They got him, with some difficulty, into the American hospital in Paris. One morning, when he was getting better, she read him, because she thought it might amuse him, a letter from Edward.

He said, without preliminary,

"Did Edward ever tell you about my wife?"

"Only—that you got married in West Africa. A terrible blow"— she tried to make light of it—"to a lovesick maiden of sixteen."

"And you never asked him——?"

"Why should I? If you wished me to know, you would have told me yourself."

"You're very incurious, aren't you? How many years have we known each other?"

"Do you mean, since I 'grew up'? Let me think; what year was it, when you came to dinner with us in Eaton Square?"

"And went on coming."

"You'd just bought the house in Queen's Terrace"—Anna blushed, wondering if she had been indelicate.

"And my sister Evelyn was keeping house for me. It didn't work out; these things seldom do."

"You were very funny and bad-tempered about it!"

"You seem to have been through most of my trials with me."

"Well," she reflected, "there's something gratifying about sharing the troubles of people one cares for."

"Yet you never asked me anything about my marriage."

"You never spoke of it. One forgets things one never talks about."

"But you must have felt—there must have been moments when our friendship didn't seem to be complete."

"No. No," she repeated, as though reassuring herself. "There are things in most people's lives that are too painful, or perhaps too precious, to talk about. And—isn't the real meaning of friendship the avoidance of intrusion on ground to which you're not invited?"

"You're a rare woman," said Evan, after a silence.

Then he began to tell her: slowly, as one tells a tale that is partly forgotten; stopping from time to time to say, "I think this was how it went," or "it may have been like this"—yet so vividly that, long before he had finished, it seemed to Anna that the Cotter girls were in the room, in their yoked blouses and bell-shaped skirts of the beginning of the century. By the time he ended, Anna realized that there was one thing that Evan had forgotten: of which, at least for the present, she would not remind him.

The old Shaftesbury Theatre; Hugh and she, just back from their honeymoon, had gone, on Hugh's insistence, to see The Arcadians. Hugh had seen it half a dozen times already, but, even in his diversions, he was a creature of habit. He always put up a resistance to a new show, and had to see it two or three times before admitting he "liked" it—which meant that he could hum the tunes, or had found some little "bit" in the chorus who captured his roving fancy.

They went in one of the intervals to speak to some friend in a box, and returning round the back of the dress circle, met Evan, strolling with a girl who, though older than Anna, was more shy and less *soignée*. An expensive gown looked tawdry on her thin shoulders; her teeth were uncared-for; she had a pair of large, dark, silly eyes she tried—ineffectively—to use on Hugh. Anna, with her amiable gift for seizing on the good points in her own sex and ignoring what was open to criticism, admired the dark hair which, though overabundant and badly arranged, gleamed like floss silk under the bandeau which pushed it down, almost to her eyelashes.

Catching Anna's eye as she passed before him into the stalls, Hugh gave a low whistle. Anna said quickly,

"She's like an illustration to my old Hans Andersen." Loyalty to Evan prompted her if possible to forestall Hugh's comment, but, inevitably, she failed.

"Phew. Old Evan has mucked it. She looks like a dago!"

CHAPTER III

*T*hey dined together, a few days after the return from Paris. When she entered the apartment, which, as usual, was crowded with flowers, a waiter was there, arranging a table for two. A little pang went through Anna; yes, of course, she was now one with the Clarissas, Patricias and Ediths. But when Evan came quickly out of the bedroom and lifted her hand to his lips, she knew she was being foolish.

"You don't mind this—for once?" Her lip twitched; the presence of the servant prevented her laughing, but she made a little face at him. "As a matter of fact, I'm dog-tired and I didn't feel like going downstairs." He took the furs from her shoulders and pressed his face for a moment into their scented warmth before laying them across the back of a chair.

"I'm glad to find you, for once, in such a reasonable frame of mind! Well; have you seen Dr. Maxwell?"

He nodded, gave her a light for her cigarette and switched the subject.

In some way, the return to this familiar room altered—a little falsified—their relationship. When last she was here, she had been Hugh Sturges' wife—or, rather, his widow. Now she was the mistress of Evan Crewe. The fact—so simple of acceptance, so wholly natural during their weeks of vagabondage—seemed, here, a little incredible. Their mutual formality, assumed for the benefit of the waiter, stressed the incredibility. Even when the man was not in the room, Anna found it difficult to break through the awkward, almost childish stiffness that had invaded their relationship.

"Where's Chadwick?" she asked abruptly, in a moment when they were alone.

"I've got rid of him," was the short reply.

"Got rid of Chadwick?" How do you, who depend on him for everything, manage without Chadwick? her eyes asked. Evan's brows rose; he looked amused, in a cold way, as though she were a stranger. She stammered, "After all these years!"

He rose, to refill her glass. She saw his long, thin hand, tilting the bottle, and it struck her for the first time that it could be a ruthless hand. She heard him say,

"One can have people about one too long——" and found herself answering quickly,

"Can one have too much, of devotion?"

She knew, instantly, that she had displeased him, although, returned to his chair, he was smiling at her.

"I didn't realize you were an admirer of Chadwick's!"

"I don't know what we'd have done without him! He was wonderful when we had to get you to Paris."

"M'm, yes, I suppose he was. The world is full of wonderful people—at a price!" He gave her again his bitter smile.

He is overtired, thought Anna; and he is not well yet. I wonder what the doctor said?

The room was a corner one, its rounded window commanding the Thames, and St. Paul's, and the city, and, on clear days, the Tower Bridge: a matchless outlook, that they both loved. When the table was removed, and Evan had switched off most of the lights, they sat in the embrasure, looking out on the glow and the glitter; the quiet hum of London made their seclusion more perfect. They sat silently, hand in hand, letting the smoke of their cigarettes melt into the warm air, knowing the peace of lovers who need no words to express their content with each other.

"Now, tell me what the doctor said."

"Oh—a lot of twaddle"—but he told her briefly. It was not good hearing. "And finished up by telling me to get out of here, back to Queen's Terrace! *C'est le comble—quoi?*"

"Wouldn't you like," she ventured, after a pause, "to be back in your own house again?"

"Why on earth? You know why I bought it; when my brother-in-law died, and my sister had nowhere to live, it seemed a convenient sort of idea, to set up house together. One of those ideas that should have worked out, and didn't. We fought like cat and dog, and eventually she took herself off to live with an old school friend, and as I hadn't time or inclination for domestic responsibilities, I closed the place up. You've never seen it, have you? Most of it's stuffed with Evelyn's furniture—Victorian Gothic."

"I've been in some of those houses; they're beautifully designed. I love the hooded balconies and those little attic windows, like half-moons. What a gracious period it was, the Regency. Queen's Terrace always reminds me of the South Coast towns: there should be the sea somewhere, and gulls mewing, and cockleshells and little rockeries!"

"You never told me you knew it."

"Some friends of Hugh's had the end house: lovely balusters and staircases, and arcaded drawing rooms!"

"You must teach me about those things; I don't know anything about period."

"We'd better begin with your house!" She spoke half jestingly, and felt him recoil.

"No, no, I've got no time for a house. This does me very well, except——"

She sensed the irritation of his glance along the walls. Of course, Maxwell was right; the apartment, convenient as it was, was a narrow cage for the nervous and physical energy of a man like Evan.

Where to hang the Rouault and the Modigliani they bought in Paris? What to do with the horseman in *terre cuite* they found in an Avignon junk shop? How to display the miniatures in wax Evan had had the luck to acquire from an impecunious young Frenchman, faced with the enforced disposal of his heirlooms? These things were the real Evan, the expression of his inner self, his line of escape; but the pleasure of possession was largely discounted by the disorder they created in the already crowded space of the apartment. These are the things that irritate a sick person, and, to Evan, whose passion for neatness and order had surprised her, they must be a growing source of annoyance.

"That"—she pointed to the Rouault—"would look wonderful in the little alcove at the head of the stairs."

"How do you know there's a little alcove?" He sounded amused, as though he were humouring her.

"I'm only guessing; there's one in the Bulstrodes' house. They've got some sort of a Chinese jar in it. Of course, I know the Regency architects didn't go for repetition——"

He got up with a smothered exclamation of impatience, to answer the telephone.

"Yes. Oh—you."

Anna's instinct told her it was a woman. A sudden embarrassment decided her to go into the bedroom, and she rose quickly, snatching up her bag, which lay on the sofa beside her. But, as she passed Evan, on her way to the door, he shot out his hand and caught her wrist. Surprised, disconcerted, Anna tried to free herself, but his clasp tightened. She was obliged, against her will, to stand there—listening to a voice that was not to be recognized as Evan's: slow, dry, casual—subtly insulting—at least, thought Anna, that was how she would have interpreted it, if such a voice had reached her on the telephone.

"How long have I been back? . . . About a week—I don't know: it might be ten days. . . . Yes, of course I had your letters; you had my wire from Avignon? . . . Well, you know what I am, about writing! . . . Yes, I'm absolutely fit; I've had a marvellous holiday—tell you about it sometime.

"Next week end—no; I can't manage that."

A thin voice at the other end of the line piped something about "dinner."

"I haven't got my diary here and my secretary's gone home. . . . No, I'm just off to Germany. . . . No, the date's not fixed—any time, I'm not sure. I see your new book's had a great success——"

A sensation of nausea and humiliation came over Anna, as she was forced to listen to a faint, chattering outburst. Evan held the receiver away from his ear, allowed the speaker to run to a finish and answered softly,

"You'd better take a couple of tablets and get to bed."

"Damn you to hell!" came with startling clarity from the instrument.

"Or you can start a new novel—all about sun and blood and lust!" He hung up. Anna, her wrist limp in his fingers, burst into tears. He caught her in his arms.

"Anna!"

"I didn't want to know—I don't want to know—about anything!"

"Can't you understand? There must be no secrets—ever—between you and me. I wanted to show you that's all over: that there's no woman in the world for me, but you——"

"I can't bear—that sort of—brutality!"

The word evidently stung him.

"I'm not brutal! But don't you know there's only one way of getting rid of a leech?—to drop salt on it, so that it curls up?" He was trying to make her smile, but she held herself aloof.

"At least you needn't drop your salt in public. It's disgusting, and I hate it."

"Ah." He loosed her, and stood surveying her ironically. "So that's what it's come to, has it? I'm brutal, I'm disgusting and you hate me."

"That's a purely childish perversion of my words." She picked up the long sable scarf and folded it round her throat. "We're both tired," she said, with an effort, "and a little overwrought. Shall we say 'Good night'?"

"Not on your life! Do you realize this is our first quarrel?—and over a woman—a silly creature for whom I don't give a snap of my fingers!"

"You did, some time or other."

"What's this?—jealousy?" He sounded triumphant.

"Now you're disparaging me!"

"Come; let's have this out, once and for all. 'As a youth I had many mistresses; now I have one—Who fills my eyes with silver and my heart with gold'—are you blaming me, for getting rid of the base metal?"

"It didn't seem base at the time. And if gold gets tarnished, you don't drop it in the gutter."

"Anna," he said, after a pause, "you don't know your own sex—or mine. Do I have to describe to you the relationships that develop between men and women—malgré eux?

"I was in love with you, from the night I came to Eaton Square; but you belonged to Hugh. I accepted—substitutes. That's all it amounted to. You must take my word for it, that I never pretended to permanence, or accepted responsibilities for any of the people who filled your place. Any 'promises' I'm supposed to have made exist only in their imaginations. Do you think I'd be such a fool as to involve myself, with all my mind and my heart set on you?"

"Even knowing you couldn't—have me?"

He smiled a little.

"I meant to have a good try! Shall I tell you something? The very night before Hugh got his pneumonia, I sat in this room, wondering if the time had come to chance my hand. It was patent—to me, at least—you didn't love Hugh. If I'd been able to offer you marriage, I wouldn't have waited so long. But—you'd lunched with me, the pair of you, that day: do you remember? And before we'd finished, Hugh said he felt rotten and he'd go to his club. I thought it was only a sample of his usual moodiness and didn't pay much attention; you wanted him to go home with you, and he snapped you up and said all he wanted was a drink and a sleep. When we were alone, I felt you were lonely and miserable, under your gaiety. I nearly spoke then."

"Oh, I'm so glad you didn't; it would have spoiled everything, and been so horrible to remember!"

"That night I made up my mind. I rang you in the morning—you probably weren't told—and the butler said Hugh was very ill; they thought he had caught a chill at Hurst Park. Anna: this may shock you. But I felt—then—I wouldn't have long to wait."

"You waited—twelve months."

"Shall we call that the measure of my love? Knowing you, I didn't want to do anything crass. You felt Hugh's death more deeply, simply because he meant so little to you."

Her eyes glazed; she groped blindly for his hand.

"And I called you brutal——"

"—and disgusting! Don't forget that."

"Dearest, I couldn't bear listening to you being—unkind! We owe something to the people who've helped us through our—bad patches!"

"My sweet, soft, silly Anna—would any have helped, do you think, if it hadn't been made worth their while?"

She felt herself shrinking, even as she abandoned herself to his arms.

ii

When he left for Germany, Anna was pledged to "look after" the house in Queen's Terrace and to have it, if possible, ready for occupation on his return.

Charmed by its structure, she was, as he had warned her, horrified by the contents, and a rather embarrassing correspondence with Evan's sister resulted in the removal of most of the furniture to storage. How deeply indifferent he must have been, at that time, ever to have suffered it! Given *carte blanche*, she bent all her invention to the transformation of a few rooms to her taste, and his. The night before his arrival, she was able, with triumph, to supervise the hanging, on honey-coloured walls, of the Rouault, the Dufys, a Soutine and the little Vuillard which was her own proud discovery in a corner of Montmartre. Remembering his passion for flowers, she gave an extravagant order to a florist, and, overcome at the last moment by an inexplicable shyness, left a note of welcome and betook herself to Helen's nursery, where the infant Belinda bubbled and gurgled in her cradle.

"Goodness, Mother, you look half dead! What *have* you been up to?"

"Getting Evan's house in order and engaging a staff for him." She was conscious of Helen's sharp look.

"Well, I'm sure he ought to be very grateful! I don't see why you should put yourself to all that trouble."

"Where are you going?" Helen was dressed to go out; she remembered noticing, in the hall, a cellophaned sheaf of flowers. She saw the colour mount in her daughter's face.

"I thought you'd forgotten the date." There was not a shade of expression in her voice or look, but Anna felt as though she had been slapped. The date? Oh, God; the anniversary of Hugh's death. Deeply ashamed, she whispered,

"You're going to Golders Green."

"I'll be back for tea; you don't have to hurry away?"

"Helen, I ought to—Shall I come with you?"

"Whyever should you? You hate that kind of thing," said Helen briskly. "Belinda's napping; don't disturb her, or there'll be trouble with Nanny. Why don't you have a lie-down until tea time? You look as though you could use it." She gave her mother a matter-of-fact kiss and picked up the flowers. "There's a good fire in the drawing room, and I'll tell them you're not to be disturbed."

"Thank you; I just came to see the baby—I think, perhaps, I'd better get back." She glanced at her watch; the plane was due in, and Evan might ring up.

She remembered she had planned to go into the electrical department at Harrod's, about some of the fittings at Queen's Terrace. When she walked into her own hall, the telephone was ringing.

"Why aren't you here?" The note of truculent resentment almost shook a laugh from her. She said meekly,

"Well—how are you?"

"The car is on its way to fetch you"—and he slammed the receiver back on its hooks.

She rushed, to make sure of her face, her hair; he must not think —like Helen!—that she looked jaded. Then she drove through the soft, autumn rain to the house which—little as she then realized— was to be her future home.

With her head against his bosom, she found herself clutching him: feeling, with horror, little but bones under the thin cloth of his travelling suit.

"Taken off weight, have I? Well, I've been damned busy—and so," he added, letting himself drop back on the sofa, "are the works going to be!"

He told her, over tea, that war was inevitable. He described the conclusions to which he had come, through his tour of the industrial regions of Germany. She tried to put aside her feminine disappointment—that he made no reference to the changes she had effected during his absence; for the time being, he was blind to them. She forced herself to pay intelligent attention to the names of Hitler, Von Ribbentrop and the Reich, and to associate herself with his preoccupation with the prospect ahead; but all of her intellectual power was sunk in the perception that she had again on her hands a very sick man.

For two and a half years Anna fulfilled, to all intents and purposes, the functions of a nurse, as well as those of maîtresse en titre of Evan's household. From the moment of his return, either from Head Office—now transferred to Pall Mall—or from one of the Crewe factories, she was at his disposal: sometimes to dine *tête-à-tête*, sometimes to act as hostess to solemn-faced delegates of British and foreign industries, mysteriously linked with Crewe's; to members of the Cabinet or of Congress; to Whitehall bigwigs— simple-seeming, owl-eyed men, with the weight of secret knowledge behind them, who, from Anna's point of view, were less formidable than the women they brought with them. She learned, for all her simplicity, to recognize, behind the deference they paid to her, as hostess, the sharp atmosphere of rivalry and intrigue that surrounds political wives. She learned to guard her tongue, so that nothing she said could be used to the advantage of Evan's competitors. And, whoever was present, the talk was all of war, war, war.

She carried, with sweetness and fortitude, what, for a woman like Anna Sturges, was a heavy burden. The artists, the writers, the charming foreigners whose company she had formerly enjoyed, had vanished from Evan's circle. There was none of the wit and laughter that enlightened his hospitalities at the Savoy. With little but her beauty and her grace to contribute to the lengthy, and often portentous, discussions that took place across the long, candlelit table at Queen's Terrace, she felt, often, a nonentity and, sometimes, an ignoramus. Her only justification was the knowledge that she helped Evan, by her presence, to carry some part of the load which had visibly increased since his return from Germany.

Sometimes they planned "a quiet evening," and, changing his mind at the last minute, Evan would take her to the opera or the ballet. Realizing that these, also, offered him relaxation, she made no demur; but, one night at the opera, he looked so deathly that, filled with alarm, she laid her hand on his knee. He opened his eyes to smile at her.

"What is it?"

"Would you like to go home?"

He shook his head. The lids closed again over his exhausted eyes, as he murmured,

"There's not much more time; we must see and hear as much as we can."

This, more than anything to which she listened at his parties, brought home to Anna that all the talk of war was not a political chimera, but an inevitability for which, morally and spiritually, they must all prepare.

She found she was very cold. The cold increased. When they were in the car, driving back to Eaton Square, she felt herself shrinking inside the mink coat Evan had given her for her last birthday. Suddenly her knee shivered against his. Mistaking the contact, he touched her with passionate tenderness. They were nearly at her door.

"Are you really leaving me?" he muttered.

Her heart gave a nervous leap; this argument had taken place before.

"It can't go on like this for ever, you know, Anna!" As she made no reply, he coaxed her. "Let me come in for an hour. You know I can never sleep, after those infernal injections."

"I—I think I must have got a chill," she stammered. "I'm so sorry—but I think I'll have to go to bed."

"A chill?" His face burned white in the darkness; his hand grabbed her wrist and felt angrily for the pulse. "For God's sake take care of yourself. Don't get ill!"

He insisted on accompanying her into the hall, to take her in his arms. Half an hour later he rang, to know if she was in bed. His last words—charged with an absurd exaggeration of panic—were:

"Don't forget: *I cannot live without you.*"

iii

Roger chose the following morning to walk into her bedroom, sling himself across the end of the bed and announce his intention of getting married.

"But—my dearest boy!" said Anna, when she had found her

breath. "You've got another year at Oxford——" It sounded foolish, but was better, perhaps, than reminding Roger he was only a few months past his coming of age, or talking about the responsibilities—inassociable with Roger!—of married life.

"Oh—that." He pulled out his cigarette case, and remembered, for once, to offer her one, before lighting his own. Neither Hugh nor Roger ever remembered that, though a mild smoker, she never smoked in her bedroom; the scent of tobacco offended the fastidiousness she brought to everything connected with her toilette. "You know as well as I do, the balloon's going up any minute."

"The war," she said, with sinking heart. Like many other women she was tempted, during those middle years of the decade, to wonder why she had ever borne a son.

"Well, one naturally wants to have as much fun as possible before one's swiped into the army! Mary and I've worked it out that we should be able to have a whale of a time for the next twelve months, at any rate; and by then she'll be in pod and I'll get a commission. I thought you might be able to give us the dope on a special license."

"Is there—all that hurry?" faltered Anna.

"Oh, it's all right—if that's what you mean," her son said airily. "But you can't put any faith in Berlin, or, if it comes to that, in our diplomacy. We thought we might get married on—let's see: what's today?—well, say Friday; and take off for Bermuda, by way of a start."

"Have Mary's parents anything to say to this?"

"She's coping with them this morning. It doesn't matter what they say; Mary's twenty-three and she's come into fifteen thou' from her godfather. That ought to go quite a way"—it was Hugh's ingenuous grin, when he wished to charm or placate one—"towards financin' a twelve-month honeymoon!"

As Anna did not reply, the grin turned to a scowl.

"You're not turnin' sour, are you?"

"Reasonable as it all seems to you—I suppose you've had plenty of time to discuss it—you must see it comes as rather a shock to me!"

"As a matter of fact, we only thought of it ourselves last night," admitted Roger, with charming candour. "We were having a bite at the Embassy, and it just popped into my head—like that! Mary seemed to take quite a good view, so we worked it out over a couple of daiquiris, and—well—what about that special license?"

"I suppose," said Roger, when Anna had supplied, to the best of her ability, the necessary information, and had refrained—she hoped heroically, but suspected weakness—from recriminations, "there's no point in askin' if you're likely to be in between six and seven?"

"Why not?—if you want me——"

"Mary said something about comin' in, to go through the mother-in-law performance. I said it was rather dated, and you were likely to be out, anyhow, but——"

"Oh really, Roger! Of course I'll be in; you should have said so!"

"Well, I didn't know. It's about six months since any of us set eyes on you"—he waived her expostulation at the exaggeration— "and if anyone asks where you are or what you're doing you've always got a date with your boy friend——"

"That's rather ungraceful—if you mean Evan."

"I couldn't very well mean anyone else, could I? There's no need to look pie-eyed about it; we all know you've been cracked on each other for years. And if you want to know," volunteered her son, tactfully averting his eyes from the flame that ran up Anna's cheek, "Helen and I both think it's hard luck you two can't get married."

"Helen! I thought she'd be the first to resent——"

Roger wagged his head with a kindly assumption of the air of a man of the world, and replied,

"Of course, old Helen's a bit sentimental about Father, but she's not as much of a dumb cluck as all that. We both realize you're getting on——"

"Thanks!" gasped Anna.

"—but you're still pretty attractive," said her son handsomely, "and lots of women of your age remarry. As a matter of fact, the only thing that rattles Helen is—well: I suppose it does look a bit funny, to some people—you, popping in and out at Evan's, as though—as though——"

"Go on: as though——?"

It was Roger's turn to flush.

"What do you take me for?" he spluttered. "I'm not a snotty little provincial, like Norman Raymond!"

Is he telling me—is my son telling me—that he knows I'm Evan's mistress? Her head swam. His next words disabused her of the fear; of the hope.

"We know that's not your line of country, and—good God! Helen and I aren't Victorians. People's private lives are their own affair." She watched him weave himself, in a cloud of incoherencies, out of the room.

Shortly before Christmas Evan was operated upon again, and the result, this time, was pronounced satisfactory, even by Maxwell. But he was advised to take another holiday. To Anna's surprise, he was complaisant.

"We're going to Portugal, this time."

"We?"

"Of course." His calmness challenged her.

"But—Evan: where does all this end?"

He seemed to be amused; crossed the room and lit a cigar.

"I've told you it couldn't go on like this for ever."

"But—what's the alternative?"

"Living openly together," he told her, as though it were the simplest thing in the world. "Why make such a 'thing' of it? It's what we've been doing, in effect, for years. All the people we know take it for granted——"

"Oh, no!"

"Are you ashamed?"

"Of course not!" But she was, inwardly. Ashamed—not of or for herself or him, but for the good faith of those who trusted her. "It's not fair, it's not playing the game," she said confusedly, "to ask people to accept, publicly, something they've taken, out of affection, in private. It's such a poor return for their tact and kindness——!"

He said, after a silence,

"I know it's asking a great deal of you——"

"It's not myself!"

"Any woman in your position," he continued, as though she had not spoken, "must feel she's making a sacrifice. There are things I shan't be able to give you——"

"What nonsense is this?" She forced herself to smile. "You give me everything!"

"I'm not a fool. Certain houses will be closed to us, and there'll be certain company you'll prefer, from delicacy, to keep out of. I'll often be angry on your behalf—though I know how little ambitious you are; and you'll make me ashamed of my anger, with that serenity of yours! It's amusing—at least, it ought to be—to see public honour paid to a whore and withheld from a woman who lives openly and faithfully with the man she loves. In fact, it's terribly funny, until it happens to touch one's own life and one's own woman. You know why I'm saying all this, don't you?" He drew her to his side. "Whatever you feel, I shall feel with and for you. If you can take it, I can."

"Neither of us can; because of the children."

"What—Roger and Helen? Both married? Both starting families of their own?"

"Exactly; isn't that the complete answer?"

"Don't be ridiculous; they aren't Victorians—or even Edwardians. In the neo-Georgian age, the sins of the parents aren't visited on the children. Neither Helen nor Roger are going to suffer, socially, because you and I choose to depart from convention."

"There are other sorts of suffering——"

"My very dear Anna: I don't wish to be offensive: but even you, I hope, won't claim sensitivity for either of your children?"

She gave him a sweet, shamefaced smile.

"No; but couldn't it be as painful, to be born stupid, as to be born sensitive?"

"We aren't accountable for other people's stupidity, and you, certainly, aren't responsible for it. I wonder," he said slowly, "how you visualize this future of ours? I said something once about 'the snobbery of success.' You didn't understand, did you? It wouldn't occur to you that, in my position, I can command, practically—anything! I'm not offering you some dubious, shadowy existence in the background of my life, Anna. I can impose you on any society—apart, of course, from that of the Court—that you choose."

"I don't wish to be imposed!" she cried indignantly.

"Of course not. A stupid expression; forgive me. You need no imposing. You don't realize the impression you make on the people who meet you. They all know what you stand for in my life, but they're prepared to accept you for yourself, apart from any privileges I might claim for you. The strongholds of British hypocrisy have fallen, since the last war. When the next one comes along, there won't be time for worrying."

"Won't you believe me? I don't care about any of that. All I mind about, apart from you, is my children. You can't expect me to hurt them! Roger might understand—one never knows—but it's too much to ask of Helen, tied up with all her provincial in-laws. Norman's people are quite capable of making her life not worth living——"

"So it comes to this: a showdown between us and your children."

"If you must put it that way."

"For God's sake, Anna, have common sense! When the war starts, what use will you be to Helen or Roger? He'll be in the army; she—if I know anything about Helen!—will be in a factory, or one of the services. Norman, of course, will be called up. You'll fool around, persuading yourself you're being useful, in some damned job for which, practically and temperamentally, you're unfitted! While I *need* you. You idiot, don't you see how I need you?"

She did her best to calm him.

"Whenever you need me, I shall be here: as I've always been."

He smothered a sigh of impatience.

"You can't even imagine, can you, what the next war's going to be like? I shall be what they call 'a key man.' I shall be obliged to go to places where I could not possibly take you, except as my wife—*en titre*. Don't quibble!" as she raised her head. "We've still got some little time for me to build you into a position which even a wartime government will be obliged to respect! And I can trust you, with your tact and discretion, to justify whatever claims I make on your behalf. But I can't do without you. Do you hear what I'm saying? I cannot do without you!"

iv

He told her casually, a few days later,

"I've asked Helen and Norman to dine with us."

He had never pretended to like Helen, or to be more than tolerant of the man she had married: a stout, serious, young barrister, whom she had got to know at the golf school where she was having some coaching. Norman Raymond recognized a young woman who could give him the *entrée* to a society for which his birth and upbringing had left him unprepared, while Helen, on her part, shrewdly aware of the limitations of choice, even for the daughter of Hugh Sturges, saw in Norman someone she could dominate, and of whose prospects people "in the know" seemed confident. Hugh did not think much of the match, but Anna saw in it the almost perfect union of two people whose minds ran on perfectly conventional lines, and who shared the same set of values. It was the only time Helen had turned to her for sympathy, in preference to her father.

Anna now hid a considerable misgiving under her reply.

"That's very sweet of you." Norman, she knew, would be pleased:
it was a feather in the cap of any young man, to be invited to
dine with Evan Crewe. "Are you asking anyone else?"

"No; I thought we might dine, for once, en famille"—which did
not contribute to her peace of mind.

Helen wore a gown of beaded crêpe—rather matronly—and
looked with a shade of envy at her mother's narrowly pleated
chiffon.

"That's nice; where did you get it?"

"In Paris." Helen had a way of making one feel guilty about
innocent things.

"Goodness, you must have paid a whacking lot! Mary got some
things while they were there; she says the prices were monstrous."

"How's the baby?"

"Belinda? She's a tough little thing," said Helen, with evident
satisfaction. "Keeps Nanny on tiptoe every moment of the day.
Do you know, this morning, in the square——" The talk de-
generated into nursery subjects; much as she treasured news about
her grandchild, Anna knew Evan was bored.

After dinner, the conversation turned upon Spain, where trouble
was imminent. Norman had a good deal to say, in his pedantic
fashion, about the bogus Republic, oil concessions and Communist infiltration; but she knew, from Evan's attention, that he was
interested and that Norman was "talking sense." He was a good-
looking, thickset young man, with a sweet mouth and small, shortsighted eyes permanently distorted by thick convex glasses. His
deference to Evan was excessive.

"We are going to Portugal," Evan told him.

"Wolfram?" said Norman intelligently.

Evan laughed.

"Nominally a holiday. Anna is due for one."

She saw their eyes, deliberately avoiding one another. Evan continued calmly.

"Don't you think, by the way, it's rather absurd for her to keep up that barn of a place in Eaton Square, since Roger got married?"

"I never thought about it," floundered Helen, as her husband was silent. "I suppose it is rather big for one person. You never said anything," she accused Anna, who murmured something unintelligible. "I don't see how you'd get all the furniture into a smaller place—and storage is nearly as expensive as rent; isn't it, Norman?"

Norman said that that was rather an exaggeration, and that there were plenty of smaller houses on the market. If Anna was serious about wishing to make a change, he would be pleased to look out for something for her. There was a good market, at present, for secondhand furniture——

"You wouldn't want to get rid of the Restoration stuff!" put in Helen, referring to the more cumbersome and least decorative furnishings of the Eaton Square establishment. "It belonged to Daddy's family, didn't it? It must be very valuable, and nobody wants to part with heirlooms!" Nobody had *better* part with heirlooms! was the implication of her tone. Anna was on the point of murmuring that Roger and Mary might like them, when it occurred to her that Mary, at any rate, had enough culture to recognize most of the "Restoration" pieces as fakes.

Taut in her chair, she felt Evan's hands press down on her shoulders.

"As a matter of fact," he said calmly, "we have decided to set up house together."

She wondered whether the tick of the clock was any louder than that of her heart. After a protracted silence, she turned towards her daughter.

"Do you mind, very much?"

"But——" Helen's face had turned purple; she dragged her agonized eyes away from her husband's face. Norman was closely examining a piece of Bristol glass. "You're not married!" she burst out.

"That's unhappily true. But we have come to the conclusion

that there are things that matter more, at our time of life, than—if you'll forgive me, Raymond, for putting it that way—a legal formula."

The room swam round Anna. She was as little prepared as the Raymonds for this discussion; she realized that Evan had forced it on them deliberately, and that there was no alternative for her but loyalty.

Norman's eyes glittered solemnly, like a young owl's, as he set the glass down.

"You may be able, if the Bill goes through, to regularize your position. Or am I wrong, sir?"

"I'm afraid you are. I suppose you're thinking of the insanity clause?"

"That was in my mind." For a rising barrister, Norman was singularly embarrassed. Evan shook his head.

" 'Incurably of unsound mind.' That means, incapable of being healed by medicine, or medical skill."

"I'd been given to understand it's more than twenty years since the—er—subject was certified."

"If, by 'the subject,' you mean my unfortunate wife"—Evan smiled thinly—"she was never certified. Her sister—who is her guardian—saw to that. Actually, there are no grounds for certification. She isn't dangerous, and she has long periods of approximate sanity."

"Long enough to qualify her to plead?"

"If there'd been the smallest loophole, don't you think I'd have availed myself of it? My wife's solicitors have had enough evidence to enable her to divorce me at any time in the last twenty years. No doubt she'd have done it, but for her sister's influence."

"What about desertion?"

"My dear fellow, I did the 'deserting'!"

At this point, Helen rose, burst into tears and left the room. Anna, about to follow her, was checked by Evan.

"Stay; I want you. Believe me, Raymond, I've been into the

matter from every possible angle. Even if they bring in this five-years clause, it's no use to us. My wife has never been in detention under the Lunacy and Mental Treatment Acts, and, so far as the present law goes, she's perfectly qualified to sue for divorce—which, unless something happens to remove the sister, she'll never do. I've got no grounds to sue on—*en somme*, it's one of those dead ends from which, through the channels of English law, there's no escape."

"A most unfortunate position," muttered Norman.

"Admittedly; and we're proposing to make the best of it."

"I don't really feel there's anything for me to say."

"I wasn't inviting your comments. My only reason for dropping this rather—disconcerting—piece of news on you tonight is to ask you (I'm speaking rather for Anna than myself) to use all the influence you can to persuade Helen to accept a situation which—as we both realize—is a very disagreeable one, from her point of view."

"I'll do what I can. But—it's not very agreeable for anybody, is it?"

The shadow of a smile slipped across Evan's face.

"I expect you'd like to discuss it with your wife privately."

"I think, if you will excuse me, my best plan would be to take her home."

Anna's heart swelled with pity for the young man, product of a strictly conventional upbringing, whose professional sophistication was so painfully unequal to the situation in which, through no fault of his own, he found himself involved. She rose to kiss him.

"My dear, I'm so sorry. Please, will you tell Helen, I'm—so—sorry!"

Helen's letter reached her the following evening.

I suppose I'll have to pretend to back you up, because you're my mother. But I'll never, never forgive you. This would break Father's heart.

Of course you both think you can get away with murder, but you'll find plenty of people who'll feel the way we do about it. Roger and I have known for years you were absolutely infatuated, but it never even entered our heads you'd be likely to do a thing like this!

Evan's tenderness and consideration during the following weeks were never to be forgotten by Anna; he had no thought, seemingly, but to prove to her the depth and permanence of his devotion. The weather deteriorated while they were at Estoril, and the outbreak of the Spanish Civil War prevented their carrying out their former intention of motoring across the peninsula into France, but Evan hired a private plane, and they swooped rather dangerously over the sierras and the Pyrenees into what, said Evan, would be, to them, for ever "the lovers' country." No word of war was spoken, for a long time, by either; but in the hearts of both each felt, with a sweet and melancholy poignancy, that they were seeing the last of the innocent and happy France of their idyll. The first time this rose to the surface was at La Rochelle.

"Have you ever seen La Rochelle?" Evan asked her. "It's a strange, grim place—and you'll find it very primitive—but it's a place you ought to see, before the Huns demolish it."

After Nantes the rain started thinly, and the cattle were being driven home off the Poictevin marshes. The mists were rising, and the backs of the cattle moved just above the mist, which they tore with their wide white horns. Anna felt chilled, and pressed into the shelter of his arm.

"Are you cold?" As ever, he was solicitous of her comfort.

"Not really: but it's eery. Do you hear them?—they're all round us: the dead men in rusted mail—and the marsh lights—and the adders. And the sun: look—it's like a burning plane——"

They got into La Rochelle by moonlight; there was just light enough to see the sixteenth-century façades, white, barred with bitumen, and the hollow, wind-swept arcades. As she prepared for bed, Anna hoped they would not stay long; there was something evil, something inimical in the air; she wondered why Evan had brought her.

They lunched, on the following morning, in a window overlooking the quays, and the towers of St. Nicolas and the Chain, and the Duperré statue. A light brume made everything pale grey; the nets, hung up to dry, were pale blue, sapphire, faïence and the transparent colour of unboiled shrimps. The food was coarse and badly cooked; she expected Evan to expostulate, until she saw that the whole of his attention was fixed on an adjoining table. The roar of rochelais and Vendéan voices made conversation all but impossible; she, too, set herself to listen. Much was unintelligible; once or twice she glanced at Evan, his face bent inscrutably towards an unpalatable dish. Not their France; a France of savages. . . .

"Do you feel like walking?" he asked her when they were out on the cobbles. He looked down at her feet. "What other woman would have the sense to pack a pair of flat heels!" He linked an arm into hers. They looked down from the top of the tower of St. Nicolas, upon the strange perspectives of the *bassins* and the boats and the fishwives collecting their boxes at the harbour steps. They were oddly silent. Then—still silently—they walked out along the *rade*. With the Atlantic wind blowing spray into their faces, and the distant thunder of the Perthuis d'Antioche in their ears, Evan asked her,

"Well, do you like it?"

She hesitated before answering.

"Am I foolish? I *don't*. To me, it's not France. I feel as though we were in an alien—and not very friendly—country."

"So you were listening to those fellows at the next table."

"I didn't understand much. What were they saying?"

He was silent. Presently she looked up, and saw his profile, cut against the white and stormy sky. He said, after a while,

"I'd bet a thousand to a ha'penny, when the war breaks, that the French will be out of it within six months."

"You wouldn't get Winston Churchill to agree with you," said Anna.

"He's Francophile. I love, and know, France," was the answer.

"Which means?" she persisted.

"I read the little local papers. I listen to what the people say. I see the game their politicians are playing."

"But they've been our allies for—how many years?"

"Not our natural allies. In temperament and ideology, we're much closer to the Germans than ever we've been to the French."

"You can say that—after the last war?"

"Of course I can. Hitlerian Germany is only a temporary madness. It's likely to prove—I admit—a disaster. For which in part, we're responsible."

"And the French?"

"Victims of a corrupt political system. They'll rat on us; but who should blame them? Forewarned is forearmed. It's a pity some of the members of our Government weren't here today. I'm sorry to have let you in for this, Anna, but we'll get away tonight."

They reached Alençon. Missing him from her side, Anna got up and found him in the sitting room, engrossed with pencil and paper. He lifted his head to smile at her.

"What are you doing?"

"I bet that means nothing to you." He pushed the sheet of paper towards her, Anna knitted her brow and shook her head. He laughed.

"Nor did it to Uncle Everett! It's only the development of a design I showed him just after the Boer War."

He explained it to her, and she found herself shrinking.

"But it's—inhuman!"

He answered her as he had answered Everett.

"The next war, Anna, will be inhuman. All wars are. The next particularly so. But things like this might help to shorten it—if one could persuade the maggot-headed sentimentalists in our Government!"

They talked till dawn. It was the first time he had taken her fully into his confidence. She strained to understand his descriptions of the modifications in the Crewe plant which would enable them, at short notice, to switch over to war production; and the arguments with his fellow directors who considered him crazy because, in the face of all the pacifist pronouncement of the Government, he insisted on preparing for war; and the motives underlying his endless conferences with foreign producers, annoyed and mystified by England's refusal to enter into contracts, with danger so plainly ahead.

"Do you wonder they think the Communists have got at us, with Chamberlain persistently playing the Communist hand? I suppose," he teased her, "you don't know that the charm you worked, in Lisbon, on Periera, may be worth a year's shipment of tungsten? Of course you don't—my beautiful idiot of a wife!"

"I have a shock for you," he told her, a few hours before they were on the plane for Northolt. "You'll find a new staff at Queen's Terrace. Don't be alarmed; if any don't suit you, you've only to get rid of them. They're all prepared to take their orders from Mrs. Crewe."

CHAPTER IV

At the time of Munich, Anna tentatively asked her sister-in-law whether, in the event of war, the children—Helen's and Roger's —could be given shelter at Camelhurst. Griselda, her long face doleful, could make no promises. "We're almost certain to be taken over by the Government. They're talking of moving all the departments out into the country; we'll probably have to turn out ourselves."

Norman and Roger were among the first non-regulars to be given commissions. When the bombing started, Helen and the infant Belinda—now known as Lin—went to Norman's people in Derbyshire, and Mary, with two-year-old Hugh and nine-months-old Simon, struggled to adapt herself to the cottage Roger had taken for them near Wantage. Their doleful letters—though Helen was spirited enough to make fun of the Chesterfield in-laws— touched Anna's heart, and, though reluctant to add to his burdens, she asked Evan if there was any hope of finding a place where the family could be collected together, and live, so far as it was possible in wartime, a normal life. It was all but impossible, by then, to find anything suitable; the rush from London that followed the first bombings, and the snapping up of all available country houses, left them with little choice.

Through his secretary, Evan sent her particulars of a place

in Berkshire, and advised her to take Mary over to look at it.

The Court, Chilton Magnates—big, rambling, moat-surrounded, its Queen Anne structure grafted on Carolean foundations—must have been thankfully leased by its owner. It was joyfully occupied by Raymonds and Sturgeses. Helen, between the devil and the blue sea, hating to accept favours from Evan, insisted on paying rent; when Anna explained that such an arrangement would offend them both, she said—Well, then, she would earn her keep by acting as housekeeper: an arrangement that suited everybody, as Mary had little gift for wartime housekeeping, and wanted to be rid of her nurse and devote her time to the boys. Anna could only be there briefly in the intervals of her attendance on Evan.

Hers, she felt guiltily, was not a very distinguished contribution to the war effort. She was only just over age for calling up, and many older women had taken on full-time service. No one but herself knew how necessary she was to Evan: how much his health and his nerves owed to her care, and how far her presence went to preserve his efficiency. The Crewe factories were distributed all over the British Isles; he was obliged, not only to keep in touch with his key men, but to attend conferences in remote areas where production was expedited by personal interest and supervision. Several of his designs had been incorporated into the national scheme of defence, and he was rated as a V.I.P.

Anna's war was spent in cars, on railways and in planes chartered on long-distance flights whose destination was kept secret until a few minutes before arrival. Her work was to secure for Evan whatever might be of comfort in the brief moments of respite from his tasks, to save him from contacts with well-meaning but time-wasting people and, in general, to control, so far as might be, his movements in his own interests and those of the powers he represented. The first two fell within the province of any well-trained secretary; but Miss Ryder, to her furious indignation, had been called up and drafted on to the staff of a film corporation. She came to Anna, in floods of tears. "I know Mr. Crewe could get me exemption if he applied!" Guessing that something more than mere disinclination underlay her distress, Anna went into the matter, and, on discovering that Miss Ryder had an old and blind aunt whom she looked after in the afternoon (employing her only for his private affairs, Evan rarely kept her after midday, and she was not on duty again until five o'clock), promised to speak about it. Evan, to her surprise, would not even listen. Miss Ryder's private life was no business of his—"Oh darling, when she's been with you eleven years?" Anna was driven to expostulate. "She's not the only one whose plans are disorganized by national service!" snapped Evan, and she had learned, by then, not to press him. Of course, he was right; yet it would have been so simple for him to arrange the matter. He had done it for other people—with less claim on his offices than Marjorie Ryder. A word in the right place, and officialdom would quickly decide that her work for Evan Crewe was more essential than typing script for a film director.

"What about your aunt?" asked Anna, when she was obliged to tell her the appeal had failed. "Could we arrange something?"

"No, thanks," snapped Miss Ryder. "I don't want anybody to be troubled with my affairs. And I hope the new secretary"—a highly specialized young man, engaged by Evan through the War Office—"will give satisfaction!" She flounced from the room with tears in her eyes. Evan might have wished her good-bye; said a few words of appreciation of those eleven years of loyal service; given her, perhaps, a present. But Anna knew, by now, that was not Evan's way. He discarded people with the same indifference that he discarded an obsolete piece of machinery, when he discovered something more effective.

Often, on their train journeys, she did not even travel in the same compartment; Evan, locked in with people whose names and missions were Top Secret, might remember to wave to her, when they reached their destination. It was left to one of the satellites—who seemed to be innumerable—to put her in a cab, or even escort her on foot, to some meeting point where, among dust, smoke and a smell of burning, she was left to possess her soul in patience until his arrival. She accompanied him, sometimes, through painful and heart-rending scenes of destruction, her eardrums ringing with the howl of sirens, her skin and hair collecting sparks and soot and her shoes splinters of glass—her notebook and her memory at his instant disposal, her eye on her watch to remind him of a waiting car or plane. She learned, in the few moments they were by themselves, not to speak, above all not to "fuss." She poured hot coffee, or malted milk, from the thermos and placed sandwiches where he could reach them; but she made no comment if he ignored or waved them aside. She looked, or uttered, no reproach if some member of the party entered their compartment when Evan was sleeping; she only made sure it was her touch that woke him, before leaving him alone with the intruder. These people had more right of access to him than she, and Evan told her once that she was the only person he could trust never to come between him and his duty. As "Mrs. Crewe" she could have claimed all the authority she chose, but prudence as well as delicacy made her refuse, absolutely, to be associated on any public occasions with her by now "famous" husband. It was the only bone of contention between them.

"You might at least be on the platform when I'm speaking!"

She shook her head, smiling.

"Well, why not? It's perfectly ridiculous—with all those other women perched up there—to see you sitting down in some corner!"

"Well, dear, I prefer it that way. I never had any kind of taste for publicity."

"So I have to be surrounded with those moulting old hens while the only well-dressed woman, who happens to be my wife, is ashamed to be seen with me."

Had he, through force of repetition, really come to believe they were married? She was, now, actually Anna Crewe. He had insisted upon her taking his name by deed poll, and the announcement had appeared—no doubt with the connivance of Evan's innumerable friends on the press—at a time when no one opened a paper except to read the war news. On her registration card she was Anna Fitzalan Crewe. But she still tried to keep their names from being bracketed together publicly. Great men have enemies, and—although Evan pooh-poohed the suggestion—not a few must know she was not his wife. Many, she realized, had been disarmed by her gentleness and her lack of assertion, but she did not, like Evan, discount danger.

At infrequent intervals, and always without notice, they rushed down for a night or two at the Court, where Lin, Hugh and Simon rolled in the long, rough grass and tumbled in and out of the moat—which it had been Helen's first consideration to have drained. Mary declared she had done most of the work herself; there was no outdoor labour to be had, but they had managed to get two Germans from a P.O.W. camp, who, taking their orders from Helen, appeared to respect her for barking at them like a sergeant major.

The Court had more than justified itself; out there, in the heart of the downs, the manifestations of war were reduced to occasional distant rumble of gunfire, to a crosshatching of searchlights after dark, to the silver bubbles of barrage balloons over depots and camps hidden in the farther valleys. The children screamed with joy at the spectacle of the trainer planes, hedgehopping over the orchards, and Hugh, who was going through a troublesome phase of sleeplessness and crying, was comforted by being carried out of doors to watch the dropping of flares. Mary was doubtful, thinking he would be frightened, but Helen, with her usual robust common sense, said it meant nothing to the child but fireworks. The experiment was not a complete success, because Hugh was boastful the next morning at breakfast, and the other two bawled their resentment at having missed the fun.

Apart from labour difficulties, their main trouble was the blackout.

"It will finish by driving me crazy! Mary and I spend every

minute at our sewing machines, but there's always some wretched little chink, and the warden's been up four times in ten days. It's not the rooms," pointed out Helen, "but the landings that we've got to keep lighted or we'd break our necks. People won't remember to close doors and there's not a key in the place. I've made a sixpenny fine for every door—and that starts with you," she announced, holding her hand out to Evan, who laughed and dropped half-a-crown—"on account"—in her palm.

Yes, the Court had justified itself; it had preserved for them what many of their friends had lost—a home. Roger and Norman could come there on their leaves, and Helen had devised an ingenious scheme that saved them from the menace of refugees. She had made over the whole of the attic floor to one of her bombed-out London friends for the storage of her goods and furniture; the neighbour and her family were hardly ever in residence, but when the billeting officer came round, Helen could claim and prove the house was full. Three children and four adults (they had had to get a nurse, after all, for the infants, who were too active and mischievous for Mary's unaided supervision), as well as the apartments that had to be reserved for Evan and Anna, and Evan's secretarial staff, took up all of the habitable space. One wing, they had found, was virtually in ruins; after a few hair-raising escapades by the children, Helen had the communicating passage blocked up.

The chief delight, Anna found, in being there was the cleanliness. Cleanliness, by then, was a major luxury. It was rapture, to toss off smoke-impregnated garments, underclothes which always felt, although they could not be, dirty, and to abandon for a day or two the dark and dreary tailor-mades which alone were practical when they were traveling. Evan shared her feeling; within an hour of arrival, he was in white—white slacks, sweaters, cardigan, shirts, even white shoes: vastly impressing Lin, who had never seen a grown-up person dressed all in white before.

"Snow man!" she observed slowly, with her enchanting smile. "Mustn't get dirty," she added, with gravity.

Anna for once lost her temper with Helen, who, with a comprehensive glance at the "snow man," thought fit to remark,

"H'm—very dandy; it's a pity there's a soap shortage and it takes about three months to get anything back from the cleaners."

"I dare say I can find you some soap, my dear." Anna spoke coldly. She thought it was a pity they kept the children in their dingy blue denims: Lin as well as the boys. It was bad training—for Lin in particular—to go from morning to night without changing; sometimes even without washing, to judge from appearances! Nobody, it appeared, changed at the Court. Helen and Mary sat down to dinner in their crumpled slacks—which, while becoming to Mary's slenderness, were disastrous to Helen's broad, squat figure. There was no excuse for it, during Evan's visits, when they always brought down with them Evan's man, an elderly ex-R.N., who was a good plain cook, and two of the village women "obliged" in the kitchen.

"Pretty!" said Lin, wandering into her grandmother's room, where Anna was slipping into the thin silk robe she had not worn since her last visit to the Court. She stood shily, leaning against the door—her hair draggled, grass stains on the knees of her dungarees, her small hands black to the wrists. The darling! It's too bad, thought Anna, that they don't take care of her. "Are you going to a party?" asked Lin gravely.

"No, darling; we're going to have dinner."

"In that pretty frock?"

"Would you like to put on a pretty frock, too?"

Lin considered, nodded and shook her head.

"I haven't got one."

"Of course you have. What about the one with the little frills I sent for your birthday?"

Lin looked at her blankly and shook her head again. She had forgotten—or perhaps she had never seen it.

"Come," said Anna, holding out her hand. "Let's see if we can find it."

"Good heavens, Mother!" Helen turned round as Anna walked into the parlour, with Lin in her arms. Lin's head was pressed close to her grandmother's, their two faces, so strangely alike, were smiling, Lin's with an exquisite, shy triumph. Her hair was brushed into floss, a foam of white muslin broke over Anna's supporting arm. Anna's eyes met Evan's, confident of approval; crossing the room quickly, she put the child into his arms.

"Snow lady to snow gentleman!"

"Well, you are a beautiful person!" observed Evan with the solemnity that endears adults to children. "Tell me: how did you get so lovely?"

"Granny!" beamed Lin, almost overwhelmed by this unwonted success, but anxious for full appreciation. "And smell"—she pushed her little chest towards his face—"I've got scent on. It's called"—she hesitated, and looked to Anna for prompting.

" 'Je——' " smiled Anna

" 'Je—t'aime!' " brought out Lin.

"And it means?"

" 'I love you!' " crowed Lin, and threw her arms round Evan's neck.

"I don't know where you dug that out from," said Helen crossly. "I was keeping it, in case she got asked to a party. I've put away everything that needs laundering. Don't mess it up, Evan! Those frills take hours to iron. Now you've shown yourself off," she said to Lin, "you'd better go and tell Nanny to put it away. And go straight to the nursery—do you hear? If you get that frock dirtied, you won't be allowed to wear it again."

Lin's face crumpled for tears. Anna spoke quickly.

"Where are her other frocks? Dinner is so early, I told her she could have it with us, for a treat, while Nanny is putting the boys to bed."

As, leaving Lin with Evan, she followed a grumbling Helen up the stairs, Anna said gently,

"Don't you think it's time she began to be trained to take a pride in her appearance? She's such a pretty little girl, and those rompers, or whatever they are called, are so ugly and unfeminine. I wanted Evan to see her at her best."

Helen's lips tightened; she was obviously controlling herself.

"I know you don't mean to interfere, Mother: but, going round as you do with Evan, waited on hand and foot——"

Anna's eyes widened; this was a new interpretation of her pilgrimage.

"—you simply don't know what it means, running a household like this, with hardly any conveniences and no proper staff. Nanny's thoroughly fed up—we expect her to give notice any day—and Mary and I have as much as we can do, to feed the children and keep them healthy, without dressing them up. As you see, we don't even get dressed ourselves. I suppose we ought to have changed, on account of Evan—but, if you want the truth, we're both too tired and bad-tempered by the end of the day to care what we look like!"

"But—wouldn't a bath, and getting into something fresh, help to take the tiredness and temper away?"

She should have known it was useless to argue with Helen; but a cotton frock was found—rather crumpled—and Lin, after some show of reluctance, accepted the substitute. She was comforted by being allowed to keep on the ruffled petticoats that formed the foundation of the creation from the White House. She sat through most of the dinner on Evan's knee, rubbing her head against his chin, visibly enraptured by her social success.

"What a conquest you've made of Lin!" Anna teased him, when they were going to bed.

"She's you, as a little girl. The likeness is ridiculous," he told her.

On the few mornings she persuaded him to spend in bed, Lin was invariably discovered, curled up on his eider down, drawing, or playing with her dolls, or being read to.

"Isn't it absurd? I'd no idea you liked children."

"I don't; I can't bear the little brutes," said Evan. "Not meaning to be offensive—how do you imagine Helen and Norman managed to produce a child like Lin?"

There was a rather disconcerting sequel to his friendship with Lin. Anna discovered that, from most of the towns they visited, Evan was having parcels despatched, to Miss Belinda Raymond, the Court, Chilton Magnates, Berks. Toys, books, trinkets, fabulous boxes of chocolates. She found it out quite by accident, when they were in an antique shop in Gloucester. Evan picked up a double string of corals.

"Wouldn't these suit Lin?"

"Yes; but——"

He nodded to the assistant, who went in search of a box.

"I have a notion she's getting too old for toys."

"You're probably right. How old the children have grown, in this war. Now you'll have to find something for Hugh and Simon."

"Why?" he asked drily.

"Fair's fair!" She smiled at him. "You're their 'grandfather,' as well as Lin's."

"There's been no trouble, that I know of, so far"—and she learned of his outrageous favouritism.

"Send them some sweets," she counselled. "No little boy can get enough of those, on the ration."

ii

At the end of the war, Evan was fifty-six, and looked ten years older. On the evening of V-Day, they went down to the Court, for a nominal fortnight's rest.

Evan ripped the blackout from the windows and leaned out to inhale the sweet air. An owl hooted. There was the sound of a cow, chewing its cud. Peaceful night, holy night. No distant wail of warning, no thud, or thin flame falling from the sky. No fan of searchlight, blotting out the stars.

"Would you like to stop here?"

She caught her breath.

"Could we?"

He drew her close to his side.

"You're a countrywoman at heart, Anna. You should have a country place of your own."

"Of our own: for when you retire."

Strange, how a place, from the moment it belongs to one, takes on a new character. The Court was vast and empty, after the children left; then, gradually, it warmed and softened; it gathered around her.

Queen's Terrace was dingy, disreputable and cheerless, after the bombing. They agreed, for a time, to leave it unoccupied. The Court was as accessible, for Evan, as London, since Head Office moved out into the country. Each night he could come back to the scented silence of the downs; he could share with her the frosty mornings, the strings of race horses, moving in the steam of their own breath over the rounded shoulder of the hill.

She sank more and more deeply into the country life that recalled her childhood at Camelhurst. As she began, shily, to penetrate village life, she found the sly, slow Berkshire folk courteous but innately distrustful—the women more so than the men.

She was there when the results of the general election swept the country, and stunned the "pastoral heart of England." "May be some of the chaps voted Labour, mum"—but none would own to it—"but we knowed it meant getting rid of Mr. Churchill!" On each of her visits, she was more conscious of the apathy that lay on a land deprived of centuries of initiative: she watched it spreading through the homes, in the form of a kind of bucolic cynicism. She sensed the desire of young and old, to escape from the land, no longer truly their own, and therefore not worth the expenditure of blood and sweat, towards the easier life of cities, even to where the abominable bubble of the observation balloon over the Atom research station offered money for nothing: and to the Ordnance Depot—known locally as the "Rest Centre"—where "they doesn't only pay you for sitting on your arse, they sends a bus to fetch you!" She wondered if there was any way of breaking this evil spell, this canker which, eating into the roots of peasant pride, robbed the land and its people of their traditional dignity.

Evan's every moment was absorbed in the reorganization of the business; in the adaptation of the plant from the production of war to that of civilian material. At the Court, she might do as she chose: that is to say, what permits and prohibitions allowed her to do in a country which was no longer free, but held tight in the grip of a dictatorship such as England had never known: its reward for "winning the war."

News went around that the Court was "a good job." Young women, bored with sitting on office stools and knitting jumpers, took to dropping in, to see if there was "anything doing." They came in peep-toe shoes and lipstick, their hair (in curlers) covered with printed squares; and eyed askance the overalls they were offered. One and all refused to sleep in; the minds of all were fixed exclusively on their boy friends, the local cinema and the Newbury shops. They spent their evenings in hanging about the crossroads, in the hope of being picked up by the motor cyclists, or playing darts in the saloon bars.

None, Anna discovered, was used to laying a fire, sewing a seam, ironing a dress or cooking anything that did not originate in a can or end in a frying pan. "Mum does all that." Gradually she weeded them out, and acquired a permanent (though nonresident) staff, which fascinated her and amused Evan. It also secured for her the animosity of neighbours at the mercy of "dailies," who were constantly "missing the bus," or stopping at home "because Mum's got one of her turns," or having to get married in a rush.

She was suspected of paying "Deppo" wages. It was not true. The Court servants were paid, on Evan's insistence, strictly on the local tariff; but, if she had chosen to go outside his orders, would she not, Anna wondered, have been justified? To give a girl an honest job, in place of a dishonest one; to prepare her for the married state on which, with refreshing candour, every village damsel's mind was set—were these things not worth while?

The difference between the hearty Camelhurst wenches and these Berkshire girls was not confined to manners or efficiency. Were all the local women thin, frail and subject, as soon as autumn set in, to coughs and streaming colds and "pains inside"? Of course they were. After scolding them for not "wrapping up," or "taking care," and pointing out that this kind of neglect was a form of dishonesty to their employer, Anna arrived casually at the truth. "Dad?—'e wouldn't eat marge!" She discovered that, although most of the local labourers had access to a canteen, they "didn't fancy" the plentiful food served there; they preferred to cycle five or six miles, to have their midday meal of the bacon, cheese and fats the women went without—either of choice or under durance.

Anna's young servants "settled down" at the Court, not only for the square meals with which, after finding out the state of affairs in their homes, she took care to supply them: but because they liked working for her. They were given a routine, and shown how to carry it out; they were praised for work well done; and each, at the Court, felt herself an individual, whose private affairs were not a matter of indifference to her employer. Anna insisted on the reference of each detail to herself. The young married couple— who, at last, by offer of accommodation for themselves and a young family, were induced to live in—though industrious and of good intent, had not enough experience to assume responsibility on major issues.

"I like it," said Anna, when Evan protested. "I don't get any of this fun in London! I like to feel all these children—really, they're nothing more—depend on me. I like it, when Muriel comes snivelling about the boy who's 'going with' another girl, and Joyce confides in me about her sister whose husband is talking about divorce, because she's 'carrying on' with a Czech. That's how country houses were carried on in our grandparents' time; don't you remember? Even Mamma—in a distant sort of fashion—made herself responsible for the younger servants."

"It was a fairly long call, by way of the housekeeper's room, to your mother!"

"*Autre temps, autre moeurs;* it's up to us to do what we can, to bring the young people back to the land and restore their belief in their own traditions."

"If you asked them, they would say they're building their own traditions, and to hell with the old ones!"

"Anything's worth while, that helps to break down class hatred, and this idea of 'something for nothing' that the Gutter Government has wished on us."

But the heart of Anna's content was Evan's pleasure, as she gradually built up a feeling of permanence in the house he had tossed her, to humour what he considered a whim; his growing habit of inviting friends down for the week end; his cautious assumption of some of the duties of a squire. "Last squoire," she learned, " 'e wur killed at Mons. Folk that comed after—they didn't take no care. They comed and they goed. Din't care for the land—rare fine land it wuz, in them days; but now, under Guv'ment, you don' know what you're at."

At the Court, Evan became a different being; he shed the irascibility which frequently tormented him in town, and during their flying trips abroad. He made suggestions it was her delight to carry out, and brought enthusiasm to bear on all her achievements.

"This is our *real* home—isn't it? When you stop working, all we'll need in town will be a flat the Humbles can run for us, without all this bore of daily women and extra help for parties." She spoke with happy confidence: sure that his love for the Court was now as strong as hers, and that the life of a countryman offered a sufficient recompense for the abandonment of his former habits.

"And suppose I die in harness?"

She forced back the chill that overcame her. What reason, after all, was there to assume she might outlive him? He was five years older than she, but his last checkup had been more than reassuring; few men of his age, Maxwell told her privately, had a better life expectancy; his recovery from the stress and strain of the war years was remarkable. She was told one thing that made her glow inwardly, though her fine smile rejected it. "And he may thank you for it. Without your help, I very much doubt if he'd have beaten that 1942–43 winter." "Oh, nonsense; Evan's will would carry him through anything." "Will's one thing"—Maxwell ducked his head in his stubborn Scotch way—"and speerit's another. It was your speeritual help that pulled him through."

She laid her hand calmly on Evan's arm.

"No, I refuse to be cheated of my picture—of us, Darby-and-Joaning it down here; looking after our land and our people, and going to sleep together on a summer day, with the larks singing overhead."

"You blessed thing," he muttered, and twitched his face away.

iii

They always spoke of the years immediately following the war as "Lin's years." If anything had been needed, felt Anna, to add perfection to her life, it was Evan's "infatuation" (the word was Helen's) with Lin. It was true, she discovered, that he did not like children; his attitude to the boys was often sharp, and always offhand; they were continually snapped up, for their behaviour or their manners, although, thanks to Mary's sensible training, they were, on the whole, good little boys, and rarely deserved the snubs Evan gave them. But Lin could do no wrong. "You really mustn't spoil her!" Anna protested, after some outrageous sample of favouritism. "Nobody could spoil Lin," he retorted, and grimaced at her. "And you needn't pretend you aren't crazy about her yourself!"

It was true; Lin was an enchanting child. Physically beautiful—at eleven or twelve she developed a kind of old-fashioned, Burne-Jones loveliness that distinguished her among other children of her age—her sweet nature, grace and politeness endeared her as much to her contemporaries as to the older generation. She was kind—and kindness was rare. "She's inherited it from you," claimed Evan. Anna shook her head. "No; she's a rather typical Fitzalan. Doesn't she remind you of Edward?" He admitted it.

Mary had another son—Peter—after the war, and Helen and Norman concealed (though not from Anna) their disappointment at their failure to provide Lin with a brother or sister. Norman was perfectly simple in his attitude to Lin: she was his only, and his treasure. Helen—whose whole life was centred on her daughter —took up a tough line: Lin mustn't be spoiled, she mustn't be encouraged to think herself important, because she happened to be an only child. Lin's eyes, sweet and wise, twinkled upon them both. But, childlike, she took naturally to Queen's Terrace and the Court, where there were no undercurrents of which, without understanding them, she was aware.

"Where's Lin?" Evan would ask, at the week end.

"They've gone down to Rottingdean, for the week end." Anna smiled at his discomfiture. "We can't monopolize her," she said quietly. "She's theirs. We must be careful. I think Helen's a little hurt, that she spends so much time with us."

"I suppose she could stop it, if she chose," he muttered.

"Well, we don't want to push it to that point, do we?"

Lin went to boarding school, and Evan raged privately to Anna. "You never went to school; why don't they get her a governess?"

"Governesses are out of date. I agree with Helen; one has no right to bring up children in an obsolete pattern. And Lin's very happy."

"They'll turn her out some sort of hockey-playing clodhopper!"

"Don't you trust Lin?" she smiled at him.

Just before the summer holidays, Helen—who had never had a day's illness in her life—was ordered, to her indignation, into a nursing home, for an operation. She was obliged sullenly to admit that she had had some inconvenience—yes, and a certain amount of discomfort: why, otherwise, would she have consulted a doctor? No, she certainly wouldn't go into hospital, until the holidays were over; she had a daughter of fourteen, and she had planned out the whole of the eight weeks; Lin was bringing two friends home with her. Warned by the specialist, Norman put a stop to all this; he rang Anna, to enlist her support.

"Of course; they must come down to the Court. Why, Norman, we'll *love* to have them! How many are there, besides Lin? Only two? But, my dear, it's easy. Give Helen my love; I'll be round to see her in the morning."

Three schoolgirls; how would Evan take it?

She need have had no misgivings, she thought, as she watched the four—Evan, Lin and her friends, Agnes and Deirdre,—on the tennis court, in the evening. Lin, of the three girls, was much the best player; the game resolved itself virtually into a combat between her and Evan, with the other two fagging after the balls. She had grown very tall, for her age, and slim; she moved like a swallow—no "hockey-playing clodhopper" about Lin!

"We must find them some young men," said Anna, after dinner. Evan scowled.

"For children of that age!"

"My dear, Agnes is sixteen!—and, as for the other two, fourteen, in these days, seems to be about equal to my age when I was coming out. The competition for your favour is really too pathetic!"

"Don't talk such nonsense."

How transparent men are, she thought, without cynicism. Stretched out on the sofa, there was a kind of innocent satisfaction about him which Anna found touching, rather than ridiculous. Excellent at all games—although it was many years since he had had opportunity to indulge in them—it was something more than gratifying, to have held his own with the children. He and Deirdre —the weakest of the players—had beaten Lin and her partner every time, and Lin was obviously proud to be beaten. They had left the court with their arms round each other's waists, Lin's head resting against Evan's shoulder, her laughing face lifted to his; and Agnes—impressively introduced by Lin as the school champion—had as little resentment at being beaten by the other two, and brushed aside Deirdre's anxious apology: "We'd never have won, but for Mr. Crewe!" "For God's sake," laughed Evan, overhearing this, "don't call me 'Mr. Crewe'!" "We-well, what do we call you?" stammered Deirdre. "Evan, of course——" Lin tossed it across her shoulder. "You've always been 'Evan,' haven't you?"

An elderly oracle, surrounded by his vestals. As Lin flung her arms about her—"Wasn't it a wizard game, Granny?"—Anna felt, without bitterness, that she was the elder of the two. Her heart warmed and lifted, to see Evan drawing youth from these happy children; and contracted a little, at the thought she had never been able to give him a child. Absurd as it was, to be "Granny," while Evan was "Evan," resentment never entered her mind. She had drawn pleasure, all her life, out of service to other people, and her chief concern was to see those around her contented.

There was one small, disconcerting development of her plan to provide escorts for the girls. She had surprisingly little difficulty: a few telephone calls to neighbouring houses, and the Court was invaded with young men who, within a few hours, showed an embarrassing inclination to fall in love—with Anna. When she thought the children were happily disposed of, and herself at liberty to go about her own affairs, she was apt to be dogged by pie-eyed youths, whose attentions she found as cumbersome as they were uninvited.

"But, Alan" (or Vivian, or Charles) "I thought you were all going over to Moulsford, to swim." She laid down her book or her needlework with patience.

"We thought you were going with us"—on a note of injury.

She tried to convey her perception of the superfluity of her presence on such outings. "Didn't Lin say I always rest in the afternoons?"

"I suppose I'm frightfully in the way!"

"Not at all. Do you like music?" Anna would ask, desperately, at the end of a creaking half hour. "There's the gramophone, and there are plenty of records in that cabinet. You'll see they're filed under their various headings; I expect you like 'swing'?"

"As a matter of fact, I prefer the classics"—loftily.

Prepared for Mozart, or Bach, Anna suffered a repetition of the *Liebestod*, and agreed that *None but the Lonely Heart* was "an awfully sensitive piece of orchestration. Of course, Tchaikovsky hasn't the purity of the higher classics, but—it's just an idea of my own, of course—are we becoming overintellectualized: don't you think? I mean, there must be some form of expression for the purely emotional."

Anna preserved an admirable gravity, as she agreed it was a mistake wholly to shut out the emotions. What would Hugh have said to this kind of thing? How, she wondered, did the feminine young—Lin, Agnes and Deirdre—respond to Wagner and Tchaikovsky? All three were demurely tactful when they returned from the river, with drenched hair and slacks pulled over dripping swim suits; she received the impression that they were in connivance with a plan to prevent her "feeling lonely" in Evan's absence. While they went to change, she was surrounded by wet-haired youths who contrived in some way to convey the suggestion that, although the river, and the girls' company, had been great fun, it was she they had been waiting for. She had enough experience, however, of youth, to divert their interest into its proper channels; she was relieved to see her erstwhile *beau* ringleader in the horseplay that developed after tea—and something more than charmed (as Evan would have been) to see the ingenuity with which Lin, with no suggestion of superiority, managed to extricate herself from the roughhousing indulged by the others.

At the week end, when Evan came down, the atmosphere changed; developed an indefinable element. The youths—warned, doubtless, by Lin—appeared in dinner jackets; Lin had a long ballerina frock, sleeveless, but with a Peter Pan collar that clasped the base of her delicate throat; Agnes, conscious of her superior years, was in "real" evening dress, her flat waist obviously clipped into a corset; and Deirdre wore a frilly nondescript, no doubt regarded by her mamma as suitable for "a little girl," that reminded Anna of her coming-out dress. Up to then, they had appeared in flannels and cotton frocks. The air of the drawing room filled itself with innocent festivity.

Anna took her place happily at the end of the table. Looking across the candles at Evan, she wondered if he were as content as she, with these gay young faces about them. Lin was on his left and Agnes on his right; Alan and Vivian flanked Anna, and the remaining spaces were filled by the other two. It was the kind of family, thought Anna, they might have had themselves—if the gods had been kind. . . .

Evan was at his most brilliant and entertaining. It was some little while before Anna realized that all of his charm was directed towards the feminine part of his audience. Gradually, the youths fell silent; they were not snubbed, they were simply made aware— by the girls, not by Evan—that their opinions and their witticisms were insignificant, in comparison with those of the handsome figure at the head of the table. From time to time Lin sparkled at her, but the brunt of the conversation was supported by her—Lin—and Evan.

So it was not true—that the younger generation had no use or respect for its elders. Glowing on Evan's behalf, Anna felt sorry for the quenched boys, and bent all of her efforts to restoring their self-confidence.

After dinner they danced. Evan's dancing was old-fashioned, but his tall, light, narrow figure, and the assurance of his movements, gave pleasure to his partners. The "ruined" part of the Court, which contained a ballroom, had been partly restored; to Anna, it seemed beautiful and "homely," as he swept her down the long floor, under the vaulted ceilings and between the fluted pillars. Several young local couples, invited by Anna, had come in, and the room, though meagrely lit, under Government restrictions, took on an air of gentle gaiety.

"What are you looking so radiant about?" They were waiting for the record to be changed. Anna lifted her face, with its quick smile.

"I don't know—I never thought there'd be, ever again, nights like this—with dancing, and open windows, and no anxiety, or hurry to be somewhere else——"

"You're a child of luxury; I wish I could give you more." He turned her again—this time into a waltz, to which most of the others were fox-trotting. The waltz; it was the expression of his age, thought Anna. Not so much of hers. One grew up, after the first war, into the one-step, the bunny hug and the tango. She was glad she had been taught properly to waltz; so few people did—nowadays.

"Now dance with Lin. Do teach her to waltz! It's old-fashioned, but, in some way, it's an accomplishment—like learning the piano, and speaking educated French."

"Why don't you say the harp, and pinprick patterns?" he teased her. "I may be Victorian, but I'm damned if you're not Regency! Put on a tango," he called, to the group that was clustered round the gramophone. Anna protested; the tango, by now, was almost as obsolete as the veleta—but, as he swept her into the inimitable rhythm, as her limbs obeyed his, as the stride and sweep of the tempo carried her with him, time mattered not. The floor had cleared; Evan and she were by themselves; a burst of applause followed the end of the music.

"Oh—teach me!" Lin rushed up to him.

Evading the urgency of a would-be partner, Anna went out on the terrace that ran above the moat. The sky was full of stars, she felt almost childishly happy. The rambling old house had become what she had always dreamed of: a real "home." No one brought up as I was, she thought, in the heart of the country, can regard a London house, however beautiful, as *home*. No house is home without young people . . . my blessed Lin. . . .

She did not know how long she had been out there; the air was like honey and milk. She leaned now and again against the stonework, trying to imagine what the Court was like when it was properly maintained: when, for instance, the rough grass was lawns, when the moat was filled with water, and its surface crusted, perhaps, with water lilies. How long would it take—and what would it cost—to restore it to its former dignity? There must be an end, sometime, to restrictions and permits. Hybrid as it was, a confusion of periods, it could be made lovely, like Camelhurst. It could become, like Camelhurst, a proud inheritance: for whom? For Lin, perhaps, and her children.

A smothered sound of voices interrupted Anna's thoughts. She looked up sharply; without noticing, she had turned a corner of the terrace—which, actually, was not a terrace, but a rough path, running above the moat—and stood outside a window which, belonged, owing to the confused plan of the house, to a room communicating with the ballroom: a room she and Evan planned to make into a study, if ever present laws were relaxed. Someone, at some time, had broken the window space down to the ground: a French window—shocking anachronism—opened on the path on which Anna was standing.

Standing in shadow, partly masked by a clump of jasmine, whose ancient roots were buried deep in the foundations, Anna heard Lin's smothered voice say,

"Oh—don't!"

She saw the child burst out through the window: pause for a moment, gasping, and rubbing her mouth with a handkerchief.

Before Anna could speak, or make her presence known, Lin was away, like a moth through the starlight.

Anna stepped quickly into the room; swift as her movement was, she was too late—the door on the farther side, not that into the ballroom, was closing as she crossed the threshold.

She went instantly into the ballroom, to find it empty; a hum of voices came from the small anteroom adjoining. They were all there, but Lin: helping themselves to sandwiches. Anna looked at the clock; it was nearly midnight.

Evan, with one of the boys, appeared, with jugs of ice and cider; there was no service at this time of night—the caretaker and her husband were asleep in their quarters, and the servants had gone back to their homes in the village. Alan? She looked at him closely, as he filled her glass. No, it wasn't conceivable. A boy of that family and upbringing would not take advantage of a little girl of fourteen. Presently Lin slid back into the room—with nothing about her to suggest the recent upset. While the guests dispersed, Anna tried in vain to determine which of the men might be responsible for the scene she had just witnessed, and decided, after some inward doubt, not to tell Evan, who would assuredly be beside himself at anything which involved Lin.

Nothing came of it: except that, for the remainder of the holidays, Anna was aware of Lin's clinging more closely to her side. Actually, their opportunities of being together were few; Helen, though offered the hospitality of the Court for her convalescence, chose a hotel at Felixstowe, and Lin, naturally, accompanied her mother. There were a few brief meetings, in London, and Anna's offer to relieve Helen of the efforts involved in fitting Lin out for the winter term was accepted. They spent hours in Lillywhite's, and Daniel Neal's, and Fortnum and Mason's. Anna's suggestion, one day, that they should join Evan for luncheon at Claridge's, evoked, to her surprise, no enthusiasm from Lin.

"Yes, if you like, Granny."

Ringing Evan, to confirm the meeting tentatively arranged over the breakfast tray, it appeared he had been obliged to make another appointment.

"Give Lin my love."

"Yes—you know it's your last chance of seeing her before she goes back to school? She'll be very disappointed."

"It's very unfortunate; but I can't get out of this date."

Had that curious kink in his character, which allowed him to dismiss anyone who did not serve his immediate purpose, extended to Lin? The thought saddened Anna; but the sadness was not reflected in Lin's radiant smile, as she said,

"So we'll have lunch by ourselves! Let's go to the Causerie—I do love all those little dishes, and helping myself!"

CHAPTER V

*S*traightening her knees, Anna took the dry touch of ancient lips on her cheek, and made a sign to the butler, who moved forward. The doors opened, a broad plank of sunlight fell across the marble flooring and the shallow flight of steps, and picked out flakes of gold on the high modern grille that cut off the former vestibule from a broad space on which opened drawing rooms, library and a small cabinet known as the telephone room, usually occupied by Evan's secretary.

The taller of the two old ladies looked round and spoke in the all-but-forgotten accents of Middle Europe.

"What a nice place you have, Anna. You must show it to me, one day."

"Thank you, Duchess; that will indeed be an honour!" But the strain had been great. She cast a desperate look at Edward; this was the moment for him to offer his arm, while she looked after her aunt—old Lady Belinda Fitzalan: very blind and rather deaf, but still stubbornly "in-waiting," still, as became one of the ancient régime, draped in the solid black abandoned by the younger generation.

"Come, Belinda."

Edward had remembered his duty, and Anna hesitated only a moment before catching the fragile little figure in her arms and pressing her cheek against the crumpled eyes, which had filled with tears; her own were not far away. She whispered,

"Darling Aunt; so touched; so utterly, utterly grateful!"

"She suggested it. She's so good! God bless you, my dearest. Are you happy?" The old eyes sought hers; were given, for a moment, vision. "Yes, I see you are!"

The small, slow cortège moved out into the sun, into the little, paved court with tuftings of blue and magenta. Step by step, very cautiously, she and Edward, with their venerable burdens. That weight of tradition on one's arms; it made one feel so young, so young! Did Edward—ten years older than she—also feel it? I'm fifty-eight, Anna told herself—and I feel like a little girl. Ridiculous.

To the small group, the curve of the terrace lent its Regency background. In an hour, or less, sports cars and taxis would invade the gloaming, the light would alter, take on the yellow and brown and green of cocktails consumed behind high windows opening on the curved balconies which first attracted Anna to Queen's Terrace. The temporary hush and quietness was like railway platforms, cleared for the arrival or departure of royalty; was the kind of thing to which her visitors were accustomed.

It took some time to establish the two old ladies in the old-fashioned Rolls, with the chauffeur and footman in royal livery. Eventually Anna and Edward stood back, and the manservant awaited his orders to close the door.

"What a gay day. What a handsome little street this is. Anna. Come here, Anna. What about that granddaughter of yours?"

"Lin, Duchess?"

"Is that what you call her? Did you hear that, Belinda? They call her Lin!" For some reason, this was amusing. "Who's presenting her?"

"Her mother, I believe, Duchess."

The distinguished old head nodded slowly. The door was closed. As Anna curtseyed once more, the car moved silkily from the curb.

She turned, grateful for Edward's hand under her elbow. The doorway, the hall, swam before her, and the figure of the butler blurred in the light from the head of the stairs.

"Mrs. Raymond is on the telephone, madam. I said Her Highness was just leaving. She's holding the line."

"Shall I take it?" Edward—scowling, defensive.

Anna smiled and shook her head.

"We'll go upstairs. Put the call through to the boudoir, please, Humble."

"Why not say you'll call back?" muttered Edward.

She smiled again, shook her head and lifted the receiver.

Edward Fitzalan dropped into a chair and picked up *The Times*. For all his affection for his sister, he could never conceal his dislike of her daughter.

"I'm sorry to keep you waiting, my dear."

"Well! Is Humble out of his mind?" General Fitzalan winced, as his niece's voice trumpeted out of the receiver.

"Not that I know of"—Anna sounded startled.

" 'Her Highness'?"

"Oh—she came with Aunt Belinda; they've just gone."

"Well! But—well—really!"

Anna was obliged to laugh.

"You sound nearly as overcome as Humble. You wouldn't remember, but the Arch-Duchess often came down to Camelhurst in your grandfather's time."

"It's not exactly the same thing, is it? I suppose someone told her you were—by yourself."

He saw Anna's lips fold into a stiff line and muttered,

"Tell her to go to hell!"—but before Anna had time, had she chosen, to follow his advice, Helen's voice rattled,

"Well, you must be very gratified!"

"I'm rather—touched." A foolish thing to say, to Helen.

"It must have been quite an adventure for her. I suppose, at that age, one can do as one pleases; but I'd like to hear Marlborough House, on this escapade! Why ever didn't you tell me?"

"Tell you—what?"

"That they were coming. Oh, it's no business of ours, but we'd have been interested." Helen sounded injured.

"I knew no more about it than you did."

"Don't tell me they just—dropped in!"

"They were driving this way—to avoid the traffic in Kensington Gore—and my aunt remembered I lived here. Imperial memory and affection for your grandfather—I suppose that accounts for the rest."

"I know she's your godmother; but—it was pretty unconventional of her, wasn't it?"

Anna said, after a pause,

"Well, dear, did you ring me about anything in particular?"

Did her own voice fit her, she wondered, as perfectly as Helen's? —which evoked the complete picture of a middle-aged woman, smart, satisfied, confident of herself and her background: intolerant of all opinions that did not conform to her own. It even conveyed something of her physical presence: thick in shoulder and waist, but well groomed and neat—the type of physique that gives a good account of itself on golf course or tennis court. Downright, direct and wholly wanting in sensitivity or tact. How successfully the Sturges blood had dominated the effete Fitzalan strain. But neither Sturges nor Fitzalan accounted for a streak of—commonness was the only word, however painful it might be, to apply it to a child of one's own. Perhaps it was infectious, between husbands and wives: though it was hard to imagine Helen, sturdily immune, not only from youthful epidemics, but from influences, good or bad, "catching" anything. And Norman's commonness was not that hard, ruthless kind; there was something appealing about it. Anna had grown fond of her son-in-law, over the years.

Helen was gabbling something about a dinner.

"Wait a minute, while I get my book. Did you say Monday the eleventh? No, dear, I can't; that's the day Evan comes home."

"I thought you weren't expecting him until the middle of the month?" Any interference with her plans, to Helen, was a direct affront, but she made an effort to speak pleasantly. "Nothing gone wrong, I hope?"

"Not a thing; but the people he had to see in California happen to be in New York."

"They're having a heat wave, aren't they? People of his age must feel it, a lot."

"Not on Long Island," said Anna serenely. "I'm sorry about the eleventh; is it a formal party?"

"Oh, I expect I'll get somebody. You know what it's like, in August—and Norman's provincial clients will turn up at the most impossible moments. You're sure you can't? Fetch Evan if you like, though he's sure to be bored; I can always scare up an extra female."

"I'm afraid it's impossible; Evan won't feel like dining out on his first evening at home." She held out for a few moments against Helen's irritable persistence, and quietly changed the subject with,

"How's Lin?"

"All right. Why do you ask?"

Why, she felt like retorting, do you make things so hard for yourself, my child? Why let jealousy and suspicion in on our relationship, which, God knows, is difficult enough? You have never forgiven me, and you never will; but whatever ill you may attribute to me, you surely know you can depend on my loyalty. Lin's love for me has never done you, or her, any harm; but, the older she grows, the more you risk, by your attitude to it.

"Didn't you hear what I said, Mother?"

"Of course—I'm sorry; I was thinking of something else. I suppose she's going down to Dartmouth next week, with the other children."

"The boys and Mary have gone already, and Lin wouldn't thank you for classifying her with 'the children'!" Helen gave her high-pitched laugh of which, as a child, Anna had tried to cure her; it made her sound like an angry housemaid. "You had an easy time,

in bringing me up!"—intended as a jest, it came out as an accusa-
tion. "At least you'll admit I never insisted on 'being independent'
and 'earning my living'!"

"Do you think," said Anna, brushing this aside, "she'd like to
come down, for Saturday night and Sunday? I'm going down to the
Court, as soon as the Humbles go on their holiday."

"I wish you'd thought of it before," Helen surprised her by
answering. "We were informed over breakfast that she's week-
ending with some friends on the river! I suppose it's all right, but
I'm very much annoyed. I can't picture myself, at Lin's age, accepting invitations from people you'd barely heard of, and tearing
off in some youth's sports car, with nothing but a swim suit and an
extra pair of slacks!"

"When you were Lin's age, we weren't wearing slacks!—and
customs have altered a good deal in the last few years," said Anna
soothingly. She heard Helen gasp.

"If you'll excuse me for saying so, Mother, you're much more
easygoing with Lin than you ever were with me! I suppose I'm
old-fashioned," said Helen petulantly, "but I don't happen to like
the idea of my daughter spending the week end in one of those
rackety riverside cottages—with peculiar sleeping arrangements—
and half-dressed young men bringing the girls their breakfasts in
the morning." (Where, wondered Anna, had she got her information?) "So far as I can gather—we're very rarely favoured with the
details!—they're writers, or actors, or something."

"It sounds very harmless and hard-working."

"Oh, you—with your prewar Bohemianism!" It was Anna's turn
to catch her breath. "It isn't what Lin was brought up to! It's not
what we had in mind, when we gave her an expensive education—
and a sitting room of her own, to entertain her friends. Friends!"
repeated Helen bitterly. "She doesn't appear to have any—except
these extraordinary people she picks up at the office."

Edward was scowling and making gestures of impatience.

"Don't distress yourself, dear; it will all level out. The job's new, and very exciting. At Lin's age, liberty is apt to go to the head."

"So it appears. Well, I've warned her, I'm not going to put up with it much longer. A girl of eighteen is under her parents' control, even in these days. I wish you'd say something, Mother; she appears to pay more attention to you than she does to me."

Edward had risen, and was standing behind her; Anna held him off with a little gesture that asked for patience.

"I will, if you wish me to; but——"

"Why couldn't she take the job Evan offered her?—as an under-secretary, or whatever they call it, at Head Office?" Helen answered her own purely rhetorical question. "Because she'd be under his eye, I suppose! Because she wouldn't be allowed to make flighty acquaintances among the staff! And I suppose," rattled on Helen, "you haven't heard the latest? She's now refusing to be presented! We're having none of that nonsense—naturally."

"No," said Anna faintly. "She mustn't let the side down. Why—what reason does she give?"

"She says it will make her look a fool at the office!"

Edward Fitzalan took the receiver out of his sister's hand, and barked,

"Helen!"

"Oh—is that you, Uncle Edward?"

"Your mother's very tired and it's time she rested." Without waiting for a reply, he clamped the instrument back on its stand.

Stretched on the chaise longue, Anna accepted, in silence, a cigarette from her brother.

"Why do you let her bully you?" he demanded, as he gave her a light. Anna's eyes, momentarily closed, opened slowly upon the person she loved—next to Evan—best in the world. Small, thin and dapper for his years—was Edward really "getting on" for seventy?—his sleek, dark head was only starting to be streaked with grey over the temples; his smooth, sallow skin was unlined, except about the eyes, which were dark as mulberries, with perpetual laughter behind them. But not at the moment. He glowered at Anna—at her face which, within the last minutes, had grown sharper and more shadowy.

"What did she mean by 'escapade'?"

An impatient monosyllable burst from him.

"You're worn out. Can't you take a draught—or something—and get some sleep?"

She smiled.

"I'm all right. Only a bit emotional. Dear Aunt Belinda."

"I didn't realize you—cared—so much."

"For an act of love and loyalty? Those things count—as one gets older."

"They certainly count—to your daughter. I suppose you realize that every single person in Helen's circle will hear, during the next few days, that you've been honoured, by the Arch-Duchess!"

"Poor dear. Don't be ungenerous, Edward; they've put up with a great deal—Helen and Roger. And they've been loyal too—in their fashion. What good luck, that you happened to be here. The Arch-Duchess adores you; she always did, at Camelhurst."

"She's the only one, so far as I know," said the General gruffly, "who's got any fun out of being 'royal'! Helen, no doubt, would call her a prewar Bohemian!"

"Oh, oh—I won't listen to you, being cattish."

"What an infernal snob your daughter is, Anna!" But he grinned at her. "I suppose Roger's knighthood upset her."

"She was bitterly disappointed, that Norman's name wasn't among the honours; he had been given to understand it would be. But she's been very sporting about Mary's becoming 'Lady Sturges.' The sun, moon and stars shine out of Roger—for Helen!"

"It's not uncommon—between only brother and sister."

"Did Evan tell you"—she hesitated—"he was offered a baronetcy?"

Their eyes met in silence. He said,

"It sounds as if someone were ill-informed—or clumsy."

"There should be some acknowledgment of his work."

"Does he want acknowledgment?"

"It could be an advantage——"

"Why? Who pays attention, in these days, to that kind of thing?" He spoke with the simplicity of one to whom "that kind of thing" was so much of a commonplace as to hold no value. "I should have said the last Government made it sufficiently distinguished to be plain 'Mister'!"

"To some people, a title stands for—authority."

"Anna, don't be a fool. What are you going to do"—he changed the subject—"all by yourself, at the Court?"

"All kinds of things!" She was illuminated. "Get the moat filled up, for one thing. Next year, I mean to have a garden; the soil must be rich, after all those centuries of mud and leaf mould. And I shall throw out a little terrace, from Evan's study, so that he can walk out there in the sun, without having to come through the hall, and down the steps, and across the bridge, and all the way round by the bowling alley. You know, he's grown to love the Court as much as I do, and to accept it as our home—for our old age!"

"Don't you find it strange—handling other people's leavings?"

"You mean, after Camelhurst. There's a difference, of course. You can't feel, about a place that is bought and given to you, the same as you feel for the land on which you were raised. But it's more of an adventure. You go cautiously—in search of the tribal fetish, or whatever it is that helps you to establish contact with people you'd never known. Poor things; how they must have hated abandoning their home."

"I thought the family petered out?"

She accepted, with a grimace, this snub to sentimentality.

"Then there's the bridge; we're going to rebuild it, but the old causeway will serve, shored up, until after the shooting. You're coming to us on the first, of course? Evan says the birds will be good, this year."

"If I'm not too much of a crock."

"You'll be rested by then. When do you join the boat? Isn't it on Friday?"

"Yes—I suppose so," he qualified his reply.

"Suppose?" She lifted her brows, that ran like thin wings over her pale, enormous eyes.

"I'm not at all pleased with the prospect of leaving you alone," he muttered. "Evan away; the Humbles on holiday; you by yourself in Berkshire——"

"For mercy's sake! Am I a child?—some sort of irresponsible idiot?" she reproached him.

"It's the first time you've been left by yourself——"

"And you know the reason for that. It's the first time, since '35, Evan's been to the States. It was bound to happen. He should have gone last year, but they found someone to take his place. And we could hardly risk being held up on Ellis Island!"

"Damned hypocrisy and barbarianism," smouldered the General. She gave him a quick look of loving tolerance.

"Shall I tell you something? It's been rather a thrill. Not being separated; we hate it. But finding how we 'make out,' without each other."

"I wonder how much of a thrill it's been for Evan; he depends on you for everything."

"And I on him! It's natural for a woman to depend—well, a woman like myself, who has always been spoiled and protected. It came as a shock; I won't pretend it didn't. We've never been separated—except for a night or two—in seventeen years. It seems incredible, doesn't it?"

"Not many are so fortunate," he agreed with her.

"And I spent twenty-four hours praying someone might be found, to take his place. But, when it appeared there was no one but Evan—make no mistake: I was proud!"

"Roman matron," he teased her.

"No, nothing like it. Six weeks seemed like eternity. As it turns out, it will be only a little over a month. Do you know"—she gave him a shy, shamefaced smile—"I'm almost—disappointed? When you've schooled yourself to heroics, it's almost a letdown to find they aren't necessary! And there were so many things I meant to do, before his return. Now I shan't have a moment."

"Take care," he admonished her, with affectionate crossness. "It won't suit Evan, if he comes back and finds you having a breakdown."

"Do I look as though I need your warning?"

"Do you want flattery? We're neither of us young."

"I've recognized that longer than you! Sixty-eight years in a man's life aren't much, in comparison with fifty-eight in a woman's. Life never exhausts its gifts to men; but for a woman—after she reaches what is called 'a certain age'—there's only one gift: content."

"And a good milliner."

She paid this the tribute of an honest laugh.

"It takes something more than genius with felt and feathers, to create something out of a mask like this"—she touched her face delicately: her lovely face! thought Edward—at which strangers, in theaters and restaurants, still turned to look. "Never mind—I have my secrets—which will be Lin's, someday. How long is it since you saw Lin?" she broke off to inquire.

He reflected.

"There was an evening at Bagatelle, when a young woman came up to my table and addressed me—with, admittedly, a charming lack of assurance—as 'Uncle Edward.' We danced. I hope I was adequate. Then she went back to her party——"

"Is that all? Didn't you admire her?" She was visibly disappointed.

"Within the limits they set themselves nowadays"—he sounded judicial—"she was, I suppose, attractive."

"Did you tell her so? Of course not. I wish you had. She's lovely; but, so far, she's been told so by the wrong people."

"It's difficult, to pay compliments to a young woman who comes dancing in a fisherman's sweater and wears what appear to be bedroom slippers on her very likely pretty feet."

"Don't say you prefer strip-tease and high heels!" She rose

lightly and held out her hand. "Come; I have something to show you."

He knew the room well, into which she opened a door: large, important and dominated by the four-poster hung in dark blue damask. A great deal of floor space was sparsely occupied by some heavy furniture—armchairs and a Knole couch, burgundy-coloured; a table or two; a converted spinet, in use as a dresser; and—outrage on its surroundings—a vast radio-gramophone and cabinet for records. One end of the room was lined with bookshelves, the other with cupboards; over the lintels were panels, painted in trompe-l'oeil designs that gave the effect of looking through glass into shallow alcoves filled with china. The ceiling was lofty, its elaborate, shagreen-coloured moulding heavily overlaid with dark gilt. And the Poussin over the Adam mantelpiece—it could only be a man's room.

"Have you any idea how hideous this room used to be?" he asked, as he nodded his appreciation.

"Of course I have! Look." She drew his attention to the carpet. "I couldn't resist it. Chinese: the only true yellow. Do you see how it lights up the damask? Those hangings were almost black before I put this down. It's 'a surprise.' Do you remember how we used to like 'surprises' when we came home?"

As she opened a cupboard filled with masculine clothing, and drew out a sleeve and a fold of cloth, she spoke across her shoulder to the short, elderly woman who, with the respectful manner of the impeccably trained servant, had followed them into the room.

"Do you think these are all right, Gertrude? There are moths everywhere, at this time of year."

"Humble's had everything out, madam, and sprayed the cupboards."

"Don't forget to hang all the clothes in a draught, and leave the doors open, before Mr. Crewe comes home. You know how he loathes the smell of camphor."

"Finished your packing, Gerty?"

Gertrude Humble stiffened, remembered and relaxed. Mr. Edward was the only person privileged to address her as "Gerty." She produced a pinched smile.

"Yes, thank you, sir—just about. Though, what with the rush, and all that's got to be done when we get back, I'm sure I'd just as soon not be going."

"Gertrude's thoroughly bad-tempered," Anna informed him, "because Evan's coming back a fortnight before we expected him. Isn't it a pity? Everyone else is so pleased!"

"I never—Miss Anna!" Gertrude's face, disfigured by the mole that spread across the bridge of her nose, turned a resentful purple. "As if I'd presume! All I say is, if I'd known, I'd never have made plans."

"Nobody knew, and it's made no difference, excepting to me. So please don't be grumpy, and spoil Humble's holiday by grousing all the time you are away," begged Anna.

"All the housekeeping to be done the day we get back, and a nice state your things will be in, with nobody to look after you for a fortnight!" Holding doggedly on to her grievance, against the suspicion that they were secretly laughing at her, Gertrude trundled out of the room.

"Aren't you taking anybody with you, to the Court?"

"Of course I am; Pulford's wife's coming. I'm rather annoyed—she won't fit in with the staff down there; but Evan seems to have fixed it up before he went away. Sweet of him, but I'd have managed perfectly; my country girls are so clean and willing."

How little she knew of "managing," he thought, since Evan came into her life. His care for her was no less sharp than her care for him, and it was typical of him to think, even in the haste and complication of his departure for the States, of Anna's comfort and convenience. To Evan of all others, thought Edward Fitzalan, he would willingly have trusted the care of his beloved sister.

They had gone out on the little iron balcony that commanded the long, pale sweep of the terrace, and the darker roofs that defined it, and the calmness of a golden sky, delicately uneven—like a piece of silk imperfectly dyed, that derives beauty from its imperfection.

"The week end is going to be fine. I shall think of you, on Sylvia's yacht——"

"You're really going to be all right, alone?" he insisted.

"If you came down this week end," she smiled at him, "you would disturb me very much. I have too many things on my mind, to be a good companion. The harvest," she murmured, "will be nearly over; it's early this year. I've missed the white and sand-colour and honey-yellow of the grain. One shouldn't, you know——"

"Shouldn't what?" as she paused.

"Miss anything, at our time of life. It was Evan who showed me the importance of gathering in, and storing, every precious moment. But I don't mind, for once, because I should really have felt very greedy, without him to share it. Do you know that silvery look, after the corn has been cut?—the whiteness of the stubble, with the thin new grass just beginning to push through? A jet plane, shooting overhead—or perhaps it's only a motorcycle along the lane; I often mistake the sounds. And a skein of swallows, getting ready for migration, crisscrossing the moat. A reaper, crawling over the shoulder of the downs, like an enormous beetle. Do you think one grows more sensitive, as one gets older? I've lost my hatred for mechanical things. I think it's a mistake, don't you, to try to force the present into the framework of the past."

"But I regret the plough horses."

"One regrets many things; but there's always something to put in their place."

"That," he told her, "is the conclusion of a very contented person. Bless you, Anna; I'm glad I happened to be here this afternoon."

"Oh—and I too!"

"If anyone deserves happiness, it is you. And honour." He repeated gravely, "*And honour.*"

She turned her head away quickly.

"How thankless one is; however much we receive, there's always —something—more——"

He understood. Whatever comes to her is valueless, unless it is linked with Evan.

"You ask too much."

"I know. Indeed, I know."

Something made him say,

"You always loved Evan, didn't you?"

"He was my first love," she answered with simplicity.

"Why on earth didn't you make him marry you?"

"Make?" She laughed sweetly. "Evan was married when I was in the schoolroom."

"You might have got engaged."

"Had he been twenty years older, instead of five—perhaps. Thirty—almost certainly. Aren't men of that age supposed to be very susceptible to schoolgirls?" she quizzed him.

"What made you marry Hugh?"

"He asked me." Her arched brows suggested that the reply was obvious. "I needed importance. No one ever noticed me!"

"That's not true; I noticed you."

"And Griselda?" she reminded him.

"She was as fond of you—nearly—as I was."

"I think I missed you. It wasn't jealousy," she hastened to assure him. "You remember—I was a bridesmaid."

Her assumption, that she was of so little account at that moment in his life—with her lost eyes and grave air of a young vestal, taking part in rites of which no one had explained to her the significance—stung him.

"But you did—like—Hugh?"

"Of course; or I would not have married him."

"Mamma should not have permitted it," he muttered. The masculine instinct, to allocate blame somewhere, drew a smile from her.

"Who but you mattered—to Mamma?" There was no rancour in the observation. "She was naturally pleased I had found myself a husband, without troubling her; she wasn't even obliged to give me a season! Don't look so grim. Hugh was very kind to me, and I was very happy.

"One of the advantages of growing old," she said, after a pause, "is being able to say things that were impossible, while one was prisoned in the cage of youth. You had an 'Evan,' hadn't you?"

"She died four years ago." He did not ask how she knew.

"Tell me about her."

When he had finished——

"Did Griselda know?" she asked.

"Never."

"How fortunate I am," said Anna, with a sigh.

"You really feel that?"

"To share the act of living, from day to day, with the one person who makes it worth while? What else could be happiness?"

"It has taken courage——"

"Don't tell me you are deficient in that!"

"My 'Evan' was. I suppose you despise her for it."

"You don't mean that." She gave him a look of forgiveness. "Does Griselda still believe you love her?"

"No."

Her candid eyes approved him.

"The least we owe to those who love us is honesty."

"Don't make it easy for me, Anna!"

"She would have divorced you if you had asked her, but your asking would have hurt, terribly."

"I thought women knew by instinct, when men were unfaithful."

"I believe that's a *cliché*," said Anna thoughtfully. "We use the word 'instinct' to cover something of which we're a little ashamed. Isn't it usually a hint?—something overheard; carelessness with an old envelope? The telephone has done away with the stock resource of the uneasy wife: the blotting pad! But people seem still to be amazingly casual about what they leave in their pockets."

"Don't say those things; they don't sound like you. You, of all women in the world, have the least cause to be cynical."

"I'm not the least bit cynical; but isn't it true, on the whole, that men are more faithful to their mistresses than their wives?"

"I shouldn't care to confirm the generalization." He smiled reluctantly. "But you're entitled to your opinion. You've certainly made a true lover out of a rake."

ii

After dinner, she got Humble to open the parcel of records she had ordered and take them to Evan's bedroom. She glanced at the labels of the *Idomeneo*, the Arensky Variations, the *Années de Pèlerinage* and Lalo's Concerto in F minor; she pictured his pleasure—his eyes filled with the fabulous yellow of the Chinese carpet and his ears with his favourite music—as he strolled about the room.

"I shan't want anything more tonight, Humble; you and Gertrude had better get on with your packing. I've told Pulford to bring the car round tomorrow morning, to take you to Northolt."

"That's very good of you, madam. A Mr. Meredith called while you were resting——"

"Oh yes?"—from the office. She took the small, sealed packet from the tray. "I'd like to have seen him!" Meredith had accompanied Evan out to New York.

"He wouldn't allow me to disturb you, madam—he's just got back, and Mr. Crewe asked him to deliver the little parcel. And there's a big one, from Mrs. Raymond; I understand it's something for the Court. Shall I post it, or will you take it with you on Friday?"

"Oh, give it to Pulford." A bundle of Lin's castoffs—bless Helen for remembering—for the gardener's children. "And don't forget the waders, and the Burberry; I'll take them now, so they won't be forgotten when we go down for the shooting. And—Humble: give Poole's a ring in the morning, and tell them to send Mr. Crewe's new tweeds down to the country, not here."

The packet contained two little boxes from Tiffany. In the first she opened was a jewel, covered by Evan's card, on which he had scribbled, "This looked like you. The other's for Lin." When she had finished examining the chunk of gold, inset with diamonds and sapphires, for which he must have paid a fabulous sum, she opened, out of curiosity, the other box, which contained a group of little diamond "scatter pins," dart-shaped, with minute feather tips. How pleased Lin would be! She put them carefully away, and, as she fixed the record-changing mechanism and stretched herself on the couch, thought how much she liked this room of Evan's, which belonged so completely to him.

More so than her own to her. He had insisted, himself, on planning her apartments, and, seeing in the desire the expression of a starved romanticism, she would not for the world have let in a breath of doubt upon his choice. Yet she often felt that her beautiful bedroom was less her own than Anywoman's. The low, broad couch, with draperies of rose-violet net gathered into a gilt crown suspended from the ceiling, did not belong to the woman who, for twenty-one years, occupied a chaste twin bed in a room shared by her husband. (Not that Hugh went in for chastity—as such; she had forced herself to thrust aside the sickening memory of scenes in which she had taken unwilling part, believing it to be the duty of a wife in all ways to surrender to her husband's desires.)

It was not difficult to imagine what breaking through the web of rose and violet meant, to Evan. The child, entranced by the fairy on the top of the Christmas tree; the schoolboy, "in love" with the Principal Girl in the pantomime, or, later, with Pavlova or Lopokova—she cast them instinctively within her own period, but Evan's initial voyages to Cytherea were more likely to have led him in the direction of Vesta Tilley, Gertie Millar and the stars of the Gaiety. To that deeply disillusioned spirit she had to be *all that*.

It was difficult, at first, to accept a rôle so alien to her diffident nature. He had allowed her to see his embittered and frequently brutal attitude to the majority of her sex, and left it to be inferred that she was the exception. Ah God, what a weight to carry . . . but she was not, she reminded herself, the first woman to face the necessity of being both wife and mistress to the man she loved. Which was the more difficult: for the wife to play mistress, or the mistress to play wife? Only time could solve this problem—whose solution, she was wise enough to realize, lay with the man.

The violin of Miriam Solovieff painted strange curves on the deep colours of the room.

To have reached, at my age, a haven of romantic love is a miracle to which no woman can ever grow accustomed, she reflected. To be lovers at the end of seventeen years of the kind of association that is supposed to destroy all illusion is the kind of thing one would pray for—if one had the sense, and the prevision! Why should these things be given to me—without even praying?

Melted into the cushions that bore the perpetual imprint of his long limbs, she found herself expecting at any moment his step, his touch, the quiet sounds that were associated with his presence: the thin sound of sherry, being poured into a glass; the "clok" of a book, put back on the shelves; the rustle, as he shouldered his way into a silk dressing gown.

His shadow between her and the lamp—its height a little diminished by the breadth of his thin, nervous shoulders; the shaded light, running its thread of silver round his narrow head, with its line of "race." Age had not diminished his beauty, but, in sharpening, added to it. In whatever company they found themselves, Evan was distinguished, by his looks no less than by his personality; it often amused her, to see the women's awareness of his approach, their efforts—transparent to their own sex—to claim his attention. It was so good to retire, deliberately to choose the back seat, the least conspicuous place in the room—and to know that he was hers! That his eye would seek her out, in whatever obscure place she had chosen, and would signal to her with relief from the heart of his immediate entanglement!

Much to her amusement, he had become seemingly irresistible to quite young girls, and took her teasing with admirable equanimity. "I can't really allow you to get a name for cradle snatching!" she protested—not wholly jestingly—when he had spent the greater part of an evening in marked flirtation with the prettiest of the season's débutantes. "Blast the cradles" (but, under the easy retort, she knew he was flattered)—"What am I supposed to do?—snub these perishing flappers?" "Now," said Anna seriously, "I know I've got nothing to worry about! The very fact that you think of them as 'flappers' takes you out of their world." "Why, what is one supposed to call them?" he asked, with a shade of disconcertion. "I believe the current term is 'teen-agers,'" she assured him, with gravity. "What a revolting expression; it's as bad as 'bobby'—what is it?—" 'Bobby-soxers'; or flappers," said Anna. "I agree with you" —but he had not spoken—"that it's too bad, that the most delicious period in one's life should be spent under such revolting labels."

In her heart she was glad, that he should draw such stimulus from youth; it made up, perhaps, for Lin, who, while passionately addicted to her grandmother, had latterly adopted an offhand— though perfectly polite—attitude to Evan. Anna puzzled over it, and worried a little, suspecting—though he gave no sign—that it hurt Evan. The child was so fond of him—perhaps, she thought, his association with her, Lin's grandmother, emphasized unduly, in Lin's eyes, the fact that he was "old." It hardly, however, accounted for her refusal of his offer of a post in the secretarial at Head Office. That had hurt Evan, and taken her—Anna—aback. Yet there was no ill feeling, on Evan's side; so much was proved by his gift to her from New York. Perhaps that was the secret of his attraction for the young; that he understood—better than many—the waywardness of youth.

Between us two there is nothing to be explained; no gap in understanding. You love the things I love, you kindle to my fires. You are, in very truth, "my other self."

"Love is the child of illusion and the parent of disillusion; love is consolation in desolation; it is the sole medicine against death, for it is death's brother." He read that to her once, out of some anthology, and they spent half a night in discussing it. He accepted it, Anna challenged it spiritedly.

"Illusion is weakness! Love demands all the strength one can bring to it!"

"Yes—because it is powerless in itself." But his lips twitched into a smile; by the time they reached this point, Anna had decided that Evan—like she and Edward, in their youth—was "arguing for argument's sake." A little later, locked in his arms, looking up into his transported eyes, she whispered,

"So love is powerless—is it?"

"That's special pleading," he muttered—and smothered her protest.

"If thou hast loved, re-ope the magic book."

There was the night of stars—like this one—when you came, without question or comment, for the first time to my arms, and, after an interlude as much of tenderness as of passion, fell asleep on my bosom, as innocently as a child.

And the morning when we sat on the rocks, hand in hand, and accepted the implications of our future.

There was the day when our wanderings brought us to a vine-smothered balcony overlooking the valley up which, while we watched, came the procession of children, wearing the white veils of première communion; and, as they passed under our balcony, a little girl looked up and, with a smile like the breaking open of a rose, held up for me her sheaf of lilies. And you bent down to take it, and lay it in my lap, while she and her companion looked at each other and murmured, "Ah, ce sont des amoureux!" Do you remember how young it made us feel? When you lifted my hand to your lips, the children nodded with gentle approval—as though the Holy Ghost were still with them.

What is it about France—apart from Paris, which is debauched by foreigners—that makes it so truly *"le pays d'amour"*? What accounts for the strange, serious disposition of its people towards sympathy with lovers? Do you think we were like that, in England, before the blight of puritanism descended on us?

. . . She wondered how long the music had been silent, when she came out of her dream. The clock had stopped. Under the open window, the drip of the fountain threaded the summer heat with ice. The amber glow of London invaded the starry pavilion. An overwhelming scent of heliotrope and tobacco flower brought regret—that he was not there to share it. The instinct "to share" was as strong in each as in their first months of love.

Anna closed the windows and trailed round the room; touching things—just to reassure herself, and them; letting her hand linger on a pillow—"Goodnight, my darling!" How foolish, she reproved herself; you're probably having cocktails on somebody's yacht, or you're in one of those conferences that go on for ever, and ever, and ever. . . . He had written to her:

> The vitality over here is amazing; I'd forgotten what it was like. Good food, all the essential vitamins; I feel horribly guilty, not to be sharing them with you. I'm working like a dynamo, and I feel as if I'd pushed the clock back twenty years!

She allowed herself to picture his return: in that gay, uplifted mood, to which she contributed only as audience. It might be hours before he remembered her as "his own true love!" (*"Le plaisir de l'amour c'est d'aimer, et l'on est plus heureux par la passion que l'on a que par celle que l'on donne."*)

iii

Her bed had not been turned down, or her night garments laid out. It must be earlier than she thought—but, referring to the little clock on the mantelpiece (Hilderson; one of Evan's most precious gifts to her), she saw it was after eleven. Gertrude, in the throes of packing, had forgotten the time. Poor old soul, it was not like her. But she would be more distressed by Anna's maiding herself than by a reminder of her duty.

Gertrude was one of the blessings of "after the war." They came face to face, with a gasp, in a registry office.

"Gerty? It can't be Gerty."

"Miss Anna!"

Camelhurst; and a gawky laundrymaid, in trouble over some faulty ironing. Her panic, the fear of dismissal in her starting eyes, made Anna plead for someone of whose existence, up to that moment, she had been hardly aware: which she would immediately have forgotten, but for the great mole blotted over the bridge of her nose. It was the mole, larger now, and deeper purple, that rescued from the farthest reaches of Anna's memory the features of the elderly woman whose name had been supplied to her as Gertrude Humble.

When, a year after the end of the war, they moved back to Queen's Terrace, Gertrude and her husband were installed as housemaid and man; as bodyguards, respectively, to her and Evan. Their old-fashioned attendance completed the security of the home.

Humble would be out. At half past ten, or thereabouts, he took the dog, Brandy, for an airing. Humble's ideas of exercise, for a gun dog, was not dawdling round the squares. Himself a country-man, he was as much addicted as an animal to open spaces, to the smell of grass and trees unpolluted by dust and petrol. He and Brandy were wont to set off, by taxi, for Barnes Common, or the Heath. It was not unusual for them to be out until midnight or later—stoically accepting, on their return, the lash of Gertrude's tongue.

Through the open door of the Humbles' bedroom she saw partly filled suitcases, open drawers, the helpless disorder of one accustomed to packing for others, but not for herself.

Anna had not been to the room for years; all the belongings, the small, sordid contrivances of connubial life, the improvisations to achieve what they called "comfort" (what was the idea of the clotheshorse, draped with an old coat of Humble's, and a bit of faded cretonne? They had only to ask, and could have had a decent screen) filled her with a compunction increased by the snapshots—all of herself and Evan—pinned to the wallpaper over the mantelpiece. Surely it had been a pretty bedroom?—and was now reduced to the den of two human beings who, bound to each other only by weary custom, had filled its air with their petty grievances, their disagreements and the heavy boredom that descends on married couples whose lives are robbed, by day-to-day familiarity, of the elements of mystery or surprise. A sudden shyness overcame Anna; a feeling that she had no right to invade the privacy of these people who, in their dealings with their employers, took so much pains to preserve their dignity, and hers.

"Gertrude."

As there was no reply, she stepped round the "screen."

Gertrude sat hunched in a chair. Her old-fashioned cap and apron and her gown of decent black were replaced by a dingy dressing gown. Her chin was dropped on her bosom and her glasses had slidden into her lap. A thin streak of saliva ran from the corner of her mouth into the wrinkles of her chin. The mole spread across her nose was like a strip of dirty plaster, and, on either side of it, her cheeks fell into ancient, flannel-like folds. Derelict, ugly and loveless. Yet, thought Anna, with a pang of horror, she can only be a few years older than I!

She forced herself to press her hand on Gertrude's shoulder. The glazed eyes opened slowly. The look of the human face in which life is present but the soul absent has a horror of its own. Anna felt herself shrinking.

"Gertrude. You're tired out; why aren't you in bed?"

"No—yes—ah-ah—Miss Anna!" She groped for her glasses, pushed them clumsily on her nose and blinked back into the present. "Have you been ringing? I just took a nap——"

"I didn't ring; I came to see what you were doing."

A sudden awareness, the instinct to defend her own privacy, flushed Gertrude's face with resentment.

"I've been packing—as I was ordered."

Anna forced a laugh.

"'Ordered'! What nonsense. I'm going to bed, and it's time you were in yours. And, clearly, high time you had a holiday," she added.

"Holiday!" burst out Gertrude. "I'm having no more holidays, if I've got anything to do with it! Bundled out of the house, just as if you was a parcel!"

"It's a pity to say things you'll regret tomorrow," said Anna, calm in the face of the outburst.

"Regret? Me? I've never regretted anything I've *said*," boasted Gertrude. "It's the things I haven't . . . Miss Anna!" She lapsed into appeal. "I don't *want* to go on this holiday."

"Whyever not?"

"All the rush—when we get back; Mr. Crewe turning up, like this, a fortnight before he's expected——" Her eyes were averted from Anna's.

"Nonsense." Anna picked a framed tintype from the mantelpiece. "What a charming, old-fashioned thing; is it your mother?"

"It's my grandma. She used to cure folks with herbs—she'd have got rid of this for me"—she touched the mole—"but she died when I was just little. They called her a witch, but she wasn't, of course. She'd got second sight."

"Well, I'm going to bed. Goodnight. Gertrude"—she saw the old woman was crying. "What's the matter? Come; don't be foolish. Tell me what you have on your mind." She tried to make a jest of it. "I suppose the cards have been telling you something unpleasant? What is it? Is the plane going to crash? Are you both going to have to take off by parachute?"

Her trembling hands folded over the girdle of her dressing gown, Gertrude faced her mistress; a dull crimson blotted out the fine purple network of her cheeks.

"It isn't me, Miss Anna; it's you."

For a moment chilled, but touched, Anna laid her arm firmly round the other woman's shoulders.

"When you see the sun setting on the Alps, you'll forget all this nonsense. Think of it: good food, good service and nothing to do but rest your poor old legs!"

In the face of Gertrude's opposition, she upheld her refusal to be maided into bed.

"You may come and turn down my blankets, and hot up my milk, and then you're to undress and go straight to bed."

No less firm was her rejection of any further reference to Gertrude's exploits with the cards.

"Second sight! It's nothing but exhaustion, you silly old thing. And if you say another word, I'll slap you!"

Although the mole made her shudder, she forced herself to kiss the troubled old face. It was not until she was stretched between the sheets and had switched off the light that Anna realized she was not going to sleep.

iv

It was at the height of the V-bombing, when he and all who carried his responsibilities were driven close to desperation, that Evan put in her hand a letter headed by the names of a law firm in Manchester.

Their client, they wrote, was shortly to undergo an operation for cancer. In view of the fact, it became imperative to find accommodation for the sister, who could not be left unattended, through their client's illness and convalescence. All efforts, so far, having failed, it was urgently hoped by their client that the addressee would exert his considerable influence to procure, in any part of the country reasonably safe from enemy action, temporary accommodation in a suitable institution, where the afflicted person would receive the care and attention necessary to her condition.

Obviously, not a letter to be passed to a secretary.

"What do you wish me to do?"

"Tell them to write to"—he gave her an address, which she noted, before giving him the injection on which, at the time, he was dependent. As she disposed of the flake of cotton wool—"I was wondering," observed Anna, "wouldn't it save time if I were to ring up this place, and make arrangements, in your name? You know how it is, now, about civilian operations; she might be sent for at any moment, and postponement might mean going on a long waiting list."

She was able, later in the day, to tell him that the matter was arranged, and that the lawyers, to whom, on the long-distance, she had spoken, were handling the "detail" at their client's end. He appeared to be satisfied. It was only a chance remark that led her to suspect that his mind was not fully at rest.

"Would you like me to go down, and make sure everything's in order, after she arrives?" The one important thing was, not to add to his burden. "Of course I wouldn't feel anything about it!" she declared, in answer to his protest. "So far as I'm concerned, the whole thing's completely impersonal. And if we know she's being properly looked after, there's nothing to worry about—is there?"

She realized, from the relief with which, eventually, he accepted her proposal, that it had been in his mind to go himself and was thankful she had been allowed to spare him the trouble and the emotion.

The car swung between white gateposts up an avenue which wound its way to a Gothic façade: so little like what she was expecting that repulsion gave way to curiosity. It was only while she waited for the answer to her ring that the enclosing trees, the embattled turrets and a long, ecclesiastical-style block to her right infected her with a fear she felt to be childish, and steeled herself to resist.

The butler who opened the door was so normal, so much the

pattern of the best type of English servant, that she was momentarily assured. She was escorted through a long hall—somewhat surprisingly furnished with a billiard table—into a drawing room conventionally furnished, overlooking what appeared to be a small park. A Sèvres clock on the mantelpiece measured off twelve minutes while she waited; during those minutes she registered, with some impatience, the sumptuous character of her surroundings. The buhl was fine, of its kind, and the *objets d'art*, though uniformly hideous, and assembled, apparently, at random, were valuable pieces of Ming and *famille verte*. The water colours—indispensable to a Victorian décor—were accomplished. A *jardinière* in the broad embrasure of the window carried a load of cineraria and petunia that suggested a competent gardener.

The only thing that disturbed the effect of a private reception room was the absence of books or *bibelots*, and the arrangement, on a centre table, of a collection of copies of *Punch*, *The Tatler* and the *Illustrated London News*. She shrank away from these—and their reminder that this was not a comfortable country house—to the window, which overlooked, not, as had been her original impression, a park, but a considerable garden, of lawns, herbaceous borders and cedars whose spreading fans, backed by a mass of beech and elm, blocked out the horizon, and enclosed, with the architectural wings of which she now became aware, a space of grass, on which moved couples whose erratic movements drew Anna's fascinated attention.

Shuffling over grass or gravel, no apparent intercourse held the couples together; one led, the other followed. No pair approached another. Once, the follower stepped quickly forward, to intercept the seeming intention of his leader, to cross another's path. Without argument, the leader turned dumbly aside, to follow the route indicated by his companion. There were one or two deck chairs, occupied by individuals who, to judge from the conduct of the rest, had drawn an invisible ring of isolation round themselves.

Almost under the window, a figure paused, to look at a dandelion, sprouting unexpectedly from the well-tended grass; bent, as with tender surprise at this rare assertion of individuality; made as though to gather it. A tap on the shoulder interrupted the innocent intention. He raised himself, with perfect meekness, and, in rising, caught sight of Anna, to whom, with courtesy, he raised his hat.

She was blinded with a gush of tears. The devilish ingenuity: this beautiful garden—in which, for their bodily health, the Lost were permitted to wander: the rose beds, the carefully planned clumps of flowering shrubs, the clustered borders and shaven lawns—all for the placation of those who consigned their belongings to a living tomb: to impress and pacify them with the belief they would be "happy." Oh God; the happy, happy dead. . . .

She was led down a gallery flanked by classic marbles ("Very fine, aren't they?"), like a museum, and was startled when her conductor produced from his pocket a bunch of keys. She found herself being presented to a middle-aged woman in nurse's uniform, who repeated her name in the American fashion: "How do you do, Mrs. Sturges. Aren't we having wonderful weather?—and we've been able to enjoy it, so far, down here!" Her teeth squared themselves into an artificial smile. "Nothing, so far—just a touch of blast and a few broken windows."

The nurse walked briskly ahead, her heels clipping on the polished linoleum which had replaced the carpet of the gallery. The ritual with keys was repeated. A powerful wave of claustrophobia made Anna pray she would not faint, or be sick! She was passed over to another nurse, who rose gauntly from a bench, on which she had been reading a newspaper.

"This is Mrs. Sturges, Nurse—a friend of Mrs. Crewe's. Mrs. Sturges has come down to see how we're looking after our patient!" A grisly brightness was not reflected on the other's face.

"This way, please."

She felt her stomach emptying and the muscles behind her knees dissolving, as another door was opened. A stifling heat pressed on her so suddenly that she involuntarily recoiled. The nurse said sharply, "Come right in, if you please; we have to keep the door shut."

The room—square, lofty and completely featureless—was furnished, against a background of cheap, mottled paper, with a bedstead, a square table, two stiff chairs and a padded one—the last turned towards a grate filled with slack giving off thin streams of yellowish smoke behind a wire screen. On the corner of the mantelpiece—its only ornament—was a very old photograph of Evan, in a tarnished silver frame. There were some dead flowers in a vase. A shaft of sunlight falling across the table—which carried a tray with the squalid remains of a meal—revealed a film of dust.

Anna's eyes were reluctantly drawn to the figure in the armchair. Sleeping, perhaps. The grotesquery of the loose-skinned face, blotched with eczema patches on nose and brow, was increased by thin grey hair dragged back into a plait. The shapelessness of the heavy body was not disguised by a dirty cotton peignoir pulled over sour underclothing.

Anna moistened her lips.

"Shall I speak to her?"

"Just as you like; but she won't know you," said the nurse brightly. "It's one of her quiet days; that's why we haven't disturbed her, to tidy her up. You can't follow routine with this class of patient." A slight edge on the voice was intended, Anna realized, to forestall criticism. "It's a pity, really, about that old dressing gown: she's got several others, but she makes such a mess of her things, it's no use putting her into anything smart."

"Couldn't there be a little ventilation?" asked Anna faintly.

"The afternoon sun will soon be off," was the careless reply. "We've got to keep the temperature even; these cases are very susceptible to change."

"She looks so uncomfortable." The furrowed brow, curving sharply back to the thin hairline, glistened; Anna watched a drop collect and run down into the channel under the jaw.

"They don't feel a thing at this stage. Of course, that's difficult for outsiders to realize. It's one reason we don't encourage visitors, to these chronic cases: it only harrows them up, and sometimes leads to misunderstandings." The note of warning, this time, was unmistakable, and stiffened Anna's resistance. "It's difficult to explain to relatives that, once they've come in, it's far better just to leave them. After all, it's our job to understand them and give them the right attention; that's what we're paid for, isn't it?"— with a flash of the teeth. "It appears Mrs. Crewe's only here temporarily. What a pity. If she was a permanent, she would have had a better room."

Anna coldly asked the few questions she had prepared, and received, as she expected, the standard answers. The patient's health, on the whole, was good. Those patches on the face didn't mean anything: there was often a minor blood disturbance following change of diet. She might last for years, or just "pop off": nobody could tell. The old lady next door had just gone off with an embolism; she'd been perfectly good the day before, walking round the garden——

"Does she ever—is she ever taken out?"

"One of the probationers pushes her out on the terrace when the wind's in the right direction. She can't be persuaded to walk; it's a nuisance—it's just what she needs. But she's so pigheaded!" The flash of Anna's eye brought a quick amendment. "Only when she's in the mood! Usually she's as sweet as sugar. My, what lovely flowers; it's a pity she won't even notice them."

She felt she was expected to say, "Keep them yourself," but disliked the woman too much to do so. She had a suspicion they would go, in any case, to the nurses' quarters. What did it matter? —no flowers could survive in the mephitic atmosphere of Margaret Crewe's cell.

She stood for a moment, looking down on the poor, unconscious head, with scalp shining through the thin strands of iron grey. A poignant memory revived, of a swinging orchestra, the hum of the entr'acte, and a girl with a mass of black hair pushed down by a jewelled band into her dark, excited eyes.

"She had such pretty hair. . . ."

A foolish thing to say; what could it matter, to the woman looking on with professional indifference, that this pitiful creature had once been young and gay?

As though the gentle comment had penetrated some dark recess of her eternal cavern, Margaret Crewe lifted her head. Frozen with pity, Anna looked down into eyes empty of all but the dull spark of life.

Could anyone do more? She forced herself, during the long drive back to town, to accept the truth. No one could do more for Margaret than was being done. At home, in her glass, she looked at her face, too obviously scarred by her experience. It took her longer than usual, that night, to compose her "mask," but, by the time Evan came in, she was satisfied of the results.

"It's all right. But I'm glad"—she caught back the words; she had been about to say, "I'm glad she'll only be there for a little while"—which would have roused his uneasiness. She amended her sentence. "I'm glad I went down."

His arms went round her shoulders, clasped her closely to his side. Her heart rose on her throat; there was so little time—in those days—for being lovers! He called her by the name he used only when he was deeply moved.

"In all the world, there's no woman like you, Anna Fitzalan!"

. . . An old body heaped in an armchair, eyes that held life but no light, had carried her back to something she had so strenuously forced herself to forget that she had almost succeeded.

A tune came into her mind, and hummed there like a bluebottle; it took some little time to identify it—"I've gotta motta"—which Hugh used to whistle in the bath, driving the car, even while reading his letters: which Helen and Roger picked up, and sent endlessly echoing through the house until she begged them to desist. Through it she saw the blackened columns of the Shaftesbury Theatre—struck by a bomb—and the blackened life of a girl who looked like an illustration to a Hans Andersen fairy tale.

CHAPTER VI

*E*ach morning at twenty minutes past eight Lin left her parents'
house in Thurloe Square, to hurry along the Brompton Road to
the tube station. Each morning the same conversation took place.

"Have you got some change for the taxi?"

"Yes, thank you." (On the first two mornings, uncertain of the
way, she took one; on the second morning she stopped it on the
corner of the block, and walked down to the green-and-black doorway of Mynte, Publishers.)

"I've got to be at Heal's" (or Maple's, or somewhere in Oxford
Street) "this afternoon; I'll pick you up when I've finished my
shopping."

"Please don't trouble, Mummy; I mightn't be ready."

"I can wait. You close at five, don't you?"

"Shutting the door doesn't mean we've finished our work."

"It's raining; why don't you let Daddy drop you?"

Lin's lips twitched; she could see the picture!—the Rolls; Cadman folding back the rug—for two pins opening an umbrella to
conduct her across six feet of pavement under the noses of the girls
arriving in their rubber boots and hooded raincoats. "No, *thank*
you, Mummy!" There was already enough to be lived down: in-
experience, the suspicion of favour, as well as trivial matters like
clothes, and the fact of being a pin-money girl, which she had

tried, but failed, to conceal. She had got the job on the very night that survived in Uncle Edward's memory. The "fisherman's jersey" (of which she guessed his disapproval) came from Lanvin, and was casually pulled over a bell of stiffened tarlatan; the "bedroom slippers," from Gamba, were economical satin sheaths she had grown used to in ballet class, and the general effect—sophisticated in the style of 1952—gave her courage boldly to tell Henry Crome, to whom she had just been introduced by her ex-school friend, Agnes, that she was looking for a job. Henry, an owl-faced but pleasant person who had cut his teeth in publishing, began by being amused and ended by taking her seriously. What was more, he took it upon himself to beard her parents and, by dint of his extreme gravity, succeeded in convincing Norman, if not Helen, that it was not unreasonable, in these days, to wish to earn one's own living. (Why Henry Crome should take this trouble for a little girl he had only just met is a mystery bound up in Lin's own personality, which frequently procured her favours to which, in the opinion of the envious, she was not entitled.)

The outcome was a desk in the draughtiest and least convenient corner of the outer office, where everyone took infinite pains to impress on her her insignificance in the complicated microcosm of Mynte, Publishers, but which afforded an unparalleled vantage point for observation of all the distinguished authors on the Mynte list. A good many of them noticed Lin, with her swinging bell of ashen hair, her delicate small face and wide, vague eyes that lent her more the air of a child lost in a wood than of a young woman embarked on a career.

She learned a number of things unconnected with her official duties: for instance, to be genuinely excited about a sale of nylons —"slightly imperfect"—at Garridge's in Oxford Street: a region whose potentialities she had never previously sampled; to be anxious about weather—"It always rains like stink when my boy friend comes to fetch me on his motorbike"; to take an interest in babies—Jenner had an infant she parked in a day nursery during office hours; and to be earnest about amateur dramatics. Morny, who belonged to a theatre group, spent most of her time memorizing parts which, sooner or later, were to bring her to the attention of the managers whose names illuminated her horizon and talked about "Noel" and "Binkie" and "Alfred" so airily that Lin, in her simplicity, was taken in. "I've got to rush home and change," said Morny importantly; "it's Noel's first night!" Lin looked up brightly. "Oh—do give him my love, and say Mummy and I are coming on Wednesday!" There was a pause. Someone tittered. She caught her lip in her teeth and blushed crimson. She should have known by now that Morny's "first nights" meant standing on a pavement, or jammed against the doors of a foyer, and their climax was to thrust her autograph book into the hand of some star emerging from a stage door.

"Here, Raymond, change this ribbon."

"Those files in the back office are filthy. Get a duster, Raymond, and clean them up."

"Anybody seen the Ryman invoice? Here, Raymond: you aren't doing anything—have a look for it."

She accepted happily her duty of fagging for anyone who had an unpleasant or tedious task to be done: recognizing this as the price of her pure vowels, the indiscreet favour of Henry Crome and her status—highly suspect—as one of the "upper class." Her sweet temper and willingness wore down suspicion sooner than she expected.

Whatever piece of office drudgery engaged her, she was conscious of every moment after the clock struck three. Not yet sufficient of an "office rat" to welcome the break for its own sake, it then became her duty to make tea, and to take the cups of thick white utility china and the biscuits laid out on a tin lid round the offices. Up went Lin to the first floor—where there were the Chairman's room, and his secretary's, and Henry's, with his secretary, and Publicity, and Distribution—at this point the office boy, Leonard, usually took over some part of her burden. Whistling cheerfully, slopping the tea into the saucers of the cups he carried with noteworthy agility, piled on top of each other, three in each hand—he vanished down the passage, leaving her at the door of the Chairman's room.

She wished there were a looking glass, to make sure her powder was even, her hair smooth and the line of lipstick sharp and clear round her mouth. Her heart quickened its beat as she tapped softly on the door.

Richard Mynte, his ear clamped to the telephone, allowed his eyes to rest appreciatively on the childish figure: on the small breasts that thrust innocently against a shirt of grey linen belted in to a fragile waist; on the matching skirt, whose voluminous folds ended a few inches above gazellelike ankles and childish feet in ankle-straps of grey doeskin. A fold of turquoise chiffon made a holder for the white flower of her face. A lovely kid—amazingly like her grandmother, who had been one of the great beauties of her own and, incidentally, his mother's day.

"—ten thousand, I think—but I'll have to check up with Miss Sanford. Make it Tuesday week, can you, old boy?—the proofs of the jacket will be along by then. Ten fifteen; splendid." He dropped the receiver back on its cradle, his right hand executed a scribble on the pad. "Tea; good," he smiled, as she put it carefully at his elbow. "Well; still in love with the job?"

"Yes, thank you." She swallowed; fascinated, he watched the faint convulsion run like water under the thin column of her throat.

"Henry tells me you're going down to their place for the week end."

She nodded; her face, struck full by the light from the window, held a polite fixity—like a schoolgirl's, up for a wigging from the Head! thought Richard, amused. He was fond of children.

"I may be seeing you—if I get back in time from Holland."

"H-Holland?" she stammered; the flame that ran up her face took him by surprise.

"I'm going to Amsterdam in the morning. A lot of our printing is done in Holland, you know." His smile mocked her ignorance.

She was halfway down the stairs, dawdling from step to step, letting her pulses settle, when he called her back. She turned, one hand on the baluster rail; her face, tender, at his mercy, glimmered up from the darkness of the stair well.

"Lin."

It was the first time he had used her Christian name; she wondered if she imagined it.

"Have you got a date at five o'clock?"

"Nothing—nothing special." She had had some idea of going round to Anna's for an hour.

"I've got a man coming in five minutes, and a bunch of letters to get off. Miss Sanford's asked if she can go at half past four. How's your shorthand?"

"Not terribly good; but I can usually understand what I've written!"

He laughed.

"Good enough. Then bring your notebook, will you, in about half an hour? I'll ring down when I'm ready."

The downstairs office, when she returned to it, appeared to be dancing with light. *My soul doth magnify the Lord.* . . .

"Hi, Raymond; you been having tea with the Chairman?" The query was not malicious, as it would have been a few weeks ago. "Check these addresses, will you"—a sheaf of envelopes poured into her basket—"and look sharp; they've got to be in the post."

As she took down the ledger, Lin gratefully recognized her excuse for staying on after the office closed; there was no need to explain her assignment with the Chairman—just enough to tip over her precarious popularity. Over her head swung the shuttle of office chatter.

" . . . so I said, If you think she can carry a part like Ellean, after a couple of walk-ons . . ."

"The loveliest pub; my friend and I . . ."

" . . . five-and-nine! For a pair of wool bootees I could knit for a bob, if I'd got the time!"

"Well, you know what he is; let one of his fancy girls come along, and he'd pack up Sybil Thorndike. . . . Good afternoon, Mr. Beamish; will you have a seat for a moment?"

Decorous silence accompanied Morny's special telephone voice on the interoffice line. The visitor put on glasses and nosed among the novels on the table; fortunately—this also was Lin's business—his own was among them. She glanced at the clock and her heart gave a tick. Miss Sanford's speed was a byword; could she, by now, have taken down those letters and rattled them off before leaving at half past four? Richard's expected visitor was at least twenty minutes late.

Sanford came in, hatted and gloved, to be greeted by the famous Reginald Beamish as an old friend. She bridled with pleasure at the public demonstration of her importance.

"Mr. Mynte's *quite* ready; shall I take you up?"

"No, no, no. I should be able to find my way—by this time!" Gurgles from three of the four desks; Lin had not yet learned the sycophancy due to a best seller.

"So you're doing the letters." She started, as Miss Sanford spoke across her shoulder. "I hope you'll manage!" with a dubious sniff. "Please don't use my typewriter; they're like fountain pens, they get used to a particular touch. Paper and envelopes in the top right-hand drawer; I've locked the others. And you'd better sit at the table; I don't care for other people using my desk. Don't forget to shut the windows when you go."

"*Well.*" Morny's voice cut like a knife into the silence that followed the banging of the door. "How long have you been understudying Sanford, may one inquire?"

"I haven't," she stammered. "I mean—I suppose R.M. asked me —just because I happened to be there."

The silence lasted until five minutes to five. Then Morny and her friend Jenner slammed the covers on their typewriters and vanished into the cloakroom. The third girl was slower in clearing her desk.

"Well, you've got Morny's knife well into you now."

Lin looked up quickly, taken aback by the edge of vicious satisfaction on the other's voice. Surely they had been friendly for the last month? Lytton had been enraptured by the bottle of "Miss Dior" Lin gave her for her birthday.

"I know. But I couldn't help it. I wasn't trying to go over her head."

"You wouldn't be here long if you did!" was the retort.

The door swung after them. Feet clattered on the stairs. Whistles, calls, a final banging of the street door. Lin sat in the silence of office twilight: a little stunned by the cloud of open enmity which had suddenly gathered around her—but a great deal more ecstasized by the prospect before her.

Richard's voice in the hall, bidding his visitor good-bye: the space filled suddenly with his height and breath, his handsome, amiable, jaded face. . . .

"Hello; there you are. Let's go upstairs, shall we."

She picked up her portable typewriter—it was her own, not office property; she had asked for it, in place of the Elizabeth Arden "beauty case" that Helen was going to give her—and followed him. Perched on a high chair, her pencil dutifully ready, a strange, listening look on her face checked Richard, about to begin his dictation.

"What's the matter?"

"N-nothing."

"What did you hear?"

"Nothing." She recovered herself. "Only—the quiet! I've never been here before, after everyone's gone home."

"Damnation." He bit his lip.

"Have you forgotten something?" she asked anxiously.

"No, I've remembered something. Well, are you ready? Let's go."

Usually fluent in dictation, Richard made—he was conscious of it—a mess of it, that night. He ought to have used his common sense. The Raymonds would be furious at his keeping the kid here, alone, after office hours. He had been a considerable fool, not to pass this job on to Morny, who, actually, was Sanford's "second string," but—well—one liked a person or one didn't; that was what it came down to. Overworked as he was, and overtired, he was not in the mood for Morny's genteel efficiency.

Lin's face was burning by the time he finished. He had let her down lightly, showing no impatience when she was obliged to ask him to repeat; but she had not been really good.

"Do you mind if I read them back to you? I think I've got it all down, but if you wouldn't mind checking it over with me——"

"Don't look so desperate!" He laughed, put his feet on the desk and relit his pipe. "Good effort," said Richard, when the slow reading came to a close. "M'm; ten past six. How long will it take you, to type those?"

"An hour? No, I'm afraid it may be a good deal longer." She missed the dismay on his face. "The Lysons letter is nearly two pages, and you'll want carbons, won't you? I promise I'll have them ready for the last collection," she assured him earnestly.

"But, my dear kid, I've got a date, and I must go home and change! What about signing them?" He frowned, pinching his lower lip between thumb and forefinger; he did not see her wince. "I suppose that means I'll have to pop back. You'll be through by half past seven, won't you?"

"Could—couldn't you sign some sheets now? I could do the typing over your signature, and you needn't come back," she proposed naïvely. Richard was obliged to laugh.

"Highly unprofessional. I suppose you could put 'p.p.' to some of them, but it wouldn't go for the rest." She looked so crestfallen that he relented. "All right; give me some paper—Christmas daisy! I didn't say a ream." He reached for his pen. "How many was it—eleven or thirteen?"

"If you wouldn't mind doing a few extra; in case I made a mistake!"

He chuckled, and humoured her.

"How you're armed for all emergencies." (Am I? Six seemed a very small margin of error.) "It's terribly sweet of you to give up your spare time—I must fly. By the way, what size do you take in gloves?"

She shook her head, her anxious lips straining into a smile.

"Oh, no; I don't want overtime pay!"

"Mustn't blackleg the union. What narrow hands you've got; I suppose your gloves are made for you?" He turned at the door. "You don't mind being left by yourself, do you?"

"Why should I?" She tried, with a little air of dignity, to convey that it was he, this time, who infringed on professional relationships.

"Blessings on you—don't forget to slam the door."

"Enjoy your trip to Amsterdam!" she called after him.

. . . She allowed herself, for a few moments, to be lost in a dream that included backwaters, punts, the bat-haunted twilight of Thames Valley and the scent of Richard's pipe, before settling to her task.

Having carefully arranged paper, carbons, rubber and ledger at her side, she glanced at the clock. Nearly three hours to go before the last collection; she could afford a trial run or two.

. . . and if it happened to be raining, there would be the Cromes' big living room, and television, or dancing, perhaps, to the gramophone. . . .

Two of the letters consisted only of a few lines, and she slid the signed sheet, with its carbon and copy sheet, confidently into the carriage. But for one small erasure, it came out faultless, and she breathed a sigh of relief.

Overconfident with the next, she forgot to press the alignment lock, and discovered the print slanting across the page. It was, fortunately, only a very little out of true, and would hardly be noticeable; but, in straightening the paper and clicking the lever forward, she omitted to advance the roller. She had not begun, yet, to type blind, and by the time she lifted her eyes from the keyboard, ten letters were superimposed on the previous line. As the ribbon was worn, and she had been obliged to type heavily, the print, dug into the paper, resisted the rubber. First there were wrinkles, then a small hole. That was the end of one of her "lives."

She dragged the sheet out and flung it towards the paper basket. Her stomach fluttered and the palms of her hands were damp. Bats and *Delicado* and the scent of tobacco whirled in her brain with a copying-ink stain on her finger and "We shall be glad to have your reaction to this project" and water lapping under a punt and margin release and the date and gloves and narrow hands. . . .

She drew a breath of relief, as she checked over the new sheet; not one mistake and "a pretty page"! It had taken a long time, but it was as near perfection as typing can be, when one is handicapped by an old ribbon and a carbon near rejection point. Sanford had left her no extra carbons—but even she would approve, thought Lin happily, as she separated the sheets—and found the carbon printed back on the reverse of the signed letter.

The clock, chiming the half-hour, threw her into a state of panic. She must ring up and let them know she would be late for dinner. As luck had it, Norman answered the telephone.

"I'm finishing some work, Daddy; ask them to keep me something, will you, if I'm not in by dinnertime?"

"You'll be finished by then—surely?"

"I'm not much good at speed!" She managed a giggle, which she hoped was reassuring.

"I'll send Cadman, at a quarter to eight," said Norman peremptorily.

"Please *no*. I'll take a taxi the minute I'm through."

"All right, Linnet," she heard him say, after a pause. "But—don't make a habit of it."

She gave a gasp; it was so evident he didn't believe her!

"I—I must get on. And—Daddy; please fix it with Mummy. Tell her not to ring up. Somebody else might answer the phone, and it makes one look such a *fool*." If she was expected to lie, she would. . . .

ii

Round her feet was a mess of crumpled sheets; her face was crimson, her hair raddled. As Richard walked in, she gasped and spread her hands over the sheet she was typing.

"Well, how's it going on?"

"I thought you weren't coming back!"

'The place I'm dining is just round the corner; I thought I'd pop in."

"I haven't finished."

"That's all right," said Richard kindly. "You've got plenty of time. But you must be infernally hungry!" he remembered. "Come on, get your coat; I've just got time to give you a drink and a sandwich at the pub."

. . . He would have taken any crying child into his arms, he told himself—while instinct warned him it was not a child he was holding.

"What's the matter, darling? Lin. Stop it, Lin!"

"I've messed them all up; all the pages you signed."

"Well, what about it? I'll sign some more."

"You shouldn't have asked *me*——"

"Come on; let's look at this 'mess' you've made." He was furiously aware that his hand was shaking as he picked up the pages. "But this is fine; what do you mean by 'mess'?"

"I took seven sheets to get that one right, and three for the other. I was doing the Lysons letter when you came in; I've done it four—no, five times; I've just spoiled it again."

There was only one thing to do. His head swam and he cursed himself as their lips met—but who could have resisted that virginal mouth, with its innocent surrender? She dragged her face away, and buried it in his shoulder. As the telephone shrilled into their silence, and Lin leapt from his side, his hand went automatically to the receiver. Helen's voice trumpeted into the room.

"Is my daughter—is Miss Belinda Raymond there?"

He heard Lin gasp, and threw his arm round her.

"I'll find out. Is that Mrs. Raymond?"

"Of course it is! Am I speaking to Mr. Crome?"

"No, this is Richard Mynte; how do you do," said Richard—drawing another gasp from Lin. Oh no! That debonair approach wouldn't go down with Mummy!

"Really, Mr. Mynte!" Helen's high-pitched voice did full justice to her indignation. "May I ask if you're in the habit of keeping your—your secretaries until this hour of night?"

"Not as a rule," answered Richard coolly. "This happens to be exceptional."

"Do you realize my daughter is only eighteen?"

"I don't require the staff to produce their birth certificates"—an agonized clutch from Lin warned him of the danger of flippancy—"but—yes; I understand she's only just left school. I'll do my best to see it doesn't happen again."

"If it does, she'll have to leave. I thought I'd made it perfectly clear—to Mr. Crome—that we were only allowing her to take this ridiculous job as a hobby!"

"I'm afraid this office doesn't regard business as a 'hobby.' Lin—Miss Raymond—understands that. Here she is. Miss Raymond; your mother wishes to speak to you."

She took the receiver, warm from his hand, in her trembling one; if he had only kept his arm round her!

"Mummy? I'm sorry I'm late. I'll be home as soon as I've finished. . . . Now? Oh, I can't possibly—excuse me: just a moment——" She clasped her hand over the mouthpiece. "What am I to tell her?"

"That you're coming immediately, of course." Furious with himself, he turned on his heel.

"But the letters?"

"I can send some wires. Oh, get on with it."

"Mr. Mynte very kindly says I may go. All right, Mummy, I'll take a taxi."

"And now," Richard snapped at her, "you'd better clear up and hurry away."

"I'm so terribly sorry."

Their eyes met; she was back in his arms.

"Mummy doesn't mean to be rude! It's just that she doesn't understand!"

"Perhaps she understands too much. Lin, do you realize this is crazy behaviour?"

"Is it?" She was something bathed in sheer light; everything about her offered itself, in innocence, to the Lord of her being! A step on the landing flung them apart.

"Hi!" Henry Crome was staring at them through his big, round glasses. Lin, on her knees, pitching balls of paper into the basket, laughed with patent relief. Henry, that nice person, wouldn't think anything.

"Hi," said Richard, without enthusiasm.

"What's cooking?" Henry advanced slowly; a rather fat, very serious young man, who reminded Lin, in some ways, of her father, his eyes were fixed on Richard, who summoned up a geniality he was far from feeling.

"Lin's been giving me some overtime. And what, may one ask, are you doing here?"

"I left a manuscript behind."

"Oh indeed?" Incredulity hummed in the air. "Come on, we'll put her in a taxi; her fond mamma has just been breathing flame on the telephone. . . . In case you're ever a mother, Lin"—he forced the note of levity for Henry's benefit—"you might remember how many a good woman has put Paid to her daughter's career by untimely intervention!"

"You—aren't—sacking me!" gasped Lin.

"Not this time. Come on; clear your baggage away."

"What the dickens are you up to?" muttered Henry Crome, as the taxi, with Lin inside, shifted into the traffic stream.

"Meaning?"

"Well—in a way, she's my responsibility!" stuttered Henry.

"That's very interesting," said Richard nastily.

"I got her in, as you jolly well know, in the teeth of enormous resistance from her family."

"I'd rather you didn't supply the office from your social diary in future; do you mind?" drawled Richard. "This business isn't run as a nursery for debs."

"It's n-n-not run as a p-place of convenience for your l-l-l-leches!"

"Henry," said Richard very quietly, "if I hadn't known you for twenty years, and wasn't aware that you're practically an abstainer, I'd say you were plastered. As I don't wish to have to knock you into the gutter, I'll credit you with one glass more than you can carry. I will also take the opportunity to point out that whatever my vices may be, they've never run to the corruption of children."

"It's as p-plain as the nose on your face," mumbled Henry, "that she's f-fallen for you!"

"In that case," said Richard, with a coolness not wholly convincing to himself, "she'll only need to see a little more of me, to get over it. Don't be a b.f., Henry; I'm old enough to be her father and my tailor tells me my waist-line isn't what it was—a depressing thought. *Hasta la vista*. Give my love to Jemima—B.E.A. permitting, I'll be down on Saturday in time for dinner."

He had got out of that, he felt, rather well. Why should he feel, in himself, not completely satisfied?—feel as though, in some obscure way, he had let the child down?

iii

"You must see, Mummy, if one's taking a salary, one's got to do the work one's asked to."

"I wish you'd stop this nonsense about 'salary'! It's simply a pose. If you can't manage on your allowance, why don't you say so to your father? He'd make some sort of adjustment—so long as you weren't being extravagant."

"I can manage, and I don't need a salary; I never pretended I did. But as they're paying me one, that's all the more reason I should earn it."

"If you'd taken the job Evan offered you, you'd have got more money and there'd have been none of this rubbish about 'overtime.'"

Lin's lips closed stubbornly. She opened them to say,

"I'd rather keep a job by merit, and not by favour."

Later in the evening she asked.

"Has the laundry sent back my spotted muslin?"

"It only went on Friday." Absorbed in her crossword, Helen ignored the urgency in her daughter's voice.

"But I want it, for the week end!"

"I thought you weren't taking any 'clothes'?"

"I'll have to take something," muttered Lin, "in case! Please will you ring them in the morning, Mummy, and say I want it 'express'? If they can't do it, I suppose I'll have to get something."

"At this end of the summer? You might pick up something in the sales," conceded Helen, divided between her "clues" and surprise at Lin's proposal to take an evening gown. Perhaps these Cromes, with whom she was week-ending, were civilized, after all; the spotted muslin was a sign of grace. "But you've got plenty of other frocks; I can't imagine why you should need a new one, to go down there."

"They're all mussed-up. Don't bother about the laundry; I think I'll get a new one, after all."

She kissed her parents good night, and went to her room. Helen directed a penetrating look at Norman.

"Do you suppose she's in love with Henry Crome?"

"That fat fellow who came to dinner? I should hope not," said

Norman, with the indignation of any father in whose estimation no male is good enough for his daughter.

"All this to-do about a dress——"

"He's years older than she is!"

"So were you, when I married you," pointed out Helen. "He's a bachelor, and he came into a lot of money from his grandfather: you remember old Harry Matlock, who made a fortune out of ironmongery and put it into that publishing business?—wasn't there a case, or something? Henry Crome's a gentleman, on his father's side, and a husband older than herself helps to steady a girl down——"

"Did I steady you down?" He twinkled at her.

"I didn't happen to require it," said Helen loftily. "But these children of today seem so"—she sought for a word—"directionless, in a way. Lin's less troublesome than most, I know, but she's got far too much Fitzalan in her. The sooner she's settled the better, in my opinion."

"If 'settling' means marrying a fellow with false teeth and a stutter," said Norman, with unwonted unkindliness, for him, "she can stay, as far as I'm concerned, unsettled. Damn it, is she really going down to those people for the week end? Can't you do anything about it?"

Helen put down the newspaper, eyed him reflectively for a moment and went out of the room.

. . . Lily ponds, a diving board, the Tudor cottage, Jem's and Henry's hospitality—all gathered about *him!* At the sound of her mother's step, Lin thrust her book—*Laus Amaris*—hastily under the pillow.

"I forgot to tell you; your grandmother wants you to go down to the Court this week end."

"Oh—what a pity. I suppose you told her I'd got a date."

"I expect you could get out of it. It's not very amusing for Granny—down there by herself."

"*Mummy!*" Lin's eyes widened with astonishment at this *volte-*

face on the part of one who consistently preached—and practised—observance of the formalities. "You know what you've always said to me about people who break engagements for their own convenience."

"It doesn't happen to be your convenience." Helen, however, had the grace to look shamefaced, and Lin puzzled; why should her mother, who was always inclined to be—well—obstructive about anything that concerned visits to the Court, be suddenly so solicitous? "Most people put family claims before those of strangers."

"But Jemima and Henry aren't strangers! They're perfect dears, and Henry——" It would be tactless, by reminding Helen that she owed her job to Henry, to revive former arguments. "I couldn't possibly. But I'll tell you what I'll do: I'll ring Granny in the morning and invite myself to dinner: then I can explain all about the week end——"

"You can't be out tomorrow, you'll upset the table. You know we have people for dinner."

"Goodness, who?" scowled Lin.

"Your Uncle Roger, and the Noel-Reids and the Huntingtons."

"Oh mercy; those deadlies! Isn't Aunt Mary coming?"

"Don't be silly; she's at Dartmouth, with the boys. And the 'deadlies,' as you call them—your new friends may be very fascinating, but that's no reason for being rude to mine."

"Well, I'll ask Granny if I may go in after dinner. You'll all play canasta, and I loathe it: it's such a mean game. Nobody'll miss me," said Lin—closing the subject.

Helen returned to the drawing room, feeling, as she frequently did, a very ill-used person. It seemed to her that she got very little satisfaction out of the daughter on whom, in her secret, almost sullen fashion, she had centred most of her life. There was something cruel in Lin's persistent turning towards Anna, and her pointed conference of confidence and affection upon her grandmother, while withholding them from her parents. Of course the Crewes were now accepted by everybody, and the Arch-Duchess' visit, the other day, was certainly a feather in Anna's cap! (But everyone knew the old lady was a little gaga, and it was not to be assumed that the rest of the "royals" would follow her lead.) But it had not always been so.

What would Lin say if she knew—not that Evan and Anna were not married, which would probably glorify her grandmother in her eyes and cause her to make Anna into a heroine!—but the burden which had been imposed on them all, by the selfishness of the woman she adored? Would she ever be able to imagine what it had been like—to hold at bay the comments and innuendoes: a situation intolerable to Anna's son and daughter?

Indistinct, also, in Helen's mind—which, like her father's, was given only to formulating the simple and obvious—was the dread that the society Lin was now cultivating would encourage in her an attitude of levity to matters which involved, to Helen's way of thinking, the whole of the social structure to which Sturgeses subscribed. Of course, it was now fashionable to be casual about the moralities; it mattered very little what you did, so long as you received your command from the Lord Chamberlain and your badge for the Enclosure! So far as these were concerned, a mysterious system of what Norman called "blinkerage" protected a great many people from the results of their indiscretions. Secure in possession of her badge, Helen was wont to raise her eyebrows on various characters whose presence in the Royal Enclosure could owe itself only to glaring favouritism. She was fond of saying that she was "quite satisfied to be old-fashioned"; her narrow integrity was rooted, actually, in the code which, as she proudly (and justly) claimed, still governed English Society. Even if people were not, to use her favourite expression, "decent," public opinion obliged them to be—at least, in their official capacity. This, according to Helen, was not hypocrisy, but a proper sense of social responsibility: which meant setting an example to the lower orders and bolstering up the shaky credit of the upper classes.

Lin's repudiation of being presented was, to Helen, a most disquieting symptom, indicating a want of the sense of responsibility she had done her best to inculcate from Lin's earliest childhood. The look she turned upon Norman was glassy with tears.

She had always liked Norman—apart from loving. He was the kind of person she could understand, and it was all very well for Anna to take up an attitude of gentle tolerance. People had to find their own level, and in Norman she had found hers. All the brilliant young men who had been introduced to the daughter of the beautiful Mrs. Sturges had failed to kindle the spark which, at her first meeting with Norman, marked the recognition of like and like. Perhaps he was commonplace; so am I, she asserted stoutly. So, in a way, was Father, though he had more "style" than Norman. But that belonged to his generation. There wasn't much time, between the two wars, for acquiring "style," and Norman—nineteen when the first war ended—was, like most young men of his age, too preoccupied with building up a career to bother much about cultivating the graces that people like Anna took for granted. Helen was satisfied with Norman, as he now was—thirteen years older than herself, substantial, settled in his opinions, capable of giving her the lead which Helen, for all her self-sufficiency, required from a man.

"She'll have to be told——"

"Who told?—and what?" He blinked at her kindly. He was very fond of this well-dressed, neat (though heavy) woman: honest—reliable, infallibly loyal to her friends and inimical to her enemies—who had most conscientiously fulfilled her duties as wife and mother; who had consistently put his interests before her own, and managed, at the same time, to do something more than her duty by a brother to whom she was devoted, his wife and his children. But he found himself, sometimes, gently amused by Helen. Left to herself, she would have made life intolerable—not only to those for whom she cared, but to herself.

"It's really exaggerated: Lin's fondness for Mother!"

Norman smiled; he—like most people—had fallen under the spell of Anna.

"Anna's got a wonderful understanding of children."

"Has she! She never understood me or Roger—I don't mean she wasn't sweet," stammered Helen, "but we never felt she knew what we were talking about. Nor did Father," she concluded defiantly.

He continued to smile. She thought—Norman's put on a great deal of weight; it can't be healthy, to carry that enormous paunch. Oh, don't, she begged of some indistinct power she thought of conventionally as "God," don't give me something else to worry about.

"Possibly not. People like us rather defeat her."

She caught at the "us" for comfort, but blundered on.

"Lin's too like Anna!"

"Is it such a disaster?" He cocked a questioning brow.

"You know what I mean. She's got to know, sooner or later; I'd hate it to come from some outside source."

He looked at her quizzically, through the thick lenses that covered his small, blue eyes.

"Isn't there something about not crossing bridges?"

"Don't be casual; she's your daughter as well as mine."

"But there's no need to dramatize it." Helen turned scarlet, at the suggestion of her—her!—dramatizing anything. "I only mean—things have altered a great deal in the last few years. 'There's been a war.' "

"Wars don't alter right and wrong!" she asserted stoutly.

He looked at her: admiring, and a little envying, her power of reducing the most complex argument to a flat statement in black and white.

"They give people more to think about and correct their sense of values. At least," said Norman simply, "one hopes they do. It's not a matter of 'change of heart'; there's no time for that——"

"Don't tell me there's any less gossip!" said Helen, with curling lip. He cocked his head and looked at her out of the corners of his eyes: a trick of Lin's, she thought with a pang.

"Not at all; but less time to take it seriously."

"What you really mean is, the moral standard is lower. You needn't tell me that!" she retorted triumphantly. "Let's get back to Lin. She's got to be told."

"Why?" He rested the tips of his fingers together—a mannerism that irritated Helen—and gazed at her across them, as he gazed at his clients.

"I've not come to you for professional advice, and I'm not under cross-examination! Lin's got to be told."

"In that case, the best person to tell her would seem to be Anna."

"No! I won't have it!"

"I think," said Norman quietly, "it would be wiser."

She winced from his look of uncomfortable understanding.

"Coming from you," she muttered, "she won't think it's malicious."

He lifted his shoulders, and allowed them to drop.

"If there were the least necessity! I absolutely can't see how it concerns Lin, at present—in fact, at all. I can't even see the line of approach; do I toss the information across my shoulder—'You know, of course, that your grandmother isn't married to Evan': to which, if true to her generation, she will answer, 'So what?'; or do I cover my eyes with my hand and say, 'My child: prepare yourself for a great shock. Your grandmother has been living in sin from the day you were born.' "

"Oh, don't be so flippant. You didn't take it so lightly sixteen years ago, did you?"

"Sixteen years ago; is it, really? We should be wiser—you, I and Roger—by now. Let's be honest—shall we? Our reason, at the time, for being shocked, had very little to do with our morals. We were afraid it would affect us in some way: socially, or through our careers. It didn't, did it? Which, of course, made it simpler. Roger has got his knighthood; mine will come—some day. Meanwhile, let's agree that, for two people in their position, they've managed very well. In fact, remarkably. Ours isn't a Bohemian society——"

"That's the Fitzalans. If Mother's family had gone back on her, it wouldn't have been so good!"

"I accept the Fitzalans." He bowed his head, with an irony so faint that it was lost on her. "I'd give most of the credit to Anna herself. She's got the kind of quiet dignity that makes it difficult for people to be rude to her."

"Well, naturally, they want to keep in with Evan. A person who can pull all those strings can get away with anything!"

His eyes covered her with a tolerant pity.

"Don't underestimate him, Helen. It takes more than string pulling to fly full in the face of prejudice and outdistance your rivals."

"Men always stick up for one another. As a lawyer, you can't approve——"

He chuckled.

"I certainly didn't approve of their proposal to put up a cock-and-bull yarn about a civil ceremony in France!"

"That was Evan! Whatever mistakes Mother makes, she never lies. And it was only meant for the servants and the office. Nobody else would have believed it."

"A good thing they wouldn't, or he might have let himself in for a bigamy action. It's a source of unending marvel to me," reflected Norman, "of what idiotic things intelligent people are capable: particularly if they're touched with Evan's infallibility complex. It's what brings great criminals eventually to the gallows: the impossibility of visualizing failure. If you've never in your life had a setback, it must be difficult not, in time, to believe yourself outside all human law."

"His marriage must have been something of a setback!" Though her condemnation of Evan was deep and bitter, it hardly justified comparing him to a criminal.

"I doubt its ever entering into his consideration. When did it happen?—in 1910, or so?"

"Well, the wretched woman's put away safely, somewhere up north."

"Where she can't object to Anna's calling herself Mrs. Crewe. M'm; they managed the deed poll very neatly. . . . My dear"—he had risen, and dropped his hand on her shoulder—"nothing's deader than a dead scandal: especially one of before the war. The world's changed; perhaps, from your point of view, not for the better. But who's to say we're not kinder, now, in our judgments of people whose lives can't be made to fit into the common pattern?

"Every day, in chambers, we're handling broken lives: people who can't make a go of marriage, or haven't the patience to try. Men and women who, outside the marriage bond, have formed attachments that compel one's respect by their deepness and sincerity. Wives who, out of malice, won't divorce husbands, and husbands who won't divorce wives, because they imagine it reflects on their sexual authority! Herbert's amendments were a step in the right direction, but they don't go far enough. It grows on one, you know: the thousands of people—either living in hell, with partners they can't respect, let alone care for, or tossing themselves into limbo and dragging the people they love with them——"

She stirred uneasily, reacting as to her habit.

"You don't support easy divorce!"

She felt him take his hand away.

"To change the present law doesn't presuppose easy divorce. Certain situations carry their own solutions; to that particular situation, the law, as it now stands, presents an impediment. You know I've always maintained"—there was a note of weariness in his voice —"that the inability of the partner, as distinct from the refusal, to carry out the obligations of the marriage should, subject to well-defined conditions that include provision for the first party, automatically absolve the second party from the contract, if he or she wishes to be absolved. Noncompliance with the five-year clause, which has blocked Anna and Evan, is only a sop to the antidivorce crowd; there's no good reason in humanity, if not in law, for refusing release. Don't let's start on this"—impatience reinforced exhaustion in Norman's voice—"You've heard my views often enough; you're bored by now. It's not morality, but humanity, that's at stake. If you knew about one tenth of the cases that come through our hands, Helen, you'd realize that misery is so widely distributed, the shifts and struggles of people to escape from their individual miseries so general, that a case like Anna's can only arouse respect from thoughtful people."

"All people aren't thoughtful"—she sounded like a child on the point of tears—"and, anyhow, I only care about Lin. What's this absurd adoration of Mother leading to?"

"Let her keep it! Adoration's good for the young; there's only too little of it today. They've got more wisdom than we had. God knows they should; there must be some progress, from the ignorance of Anna's youth, through the mock sophistication of ours."

"Were you sophisticated?" She spoke like one uncertain of everything: so different from her usual, positive self that he had an impulse of almost unbearable tenderness towards her. "I never noticed. The thing I liked was, you were so different from most of the boys I knew; you didn't have any poses, or appear bored, or quote French poets at me and expect me to know about Picasso's 'blue period': whatever that meant!"

"I wouldn't know!" He smiled at her. "Most of the fellows who came through the first war and had to make up their time were too concentrated on their jobs to go in for poses. I was one of the few who came into a ready-made job, and considered myself lucky. If you'd met me a few years earlier, you'd probably have put me in your category."

"I hadn't started a category, in those days." She gave him a shamefaced kiss. "All right; I'll leave Lin alone, for the present."

"You would be wise." His arms were round her. "At that age,

one has a gift for misunderstanding. Especially where the affections are involved. Why risk it, for the sake of some stale rag of gossip that may never blow across Lin's path? Has it ever struck you," said Norman, with his kind smile, "how unimportant, and how uninteresting, our affairs are—to her generation?"

She was in bed when he came through from his dressing room, enormous in a quilted, crimson robe Lin had bought him—"If Daddy likes it, why shouldn't he have it?"—against Helen's protest.

"Well, did you make her put off the week end?"

She shook her head.

"You know what she's like, when she sets her mind on anything."

He sighed.

"Well—Anna can deal with it, probably, better than we can. I'll have a word with her, in the morning."

CHAPTER VII

*T*he Humbles departed—Gertrude barely glancing at Anna as she muttered good-bye, Humble with an air of resignation to circumstances too strong for him. Gertrude, who had a very nice tweed overcoat, a castoff of Anna's, had elected, for her own imponderable reasons, to travel in dead black; whether under pressure or infected by example, Humble, though addicted, when off duty, to the livelier heather mixtures, wore his darkest suit. Anna went down the hall, to see them off. As they climbed dumbly into the car, Pulford, the chauffeur, a pleasant, cheery person, came back to ask if Anna had any further orders. He did not quite wink at his mistress, behind the backs of the departing couple, but he grinned.

"Might be a funeral, mightn't it?"

Anna did not hold with discussing servants with one another, but her lips gave an involuntary twitch.

"Look after them, Pulford, and do try to cheer them up! Good morning, Emily." The old daily housemaid who had worked for her since the end of the war came respectfully forward to close the door.

"Good morning, madam." There was a twinkle in the gentle old eye; Emily knew she was a favourite. "Poor Mrs. Humble!" she ventured. "She'll be better when she's on the plane. She's really upset at leaving you, ma'am; I had to promise we'd do our best to look after you till she's back!"

"I don't think Gertrude has got out of the habit of regarding me as a little girl," observed Anna.

"No, madam. Mrs. Pulford is upstairs—if you should wish to speak to her."

Pulford's wife, in a grey tailor-made with low-heeled shoes, had entered upon her duties and was stripping the bed. Anna said pleasantly,

"Haven't you got an overall, Mrs. Pulford?"

"Oh—certainly, Mrs. Crewe, if you prefer it!"

Anna turned away quickly. Yes, Gertrude has spoiled me. There's no reason she should say "madam"—even Pulford sometimes forgets; it's the modern school. But even Evan had pulled a face over Pulford's marriage to an ex-schoolteacher—allowing that, apart from her self-assurance, she seemed to be a capable young woman, who would make a good wife.

Oh yes; she was going to miss the Humbles, who, for all their irritating habits, brought a kind of warmth into life which paid service rarely provides. I must be getting old, Anna reproved herself; old and unreasonable. The people who work for us nowadays don't build their whole lives round us, as they used to do; why should they? We never deserved it. It's our own fault, now, that they put their own interests before ours. The Pulfords will do everything in their power to fill the place of the Humbles while they're away, but oh! I shall be glad to have my bad-tempered old Gerty back again!

She was out most of the day and dined with friends of Evan's before going to the play. When Pulford opened the door, she thought, as she invariably did on coming home, how pretty her hall was, with its effect of shaded candlelight, and the iron trellis between the upper and lower levels, which, following his instructions, Pulford proceeded to lock, after closing the street door.

"Miss Lin rang, just after you'd gone out."

"Did she leave any message?" Disappointment at having missed the child slightly chilled the evening's pleasure.

"I said you'd gone to the theatre, but she came round, all the same."

"She's here!"

"She's been here about an hour. She said she'd wait till you got back. I took some coffee down to the basement room."

Dropping her cape on a chair, Anna ran lightly down the stairs. The broad room, with its shining floor and clusters of wall lights, was empty, and the doors open into the garden. Round the fountain, like a large white moth, Lin wove a mysterious improvisation which finished, as she saw her grandmother, in a sharp arabesque. Anna caught the child in her arms.

"You don't mind? Mummy's dining one of her 'lethal' crowds. I made it my excuse, that I had to see you before you go away. Isn't it the divinest night?" She stretched her bare arms and bosom towards the stars—as though, thought Anna, she might at any moment float out of her strapless bodice and drift naked over the roofs: a peri in search of paradise! "I do think August is the loveliest month—in spite of the end of the season and everything."

"All our childhood was August," murmured Anna.

"What did you say, darling?" Lin sounded puzzled. "Is it a quotation?"

"Yes, from Anna Fitzalan!" She smiled. "Haymaking; strawberries and cream; the seaside; sand castles——"

"I know," said Lin quickly. "Harvest, and village fêtes; the biggest marrow; the best tomatoes; 'country bunches'——"

"The time of fulfillment."

"How like you, to find the right word. That's it—exactly: the time of fulfillment!"

She's in love! It came to Anna in a flash, and filled her with a curious sadness. Eighteen; so early to fall in love! Yet who was she, to question it?

"You're very smart, for dinner at home." The crisp whiteness of seersucker, the narrow inlets of lace; the monster bow of black velvet, poised, like a butterfly, on one hip.

"I put it on to show you. Mummy doesn't approve of it: she says it's 'too old.' Cotton isn't old! And I do think, if one's old enough to earn one's living, one might be allowed to choose one's clothes."

Only a few months ago, the child had been in school uniform.

"Tell me about the 'living,' " smiled Anna.

"Oh, it's wonderful. *Terribly* interesting." (Not someone she has met in the office?) "It's such fun—seeing all the famous authors we publish, and wondering how they got that way!" Lin let out a small giggle. "All the women *deadly* smart, and the men—well, tatty, rather. Except the young ones, who're smooth and silky, and call everybody darling, and are just rushing out for a date with Princess Margaret." Lin grinned. "Don't you know, Granny?—you just don't grade, if you haven't had one cocktail in the same room as the Princess. You should see Lytton's heart beating, right through her Swan and Edgar model, when they say 'Margaret'!"

"Have you anything in particular to do? I mean, apart from social chitchat and gazing at authors?"

"Oh, it's the dreariest stuff," admitted Lin cheerfully. "Practically scrub woman!—cleaning type and washing teacups and tearing up and down stairs about fifty times a day; really a sort of office-boy job—but don't tell Mummy! She thinks I'm private secretary, or something, to Henry Crome. I wish I were; he's a terrific person. He does all the editing; that means, he practically writes the books. I once," said Lin, in a hushed voice, "saw a manuscript immediately after it came in, and then after Henry'd been at it: honestly, I don't know how the author had the *gall to sign his name to it!*— and it turned out one of our best sellers—and I do think it's mean Henry shouldn't get any of the credit"—she paused to draw breath.

"And what else?" prompted Anna—too wise to assume that this "Henry," whoever he was, was the person engaging Lin's affections.

"Oh—addressing envelopes and dusting shelves——"

"It wouldn't have been quite so 'slavish' at Head Office." Grateful for the opening, and mindful of her promise to Helen, Anna put in a smiling word.

Lin's face closed; it was as though a little wooden mask slid over her brow, and her mouth, and her sweet, candid eyes.

"No, probably it wouldn't."

Head Office: yes. The little room opening out of Evan's, that one would have shared with the secretary. Flowers, cosy carpets, a coal fire, cigarettes; immunity from the restrictions imposed on the rest of the staff. Favouritism. Ten-in-the-morning duty, instead of nine. Free on the tick of five.

"It—it was terribly nice of Evan to ask me. But—I like it better, where I am."

"I suppose it feels more independent," offered Anna. Lin snatched at the evasion.

"Well, yes—there's that. And I am interested in publishing. I don't think I could work up any enthusiasm over shipments of ore, and tungsten contracts, and railway plant! I do think one ought to mind about one's work; don't you?"

"I certainly do." Anna admitted it rather guiltily, wondering if she was letting Helen down. "I was just sorry—for Evan's disappointment."

"It was terribly sweet of him; but he only offered it from a sort of—sort of family point of view, didn't he? He really wanted somebody much more experienced——"

Had Evan and Lin ever had a disagreement—it would be too much to call it a quarrel—about which she had never been told? Anna wondered if she had imagined, latterly, a curious aloofness between them. After all those years of devotion? On a night when they took the four children to the circus, and it should have been Hugh, Anna, the small but excessively precocious Peter, Lin, Evan and Simon, Lin upset the seating arrangements by insisting on sitting next to her grandmother, leaving Evan with a boy on either side. And later, over supper (Peter, loudly protesting, having been delivered into the hands of his nurse), how had Lin managed, somehow, with perfect politeness, to split the company into two camps—herself and Anna against Evan and the boys—returning absent little smiles to any remark of Evan's, and lending rapt attention to Anna's smallest observation? Evan noticed it, of course; rather apologetically, Anna remarked on it afterwards.

"Wasn't Lin a little 'odd,' tonight?"

He raised his brows and his shoulders, but did not trouble to lift his eyes from the evening paper. He laughed.

"The age, my dear; 'uncertain, coy and hard to please.' "

"But—she's not like that."

"One hardly expects one's senile efforts at entertainment to hold much attraction for a damsel who has just discovered the charms of her own generation."

It was not merely pique; Evan was never vain! she told herself. He was genuinely hurt, as he had a right to be. Anna had often felt grieved for aging beauties, made conscious of the withering of their charms by the withdrawal of their younger admirers. She, too, she supposed, was "an aging beauty"!—but he had filled her life so full with contentment that she never had cause to regret the vagrant attentions that came, perhaps, a little less frequently her way than they had done in the past. It must be just as painful for the man who, all his life, has been courted by women of all ages. . . . She blamed herself, that all her devotion had not rendered him as immune as she was herself to the trivial stings that accompany the fading years. That Lin should be the one to inflict them puzzled and troubled her a little—remembering the devotion that had linked those two in Lin's not so far distant childhood; and the affection he had always expressed for her. . . . It was inconceivable that he would have been hurt by the slight on the part of any other chit, as, she suspected, he had been hurt by Lin.

"I'm terribly sorry about the week end"—Lin had gone off at a tangent. "I'd have adored to come, but the Cromes—Henry and his sister Jemima—asked me, oh, weeks ago. I suppose you couldn't possibly come over for lunch on Saturday? They'd love it!"

Anna dismissed with a smile this casual, modern disposal of other people's hospitality.

"I'm not quite the age, to tear fifty miles to lunch with people I don't know, who've never heard of me!"

"Of course they've heard of you. I find it terribly hard," sighed Lin, "sometimes, to remember you're my grandmother. In fact, I often feel like calling you 'Anna'; is that *frightful* cheek?"

"It's the best compliment I've had in years. You might call me 'Anna'—if you had anything particular to say."

"Thanks; I'll remember."

But she was conscious of a withdrawal. If Lin had anything to say, the time was not yet. But she recognized, with sadness, all the signs. Lin was—luminous. Her very flesh gave off the glow of her spirit. It was like the annunciation.

Lin said awkwardly,

"I suppose Evan will be back soon."

"In just over a fortnight." Perhaps she was glowing too; Lin's hand shot out unexpectedly and caught hers.

"Darling, has it been very lonely?"

"Just a little strange: to be without somebody one——"

"I don't know why he didn't take you," interrupted Lin. "You've always gone everywhere together—haven't you?"

"I'm not quite as young as I used to be"—it was the first excuse that came to her—"and days and days in trains is not much fun, you know, for a person of my age!"

"I can never remember you're any older than Mummy. I suppose it's because you never try to make yourself out young. Am I *really* like you?" asked Lin earnestly.

"Very like me, forty years ago: at least, Evan says so." She deliberately ignored a faint gesture of impatience. "That's partly why he became so fond of you"—the old and the young Anna; was

Lin sensitive enough to catch the implication? "Things you say often remind him of me, when he first met me, at Camelhurst."

"Dozens of people must have been in love with you, in those days," said Lin hurriedly.

"Dozens?" Anna smiled faintly. "I wouldn't know. At your age I was married, and I never noticed anyone but Evan—after that," she concluded, somewhat lamely.

"What was Grandfather like?"

"Very much like your Uncle Roger," said Anna, after reflection.

"Oh." Lin was too polite to express disappointment. "If he hadn't died," she burst out, "would you have fallen in love with Evan?"

"Darling—what a question!" Anna forced a laugh. "I think—I hope" (why had she to feel a hypocrite?) "I wouldn't have done anything that would have hurt my husband."

"You mean, Grandfather. But you weren't in love with him."

"What makes you think that?"

"You wouldn't have fallen in love with Uncle Roger!" said Lin absurdly. "How is one supposed to know if one's 'in love'?"

"Darling, that's really silly!—and I'm sure you could tell me as well as I could tell you."

"I know; but I'd like to hear what you think."

"Being 'in love' and 'loving,' " said Anna, after a pause, "are two different things; one's like—like the striking of a match, and the other's—permanent. If you're 'in love,' you're inclined to give way to all sorts of foolish impulses; you're careless of everything but the attainment of your immediate desire. Being 'in love' is like having pneumonia, or what we used to call 'a growth'; it could be the death of you, if you didn't take care——"

"Like going to live with the person, or divorce?"

"Oh, I see; you mean, if you're unlucky enough to fall in love with somebody who isn't free to marry you," said Anna, with a pang.

"Well, what about 'loving'?"

"It's just as painful, but—I don't know if you'll understand what I mean: it's a life bearer. It means—wanting only the very best—not only for the person you love, but for all who love you. It means putting the interest of the ones you care for before all personal considerations. It means you'd hang, or burn or die—but you'd never demand anything that didn't come to you in the way of nature. If you really love," said Anna, "your first desire is not to hurt anybody; or, if hurting's inevitable, to take it all on yourself."

"I hadn't worked it into words," said Lin, in a hushed voice, "but that, more or less, was my idea. Divorce is awfully shabby—isn't it? I mean, this business of scrambling into bed: I think it's just *sordid!* Loving's a sort of—privilege——"

How little, thought Anna, we know the young—with their apparent cynicism, their toughness, their small faces conventionalized into a standard beauty. How lovely they are, the young, with their solemn conviction of righteousness, their grave condemnation of the follies of their elders.

She said,

"Darling—do you mind?—I'm terribly tired."

Lin rose instantly.

"I'm sorry! But I did want to see you, before you went away. You're leaving in the morning, aren't you?"

"After luncheon. I promised to meet your uncle; he's feeling rather deserted, with the family away."

"He dined with us tonight. It's so funny," said Lin reflectively, "how different you are from your children. Good night—darling 'Anna'! I'm glad you like the frock. You don't think it's 'too much,' do you, for the week end?"

"I don't know what kind of a place your friends keep up; but people don't wear much, now, in the country."

"Oh—but there's sure to be dancing."

"Come down, if you can, next week end. I'll be rather dull by then!" Not true, for each day brought Evan nearer. "I suppose I'm crazy, to plan house parties without a real staff; but so many of our friends want to come, this autumn, and he's bringing a couple of men back from the States. I'd be truly grateful, if you'd lend a hand—if it's only planning menus and writing cards for the bedrooms."

"Of course I'll come. Oh dear, I feel such a beast, for letting you down this week end——"

"Who's the party?" asked Anna, with careful carelessness.

"Oh, well—Henry and Jem, of course, and one of the Lygon boys; he's a relation of Henry's. He's at Oxford and we're supposed to play together!" Lin pulled a face. "And a girl who's written a book we're publishing this autumn, and her husband, who's at the Atom research. Sounds rather dire, doesn't it?—but I expect we'll have fun. And Mr. Mynte may be coming down on Saturday," said Lin, in a high, offhand voice.

"Dick? I knew his mother. I haven't met him for years!"

"He mentioned you, the other day."

I might have known. The stiffening up. The sudden, silver edge on her voice. Richard—with his easy charm, his good looks and popularity—especially with women: who call him "sweet," and make allowances for his outrageous forgetfulness—which covers a keen eye to the main chance! Whom did he marry? Anna could not remember, but some time during the war there had been a divorce. Not for Lin. Oh, please, not for Lin!

ii

"It sounds like something's gone wrong with the car. Mr. Pulford's taken it to the garage; he says it was quite all right yesterday."

"Well, is it anything serious?" Anna concentrated on her breakfast tray—overlooking the "Mr. Pulford." She had a premonition that her careful organization was going to break down.

"I'm afraid I couldn't say. But they're going to ring up." Mrs.

Pulford minced across the room to draw the curtains. "I wonder if Mrs. Humble's got over her troubles by now!" The implied sneer stung Anna, to her surprise, to Gertrude's defence.

"People who aren't accustomed to travelling by air usually find their first flight rather alarming. I'll have my bath in half an hour, please."

The telephone rang as she was leaving for lunch with Roger.

"They've taken her down, madam, and it looks as if we've had it. We'll be lucky if we get off tonight."

"What about the Bentley?"

"They're just in the middle of the cellulosing; but they can send a Daimler. I know the driver; he's a real smart chap. He'll get you down nearly as soon as I can."

"No, I don't care about rushing through those lanes with a strange chauffeur. I'll go down by train, and you and your wife had better come on as soon as you can."

Somewhat surprisingly, Mrs. Pulford's view was that she preferred to travel with Anna. "Mr. Crewe would rather," she said, in a prim and final way that appeared to settle the matter.

"Then you'd better put a call through to the Court, and tell them to send a taxi to meet the 4.30."

"Isn't that Abingdon line terrible?" sniffed Mrs. Pulford, returning from the telephone. "They don't seem to have any training on these country exchanges. I can't get through. What had I better do?—send a telegram?"

"It probably won't arrive before we do." Anna shrugged her shoulders. Breakdowns were a commonplace on the line to the Court; she worried a little about whether this one would be repaired in time for Evan's call on Sunday—the weekly four minutes that meant so much to them both—but decided this was meeting trouble halfway. "Yes, send a telegram."

Roger—immensely broad now, heavy and pompous—lunched her at his club, and informed her he was joining Mary and the boys on Saturday. The war—during which he reached major's rank and was twice decorated—combined with his knighthood, had completed his transformation from the irresponsible youth to one in training for the roles of country landowner and political leader. He informed Anna that they had decided to buy a property in the West Country, and that he had been invited to stand as the Tory candidate in a forthcoming by-election.

"Mary must be very pleased! She will be glad to think of your carrying on her family tradition."

"It's a frightful grind, but you've just got to face facts. We lost that seat at the last election because the other side, as usual, went in for muckrakin'," scowled Roger. "Noel-Reid: an excellent chap, but a bachelor, and a bit of a blade. Enormous nonconformist element in the constituency, and, of course, the Reds made play with it." (Any adherent of the left wing, to Roger, was a Red.) "So they decided to put up a sound family man this time." Anna had to lift her napkin to her lips, to conceal a smile at this description of Roger. "I haven't been adopted yet, but Mary's puttin' in some useful spadework; that, actually, was the idea of takin' the boys down there for the holidays."

"You had better get Evan to come down and speak for you, when you start your campaign," she suggested. He eyed her with cautious approval.

"That's not a bad idea. I'll put it to my agent." He scowled again, laying down his fork and reducing a piece of toast Melba to crumbs with his left hand. "Helen was saying last night that Lin's bein' a bit of a nuisance." His manner suggested that she, Anna, was implicated. She raised her brows and spoke quickly.

"It doesn't sound at all like her."

"You know what I mean: runnin' about with all these writin' fellas and publishin' fellas—I don't see it's anything to laugh about," he broke off on a note of offence.

"Oh, my dear, excuse me: but it sounds so like your father." (And, of course, she should not have said that; neither to Helen nor Roger was Hugh a subject for jokes.) "But, really, they seem very harmless people, and she doesn't see much of them outside the office. I suppose Helen is worrying about this week end."

"Reds!" exploded Roger. "Red as bulls! Everybody knows—and you ought to!—that the whole of the writin' crowd's riddled with Red propaganda."

"Oh, surely that's an exaggeration. I've met quite a number of authors, and they all seemed to be nice, mild people, quite unpolitical. Apart from that, Lin's politics, such as they are, are quite what you'd call 'sound'——"

"Don't you believe it; those fellas are as sly as weasels and it would be a feather in their caps to get hold of a name like ours. They'll play her along until—mark my words—one day it'll come out she's a Party member. A nice thing that'ud be—in the middle of our election campaign! 'Tory Candidate's Niece takes lead at Communist meeting——' "

"I think, dear, I wouldn't worry; it's the kind of thing they grow out of," said Anna peacefully.

"Grow out of it—after losing me a couple of thousand votes!" Roger's bellow brought the heads of several parties up in astonishment from their plates; he sank his voice to a furious mumble. "Mother, this isn't any jokin' matter! A pinch of salt, in this constituency I'm fightin', 'ud be enough to curl up the Conservative vote for good an' all; might as well hand the beggars the seat on a plate. They're out to tear strips off us, and any mud they can sling at our candidate's worth gold to 'em!"

She spent the rest of the time in soothing him, in promising to put Lin on her guard; and he drove her to Paddington, where Mrs. Pulford met them with the luggage.

"And don't forget, Mother," were Roger's parting words, "the whole lot of you, from now on, have got to mind your steps."

"Darling!" she protested. "I don't keep funny company, and I'm not addicted to getting tight in public—if that's what you mean."

He suffered this with an uneasy smile.

"Well, you may think I'm overfussy; but I've tipped Helen off about takin' Norman's customers to the night clubs and told them both to lay off the racecourses for the present. Dammit—I'm havin' to! I tell you—I've got the psychology of that gang down there, and to my way of thinking it's worth some sort of sacrifice, to snatch that seat out of the claws of those sewers!"

He's absolutely sincere, thought Anna; adolescent, but sincere, the way Hugh was. He's my boy, and I care about him——

They had a compartment to themselves. Anna, who would have chatted happily to Gertrude, opened *The Tatler*, not feeling equal to Mrs. Pulford's conversation.

"I thought it was you! We don't often see you on this train."

She started, then smiled: recognizing one of what was locally known as the "riverside set," who rented summer places round the neighbouring villages, and, over the postwar years, had formed a society of their own, not too amiably viewed by the "permanents." She rescued a name from the farther recesses of her memory.

"Good afternoon—Mrs. Archibald."

"All by yourself!"—a comment ill received by Mrs. Pulford, who did not care—Anna felt, not unreasonably—for her dismissal as non-existent, or, at least, invisible to the naked eye. The newcomer settled herself in a corner. "Well, perhaps, for once, we can coax you over to Goring! Do come to lunch on Sunday; we'll be quite a lively crowd."

Not doubting it, Anna excused herself by saying that she was expecting people to luncheon on Sunday. It could happen. It was not unusual for Evan's friends to drop in for a sherry and remain for a meal.

"So Mr. Crewe's in on this big Anglo-American railway deal—— Oh yes, it was all in the papers. I'm surprised he didn't take you with him; I thought you went on all his trips."

"The United States? Dollars, you know!"

"What—for people like you?" An envious incredulity twitched the speaker's lips. "But you always keep yourself in the background, don't you!"

Anna replied, quietly, that there was not much scope for women, in railway conferences.

"Ho—isn't there! American wives are in on everything: just let their men try keeping them out. I noticed it particularly when Arch and I were over in '48. You should see them—the way they turn everything into a party! I learned a lot, that time we were over, and, in your place, I wouldn't have been left behind! Talk about Paris—I'd trade a month in Paris for a week in New York any time; and I'd give my eyeteeth for a couple of hours in Saks Fifth and one lunch at Twenty-One."

"You know New York." She made a polite statement of it.

"Don't you?" gaped the other.

"No."

"You mean—you've never been?"

"Never."

"My dear! I thought Big Business spent the whole of its time rushing backwards and forwards across the Atlantic."

"You must know more about 'Big Business' than I." Anna concealed her annoyance under a smile, although conscious of Mrs. Pulford's ears, pinned back, though she continued to stare ostentatiously out of the window.

"You've been to Germany and Italy; and it's only a few weeks since you got back from South Africa——" Before Anna had time to ponder on the dissemination of news from her own household, Mrs. Archibald blurted, "If Arch dragged me round all those deadly places, he'd jolly well have to make up by taking me to New York!"

Am I touchy, or is she trying to be rude? Anna changed the subject—she hoped—by pointing out that they had just left Reading, and asking Mrs. Pulford to get the suitcases down.

"Is that all you've got? Good; they'll easily go in the back of the car."

"Thank you, I've ordered a taxi."

"You don't want to drive all the way to Chilton Magnates in

one of the local hearses! They charge the earth and then they've got the nerve to expect a tip. It's only a mile or two out of my way."

"Thank you very much," said Anna, with the decision that frequently disconcerted people misled by her mildness. "I couldn't possibly go back on an order."

"Smart, isn't she," observed Mrs. Pulford, as they waited for the porter to arrive with the luggage. "I always mean to get myself a pair of those Brevitts; such good style, aren't they?"

"Put the cases in the boot. Do you mind riding in front?" said Anna crisply.

"Oh—certainly!" Mrs. Pulford slid in beside the driver; her shoulders expressed reserve, but no patent resentment of her relegation to the role of lady's maid.

My new little housemaid, thought Anna, would be capable of all the attendance I need. Now, if I have Joyce about me, Mrs. Pulford will be offended, and Pulford will be placed in an awkward position. Why do nice men have to make such silly marriages? Not, she reminded herself, that there's anything to dislike about her, but—one can't help disliking servants who aren't really servants, and keep on reminding one of it.

What a to-do, she thought, I'm making about a little disturbance in my plans. The car: that began it. If Evan had been here, I wouldn't have had to decide between a hirecar and a train; that would have been settled for me. Indeed, I am hopelessly spoiled!— and I have no right to take it out on an unfortunate woman who is trying to do her duty, and whose very presence is proof of his care for me.

This, instead of comforting, sent so sharp a stab through her that she caught her breath; it was almost physical. Journeys with Evan—lightened by his wit and his gift for extracting amusement from trivial happenings. . . . . For the first time, his absence hurt: hurt, and filled her with a brief panic, the more disconcerting because she knew it to be irrational.

The woman in the train. Things like that never happened, when Evan was there. It was easy to imagine how he would have handled the situation—with a lightness, an absurdity, which would have driven the woman, in embarrassment, out of the compartment. Knowing she was enlarging the incident out of all proportion to its importance—it yet became part of her foolish panic. Evan, please come back! She found herself clutching the strap—it was an old private car, converted into a taxicab—and that the palms of her gloves were wet. Making a tremendous effort of will, Anna forced herself to relax.

She drew a deep breath, as the calm sweep of the downs opened before her; the eternal beauty of those folds of bone-white, honey-yellow and the golden-brown of sand. The vast blue sky, puffed with white cloud, with larks trembling in it. The low trees, the small, kind houses under their mouse-coloured thatch. Above all— the deep benevolence of the English countryside.

She let down the window and inhaled deeply of the pure air, heavy with the scent of cut grass. She shortened her vision to the blue flax flowers, the pink of campion and quivering white of Queen Anne's lace; the innumerable and beautiful green things curled in the depth of the hedgerows. . . .

iii

The young maids welcomed her in their clean print overalls; only two should have been on duty, but the others, even if they bolted within minutes, did not mean to be done out of the reception to "madam"—as, at last, she had become, after perky months of "Mrs. Crewe."

"The telephone's working, madam! And Mr. Pulford's just rung up to say he'll be down with the car tonight."

She went out on the drawbridge, to look across the cornstooks, peacefully uptilted against the slope of the down. The sky was a dazzling blue, and the air tasted like a fresh young wine. She raised her hand in greeting to the gardener, who paused in driving the motor mower across the green lawns sloping to the moat. He stopped the engine and touched his cap; one of the older men, of course. If it had been one of the youths, he would have grinned and expected her to bawl to him against the running of the motor.

"The new mower hasn't come yet, Dale?"

"Not yet, mum; I rung up and asked the station."

"It looks like being a fine week end." She narrowed her eyes to the trees on the horizon.

"Ay, but it speaks of rain." "It" being the radio. Anna smiled. "Do you speak of rain? That seems more to the point."

His solemn, peasant's face stirred a little, but he wagged his head.

"Zeems like them scientific chaps has got us beat."

She set Mrs. Pulford to check over the contents of the linen room—more to keep her out of the way of those liable to be ruffled by her assumptions of superiority than for her usefulness—and took the resident couple round with her on an inspection of the rooms.

"We'll be using these five bedrooms, when the shooting begins, and the small room and dressing room in the east wing. Is that woodworm?" She pointed to a corner.

"Looks like it wur——"

"Something will have to be done about that, won't it? You understand carpentry, Smallbone; can you see to it?"

"I durrzay I can, ma'am."

"And these curtains! Isn't there anybody in the village who could mend them? It's such beautiful old needlework, it deserves better than patching."

"Zeems the maidens don't care for stitching, the way they used to when I wur in school," the wife said shyly. "I can ask my old granny—down boy the mill."

The bailiff was waiting for her, when she came downstairs, and invited him, as Evan would have done, into the library, for a glass of sherry.

"What about the Downside cottage?"—which they had "done up," rather expensively, but Evan agreed with her that there should, in these days, be a bathroom and indoor sanitation; it was what all the council houses had. "I suppose that's gone, by now?"

"Well, Mr. Crewe said he'd rather let, or sell, to local people——"

"Naturally, our own people come first."

"You know how they are, round here. There's the council houses —they're right on the main road, close to the buses. And the war's made people used to community living. They like being next door to neighbours—popping in and out."

"Don't tell me you've had no offers! It's such a charming cottage —I wouldn't mind living there myself."

"No offers?" He chuckled. "I've been pestered for it. As you know, Mr. Crewe wouldn't have it advertised, but it seems there's a sort of grapevine, when there's a house for sale in these parts."

"Oh—'foreigners.' No; that's why we put the rent so low; we didn't want to get the 'riverside' crowd up here. But—I don't understand; so many of our young couples are looking for houses. Two of my girls are married, and they're living—rather miserably— with in-laws——"

"They think Downside's too lonely; it's too difficult getting back, after the pictures. We got one bid——" He hesitated. "I don't suppose you know him: Bennett. He's a gardener. Works for two or three people round Aumbury and Great Beare——"

"Reg Bennett? Of course I know him. He's a very good man— and his wife does some laundry for us, from time to time. They're exactly the sort of people we had in mind. She told me they were hoping to get a cottage in Aumbury—one of Lady Connard's——"

"Well, they didn't get it." As her eyes questioned him, he continued, "It's no business of mine—or anybody else's, to my way of thinking; but Reg and his 'wife' aren't married. Everybody knows and nobody cares—except Reg's parents, that are old-fashioned and strait-laced for these times—but it knocks them out for the council houses and it doesn't suit some people, like Lady Connard, that try to set an example——"

"Why didn't you let them have it?"

"To tell you the truth, I didn't like to, before having a word or two with Mr. Crewe." He waited for her to speak, and, as she was silent, continued, "You're good people, Mrs. Crewe; you've done more for the village than anybody that's been at the Court since the old squire's time. But, naturally, you've got to keep on the right side of your own kind. I'm bound to tell you you'll pull down a lot of criticism, if you let Downside to the Bennetts."

"I recognize loyalty, Hampden, and I appreciate it; so does my husband. Thank you for being direct with me. But we don't care—either of us—about local criticism. We don't happen to think that morals have anything to do with people's right to have somewhere to live."

"Well, Mrs. Crewe, if that's how you look at it——"

"It is. See Bennett sometime, will you?—and tell him that, so long as he can pay the rent, and his wife keeps the place clean and decent, they can have it."

He looked at her doubtfully.

"You'd have a good deal of trouble, to get them out, if they didn't stick to their bargain."

"Well, that's our responsibility, isn't it? Bennett's a decent fellow—come, you know more than I do about local reputations. And she strikes me as a nice girl, who would take a hint if one wasn't quite satisfied. Don't keep them waiting," she said, with the authority she exerted so seldom that it invariably made an impression. "They must have been very disappointed about the other cottage—and if there's any question about it when Mr. Crewe comes home, I'll tell him you acted on my instructions." He knew as well as she that Evan would never gainsay any decision of hers.

She went early to bed, in her room that smelt of old apple wood and the lavender stalks someone had pushed at the back of the chimney. She lay in her broad bed, watching summer lightning play gently along the distant horizon, and trying to picture him in his strange, artificial, elaborate world of New York and Long Island.

In a little more than twenty-four hours he would be speaking to her, his voice would bring him into this very room, space would contract. . . .

She awoke to a steamy morning. All the brown and yellow fields were misted with dew. She sprang out of bed, eager to be at the tasks which awaited her, in preparation for his return. All that was lacking, in the enchanting summer morning, was Evan's smiling face, his morning greeting, his company as they sat in dressing gowns at the small table drawn out on the balcony and his short comments to enliven their perusal of the morning papers.

By evening she was obliged to admit she had overdone it: the sweltering heat, the hours she had spent, out in the full blaze of the sun, discussing with a young man from the local nursery gardens plans for the already partly filled-in moat, ordering the removal of some buddleias—Evan's prime aversion!—which someone, in her absence, had planted directly opposite his study window; checking the yield of the cherry orchards with the gardener and listening to long, doleful complaints about the condition of the hives—had taken it out of her. In the afternoon she had intended to rest, but there was trouble, it appeared, about some fencing along a part of the stream which cut through the village; it was Hampden's affair, but it was not Evan's way to grant license for the carrying out of estate repairs without looking into them himself. So that was another long tramp in the sun, to examine the stakes which, as had been claimed, probably endangered with their rottenness the lives of village children playing on the banks of the swift-running stream.

Once more indoors, she rang up the local representative of the Beekeepers' Association; saw a police inspector, who had come to deliver a Foot and Mouth warning, and stayed for an hour of local gossip; went over the household books; checked the stores list; confirmed in the course of an unnecessarily long conversation on the telephone the loan of one of the paddocks for a village fête—a matter she believed had been settled months before—and decided, eventually, for dinner in bed.

In the night there was a heavy downpour, to which she listened with relief; but once again, day dawned serenely, and Evan's call, coming through at the hour they had agreed upon, made her forget her weariness. The delicious smallness of the things she had to tell him emphasized, for both, the security of his return.

"Did you get the trinkets?"

"My darling"—she gasped—"the pendant is too beautiful!" How could she have forgotten to thank him?—except that lacking his presence, the Kohinoor itself would mean nothing. . . . "I don't know how to tell you," she stammered, "but I forgot to give Lin her present! Will you forgive me? She's coming here next week end, and I promise I'll remember——" He seemed to make little of it. Her eyes on the clock, she ended hurriedly, "Pulford's altering the wiring in your bedroom—and I'm just going to church"—and, a moment later, felt the great blankness that followed his "God bless."

At half past ten, the bells sent their music across the downs. Anna laid down her pen, to find Mrs. Pulford at her elbow.

"Isn't it a nuisance? I've just been trying to ring up my sister-in-law, but the line's out of order again."

"Are you sure? I had Mr. Crewe's call only a little more than two hours ago."

"All the way from New York? Fancy! I expect that's what broke the line down," said Mrs. Pulford naïvely.

"I'll report it from the village, on my way to church," said Anna, rising.

"Do you want your gloves, or anything?—and don't you want the car?"

"No, I enjoy the walk."

"Fancy!" said Mrs. Pulford. "I never know what people see about walking in the country. Nothing to look at, is there?"

Anna usually went to church, and Evan sometimes went with her, although it was not for him, as for her, part of the formula of country living. No; something more. It was the opportunity to go on her knees and give humble thanks in the House of God for all the blessings vouchsafed to her over so many years. Brought up to observation of the rules of her church, she had grieved, sometimes, that conscience debarred her from the mass. One day, realizing she was fretting, Evan questioned her, and she confessed her trouble to him.

"But—do you mean you're living with a sense of sin?"

"No, I'm not; that's the worst of it!" She gave him her smile, triumphant yet half shamefaced. "I suppose I'm just one of the people who want to eat their cake and have it."

"I don't think there's anything in the Protestant religion to prevent your going to Communion," he frowned.

"Only conscience. That's all we have, anyhow, isn't it—we Protestants? It's our weakness—and, perhaps, our strength."

"Then you *have* got a sense of sin."

"But no intention of abandoning it. To receive the Sacrament you must repent, and promise to 'sin no more.'"

"Do you mean, you regret?"

"How could I! A sense of sin and a sense of guilt are separate things. I think, perhaps, I could not live with a sense of guilt; it would seem so—shabby, somehow," she concluded calmly.

The little Norman church was thinly sprinkled with "gentry." Methodism had hold of the few villagers who had time for religion. Anna went on her knees and said her usual prayer: "Lord, according to Thy laws I have done wrong, and I am not ashamed. Forgive my want of shame, and receive my constant and humble thanks for all Thy loving kindness. . . ."

When she had laid her envelope on the offertory plate, and the service was over, she lingered in the porch, exchanging greetings with her neighbours, answering enquiries for Evan.

"Yes, he'll be back in about a fortnight. . . . Yes, of course, take whatever you want for the harvest thanksgiving; I'll tell my gardener to come along, shall I, and find out what you'd like us to send. . . . I'm so sorry I missed the Institute last week, Mrs.

Ripley; I hope Joyce brought along the buns and things I ordered?
. . . Good morning! How's Priscilla? Oh, poor dear—her hay fever
again; I do think it's too bad, not to be able to enjoy the summer."

She nodded to several couples who happened to catch her eye,
and, at the gate to the churchyard, was overtaken by the vicar. She
gave him her kind look, and wished she could like him. There was
pathos, somewhere, in his pinched, uncharitable face, which, perhaps, when he received his induction, was full of shining faith, of
the love of God and man. Who should condemn those who bear
the burden of their calling against doubt, discouragement and,
often, privation? Chilton Magnates was one of the poorest livings
within the see; as frequently happens, its incumbents were invariably appointed from those ranks of the clergy which, lacking personal means or influence, are presumably supposed to make up for
their want of other blessings by the saintliness of their behaviour.
But was it fair to expect any man—even if ordained by the church—
to possess the virtue of saintliness on that scale? Looking at the
meagre figure in a suit that showed green-black in the sun, Anna
wondered if it had come to his ears that she, with Evan's support,
had been trying hard to raise a fund to augment his stipend. She
hoped not; gratitude was embarrassing; at any rate, she would prefer
that Evan were there, to relieve her of its burden.

"Good morning, Vicar. It looks as if we might have lovely
weather for the flower show," she observed pleasantly.

"The weather reports have been very inaccurate lately. Speaking
of the flower show—I am commissioned by the Ladies' Committee
to ask if you will give away the prizes, Mrs. Crewe."

He hates asking, because he does not like me, flashed across her
mind. Why should he? It's less than human, not to be envious of
someone who lives in conditions which, to him, represent luxury,
while his wife and five unhealthy children are crushed into that
ruin of a vicarage, without even main water or drainage, and no
lighting but lamps——

"It's very kind; but wouldn't it be better to ask someone else?"

How could she make it easier for him? "I'm not a very reliable person; I have so many engagements—especially when my husband is here."

"The Court is very popular—I mean, with the village," he corrected himself. Anna concealed a smile. "I understand that Mr. Crewe has offered a number of prizes and that you both interest yourselves in village life. I mean, in—in the gardens, and so on," he concluded lamely.

If you had less to contend with, you would be more generous; or, at least, more gracious—or is that my foolishness? Evan always says I'm a terrible fool about people. . . .

"Well, but, as residence goes, we're relatively newcomers. What about Miss Antell?—or Lady Connard?"

He cleared his throat irritably.

"The committee, as you probably know, is somewhat—mixed." *And your accent, she thought: the Midlands?* "Several of the local —er—tradespeople, and farmers, are on it. Very worthy people. But—naturally—biased in favour of—well, in these days, one need not talk of bread and butter!" His mirthless grin exhibited a row of unnecessarily bad teeth. "Shall we say their television sets, their jaunts to the seaside and the latest equipment in their homes."

Anna felt herself stiffening. Was this intended for a side shot at Evan? Then she remembered that the patronage of the Court, which had long lain uninhabited before they rented it, must stand for a good deal with the countryside.

"A strong wish was expressed——"

"It's very kind of them, but——"

"I'm only following instructions," he hastened to point out. "The general feeling seems to be that—er—you have an excellent— er—platform presence, and that you would undoubtedly—er—grace our little function."

"Let's leave it at that, shall we?" She took pity on his confusion. "Tell them, I'll give away the prizes with pleasure, unless, in the meanwhile, they find someone more likely to lend lustre to the occasion—and the village—than I."

She had absently been watching a figure which, leaning on a stile farther up the lane, vanished as they took a few steps towards it.

"I'm sorry; did you say something—Vicar?"

"I think that's the Cherible woman," he muttered. "Hilda Cherible."

"I don't think I know her." She was surprised; she thought by now she knew all the village women.

"She calls herself Mrs. Bennett. . . . By the way, I assume there's no truth in the rumour you've let one of your cottages to the Bennetts?"

"Why?"

"Why? I don't quite get your meaning," he stammered.

Leaning lightly on her stick, Anna sent the full light of her eyes into his face.

"Why should you assume anything? Should I say that I assume we're at liberty to dispose as we choose of our own property," she said quietly.

"I suppose you've heard Lady Connard refused——"

"Lady Connard's refusals are her own affair. If you have anything to add to her decision, perhaps you would like to speak to my husband—when he returns?"

"I—I don't wish to cause any unpleasantness," he blundered. "I merely—it is my duty to point out that it is a mistake—for people in your position—to give an impression of—of laxity in matters involving moral conduct!" He brought it out in a rush.

"Thank you for reminding me." She spoke gently, without irony. "One always respects people who do what they conceive to be their duty—no matter how disagreeable that may be. It takes a lot of courage to be unpleasant"—she checked herself; she had almost said, "to people like us," people whose good will carried so much weight in the countryside. "Good day to you, Vicar."

She found herself looking into a face, square-boned, coloured like a tea rose, framed in lustrous hair, that was removed only by the uncared-for teeth of the peasant from the category of pure beauty.

She remembered she had never seen Hilda Bennett by daylight before; that their chance meetings had been, as it happened, in the dark dusk, outside the Court laundry, or at twilight, when, from the terrace, she had watched a statuesque figure, bearing its bundle up to the house.

"Mr. Hampden told Reg last night. It *is* good of you! Oh Mrs. Crewe, excuse me, but we're that grateful! Baby's going to be born soon, and we was just desperate. His mother was going to turn us out, and we didn't know where to go." She bit her lip, dropped her head, and fumbled in the pockets of the coat that did not close over her heaviness. "Vicar's properly got his knife into me, but I haven't done any harm! My husband got out on me the year after we was married—that's nearly seven years ago——"

Anna put her hand on the woman's shoulder.

"It's all right. We shan't go back on our word."

"Oh mum!" An indescribable look, a look of benediction, dawned on "the Cherible woman's" face. "I was scared when I saw you talking to vicar. He'd do us a bad turn, if he could!"

"Don't say that; don't even think it." Anna added uncertainly, "He's a good man—but there are different patterns of goodness, you know, and we all have to find our own. Let me know if you want anything for the baby. . . ."

"Oh, mum, thank you. Reg's mother's been that unkind—she's upset us proper. He's started to say he doesn't want it. Wouldn't you think anybody'd want a little baby?" She drew a deep breath. "But he'll feel different—now we got a home!"

iv

Two years after they were together, Anna discovered, with incredulity, that she was with child. Evan took it with disconcerting calmness that covered—she did not realize it at the time—immense satisfaction. She should have realized the natural urge of the male towards reproduction—increased, in Evan's case, by knowledge of the vast resources, intellectual as well as material, he had to bequeath to a child.

They had taken, by tacit agreement, "precautions," and these, for once, had failed. He took the failure easily; it was the first time their minds had not run parallel, and she had a sharp sense of solitude and loneliness. Infected, despite herself, by his assurance, she tried for a while to take it equally for granted; until, one day, her innermost doubts broke out with,

"But we can't!"

That he did not even dispute the matter she took, at the time, as proof that his sentiments were in abeyance to his sense of what was practical. The few observations he made were cool, reasoned and kindly. He said,

"If you really feel that way about it——"

"How otherwise could I feel?" Helen; and Roger. Surely their unspoken names were painted on the air? But it was no moment to indulge in emotions; to cry out for bitterness, that her two children born of no-love must come before the one she longed to give him, her lover.

"—there is a Mrs. Timson," he continued calmly. "Everyone goes to her." He mentioned some names that startled her; he seemed amused by her obvious astonishment. "What a naïve person you are, Anna! Leave it to me—and Bell Timson; she's to be depended on, absolutely."

Instinct told her that the matter-of-fact solution was founded on experience. Their friends—even Edward!—had spared no pains to remind her that Evan, down the ages, had had much to do with women. She remembered the teasing thrust of her cousin, Judy Fitzalan.

"What a reformer you are—and you needn't lift your eyebrows! We all know Evan was a raging Don Juan before he met you, and he's never so much as looked at a woman since. Of course, you've been terribly clever——"

"Clever? I?"

"It was so cute of you, to make friends with all the women: I mean, you just knocked the chocks from under them."

"But I never—I *liked* them!—most of them."

"Evan had a funny thing, you know; he always made them care. Clarissa Mellon: she was supposed to be quite nymphomaniac and now—my dear! She's virtually a nun. And Maria, and Edith——" She ran off a string of names; names that Anna wrote weekly into her engagements diary. "How we love sacrifice, don't we," grinned Judy. "I mean—as a sex. Not that you'll ever have the chance to practise it, by the look of things!"

Anna remembered a raw morning of fog when she dragged herself out of her chair to receive a good-looking, hard-faced woman with a pair of direct eyes that disposed of subterfuge. While they drank coffee, and Anna, rather defiantly, smoked a cigarette over her bedroom fire, she had time to observe that Bell Timson's mink was the equal of her own, and the diamond spray on the lapel of her tailored coat clearly authentic. Little impressive as such details usually were, to Anna, they helped, in this instance, to reassure her —in conjunction with a hard, handsome, unsmiling face and the general air of neat efficiency of her visitor.

The conversation was as casual as might have been between two women meeting in the powder room: the weather, the imminence of war, the Prime Minister's latest utterances, events in Berlin. She was conscious of the unremitting, though polite, scrutiny of a pair of clear eyes with lashes so long that they were pushed up by the lenses of tortoiseshell-rimmed glasses. She did not like Bell Timson, but felt she was to be trusted; in some curious way, the fact of not liking her as a person increased the feeling of confidence. She's strong, thought Anna. And perfectly ruthless. She's leaving it, on purpose, all to me.

She broke a silence by saying bluntly,

"I suppose you know I'm going to have a baby?"

"Who says so?"

Anna laughed involuntarily; the statement, to Bell Timson, was so obviously an affront.

She answered some short, sharp questions; embarrassed, she had turned her head away; when she looked round, her companion had slipped out of the mink coat, her gloves and bag were tossed on a table.

"Is that the bathroom, through there? . . . All right; get your stays off, and lie down."

Twice weekly, stretched on her bed, Anna submitted to the violation of her inmost modesty. It was like that every time, although she became used to, and even took comfort from, the deep almost manly voice, which was warm and kind, without a flicker of imagination or emotion in it. She tried hard to see the whole degrading business as Bell Timson saw it: as a commonplace necessity. Sometimes she was nervous and doubtful.

"How, now, what's the matter this morning? That hurt, didn't it? Loosen up, Mrs. Crewe; you're only making it harder for yourself—and me!"

Once or twice she was paid compliments—from which she shrank, with so instinctive and visible a disgust that Bell Timson was instantly aware of it and moved quickly on to other ground. She's clever, thought Anna, in adjusting herself to her subject; but is it possible that any woman could enjoy, in such circumstances, the compliments of her own sex? Apparently it was. Behind her closed lids she tried, and failed, to imagine others who had submitted to those cunning hands; others caught, like herself, in the toils of love.

At last it was over. She could not bring herself to speak of it to Evan, who was abroad when her "treatments" started. He told her, casually, that Bell had rung him up. He was very gentle, very solicitous; he insisted on taking her for a holiday to the South of France. Not to the scenes of their early raptures. They went to Nice and Monte Carlo, living very gaily and lavishly for a fortnight.

She tried to find out, once, if he were disappointed, or regretful, and found it impossible to penetrate an indescribable sheath which had grown over their former relationship. It was as though—although no less passionate a lover—he disclaimed the past. He wanted no more of it. In time the sheath melted; she again found herself close to him spiritually, as well as physically. But she could not forget it. For years she could not forget it. In their moments of utmost nearness, it was there: a faint, all but invisible wraith, a trace of smoke, blown across their empyrean. She became used to, and accepted, it.

During the war, against a background of blast and smoke and transigence, Anna conducted what women call "the change of life." None of the revolting things she had heard of happened to her—or perhaps there was no time to think about them. Certainly there was no time to be ill, or even to complain of small discomforts. Some time after the war was over, it occurred to her that she had ceased—without mental or physical disorders—to function as a woman; she was mildly surprised, and pleased—as an athlete might be pleased at negotiating some difficult hurdle. She felt better than she had done for years; had more endurance; her beauty took on a fresh flowering. It did not occur to her for several years that she was now old. When she realized it, she was content; it brought her more completely into line with Evan—who had shown, latterly, some consciousness of the disparity in their ages. From now on, they could just move quietly, together, into the twilight. In the natural way of things, Evan must die first; she had steeled herself to acceptance of this from the beginning of their life together. What really mattered was to secure for him the serenity which, deep-rooted in herself, she had failed—largely owing to the circumstances of their lives—to communicate to her lover. At first sight of the Court, something within her said, *Here is the answer.*

He came on her one evening, with arms crossed on the window sill, gazing across the downs. She turned to him a face so unconsciously rapturous that his heart—that guarded organ—seemed to melt and flow out to join with hers.

"You foolish thing; must you be so happy?"

She nodded, her lower lip caught in her teeth. She let herself lean into his side, and they were silent; looking towards a yellow sunset, against which the pearl white of the cherry blossom turned to the vivid blue of jacaranda.

"Magic. Spring, summer, autumn, winter; if there were nothing else left in the world, life would be worth living—just for these. You know—it sounds so foolish; but, when I was little, I used to think it would be nice to be an animal: a deer, or a hare, or even something very tiny, like a vole——"

"And what about the hazards?"

"Are they worse than ours? Death comes to all; more harshly, more sharply, perhaps, to them—but quite simply. We agonize our way through life—but, after all, we're given our compensations."

"And what may those be?" She felt him gently mocking her.

"Well—vision, for one thing!" She flung her hand towards the banks of amber and saffron in the sky. "That doesn't mean anything to a hare; to a field mouse, swinging on a blade of corn! Why don't we ever stop to think how wonderful it is—just to be human? To carry the burden of humanity, and enjoy all its privileges?"

"We don't all share your—perception."

She turned on him.

"You love this just as much as I."

"A great deal"—he paused—"most of it—comes to me through you. Without you, it would mean nothing. Nothing," he repeated, with finality. Could I, thought Anna, could I, with sincerity, say the same? The thought troubled her.

That night he made love to her as he had not done for a long while. When, at last, they lay quietly, face to face, her cheek in the palm of his hand, he discovered she was weeping. Evan was surprised, and a little repulsed. For some women, he knew, tears are part of the act of making love; almost, it seems, a necessary ingredient in the fullness of their satisfaction. It had always seemed

to him a bore—this dreary little codicil to pleasure, this hint of
sacrifice, with its tacit demand for patience and its call on a range
of emotions at variance with his own mood. It offended him aes-
thetically—like a piece of music into which, without proper gradu-
ation of harmony or character, the composer suddenly introduces
a phrase that interrupts, without enhancing, the main theme. It
was not typical of Anna!

He could feel the little pool of her tears gather in the palm of
his hand, slide tickling down his wrist. He wondered if he should
pretend to be asleep. No; this was Anna!—not just any crying mistress. He lifted his other hand and laid it gently across her eyes,
feeling the long, wet lashes tremble like feathers under his fingers.
He said sharply,

"Anna?"—and felt her lips curve into a smile.

"Yes—I'm here!"

"What's the matter?" As she made no reply, he waited, then,
abruptly, switched on the light. Her smiling face, glistening with
tears that did no damage to its beauty, broke from the darkness.
Her eyes met his without evasion.

"I'm sorry."

"But why?—why?" His voice sounded angry, because of his
anxiety.

She laid her hand over his; he looked down at the lovely, narrow
hand, and wanted to kiss it, but would not. He felt, as a man in
love sometimes feels—but Evan Crewe rarely—like a child: baf-
fled, afraid and a little angry, faced by an adult emotion it cannot
understand.

"I have let you down so——"

"What nonsense are you talking?"

"I ought to have given you a son."

He stumbled into an incoherency of speech. Lost, dragged away
from his moorings, hating the sensation of being naked and ex-
posed, even to the one he loved—it was she who lulled him back,
on her bosom, to security.

CHAPTER VIII

*L*in ran out on the doorstep with a suitcase in one hand and a camera in the other, pitched the suitcase in the back of the car and crawled in at Henry's side. Henry Crome, confirmed bachelor, and by no means susceptible to young women in pull-overs and slacks, had an unaccountable feeling that the car had been invaded by a shaft of sunlight.

"Do you mind stopping as we pass Boots? I left some rolls of film there last week, and I've got another; I'm sure to forget if I don't do it now."

"Smashing camera," observed Henry, as they swung away from the curb.

"Rather; it's a Leica—they brought it back for me from Germany. Oh, and I brought one of my albums; you said Jemima was interested in photography, didn't you? I expect she can give me dozens of tips about exposure and lighting, and things like that. They're mostly of the Court; I do want you two to come over, one week end. It belongs to Granny, actually, but we lived there through the war and my cousins and I always look on it as 'home.' "

Although the day was brilliant when they left town, Windsor Castle was invisible from the loop they took to avoid the Slough bottleneck.

"Blast; I bet it will be raining by the time we get home."

"So what?" She had waved gaily as they passed the airport; there, at any time now, Richard would be arriving. "Wet days in the country have a special kind of cosiness, don't they? It's fun to sit by a wood fire and watch the rain slooshing down outside!"

"It'll be maddening, if we can't swim."

"Don't you adore swimming in the rain? I do!"

"I believe you 'adore' everything," mumbled Henry. Youthful spirits were all very well, but they made him feel elderly.

"Oh no; but I just feel this is going to be a perfectly blissful week end!" She leaned back, accepted a cigarette from Henry's case and pushed it into the small, red core of the dashboard lighter. "Shall I light one for you?"

"Please," said Henry—feeling ashamed of his grumpiness. She was really a very nice, civilized kid; it was not surprising Jemima had taken a fancy to her.

He was right in his prognostication; it was pouring by the time they reached the cottage. After luncheon, Jemima proposed canasta; Lin and Henry exchanged glances. He said amusedly,

"We don't have to entertain her!—and she's got some photographs to show you."

Studies of the cherry orchards, mainly—she had taken a great deal of trouble over the angles, and the lighting. One or two bits of architecture—the best of which was the drawbridge, taken from below, in the moat. And the usual family groups. . . .

"Who's the handsome old wolf?"

Startled, Lin glanced across her shoulder.

"Oh, that's Evan: Granny's husband."

Jemima's apologies passed over her head. Handsome—old—wolf. I never thought . . . Anna; darling Anna. . . .

When they went up to "change," it did not occur to Lin that "changing" meant anything but putting on evening dress. It was impossible to visualize the neat, conventional Henry in anything but a dinner jacket; but she wondered what Jemima would wear—Jemima, who lived in slacks or jodhpurs, and had always an air of faint discomfort in a skirt.

And Petula Wimbleby, the Mynte author, who arrived with her husband in the middle of the afternoon—rucksacks on their backs and the beam of virtue (assumed, for some reason, by people who, without rhyme or reason, have tramped stubbornly over a distance easily covered by bus or rail) on their earnest faces. With wet hair, cheekbones freckled with rain and bare calves encased in Berkshire mud, they smiled innocent confidence of welcome, dripping water on Jemima's Persian rugs.

Of course, one did not have to be taken in by that kind of thing; wise through experience, Lin knew that Miss Wimbleby was quite capable of producing from her rucksack some little creation which would cast the blight of envy over the rest of her sex for the evening. Petula Wimbleby's column in *Boudoir*, newest and glossiest of the glossies, provided a *vade mecum* for every young woman with sartorial pretensions; Lin herself, more than once, had had recourse to its guidance. It was a little unnerving, to contemplate submitting the black-and-white gown—flung like a magpie, with spread wings, across the bed—to that formidable scrutiny; although it had been even more of a shock to behold the fabulous Petula, in corduroy shorts and a lumberjacket tramping in out of the rain.

No matter; everything was lovely and perfect—even the rain, which made a soft grey curtain round the cottage; the cottage which, at dusk, with the lighting of fires and innumerable lamps, transformed itself into a glowing shell.

Steeping in the bath, eyes closed, freshly set hair tight-bound in its coloured net, Lin counted the minutes: an hour, or a little more?—until she heard his voice. Through the open window came the hoarse whisper of the rain. Presently she heard a car start up, and squelch out into the mud: that would be Henry's nephew, Oliver, going to meet the train at Reading. She leapt out of the bath and whipped a towel round her; there was just time to re-varnish her nails, which she had chipped, helping Jemima to pull the vegetables for dinner. As Petula Wimbleby told her readers—there is nothing so squalid as a chipped nail.

The black-and-white gown was, perhaps, a little "grand"—but it was a dinner party! Henry and Jemima, herself, the youth Oliver, the Wimblebys and an extra woman—"scared up for Richard," so Jemima informed them. Somewhere the telephone trilled faintly; allowing the varnish to dry, Lin amused herself by inventing disasters for the extra woman: a cold, a breakdown, a sudden message—no matter what. Her hair, shaken out of the net, was like floss; her breasts were two small white roses, lifted by a strap of lace; the petticoat of white net, with its lacy encrustations, foamed over the stool and her insteps. She had been, perhaps, a little lavish with scent—but it was thrilling!—almost as thrilling as one's first ball. No, more so. Because the first ball is so complicated with anxieties and shyness and moments of obscure doubt and dread that one has hardly begun to enjoy it before it is over. And at the first ball—her first ball, at any rate—there was no one, no special person, to collect and concentrate the excitement. . . .

Jemima Crome, full stride into the room, was checked by the burning transparence of Lin's face; its sheer, unconscious rapture.

Six feet high in her size-eight moccasins, Jemima's life was dedicated to her brother Henry, to the maintenance of his home and the care of his guests. This seemed a reasonable solution of the life problems of a young woman whose normal aspirations were persistently checked by a physique which acted as a prophylactic to the tender passions. The only men who ever paid attention to Jemima were, to use her own description, little squits round the five-foot mark, whom she candidly informed she did not want a husband she could dandle on her knee like Charlie McCarthy. Big-bosomed and broad-hipped, with a face like a Dutch doll, Jemima effectively concealed her emotions—which were deep and various—behind a roughcast façade that alarmed strangers and amused her friends.

"Inside that shell of yours, you're nothing but a great, sloppy oyster!" Henry told her affectionately.

"All right," snarled Jemima, whom, at the moment, something

had happened to upset. "Then you'd better remember that when the shell's opened the oyster dies!"

"Goodness, you haven't changed——" Lin caught back the words: for, of course, blue denim had become blue velvet, and a cotton shirt had turned to silk. One might have had the intelligence to recognize Jemima's interpretation of "changing." "You do look lovely, Jemima; you always look so clean! Nobody was ever as clean as you in all the world."

"Gammon. What do you think you are?" inquired Jemima kindly. "The sugarplum fairy?"

"It's not 'too much,' is it? I thought, as it was a dinner party——"

"It's a humdinger." Jemima's big hand lay lightly on the black and the white. She smiled slowly at her young guest. "It must be all sorts of fun, to wear things like this."

"You'd look wonderful in it, Jemima," said Lin, with earnest sincerity; she had a sudden vision of Jemima. . . .

"Me? I'd look like the Matterhorn. . . . Richard's not coming," said Jemima, as casually as though she were saying, "It's stopped raining."

It felt like a blow on the back of the neck. The room spun and darkened.

"Oh. What's happened?"

"You know Richard." Did she? Did she? "He got into some kind of knit and missed the plane. His secretary's just rung through. He's stopping overnight in Amsterdam and coming down to lunch tomorrow."

It was difficult, for the rest of the evening, to keep one's end up—with the whole meaning of it wiped out; with the consciousness of being overdressed (Petula Wimbleby's solution turned out to be an exquisite but throat-high "little number" redeemed by lumps of jade and marcasite, and the "extra woman" wore what amounts to uniform at summer dinner parties: a limp, salad-patterned chiffon); with the whole of the long-studied picture disintegrated, and the necessity of adjustment to a new and different picture—Richard's meeting her in a checked shirt and pedal pushers. Is it possible, to feel romantic about a girl in pedal pushers? Possibly, for a person of one's own age; but Richard. . . .

Sitting on the edge of her bed, the dress was like broken snow round her feet, and her cold shoulders prickled with goose flesh.

If you really cared, you wouldn't have missed the plane . . . if you really cared. I know there's no future in it, but I love you—the way Granny loves Evan. *Love is its own reward.* There can't be any harm in it, so long as you take care not to hurt anybody else. To love is to live; by inference, if you're loveless, you might as well be dead. And you do love me, in a sort of way; it wasn't the kiss, it was the way you held me. . . .

. . . The sun was blazing on her face, when she awoke, after confused and painful sleep.

"Hi!" Henry was shouting. "We're going up the river; come on!"

The time? After ten. Soon he must be here. She dragged something over a swim suit and leapt downstairs. Everything sparkled—Lin too, as she sprang out on the paved path, where the others were waiting. A shaft of gladioli lashed her knees and emptied its load of rain water into her shoes.

"Where's Jemima?"

"Chores," said Henry briefly.

"Oh no! I must stop and help her."

"No you don't." Jemima's head came through the thatch. "The only bearable thing about Sunday morning is getting the house to myself. Don't be late; I want to get lunch on early and loll while you men are washing up."

Lin and Henry, and the Wimblebys and Oliver, chased each other down the lane, found the punt and jumped in. The water clucked away from the paddles in folds of dark-green silk.

"Hoo—it'll be icy!"

With a regretful thought for the cap she had forgotten, Lin was first over the side; diving head down under water until she came up for breath. Oliver broke water almost under her arm.

The others—with loud cries of "Oh, Jesus, it's cold!" from Henry—struck off into midstream.

Oliver—to whom she had paid hardly any attention—was more than ever unattractive; purple and spotty, his hair lay across his nose like seaweed, thin and much too long. His ideas of swimming included, it appeared, pulling one under by an ankle. This kind of horseplay which, although annoying, was legitimate, he varied by unnecessary contacts—forcing one, with an arm across one's shoulders, to dive with him; performing porpoise leaps across one when one was floating, and failing sometimes—Lin suspected, deliberately—to make it, so that the pair of them were borne down, in a tangle of protestant arms and legs, into the weeds. She surfaced and shook him off furiously.

"Don't do that! I hate it."

"Scared?" he mocked her, through a splather of hair.

"Of course not."

"I vote, when the others go back for lunch, we take the punt up a bit farther; there's a hotel where they give you quite a fair meal, and a much better place for swimming—less current and practically no weed."

"But we can't cut lunch; we're visitors."

"Rot. The Wimblebys are going, anyhow (isn't she fearsome?), and it's not very amusing to sit around while Jemima does her crossword and the old boys snore."

"What 'old boys'?"

"Henry and Richard; you know what it's like here on Sunday afternoons; they start chundering about sales and libraries and advertising space, and end up by going to sleep in their beards."

"Oh—well—I can't afford to be as rude as you." The shock of hearing Richard referred to as an "old boy" had nearly carried her down to the river bed. She dropped her ear towards the water, swung her arm over her head and shot away.

She did her best, while Henry paddled them back with annoying slowness, to make herself presentable; there was a hope that, if he were not waiting at the mooring, she might be able to rush in and bind something round her hair. But it was a blow, to see no long, loose-jointed figure propping the wooden post to which the punt was tied.

"He hasn't turned up yet," called Jemima, as she flew past the window of the kitchen. "Where's Henry—tell him to lay the table. I'm a bit behind—had to cut sandwiches for those Wimblebys. I don't mean I *had* to, but you can't send people off on a fifteen-mile tramp with a bunch of dahlias and a kick in the pants."

"I'll lay the table," offered Lin.

"No, you won't." Sandwich cutting had shortened Jemima's temper. "Take the Sunday papers, go dry your hair and keep from under my feet until you're called—honey-pie."

She peeled off the swim suit and pulled on a clean shirt—regretting the pedal pushers, which, however, with their little plaid turn-ups, were more original and amusing than the wet and crumpled slacks; tossed the counterpane over her unmade bed, picked up the papers and sat in a patch of sunlight to dry her hair and watch for Richard. Each car that swung from the market place into the broad country street made her heart stand still—until she remembered something Henry had said, about "running in" a new car. Of course, she wouldn't know it, even if she saw it; what a fool—not to have asked Henry, quite casually, what make it was.

A little more of this, thought Lin, at the end of half an hour, and I'll faint right out through the window and be picked up out of the gladioli with a broken neck. She gave a titter that ended, to her dismay, in a hiccough; held her breath, pressed both hands hard into her solar plexus, then stretched her arms stiffly above her head. Mercifully, that did it. The averted danger of greeting Richard on a burst of hiccoughs sobered her sufficiently to fix her attention on "What the Stars Say."

" 'VIRGO,' " read Lin. (I wonder if it's bad luck to be born under the sign of the virgin?) " 'A difficult week for love affairs. Go cautiously, and do not commit yourself until you are perfectly certain of your feelings. A good week financially, with prospect for future gains.' What piffle." She let the sheet slide to the floor, and, with an access of conscience, picked up the *Sunday Times*: the first newspaper she had been allowed to read. Daddy still cross-examined her, sometimes, on the leader.

She had latterly, of course, a proprietary interest in the reviews; she turned anxiously to see if there was anything "nice" about any of the Mynte books, but only a tepid line or two, in the "also rans," rewarded her search, and she remembered Henry's complaint that they were not buying enough advertising space. How differently one learned to look at things, after one was "in publishing." Dismissing reviews and reviewers with a sniff, Lin turned to what Mummy called Hatches, Matches and Despatches. . . .

ii

"If he's much later, I'll just have to dish up. What a nuisance he is; anybody knows to allow extra time for running in a new car."

"I'll take a look down Market Street, if you like," offered Henry.

"Meaning, you'll have one at the Red Lion. All right," muttered Jemima. "We've run short in beer; you'd better take Oliver, and bring back a dozen between you."

"Where's Lin?"

"Upstairs, drying her hair."

"No, she isn't," contradicted Oliver, who had followed Henry into the kitchen. "I heard her just now on the telephone." He stepped into the hall to yell, "Hi!—we're going for a drink at the pub; are you coming?"

"No," came Lin's voice faintly. "I'm trying to put a call through——"

Henry's suggestion, that they should wait, was vetoed by Oliver with the want of chivalry of his generation.

"What for? She knows the way to the local, doesn't she? I can use a shandy."

They vanished; a few minutes later, footsteps on the flagstones jerked Jemima's head towards the doorway. She turned petulantly back to the stove, on seeing it was Lin. When one regards oneself, with reason, as something of a *cordon bleu*, it is mortifying to waste one's skill on an unpunctual guest.

"When you're married, don't fall for love in a cottage—even at week ends. Unless you've got an iron-riveted, copper-bottomed staff, guaranteed to work on Sundays, and *like* it——"

"Please," said Lin, "may I borrow the car?"

"What on earth for?"

"I—I've got to go over to my grandmother's," she stammered. Basting spoon in hand, Jemima's Dutch-doll eyes widened upon Lin's white face.

"I took the car into the garage while you were all up the river—Henry was grumbling about the tappits, or something. They promised to drain it and clean the plugs, and all that, by tomorrow morning——"

"Then I'll have to hire one," said Lin, deadly calm.

"I doubt you'll get one; they don't do Sunday work, except for church. . . . What's the matter, kid?"

"I'm afraid I can't tell you—just now; but it's—rather—important." The stiffening of her jaw and fingers twisted into her belt filled out the understatement.

"Well, you'd better have lunch, and Oliver will run you over on his motorbike."

"I'll borrow it now. Please, I must!"—as Jemima started to protest. "Tell Oliver I'm so sorry—and I'll take the greatest care of it." She flashed out of the door before the other could speak.

Jemima, inwardly cursing, found her in the garage, struggling with the heavy machine, and, recognizing the futility of argument, helped her to push it out on the road.

"Do you know anything about those things?"

"Of course I do." She had ridden on the back of one; she had ridden a bicycle all her life, and driven Evan's cars since she was fourteen. The fact of not possessing a license had nothing to do with one's ability. Head down, she fought with the starter, and, after some moments of unavailing effort, looked up, crimson-faced. "Please—you make me nervous! Could you lend me a pound—in case I run out of petrol—and—and"—her wild eyes scanned the sky—"a mack? It looks as if it's going to rain again."

Wondering what she should do, wishing Richard and the others would appear, hoping Oliver's machine would not start—Jemima trudged back to the house. As she groped in her housekeeping purse, she heard the shot and roar of the engine. Lin was waiting, astride the saddle: white as a ghost, but with the tension gone from her brow and jaw.

"You're an angel, Jemima." She slid her arms into the old trench coat which had come first to Jemima's hand and pocketed the pound note.

"It's miles too big for you—bunch it up, for God's sake, and pull the slack up between your legs! I think you're absolutely crazy!" muttered Jemima.

"I'll be all right—don't you worry!" She flung up her hand as the motorcycle shot away at a perilous angle, righted itself and roared round the corner. It was like seeing someone off on a death ride. Jemima felt slightly sick. The puddles disturbed by Lin's departure had barely subsided when Richard's car, with the other two on the running boards, purred, from the opposite direction, up to the gate.

"Do you know," said Oliver amiably, as he unloaded beer on the kitchen table, "just for a moment I thought that was Boadicea— my motorbike," he added, for Richard's benefit. "One gets to know the sound of their voices, you know: like a mother and child."

"I know I'm in the doghouse," said Richard, having greeted his hostess and been brusquely ordered into the parlour to get himself some sherry. Henry shambled after him, to see to the requirements of the guest. "I was the best-hated driver along that stretch near Pangbourne; I had to let everything pass me and usually it couldn't;

the road's lousy with traffic. . . . No, not sherry, old boy, I'll have some beer." He lit his pipe and stretched his limbs; it occurred to him to ask, "Where's Lin?"

"Somewhere about." Henry, who had not quite Richard's majestic capacity for ignoring the past, answered shortly.

Richard walked into the hall and roared up the stairs,

"Lin!"

Jemima appeared in the kitchen door, with dishes, followed by Oliver, pushing the trolley.

"She's gone."

"Gone where?"

"Over to her grandmother's."

"Without having her lunch?" Henry's jaw dropped; Jemima shot a glare at him that indicated the subject was closed for the present —and Henry wondered if he had seen, for a fraction of a second, a look of relief on Richard's face. "But how did she go?" He glared back at Jemima defiantly.

"I forgot. On Oliver's motorbike. She said she was sorry and she'd take care of it."

"That's the damnedest thing!" Oliver whirled round furiously. "I knew I wasn't mistaken—it was Boadicea! And you allowed her! I'll never, never forgive you, Jemima; I never lend my bike to anybody."

"Oh, shut up and sit down."

"And I hope she breaks her neck!" muttered Oliver.

"I suppose we might give Mrs. Crewe a ring, a bit later on"— Henry pointedly ignored his young kinsman—"just to find out if she's got there."

"You can't; the line's out of order. She'd been trying to get through—Lin, I mean."

"Does she know anything about motorbikes?" inquired Richard —as it seemed incumbent on him to say something.

"She says she does," shrugged Jemima.

"She's probably run slap into the back of an R.A.F. wagon at

Rowstock corner," said Oliver, with vicious satisfaction. Henry snarled at him to stop being bloody-minded, to which Oliver retorted, with a high, theatrical laugh, that he—Henry—would probably be bloody-minded if he had just paid over two hundred pounds for a super racing model like Boadicea.

Before lunch was over, the rain was descending in torrents. Oliver, unconstrained by courtesy to his relatives, took himself off in a dudgeon, and Jemima, after hunting for the newspapers, discovered them in Lin's bedroom and stretched herself on the parlour couch. The two men, glass cloths in hand, embarked on Henry's usual Sunday-afternoon task of washing up.

After a protracted silence, Richard—in an apron of Jemima's, which had somehow failed, in spite of its bows of scarlet tape, to strike the usual comedy note—faced Henry across the table.

"Well?"

"Well, what?"

"I take it this is supposed to be my fault!"

Not pretending to misunderstand, Henry mumbled,

"It probably is."

"Don't be such an ass. I wouldn't have come down, if I'd thought —look here; she was delighted at the prospect of this week end."

"Oh, you'd told her you were coming."

"Why—didn't she say anything about it?"

"N-nothing in particular; I think your name came up, when Jemima was saying something about the places for dinner—but she didn't seem to make anything of it."

"Good girl. You see, all that fluster of yours——"

"Hang it," said Henry, "what would you have expected her to do: shriek or faint dead away? As a matter of fact, she was pretty quiet for the rest of the evening. It might have been disappointment, when you didn't turn up—or relief."

"Damn you, Henry! You remind me sometimes of an old maid at a sewing meeting!"

"It wouldn't occur to you, would it, that she'd thought better of that little interlude of yours, the other night? If you want my opinion——"

"I don't——"

"Then you can have it!—the kid probably felt she'd made a bit of a fool of herself and bolted——"

"I wish, Henry," said Richard, after a pause, "instead of puttering about with other people's work, you'd call yourself Henrietta Cromwell and settle down and turn us out a regular line in romantic novels; we could do with it, old boy—we really could! I've been saying for months that our list's a bit too rarefied, and we need a Denise Robins or Dorothy Black to lend the bank confidence——"

Henry muttered something and turned his back, to hide the degrading glitter behind his glasses; good-natured as he was, and impervious to most forms of teasing, there was something about Richard's that got under his skin—probably because he was fond of Richard.

"Look here," continued Richard quietly. "We've been into this before—if you remember? I can only repeat, nothing happened the other night to embarrass Lin, or to make me feel like a villain. She may be only eighteen, but she's not green!—not green enough, anyhow, to think that a kiss——"

"So you did kiss her!" roared Henry.

"Of course I did!" roared Richard. "So would you have done, if you'd found her blubbing like a child of two over that wretched typing——"

"That you ought to have given to Miss Morny!" shouted Henry.

"Who's the head of this firm—you or I?" bellowed Richard. "I—don't—have—to ask—you—or anyone else—who I give my work to!"

"When you two have finished bawling at each other," said Jemima's voice behind them, "you had better take a look at this." She handed a newspaper to Henry, who read, slowly, the lines at which she was pointing. And read them again.

"Somebody's going to catch hell's bells for that, surely? Richard, come here—where are you going? You know Lin's grandmother, don't you—Mrs. Crewe?"

"She was a friend of my mother's——" Richard took, reluctantly, the paper Jemima had pulled from Henry's hand and was holding out to him.

" 'CREWE,' " he read.

> "On Friday, August 1, after a long illness, Henrietta Margaret, younger daughter of the late Cyril Cotter, and wife of Evan Everett Crewe, of Queen's Terrace, S.W.1, and The Court, Chilton Magnates, Berks. Interment private. Service at SS Peter and Paul, Winchester Square, S.W., on Wednesday, August 6, at 11.30 a.m."

"What do you suppose it means?" Jemima was asking.

Richard shrugged his shoulders; his eyes met Henry's, and in the latter he read apology.

"I suppose there'd been a divorce," Jemima was saying. "But it's not usual, is it, to announce the death of an ex-wife in quite those terms? I suppose that's what upset Lin."

"It's rather upsetting for her grandmother. I should think that sort of thing's actionable, isn't it?" Henry referred the point to Richard.

"Well, her son's a lawyer, isn't he?"

"Her son-in-law," Henry corrected. "Lin's father."

Jemima, who had reclaimed the paper, had slung one leg across the end of the table and, biting her thumbnail, had returned to her study of the close print.

" 'Of Queen's Terrace, S.W.1., and The Court, Chilton Magnates, Berks.' Whoever thought this up didn't mean to leave any room for doubt." She fixed her doll's eyes on Richard, and, not for the first time, he was struck by their shrewdness. "I wonder what that handsome old wolf's been up to? If it were me, I wouldn't trust him from here to the sink."

iii

The hollow thunder of a motorcycle across the old drawbridge brought Anna, who was in the hall, trying to decide where to hang the Italian primitive that Evan had bought at Sotheby's just before going away, to the door. In the figure that stumbled away from the falling machine and reeled towards the steps she recognized, with incredulity, her granddaughter—wearing a stained and tattered raincoat that swallowed all but the little white wedge of her face.

"*Darling*." She drew the child into her arms.

The vibration of the engine still in her limbs, her teeth full of grit and her eyes full of dust, Lin tried to pull herself together. She felt suddenly foolish. Her wild ride, her sodden hair—yes, there had even been a cloudburst to heighten the drama—appeared ludicrous in the face of this familiar serenity. The sunlight lay calmly across the threshold, there had evidently not been a drop of rain; the weather itself was no less tranquil than Anna's white brow and the deep translucence of her pale eyes. As she kissed Anna, a breathless laugh escaped from her—it was so plain that she had succeeded, as she prayed to do, in outracing the news. What luck—that the Sunday papers never reached the Court before noon. What luck—that Anna never opened them until she went for her rest. Usually, when one relies on such things, something happens. . . . It was possible, for the moment, to thrust into the background the prospect of telling Anna oneself. . . .

"I tried to ring you."

"The line's been out of order again—ever since Evan's call came through. Mrs. Pulford thinks we wrecked the telephone system."

"I'll have to borrow a dress from her—Granny, I'm sorry I'm such a sight! I know you hate these things"—she cast an apologetic glance at the plaid turnups—"but I got my slacks wet in the punt——"

"Is anything the matter?" Anna interrupted the outburst. "Are you all right, darling?"

"Of course I am. I just thought I—I'd rush over and see you——"

"On that fearsome-looking object!"

She hoped her giggle did not sound hysterical.

"It's a good thing Oliver can't hear you; he calls her Boadicea; she's the light of his eyes."

"You had better come upstairs and get clean," said Anna, after a pause. Something had happened, something at the Cromes'. Helen had been right, after all, in her reluctance to Lin's spending the week end with people she hardly knew. "Here's Mrs. Pulford—can you lend Miss Lin anything to put on?" Lin, with a grin, indicated her disarray.

"I dare say I can find something; she's about the same height as I am, isn't she, though she's not so full."

"And you can take the papers; I shan't want them before tea time——"

"No!" cried Lin.

Anna turned to look at her in astonishment. Lin's face had crimsoned; she stammered.

"I beg your pardon, Granny. Could we keep the papers, just for a while? There's something I—I wanted to look at—specially."

Evan: flashed into Anna's mind. No, it was impossible. It was only a few hours since he had spoken to her, with no note of disturbance in his voice. Lin?—could Lin have "got herself into the papers" in some unfortunate way? Her dismissal of Roger's misgivings came back to Anna's mind, but the suggestion seemed no less absurd now than at the time he made it. Yet—Lin had snatched up the papers, which were lying on a chest at the top of the stairs, and stood clutching them, as though fearing they might be taken from her! Whatever it is, she wants to tell me herself. Well, I shall have to do my best to calm Roger.

"Be as quick as you can; I've finished my luncheon, but I'll tell them to send a tray to the Green Parlour."

"Oh, please don't, Granny! I don't want anything—I'm not a bit hungry"—Lin's distressed voice floated after her.

. . . She watched Lin pushing the food about her plate and finally laying down her fork. Anna made no comment, but rang for the removal of the tray.

"Were the cherries good this year?" Lin had wandered into the embrasure of the window.

"Not very; the trees are getting old. We plan to set some more, for next spring."

"Oh—I'm so glad. Planting trees sounds so—so safe, doesn't it? I often think it would be fun to come back, after we die, and see what kind of people are sitting under the trees we planted. . . . Oh, is Downside let at last?" She pointed to a thin streak of smoke rising steadily into the motionless air.

"Yes; the Bennetts—I don't suppose you remember them. She's going to have a baby soon; the first baby born on the estate since we bought it."

"Oh, what fun! We ought to have a terrific christening party. Do you think I could be a godmother?"

"Lin." She put her hand on the girl's shoulder and turned her towards the light; the door had closed behind the servant. "Now let's stop pretending. Why did you come to see me?"

Her heart melted as she watched the child's pitiful attempt at self-control: the bitten lips, the sudden draining of colour from her cheeks.

"I know it's a mistake; a wicked, horrible mistake. Please don't be upset, Gran. I was afraid you might be. That's why I came." As Anna took the paper from her, she gulped—"There it is—under 'Deaths.'"

She read, let the sheet slide from her fingers and turned.

"My poor dear!"

She should have known, thought Lin, as they clung together,

that Anna was too lofty to let a thing like this get her down! She caught joyfully at anger, as an outlet for emotion.

"It's such a filthy trick! Somebody ought to be prosecuted. Goodness, won't Evan be mad! I never knew he had been married before; just like Mummy, not to tell me! My word, won't *she* be furious!" Anna stiffened. Poor Helen. Poor Roger and Mary. "She can't have seen it, or she would have rung you up."

That was it. Mrs. Pulford had complained that the telephone had been "ping"-ing all morning. ("I expect it's my sister-in-law. Considering what we pay for the telephone these days, I'm surprised somebody doesn't make trouble." "Mr. Crewe has been 'making trouble' for months." "Fancy! Anybody as important as him——" "Most of the country districts are suffering from shortage of materials or labour." "I dare say," sniffed Mrs. Pulford, "but somebody like *Mr. Crewe!*" Anna was tempted to say, "So now you see capital can't command everything": she had long had suspicions that Pulford's wife had Labour leanings. She said quietly, "The trouble probably isn't on our line at all; we're linked up with several others, and they have to put us out of action while they're working somewhere else.")

For once the shortcomings of the local service had proved a blessing; she was spared Helen. Poor Helen.

"I wondered if you'd like me to send a cable to Evan—or anything?"

"A cable; why?" Anna smiled faintly.

"I'm positive he'd come back—even if it meant chartering a special plane. Why, darling, it looks—it makes it look—as though you and Evan weren't married!"

Anna sat down quickly.

"Are you going to faint? Shall I get you some brandy?"

Again Anna's lips twitched. She lifted her hands slowly and pushed back the soft ashen waves from her brow.

"It hadn't occurred to me, to faint. Yes, that's the solution, isn't it—according to literature?" She caught back the words; it was no moment for cynicism.

Her eyes met Lin's, and held them. She saw the simple, clear emotions in the child's face quiver; break into uncertainty, fade into blankness.

Lin said,

". . . I . . . see. . . ."

"Are you hurt?"

"No. No, of course not," repeated Lin, on a louder note.

With a gesture that reflected Anna's, she thrust the hair back from her brow. The effect of the hair, dragged back from the pure, square brow, was startling: it sharpened and aged her face into a replica of her grandmother's. She kept her palms pressed to her temples, as though to steady the confusion within.

That was the moment, Lin was wont, in after years, to say, when she definitely crossed the bridge between adolescence and maturity. How many people, she wondered, could actually put their fingers on the very moment when they "grew up"?

Presently she let her hands drop, and the soft curtain of hair fall forward, as she laid her cheek to Anna's; but the face it framed had changed, permanently. May God forgive me, thought Anna. Whatever pains one takes to protect oneself, and those one loves, from The Enemy, someone must suffer in the end. That it should be Lin was her complete punishment for what, even now, her pride and her honour supported.

"It never even occurred to you, that it might be true?"

"No. No," repeated Lin. "It never struck me it could be anything but a filthy, malicious trick on the part of somebody who wanted to hurt you and Evan. I suppose it was silly of me," she said humbly. "I should have known nobody would be likely to—to invite an action, by putting a thing like that in the papers. I think I'd like to stay the night—if I may."

"But—your friends?"

"I'll get a call to them—from somewhere. That is, if you'd like to have me."

"You know I would—if it won't upset the Cromes."

Lin expressed her indifference to Henry's and Jemima's feeling with a gesture.

"There's only one thing—Pulford's down here, isn't he? Do you mind if I ask him to organize the bike back to Oliver? He'll be quite mental, if he doesn't have it in the morning."

"You'd better go and see what Pulford can manage. . . . Come in," said Anna, to a tap on the door.

"I wonder if I might just have a peep at *The Times?*" It was Mrs. Pulford. "I'm writing to my brother in New Zealand, and I usu'ly copy any interesting bits from the theatre page—my brother's a great theatre fan!"

"Miss Lin is stopping the night; tell them to make up the bed in my dressing room. . . . The paper?" She picked it up, was about to give it to the woman and remembered. "Here's the theatre page; I want the rest, for the present."

"Thanks a lot," said Mrs. Pulford nonchalantly. "Aren't you feeling quite up to the mark? Your eyes look funny—don't they?" she appealed to Lin. "It's time you had your lay-down; would you like me to slip the electric blanket under your rug?"

"No, indeed, thanks." She tried to sound appreciative. "I haven't yet taken to a blanket in August!"

"Oh well, Mrs. Humble said I was to ask you, and they say there's nothing like heat for helping you to relax. Not that I believe in it, but elderly people often fancy a bit of extra warmth—even on hot days. Anything I can do before I go?"

"Nothing, thank you," said Anna faintly.

"Well, have a nice nap. . . . You know to draw the blinds and tuck your Granny up?" was her parting shot to Lin.

"What an ass Pulford was," observed Lin, as the door closed. "Do you want me to draw the blinds and tuck you up—really?"

"Of course not; I must write some letters." Write to Helen. And say—what? What words could make up to Helen for the revival of an ancient scandal which—forgotten by everyone else—trembled constantly in the depths of her consciousness.

As the door shut softly behind Lin, she drew a sheet of paper towards her.

"My Dear Child——"

How to imagine that deep sensitiveness of the bourgeois inherited from Hugh; that horror of the slightest departure, on the part of oneself or those belonging, from the common code.

It was not the act itself—though this, as an infringement of her personal code of what was sporting, carried its own condemnation—that stung Helen: but the linking of her own name and that of her family into common gossip. Proudly conscious of being, personally and in her family life, above criticism, Helen had buried, as passionately as a dog burying a bone, the shame her mother had brought on her: hating Anna for it, but stalwart in contributing, to the last breath in her body, to the false position Anna held in Society. The blow struck at herself, Anna knew, would fall even more ruthlessly on one unprepared by temperament or experience to support it.

There would be few, in these days, to sympathize with Helen; the majority would regard her as completely "behind the times," and find her distress ridiculous. This, in itself, made Anna more tender, more full of compunction towards her daughter. How can one help one's nature? Helen's were the typical, traditional views of what she herself would call the "decent" Englishwoman: unmodified by training, and reinforced by a character that resisted latter-day influences no less staunchly than it prided itself on the maintenance of old standards.

As she sat there, helplessly holding her pen, Anna knew that she, of all people in the world, was least capable of bringing comfort to her daughter.

iv

"Pulford; I'm stopping the night. But I'm in rather a bind. I borrowed a motorbike, and I've got to get it back, somehow, to a place near Moulsford. Can you do anything?"

"That's quite a way, miss." My word, how they grow up. Lin—
she's quite a young woman. Next thing, we'll be having a wedding.

"Well, yes; it is, rather."

"It's getting back."

"I know." She found herself speaking with Helen's authority.
"You'll have to borrow the Jacksons' lorry and pile the bike on it.
I know it's rather a 'thing,' on your Sunday afternoon, but the
person it belongs to will be in a frightful sweat if he doesn't have
it back tonight. You can make it there and back in an hour—or a
bit over."

Pulford agreed, reluctantly, that it could be done.

"I should jolly well think it can! And the phone's off—as usual;
where's the nearest call box?"

There was a call box at the crossroads; or, if she didn't want to
go that far, Miss Antell, at Green Maze, usually "obliged" the
Court.

All right; and she supposed one of the girls had a bike?

As she pedalled towards the village, Lin's thoughts turned
towards Helen. She would be furious. She would be terrible! Lin
felt her heart hardening in Anna's defence; felt suddenly old, protective and responsible.

Green Maze, a cottage at the bend of the lane, came in sight,
and, on the point of dropping off, she swerved. She was not inclined to do her telephoning within earshot of Miss Antell—one of
the local tabbies, with a tongue the length of the downs. Also—the
thought struck her—Miss Antell might have read her Sunday paper
and already be agog with the news. With this situation Lin did not
feel prepared to deal, and made for the crossroads.

Her thumb almost missed Button A, as Richard's voice came
over the line; she had not taken into account this possibility.

"Well! What do you think you're doing?" Deeply and lazily, as
from the depths of an armchair. Taken off her balance, she could
only giggle and foolishly reverse the question.

"What are you doing?" She must have time to steady her heart.

"Well, Henry's in the study, nominally proofreading, but I strongly suspect sleeping. Jemima's snoring on the sofa—if you listen, you'll hear her. And Oliver—I wouldn't know; probably burning up the thatch about the purloining of his precious Boadicea. If you want to speak to Jem, I'll drop a paperweight on her face."

"Oh no!"—anything to keep him there. "Will you tell her—please —that I'm stopping the night with my grandmother, and—and I'll write this evening."

"All right." She could see his frown, his elbow on the desk, his other hand in his pocket, or working over the bowl of his pipe. "We've all read the paper."

"Oh——"

"Give Anna my love—if she remembers me. And—look; if you want to stay a few days, that's all right by me."

"Do you really mean it?" The kindness; the heavenly kindness. The ordeal of returning to Thurloe Square had not, up to the moment, occurred to her; now her heart swelled with gratitude for the postponement. "Oh—thank you; it's most terribly kind——"

"Don't make heavy weather of it." (Of what?—of the gratitude? —or of the notice in the Sunday Times?) "We'll see you—when you turn up. By the way, Oliver, as I mentioned, is flaming; anything to be done about that?"

"Granny's chauffeur—Pulford—is bringing the bike back this afternoon. It's in rather a mess, but I don't think I've done it any harm." She waited, hoping . . . and ended awkwardly. "Well, I'm talking from a call box; I suppose I'd better get back to Granny."

"I'll give Jemima your message."

She waited for the click of the receiver, swallowed hard and pulled the bicycle out of the ditch.

He was a darling; just a darling. But the person who counted was Anna. The discovery was so giddy-making that she found herself rocking about the middle of the road. Wasn't it, after all, "love"? Of course it was; but not "like that"! It had been a kind of reaching out, in search of—Lin found she was not sure, of what. She only felt dimly that Richard's kindness did not stand for "love"—on her side, or on his. Love and kindness, of course, must go together; but—she could not define it, but within the last hour or two she had, somehow, grown up. She had acquired a new set of values. If Anna's needs had clashed with those of Richard, there would have been no question as to which would have won. She had proved that, instinctively, in bolting to Anna's side; but now—it wasn't just a matter of instinct. She felt herself capable of judging, coldly, which had the greater claim. Perhaps someday it would not be Anna. But, for now. . . .

The Green Parlour looked just the same. When things happened —good or bad—one expected, in some way, the whole world to alter its colour. The little anteroom was their favourite—Anna's and Evan's; when alone, they sat there after dinner, she with her tambour frame, and Evan—frequently—reading aloud. It must be nice, to share a room like this, just with the person one cared for most. Only the privileged were invited there. Photographs of Evan, of the children and grandchildren, snapshots at Camelhurst, foolish trophies—meaningless, save to those who knew their history— were scattered among objects of beauty and value, against the sanguine garlands, harps and horns, shepherdesses and milkmaids, of *toile de Jouy*. Lin wondered how it had got the name "the Green Parlour"—save that it looked out over the smooth lawns, the trees and pastures, in which she and the other children had played. It gave, through double doors, upon the ballroom. . . .

Anna was still writing. Lin sat down quietly and picked up a book, but used it as a shield to observe her grandmother.

How beautiful she was. Of course, fifty-eight was not old, and it was impossible to associate age with Anna. Her skin and hair looked younger than Mummy's: softer and fresher, though Helen never put colour on her eyelids or pencilled her brows. The delicate fall of Anna's hair concealed the thinness of her temples, while Helen's carefully "lifted" coiffure hardened her handsome, healthy face.

What was it like, to be old, and to have a lover?—to have had a lover all these years, before she—Lin—was born? How different was it from marriage? To the pair of them, sharing their secret, there must have been something—something untranslatable in common speech; something that accounted for Anna's agelessness, and set her apart, in the eyes of a child, from the dull and stupid limitations of grown-up people.

In senior common room, living with someone you were not married to was considered bad taste; rather flashy; extremely—unnecessary! Above all, terribly old-fashioned. Even actors and actresses, nowadays, got married (and put up a tremendous act about it, and the men were created Knights Bachelors and their wives were touchy about being addressed as "Milady," and—well, perhaps it brightened Society up, but it certainly made it look rather silly). Lin remembered the comment of a little cynic in the sixth form: "Of course, you've got to get married; if you don't, how do you suppose you're going to have 'affairs'?" Very Regency. As a senior prefect, Lin dealt with that loftily. Confirmation, and Holy Communion, and the Seventh Commandment were taken seriously, at The Lodge.

Were they, she wondered, after all, not as wise as they thought? All that about "the wages of sin"—but you couldn't connect the idea of "sin" with Anna and Evan.

"Well, darling?"

"I was only wondering"—Lin stammered, taken by surprise—"if you'd mind telling me all about it, sometime."

"Yes, if you like: though there isn't much to tell."

"I'd only like to know—why Evan couldn't get his divorce and marry you."

CHAPTER IX

"Quite a mail this morning! I said to Mr. Pulford, it's never Mrs. Crewe's birthday? Fancy if we'd overlooked it!"

Anna picked up the paper knife Evan had given her, to break her disorderly, feminine habit of ripping her letters open. She had glanced through the envelopes, for Helen's or Roger's writing; nothing from Helen, but Roger—yes, with the Dartmouth postmark.

> My dear Mother,
>
> As you may imagine, Mary and I are very much upset by this unfortunate announcement.
>
> The Party is already at a sufficient disadvantage in this locality for me to feel considerable embarrassment at the prospect of adding to the "legend" which, as I told you, in the case of the last candidate undoubtedly contributed to our defeat. I am seriously considering withdrawing my name; meanwhile, as I had unfortunately, at your suggestion, put Evan's name forward, as a speaker at the adoption meeting in September, I am, of course, withdrawing that. I think I made it sufficiently plain in our conversation on Friday that our credit here is at the mercy of the least breath of gossip. . . .

My poor boy, must you be so pompous? Anna sighed, as she tore the address from the head of the sheet, clipped it to the appropriate page in her address book and destroyed Roger's letter.

Best thoughts, darling. Mind you invite us to the wedding.

This will give two or three people a jolt, but I just want you to know we're with you all the way.

You and Evan have certainly sprung a surprise on us!—but what's a wedding ring worth in these days? It certainly becomes you better than a few people one could mention!

My dearest Anna,

As one of your oldest friends (I find it difficult to believe I was eighty last week), allow me to assure you of my constant and devoted affection. It may be some horrible mistake, but whatever is the explanation, your love and your dignity will carry you proudly through this difficult hour, in which you have the support of all who have learned to admire and respect you both.

Tears came to her eyes. Flippant or grave, astonished, or knowing, or prepared, the letters were uniformly kind. Those who condemned (there would be not a few) so far had grace not to put pen to paper. Almost she could persuade herself, in this glow of loyalty and affection, that her friends took the matter more seriously than she did!

I'd like to get hold of the bitch who put that notice in the paper! Of course it's a woman. Which of Evan's ladies, after all these years, would be likely to turn sour?

Ugly as was the suggestion, and coarse in its expression, it indicated the solution. But to have waited so long for vengeance; to have taken it in so despicable a way. . . .

All her life, she had shrunk from enmity; she would have said she "had not an enemy in the world." She felt like a child that has fallen and hurt itself, but cannot quite locate the pain until the bruise appears. She wondered how soon the bruise would show, and whether she would be able to hide it.

Lin came in, wearing her own clothes, which Jemima had packed and sent back with Pulford; the frock, intended for office wear on Monday morning, was the colour of dogtooth violets; a delicate freshness about her brought light into the room. Her deportment was perfect; taking her cue from Anna, she was behaving as though she were there only on an unexpected holiday. Blessed child; fragile barrier. She laid a bunch of wet lavender on Anna's table.

"I oughtn't to have gathered it with the dew on it, but it smells like heaven. Granny; can I drive you into Wantage? Mary's grousing for curry powder, or something. It's heavenly out, and I want to hear the larks before I go back to town."

"All right, darling; that's a nice idea. You'd better go and tell Pulford to get out the little Austin. . . ."

Lin trailed out into the sun. She was "playing it light," on purpose; but Anna looked awful. Clearly she had not slept. Evan ought to be here. Possibly, of course, he did not know—but they always got the English papers. Should I, wondered Lin, send a cable? What should I say? "Please come back Granny wants you"? It was asking for trouble; it was impudence, in a way, to meddle in grown-up people's affairs—especially in the affairs of someone like Evan. But he must realize that Anna could not be left to go through a thing like this by herself! He must realize. . . . How much did Evan realize? How much did he care? . . . Lin stood still: things crowding into her mind which formerly she had never admitted: from which, even now, she felt herself shrinking. . . . No. However Evan was with other people, with Anna he was to be trusted. . . .

"Granny wants the Austin, Pulford—in about half an hour."

"The Austin? I just got orders to go to Reading, to pick up the lawn sand——"

"That's all right; I'm driving her into Wantage."

"No, you aren't," said Pulford, heavily, after a pause.

"What do you mean, I'm not?"

"You aren't driving Mrs. Crewe into Wantage, nor anywhere else."

"Don't be an ass, Pulford; of course I am."

"No, you're not," said Pulford stubbornly.

"Oh—I suppose you mean, because I haven't got my license. I came over from Moulsford, didn't I, without any bother? You're just being cuckoo. I've been driving the cars for years!"

"Not outside the village. And what you choose to do when Mr. Crewe's at home's no business of mine; but you aren't taking your Granny to Wantage, Lin—not while I'm here."

"Oh—to hell. Then fetch one of the cars up—you can go to Reading later. And I think it's high time," said Lin loftily, "you called me Miss Raymond! You'll have to, when I've got my license."

"You haven't got it yet," was Pulford's parting shot. "I'll fetch the Bentley; it's more comfortable for your Granny."

"I don't believe I've ever seen Wantage in the morning; it's quite a different person," observed Lin, as, having parked Pulford, with the Bentley, under the statue of Alfred the Great, they strolled round the market place, spread with morning sun. "Light's like those kaleidoscopes we used to have as children; it takes things and shakes them into different patterns; it gives them a different meaning—lord save us, Charles; here's that awful female who lives in that ghastly gingerbread-style villa outside Goring——"

Anna recognized her companion of the railway journey, and prepared a smile of greeting. Their eyes met. Within ten paces, Mrs. Archibald stopped dead and stepped sharply off the pavement, all but under the wheels of a car.

"Did I tell you she turned up at the Cromes' pub on Saturday morning, with the most septic bunch of spivs?" chattered Lin. "So I borrowed Henry's hat, and pulled my hair round like a moustache —funny business, see?—and Jemima says her husband's one of the biggest shots in the car racket——"

Funny, to be cut by Mrs. Archibald—who had been defined by Evan as "not the sort for you to know." Not so funny, that Lin should be included in the snub.

"Hello," said Anna lightly, to a pleasant though distant neighbour, who dined two or three times a year at the Court, and was always invited, with her husband, for the shooting.

"Oh—hello. Lovely morning, isn't it?—though we need some rain desperately. Hello, Lin; on holiday? I must rush; I forgot to remind George about the dog meal," she gasped, and shot through the doorway of the corn merchant's, from which Anna and Lin had just emerged.

Lin—who had been painfully silent—wound up the window between them and the driving seat.

"Why," she burst out, "do people have to be so rude?"

"They don't mean it; they're taken by surprise." Anna realized the lameness of the excuse, but—it had never occurred to her it would be like this. She blamed herself for falling in with the proposal to drive to Wantage; it had seemed to her that the dignified thing to do was to show herself, not to give an impression of being in hiding. She should have remembered that one of the main sources of entertainment in the countryside is making scandal; taking sides.

"What do they expect? That you'd have turned black in the face overnight, or—or be wearing a yellow patch on your arm, like the Jews in Germany?"

"Don't." Anna touched her lightly. "It's a shock—to find people you know have been deceiving you."

"What business is it of theirs? It hasn't altered you. They liked you well enough to come to your house, and invite you to theirs. They know the kind of people you are—you and Evan. This doesn't make you into something else!"

"Perhaps, from their point of view, it does."

"What hypocrisy!"

"No; it's a kind of defence they feel obliged to put up, for the preservation of the things they believe in." She must find some way of taking the bitterness out of Lin's soul.

"You've done them no harm," Lin muttered.

"It depends on what you mean by 'harm.' I suppose people like us are more danger, in a way, to the community than those who live what they call 'bad' lives. Most people see the harm, the dis-

order, the—vulgarity, of open immorality. It usually carries its own"
—she was going to say "punishments," but realized that the word,
with its puritan connotation, would not appeal to Lin—"incon-
veniences. Evan and I, living together for all these years, have
enjoyed all—almost all—the privileges of legally married couples.
We've set a dangerous example. And, when you come to think of
it—that's not quite fair."

"You mean," said Lin succinctly, "they're jealous."

Anna smiled faintly.

"Let's put it another way: they resent it, for a number of reasons.
Some of the reasons are good and pure. Some of our friends will
be truly grieved, because we've broken a law that exists for the good
of society as a whole. I don't have to tell you about the disasters
that would happen if everybody lived promiscuously: if, for instance, you couldn't be certain about the legitimacy of your own
children! Now all the old estates are broken up, and there's very
little to inherit," said Anna simply, "perhaps it doesn't mean so
much. I mean, to the country at large. But legitimacy isn't only a
matter of inheritance. It's part of the honour of every peasant;
every little man, clerking at a few pounds a week——"

"Tell Pulford to stop," said Lin suddenly. "I want to get out and
sit in the grass. I want to listen to those larks."

The grass was deep and dry, tufted with scabious and the silvered
calyces of summer flowers. The sky was a frail bubble of turquoise,
the folded downs a pattern of eternity. An endless melodic twit-
tering fell like dew from the pale arch overhead.

"Go on," said Lin.

"What were we saying?"

"You were justifying the people who are beastly to you."

"Was I?" She smiled. "It's very human, to be jealous of people
who get away with something to which they aren't entitled, without paying for it."

"Human? I suppose it's English; what did they call us?—'a nation
of shopkeepers!' "

"Well—perhaps; it's the old commercial idea—that payment straightens out anything," conceded Anna.

"And you've not paid anything?"

"Nothing that counts," she answered candidly. "My family has never disowned me. I've lost none of my friends; I've gained in fact, a useful touchstone, to distinguish between the true friends and the false. I've never been 'cut'—except by Mrs. Archibald!—or struck off people's lists. I don't miss my badge for the Enclosure; I don't mind about not going to the Courts—though"—Anna paused—"I'd like to have presented you."

"I'm not going to be presented," muttered Lin, chewing a grass stalk.

"Yes, darling; you are." Anna turned over on her side, to look her granddaughter in the face. "Of course you are. It's not a matter of snobbery; that's finished. But people who believe in the Throne, and are privileged to show their belief in that particular way, must prove their recognition of the privilege. When you make your curtsey, you make it an asseveration of all our people—yours and mine—lived, and died, for," said Anna earnestly. "That's one of the ways, if you like, in which I 'pay'; in not being allowed to make my act of allegiance. But I've been counting on you, to make it for me."

After a long silence——

"All right; I will." Lin grimaced. "And won't it be a triumph for Mummy!" She was silent again. "I don't know what it is about Mummy; she seems to have all the wrong sort of values. She's got stuck, somehow, in 'before-the-war.' What was it really like, before the war, Granny? Did people really worry themselves puce about 'class,' and being 'de race' and all that kind of thing?"

"You should have lived before the first war," Anna told her, half humorously. "A few people—like us—tried to bring our standards forward, and plant them in that extraordinary quagmire between 1918 and 1939; I think we probably only made ourselves look silly—

to your generation. Perhaps we were silly; but not the things we stood for."

"I believe," said Lin, with the valiance of youth, "the war was a good thing. It made people realize the things that matter—the stark things: the things human survival depends on. Housing—and things like that; what's the good of preaching morality, unless people have got homes to be moral in? Of course, you might as well talk to a stone wall, as expect Mummy to understand——"

How to extend the range of Lin's sympathies towards her mother now presented itself to Anna as her immediate problem: as the only way in which she could atone for the pain she had inflicted upon Helen. In fact, the whole of her future gathered itself into some vast act of atonement to those she had injured.

Hands clasped behind her head, lying in the long grass, she thought: nothing matters, but to find some way of making up for the damage I have done; to put in proportion, for Lin and Helen, this act of disloyalty I have committed against my society and theirs—so that they neither condemn me, nor the law, nor the people who subscribe to the law: for each of these condemnations, in the long run, will hurt them and involve them in consequences with which none of their experience has fitted them to deal.

She heard Lin's voice murmur from a tuft of grass,

"Isn't it heaven? Do you think, perhaps, this is how we're meant to live?—looking up in the sky: not letting anything matter but the sun, and that curve of the hillside, and these bits of weed, prickling in our ears? That was how the world was, wasn't it, in the beginning?"

"Perhaps; but, with the advance of civilization—don't forget: each one of us has got his obligations, his responsibilities."

"And what a mess—what a mess," repeated Lin, on a note of sad wonder, "we've made of them."

"I think," said Anna presently, "you should go back to work tomorrow."

"Oh—why? When does Evan get back?"

"A week today—if all goes well."

"That's a comfort. I hate leaving you by yourself. I'll come down next week end, if I may."

"You know I'll love to have you."

"And I suppose"—Lin turned her head away—"you'll be getting married."

"I hadn't thought about it." Anna was taken by surprise. "After all these years—well, darling, we couldn't feel more married; but I suppose—if Evan wishes it—we will."

"I'll take the stuff through to Mrs. Smallbone," said Lin, as they unloaded the parcels from the back of the car at the foot of the steps. "And you needn't think you're such a swell driver, Pulford; I'd have taken the car up to the top of the hill without changing down." The face she pulled at him was hardly in the character of "Miss Raymond."

"I bet you would," grinned Pulford, as he backed along the margin of the moat.

"Oh, Mrs. Crewe! Mrs. Raymond is here. She arrived just after you'd gone off to Wantage."

"Well, my dear."

In the short journey to the library, Anna had time to prepare her resistance. I will not be humble, or let her feel I'm apologetic; that would be disloyalty to Evan. Her lips lightly brushed Helen's cheek.

"I'm sorry we were out. I see"—her eyes went to an untouched tray—"they brought you something——"

"I had your letter," said Helen stiffly.

"Yes. I heard from Roger——"

"Mother!" burst out Helen—and made a visible effort to control herself. "How like you," she muttered, "to take it so calmly."

Anna lifted her shoulders, and let them drop, gently.

"I suppose," said Helen, on a frozen note, "the wedding will be quite private."

"My dear child!"

"Lin's here, isn't she?"

"She came over yesterday."

"She'd better come back with me."

"As you please. She was going back, anyhow, tomorrow."

"She ought to have been home last night! I think she might at least have rung up."

"The line was out of order. But you got her telegram?"

"Not until this morning. Mr. Mynte rang us, or we wouldn't have known what to think. Mother, I don't want to be unpleasant—but I'd rather she didn't come down here for a while. Not until you and Evan have—have arranged things!"

Anna waited: not to make things more difficult for Helen, but because there did not seem anything to say. It had all been said. Helen's face filled suddenly with crimson, and her eyes with tears.

"Oh—it's mean: obliging me to speak like this!—but, at Lin's age, you wouldn't have liked me to stay with somebody in—in your position!"

"Lin has been staying with me, off and on, for seventeen years," said Anna quietly. "You've always known about the 'position,' which is exactly the same as it was when she was a baby and you all lived here as Evan's guests." She bit her lip; ungracious, to remind Helen, at this point, of her obligation. "I'm sorry; I understand."

"People can take anything, so long as they can *pretend* to be blind; it's different, when their noses are rubbed in it!"

"Perhaps," said Anna, shrinking from the vulgarity.

"She's coming out this year. You know, Mother," blundered Helen, "it's much stiffer than it used to be. All the girls of Lin's age are going to church, and taking religion as if it really mattered——"

Anna took pity on her.

"You needn't say any more, my dear; but I ought to remind you, in fairness to us both, that Lin's principles don't seem to be affected by her association with us."

"I don't think this is much of a time for sarcasm!"

"When was I ever sarcastic?"

"That's true; you aren't," mumbled Helen; she was fumbling some powder onto her flushed face. "Well, I suppose you've told her?"

"It wasn't necessary; she understood."

"One never knows what they know, nowadays!"

Lin came in: head up, shoulders squared, back like a ramrod, her jaw set in a prepared antagonism. Anna's heart ached for Helen.

"What on earth are you doing here, Mummy?"

"I should think I might ask you that!" floundered Helen. "It's a peculiar way to treat your friends—rushing off, in the middle of a week end."

"You weren't so keen on my going to the Cromes; and I'm coming home tomorrow," said Lin, tight-lipped.

"We both think," said Anna quietly, "it would be a much better idea to go back now, in the car, than to rush off on that early train——"

"I like getting up early, and I'm stopping the night." Lin continued to address her mother.

"No," said Anna.

Lin whirled upon Helen.

"What have you been saying to Granny?"

"Please." Anna raised her voice. "I won't have quarrelling, and I won't listen to you two being rude to each other." She moved towards the bell.

Lin gasped,

"Are you sending me away?"

"Don't distort my actions. Your telegram only arrived this morning; what time did you send it?"

"Well—well," stammered Lin. "I forgot, till after I'd gone to bed. I'm sorry; I meant to go down to the post office. I sent it this morning, by wire. But I don't mind in the least—about getting up early! I'd rather stay down here——"

Anna turned to the girl who had answered the bell.

"Get Miss Lin's things packed, Joyce, and put them in Mrs. Raymond's car. And you"—she turned back to Helen—"must excuse me, my dear; I have a good many letters to write——"

"I could post them for you in town," scowled Lin. She stalked out of the room. Helen looked at Anna, with a short laugh.

"We've got a pleasant journey before us!"

She waved them off, presently, from the steps: a shamefaced Helen, a sullen Lin. And went back to her occupations.

At dusk, she laid down her pen uneasily.

She had never been lonely, at the Court; an endless preoccupation with domestic matters, and the companionship of so-called inanimate objects that made a framework of content about her inner life, had kept her busy and happy. Yet Lin's departure was like the removal of a vital force, of a reason for doing things.

She glanced down the list on her desk; two or three items were ticked off, but there was enough to occupy every moment of her time, to his return. The library to be turned out—paintwork cleaned, cornices washed: matters that called for close supervision, with only a part-trained staff. She was to go over all the bedding, with Mrs. Smallbone, and the contents of the linen cupboards lay out on the long tables of the linen room for her inspection.

She had to visit the old sempstress who was darning the tapestries in the Falcon Room, and keep her eye on the bricklayers who were at work under the bridge. Usually stimulated by such projects, she found herself tired and a little depressed; doubtful, even, about getting all completed before Evan's return. Jealous of her company, he would claim every moment of her time and resent any other calls on her attention. A youth from Oxford was coming, to check the library catalogues, and would certainly need her guidance; Evan had asked her, personally, to supervise the rearrangement of the pictures on the north wall of the ballroom, according to a plan he had left with her. . . .

It must be my age! In two years I'm going to be sixty. Sixty is nothing!—but it means a change in the metabolism. The surfaces can be as good, or better than ever; but, deep down, changes are going on. There's less resistance. Recuperation is slower. It's foolish to ignore these things—though many do; imprudent, not to make allowances for time's inroads on a hitherto flawless constitution. I've always been crazily healthy; even tough! The war years brought out the toughness. But perhaps I'm beginning to pay for it. To-morrow I'll get down to everything; tomorrow, she told herself, all these things that seem nuisances will matter. I'll have the library shelves cleared, and get Smallbone to help me with the pictures. I'll stop the bricklayers putting in those rough courses they call "Temp'ry," and make them follow the old design. . . .

Tomorrow the lethargy was still with her. She forced interest in the bricklaying, and in the bailiff's report on faulty drainage in one of the cottages. She looked in on the library, and made sure the books were being piled in a way that left them accessible to the young man who had arrived to check the catalogues. She found her favourite girl, Joyce, at her elbow.

"The vicar's called, ma'am; I showed 'im in the study."

Some kind of warning hummed in her ears, as she entered the room.

"I'm glad you came, Vicar; it has saved me the trouble of writing to you."

She affected not to see his clumsily extended hand. She felt sorry for the little, ill-bred man, faced with a situation too difficult for him to handle; she wanted to help him—above all, to spare him the necessity of being rude. To Anna, as to most people of her breeding, the next worst thing to being rude oneself was to place other people in a position which obliged them—or made them feel obliged—to be discourteous. She had no doubts about the object of his visit, and was therefore prepared to lie, in the defence of this little man against his own principles.

"I should have known I had an engagement, on the day of your flower show! You caught me, I'm afraid, without my engagement book, and I've got the least reliable memory in the world." So blatant an invention!—but it offered escape from what she had always imagined to be one of the more distasteful duties of a parish priest. Handicapped by inferior education, want of social standing and total lack of experience in dealing with any but his humbler parishioners—it could not, she felt, be easy to stand up to people like herself and Evan, whose generosity—in a parish largely dependent on its "gentry"—must be difficult to discount.

"It's as good an excuse as any, I suppose—for the village."

She found herself staring at him. If he was inexperienced, so was she—in dealing with impertinence.

"One doesn't want, in a community like ours, to encourage criticism of the upper classes. What with the picture houses, and foreign labour, and unemployment pay," he stuttered, "it's hard enough to establish authority. One naturally looks to people like yourself for an example——"

"You will excuse me." Anna moved towards the bell. "I happen to be very busy."

"I think your conscience might have prevented you——"

"My conscience?" She lifted her head. "My conscience, Vicar, is my own affair. If you were a Roman Catholic, and I a member of your congregation, it might be yours; I believe the true Church assumes responsibility for its people. No, I'm not a Catholic; not even a renegade. The most I try to be is a Christian; and, as such, I've done nothing to invite your insolence. Good day."

—A fine, highhanded exit, which would have pleased Evan; but need it leave behind this sensation of fluttering, of fear? What had she to be afraid of? Evan would soon be back; with him at her side—for the first time, she found herself contemplating seriously the question of marriage. Through all these years, it had never seemed to matter; but, if she—which God forbid—were to be left alone, she suddenly perceived in it a security against the repetition of scenes like this. It would protect her, in perpetuity, against the attacks of ignorant or vulgar people—and she was conscious, for the first time, of the need of such protection.

"Mum's here!" Joyce had burst into the room with a crimson face.

Anna felt slightly dazed; after all her careful training—Joyce, of all people; Joyce, whom she regarded as her major success—more responsive than any of the other local damsels to instruction about manners, personal cleanliness, respect to her superiors and the neatness expected of a young person in service on "a good family." The daughter of a sometime gamekeeper, now working at the Ordnance depot, and a decent, wholesome mother, who had been head housemaid to old Lady Connard, Anna had recognized Joyce as good material and taken more pains over her than over any of the young maids.

Joyce now stood before her, eyes bulging with tears, the cap she had snatched from her head crumpled in a dirty hand; over her shoulders fell the sheaf of corn-coloured hair Anna insisted on the girls' confining within their ribboned mobs—she remembered that Joyce was the only one who had taken to it willingly, without sulks or protests.

"It's nothink to do with me! Mum says——"

"Suppose you ask your mother to come in here?" said Anna; and within a few moments found herself facing a stout countrywoman, shamefaced and nervous, whose likeness to Joyce was so marked that Anna found herself giving her the same smile of kindly encouragement with which, in the beginning, she had overcome Joyce's peasant shyness.

"Good morning, Mrs. Chaplin. How's your husband? Joyce says he's been having lumbago."

"He's better, thank you, ma'am. I just came up"—she swallowed; the strained look in her innocent, country eyes apologized for the bluntness of her speech—"my 'usband says I was to say Joyce'll be leaving at the end of the week."

"That seems a pity." Anna waited for an explanation, and continued, as none was forthcoming, "She's training up very well—it's easy to see she comes from a good home!—and I thought she seemed interested in her work. Hadn't you better talk it over with her? She's old enough to have an opinion of her own."

"Well, that's what her father says. He says it's time she had a change."

"There isn't much point in 'a change,' is there, if one's in good service? She's shaping into a very smart little parlour maid, and she is due for a rise at the end of the month."

"Yes—well—it's her father."

"What would she do? She always says she would not like to be back with the Ordnance people, and that she wants to stay with us until she gets married. I think," said Anna, "Mr. Chaplin had better come up and have a talk with me."

"It wouldn't do no good. He's not the sort that changes his mind. And Joyce—he's told her she's to give her notice——"

Recognizing the note of peasant obstinacy, Anna gave up argument.

So gossip, at last, had reached her household.

Not all the village parents were as strait-laced, she knew, as the Chaplins—and the village, by now, was surely inured to scandal! Apart from their own, there was plenty of entertainment to be had out of the week-enders and "theatricals" for whom most of them "obliged." What would shock the village would be the unexpectedness—she should have recognized the signs, which, for the last forty-eight hours, had been visible enough in her own staff. One of the "ladies"—the obvious suspect was Miss Antell—had said something, probably within hearing of her daily woman, and the village grapevine had done the rest. There was no animosity, no pertness or familiarity, but her young girls had been awkward, nervous and more than ever forgetful since the week end.

She came on the Pulfords: he completing the wiring for the lamps in Evan's bedroom, she—doing nothing, apparently, but watching and talking to him. At Anna's entrance, Mrs. Pulford turned red and made to hurry away.

"Don't go, for a minute."

Pulford had laid down his tools; his honest, perplexed face was turned towards her; he seemed, by his silence, to beg her pardon.

"I'm sorry to have upset you all," said Anna slowly. "I know it has been a shock—after all these years." There seemed no more to say; she felt she was embarrassing them.

"I really—I don't think we know what you mean," faltered Mrs. Pulford, with a glance at her husband, who silenced her with a gesture and looked straight into Anna's eyes.

"It's no business of ours; that's just what we been saying. I'd like to get hold of some of these so-and-sos and push their bee tongues down their bee throats! And I bet Mr. Crewe'll do it, when he gets back!"

"But it's true."

They stood gaping at her.

"Mr. Crewe's wife died last week," she told them calmly. "She has been insane for nearly forty years. The announcement in the papers was quite correct."

Mrs. Pulford cried "Oh!" and burst into tears. For whom, wondered Anna, was she crying: for Evan, or Evan's wife, or herself—Anna?

"It's none of our business." Pulford seemed unable to find any other words; his strong, square-cut head of an English yeoman, his fresh cheeks and sober, common features stood—gratitude welled in Anna's heart—for loyalty. What a good chooser Evan was, of human beings. "That's what I say, and what I'll stick to! Mr. Crewe's a good master; he's been a good friend to us—and so have you, madam. And if I could lay my hands on them bees——!"

"We both feel the same, dear!" Anna tried not to shrink as Mrs. Pulford flung her arms round her neck and kissed her. "I can't help it—it's the way I feel. We're all human beings, aren't we? And everybody knows there's not enough men to go round, so we can't all be lucky——"

She's glad, shot through Anna's mind. She's glad. It has brought me to her level—no, lower. She can rise above me now, and patronize me—and Pulford knows it. Poor soul, he's ready to die of shame. She's taken a liberty that would never have occurred to my dear old Gertrude: taken it, not maliciously, but instinctively. She gently disengaged herself from the clutching arms.

"Thank you—both; you're very kind, and very loyal."

"Circumstances alter cases, don't they? Nobody holds with loose living, but I've always said to Mr. Pulford, it doesn't do to be narrow-minded. The world's made up of all sorts——"

"If you're not doing anything in particular"—Anna interrupted the flow of cliché—"shall we find Mrs. Smallbone and go through the linen?"

ii

"I just happened to be passing, so I thought I'd look you up——"

Anna smiled at her young cousin, Judith Fitzalan. Chilton Magnates being, literally, "on the road to nowhere," Judy could not possibly have been motoring through.

"Sweet of you."

"Evan not back?"

"Not just yet."

Judy, tall, thin, nervous, was lashing about the room rather like a distracted bird.

"I had tea with Aunt Belinda yesterday."

"How was she?"

"Oh—a bit liquescent. It was a relief when the Arch-Duchess bobbed in."

"Ah; aunt's still in-waiting?"

"What a deadly time they have—the 'royals.' The female species, at any rate. It must be enormous fun, at seventy, to take the bit in one's teeth."

"Is She doing that?"

"You know her secret vice?—servants'-hall novels: the kind that come in paper backs, with a young woman in pink and lots of 'uplift,' and titles like *She Loved Too Well* and *A Kiss in the Dark*."

"Judy, don't be such a fool!"

"It's God's truth. Natural reaction from Carlyle, Ruskin and Mrs. Humphrey Ward. I suppose you know you let Her down horribly?"

"When?" asked Anna, startled.

"When they came to tea. You ought to have been lolling on a divan, smoking scented cigarettes through a long holder, with the Wages of Sin, the size of gooseberries, round your neck. You let me in for a beautiful cross-examination——"

"You're making this up."

"Cross my heart—no, honestly, I'm giving you the facts. Aunt Belinda, of course, burst into floods at the sound of your name, and her employer turned on her and said what you've just said to me: 'Don't be a fool.' Poor soul—I expect it's the first time in her life she's come face to face with a Scarlet Woman. Then she turned the steam on me—I suppose royals can't be vulgar: question mark and period? Aunt B. always disapproved of me, in rather a cloudy way, but I went over big with the Arch-Duchess. She simply loved hearing about how you and Evan had been living in sin all these years——"

"But She knew; She must have known, when they came."

"Yes, but she's had enough practice in dealing with morganatic wives and the antics of the younger generation, not to let on. And you can imagine how Aunt Belinda would handle it; she'd make it out to be duller than any marriage. What the old battle-axe adored was all the dope about the mad wife—I bet She thought it beat *Jane Eyre*—and——"

"Judy darling, you're the first person who has made me feel slightly murderous!"

"You *would* pick the wrong person," said Judy Fitzalan calmly. "There's something I always died to ask you: why 'Mrs. Crewe'? I mean—in times like these!"

"I know; I'd have preferred to keep my own name."

"It's the only way you've laid yourself open to criticism. Look at the people we know"—she ran off a string of names. "All living together under everybodies' noses—and who cares? Perhaps a few stuffies. But you and Evan——"

"Don't forget how large a proportion of Evan's affairs is linked up with the 'stuffies.' The standard of morals in the Big Business crowd is—ostensibly—remarkable!" Anna's eyes twinkled. "But I don't think that was ever a serious consideration. It's just something that goes with Evan's generation—and even with mine. One doesn't like to put one's friends—or even acquaintances—in awkward positions. When you come to think of it, that's the underlying principle of most social hypocrisies: covering up some kind of gaffe——"

"Very out-of-date," scowled Judy.

"Well, everyone knew——"

"That's just it; they didn't." She dropped on the arm of a chair. "You and Evan set up house years before the war. In effect, you're a married couple; your friends have always taken it that way, and other people took their cue from us——"

"Do you think so? Even in this casual, postwar world, I should imagine most people take the trouble to check up."

"You're too simple, honey! Haven't you grasped that Who's Who and Debrett, as part of the furnishing of every writing table, have vanished?—that the old game of Happy Families the aunts used to play in the library at Camelhurst is as dead as mah-jongg? Perhaps a few old girls play it in their clubs, and I believe it's still kept up among the British colony in places like Madeira and Tenerife; but the young fry couldn't care less. They don't know a family tree from a monkey puzzle. Not taking into account the fact that recent événements have made most people a bit shy of poking round in the Peerage and Landed Gentry—who's got time? You'd be astonished," ran on Judy, "if you knew how many people—even some of the family—take it for granted you and Evan just got quietly spliced sometime during the war. Probably it's what they *wish* to think—and, from their point of view, it's cosier all round."

"You may be right——"

"So Sunday's bit of work came as a bombshell. . . . I suppose you've no idea who was responsible?"

"Yes; it could only be the sister—Evan's sister-in-law."

"What a bitch."

"No. We must give people credit for their loyalties."

"Shut up. People who turn the other cheek make me vomit. In your place, I'd feel like slipping arsenic in that female's dry Martini."

"Perhaps I do." She said it with a feeling of vague surprise. "Not so much on my own account, as——"

"What I really mean," interrupted Judy, "is, if anyone's particularly nasty, it's not personal. Everyone I've talked to thinks the announcement was a dirty piece of work, but several have admitted they didn't like the feeling that they've been made fools of. One in particular—I'm not going to give away names, but you're sure to guess—seems to have been living in a blue-eyed state of illusion, that she was your dearest confidante——"

"Oh, that's Violet Tallant! We only met a few years ago in Italy, and I never dreamed she didn't know—how absurd! Is one supposed to go about announcing one's married, or not married?"

"Now you're angry," said Judy, with satisfaction. Grinning, she tossed the butt of her cigarette into a bowl. "That's just what I came for! I had a hunch I'd find you being lofty and ethereal, with your bones sticking out and the skin tight round your eyes. Go on, honey; it will do you good, to lose your temper; only"—she dropped a light kiss on Anna's cheek—"save a little bit, to lose at Evan, when he gets back. Has he cabled you, or anything?"

"He probably hasn't seen——"

"Nuts. . . . Where's Edward? I thought he was sure to be rallying around."

"Cruising, with Sylvia and Noel; they should be somewhere off the Hebrides, by now."

Judy grimaced.

"That woman surely chose a neat moment to die. Would you like to come back with me, to town? The spare room's empty, and considering the season's over, there are a surprising lot of blithe spirits, round the highways and byways——"

"No, dear, thank you. We've got rather a large party for the first, and I must have everything in order by the time Evan gets back."

She wondered, after Judith had gone, whether she had made a mistake: whether she might not have found it easier, in Judith's bright, heedless world, to pull herself together. Two or three days would be enough, to steady her nerves and restore her balance. But two or three days were not to be spared from her task at the Court. Nor—and this decided it—could she take the risk of not being at home, if Evan rang. Each hour, since Monday, she had thought there might be a cable: just one of his cryptic messages to show she was in his heart and mind. Years ago, they had invented a code: Blue, I love you; Red, I want you; White—why the devil don't you write? On his arrival in New York, she had received a cable that read: *Blue red white white white*. She smiled, realizing that he would have her letter—air-mailed before he left—before he received her answering cable: *Blue blue blue*.

She picked up the schedule he had sent her, netted with train and plane routes, covering thousands of miles. And, to all these would be added frantic, last-minute hospitalities. It was not to be doubted that, in this final rush, he had either missed the English papers or skimmed only the financial pages. But it was a little too bad, that, this week of all others, their customary communications should fail.

Her week-end letter was posted before she had the news; his in reply should arrive on Friday, or, at latest, Saturday morning. Supposing he had not seen the notice? She wrote, in imagination, the short line, at the end of her next letter—should she make it a post-script?—"Margaret's death, on August 1, was announced last Sunday." It could rouse in him no emotion, cause no pang; yet, thought Anna, if only someone else could have told him—instead of I!

CHAPTER X

As the week wore on, with no word from Evan, Anna found herself obliged to put a strong control on herself. Nervous tension broke out in strange flutterings of the heart and in the solar plexus; she bent all her will to subduing them. She, normally so neat-handed, took to dropping things, to fumbling in ways she would have reprimanded in those who waited on her, and, for the first time, she found herself dependent on glasses, which she had used, so far, only for her fine needlework, or for the smallest print. Her face looked at her haggardly from various mirrors, shocking her by the change in the skin and the contours. She moistened her lips, pursed them and dragged them into a grin—"Yoo—ee, yoo—ee!" That, she had been told by a woman she had gone to in Paris, was a way of bracing sagging muscles. She drew in her chin, pressed the nape of her neck hard back against her clasped hands, jerked up her spine—and the lines of which she had once been proud seemed still to be broken. Flesh hung loosely on its beautiful framework. At last, thought Anna, I "look my age." Somehow she must make time, between now and Evan's arrival, for a visit to her woman in Davies Street.

Pulford came up, with a suit of Evan's over his arm. He valeted Evan at the Court, as Humble did in town.

"Poole's have sent down Mr. Crewe's new clothes; I thought

you'd like to look at it, madam—it's a smashing tweed!" His grin, which Anna, who had old-fashioned ideas about service, would customarily have ignored, seemed like a hand held out in friendship. She answered, with almost a child's eagerness,

"Oh yes; it's beautiful, isn't it. He will look very well in it!" Like the majority of tall, thin men, Evan never looked so well as in country clothes, with a gun under his arm; with Brandy at his heel and his tightly smiling lips and narrowed eyes directed towards a misty horizon. A few more weeks, and it would begin again—the routine she had known from childhood: first with her father, then with Hugh, who, from the moment he took up his stand, with her behind him, never knew, or cared, if she was alive or dead; then with Evan, who, for all his keenness on the birds, would ask a dozen times in the course of a day's shooting, "Are you cold?—are you bored?" For the first time, she found herself wondering whether she would have, this year, the stamina to stand up to those hours in the frostbitten stubble, and whether he would mind if she defaulted. For all her love of country living, and country occupations, she had never become one of those hard-bitten countrywomen, impervious to rain, frost or fog, who followed the guns—and handled them themselves—from the twelfth, up to the end of the season. She felt herself shrinking from the prospect, towards the log fires, the centrally heated rooms, where, at the end of the day, she would dispense hospitality to Evan's guests.

"I've been having a tidy-up," Pulford told her. "And there's all that stuff down in the cloakroom; I was wondering if you'd like to give it a look-through?"

—overcoats, raincoats, leather-bound jackets; innumerable ancient scarves and sweaters; gum boots, waders—the masculine clutter of half a lifetime. Some, she decided, must go to the cleaners; others be thrown away, or used to deck the scarecrows; one of the farm lads might be glad of these old jackets—"Take the stuff for the cleaners now, Pulford—and be sure to tell them we want everything back in a week."

Alone, she looked round the small, square room that held the very essence of Evan; the Evan so essentially her own. The clothes pegs, the hangers, the shoe racks were as much part of him as the garments they carried; and the gun room beyond, with all the sleek weapons glassed into their shining cases, and the fishing tackle, and the pungent smell of oil and varnish. Anna drank in the scent as if it were a tonic; it was as good—almost—as his visible presence. Only six more days!

On Thursday morning, while she was breakfasting in bed, they brought her the cable. Her fingers shivered as she opened it—and confirmed the premonition of evil which had shot through her at the sight of the yellow envelope.

OBLIGED POSTPONE RETURN STOP IMMEDIATE MOVEMENTS UN-CERTAIN STOP CALL SUNDAY AS USUAL.

She lay, staring at the ceiling, waiting for the numbness to pass.

I've allowed myself to depend on him so completely, got so utterly out of the habit of dealing with anything out of the ordinary, that I've lost everything—even my common sense.

Of course, by now, he has seen the announcement—or someone has told him. And this is his way of telling me that he attaches no importance to it. How right he is. What difference does it make to us? It's not as though that poor creature's death stands to us for liberation, after years of constraint, or deprivation—and misery! Nothing's altered: except that Evan and I are now free, if we choose, to walk into some registry office and make a formal and rather absurd ratification of all we have been doing and saying and thinking for eighteen years. He knows that, if it were not for the children, I would probably choose not to be married; it's a falsification, in a way, of our relationship. It lays unnecessary stress upon something we've always accepted, absolutely, between ourselves. We've said these things to each other, often—and this is his way of reminding me that he, at any rate, stands by his word. Margaret's death means *nothing*: so far as we are concerned, she has been dead these forty years. Why should it occur to Evan that the announcement means any more to me than it does to him?— that it causes me any distress, or inconvenience? A man's mind is more logical than that of a woman, and less liable to be disturbed by emotional undercurrents. Evan's mind, just now, is centred wholly on his work and on the people with whom it brings him in contact; every bit of his perception has to be centred on them. He simply relies on me, as he has always done, to hold by the opinions we have always expressed to one another; he trusts, as he has always done, in my complete understanding.

Presently she sat up and groped for her glasses. The letter she had begun lay on the writing board she had pushed aside to make room for her breakfast tray, and she read it through slowly. There were innumerable crossings-out—and how stiff the sentences seemed! She had felt, while writing, as though she had lost that contact with him that made their letters, ordinarily, like conversations. She knew the reason lay in her determination in no way to betray to him the discomforts of the past week. She had tried to fill up the space with a description of her recent occupations—and the sentences stood there, trite little statements, hard and neat as nail taps!

On an impulse, she tore up the page and took a fresh one. Not stopping to think, driven only by the ache in her heart, she let her pen race across the paper:

> Your cable has taken the sunshine out of the morning. Let Sunday bring better news,

—and signed it, "Anna."

At least—while dressing, she forced herself to accept the consolation—the extension of his absence left her with more time for her preparations. She could be sensible, and take things a little more easily.

"Mrs. Smallbone wants to know which room to get ready for Lin."

Lin? Anna turned her head vaguely.

"She mentioned she was coming down this week end. She had your dressing room last time, didn't she? We were just saying it would be more convenient, for you, if we put her in the Amber Room," proposed Mrs. Pulford.

What day was it? Anna glanced at the calendar, and saw, with a shock, it was Thursday. Yes, Lin was expecting to come tomorrow, or Saturday morning.

That must be stopped, thought Anna; whatever happens, I must not be responsible for trouble between Lin and Helen; Helen must not be put in a position of having to forbid Lin's coming to the Court, or Lin driven to defiance.

"Tell Mrs. Smallbone I'll let her know later."

The telephone offered too much scope, on Lin's side, for argument. Anna drew a writing pad towards her, and, after reflection, drafted a telegram.

> Have arranged to go away for week end so sorry darling hope this reaches you in time to alter your plans. Evan's return postponed.

Only after she had telephoned it did it occur to her that she would be obliged to implement her message; no sooner would Lin receive it than she would be on the wire, demanding to know where Anna was going. How very stupid, not to have waited, not to have taken time to think up some other excuse.

Well, having burnt her boats, there was nothing to do but act accordingly. A few names passed through Anna's mind: Judith Fitzalan, Cicely, Honoria . . . Griselda was staying with her family in Scotland, or she would have invited herself to Camelhurst (Edward came to her mind; if only he had been available—dear Edward—all would be well). Strange, how few of the names that stood for "friend" fitted themselves into the present situation. She found herself shrinking in prospect from the sympathy, affection and carefully restrained curiosity that were the accompaniments of feminine friendship. "When are you going to get married?" Few, perhaps none, would be crass enough to say it, but the question would be implicit in every kind look, every delicate attention.

I could go to a hotel.

This—the obvious solution—presented in itself unique difficulties. Ridiculous as it might seem, Anna had never in her life stayed alone in a hotel. Her immediate instinct—to take Gertrude—was defeated by the fact that the Humbles were still in Switzerland. Mrs. Pulford's companionship was out of the question. Prisoner of Evan's solicitude, with each member of the staff pledged to "look after" her, her departure, unaccompanied, would in any case create a sensation; the Pulfords or the Smallbones might easily take it upon themselves to ring up Helen, giving as their excuse their responsibility to Evan! What a bore devotion could be. The staff, both indoor and outdoor, would, of course, excel itself in gossip, and her departure would be linked up throughout village and county with the recent scandal. Apart from the tiresomeness of having to inform Pulford she did not want the car, and his wife that she was capable, for a few days, of waiting on herself—pride would not stand for that!

On the point of abandoning the project, another thought came to Anna. Had Evan's love and care really made so feeble a creature of her that she was incapable of asserting herself towards people who, in actual fact, had no authority over her whatever? It was assuredly not what he intended.

"Mrs. Pulford; I want you to pack a few things for me. Nothing for the evening. No London clothes. I'll only be away for three or four days."

"We shan't be leaving before lunch, shall we?" She was obviously disconcerted. "And Mr. Pulford's just gone out in the Bentley; if he'd known——"

"I don't want the Bentley, and I shan't want you, or Pulford." Mrs. Pulford's eyes widened, with astonishment, then doubt.

"You mean, you'll have the Austin, for the station?"

"I'm not going by train—and I'll take the Austin."

"Never—not driving yourself!" gasped Mrs. Pulford.

Anna's lips twitched. Why had she not thought of it before? "I can drive, you know. Pulford taught me."

"Well, I'm sure I don't know—what about your license?"

License? Oh, of course; license—a little booklet Evan took care of for her. Where was it likely to be? She had no remotest idea; probably in London.

"Suppose it's not current?"

Anna produced with some concealed triumph the answer to that, from the recesses of her memory: her license was sent for renewal each year with Evan's; her reason for knowing, that she had to sign the form. Evan had never approved of her driving, and it had taken much persuasion before Pulford was allowed to give her lessons. "Think how pleasant it would be, to be able to go away by ourselves." "If it comes to that, I can drive." "But you don't enjoy it," she had taken him up quickly. "Why should you? Your only time for relaxing is in the car." She felt him humouring her. Actually, he preferred one of his big saloons, with Pulford at the wheel. No, Evan was not a small-car man. Growing bored herself— for anything that failed to give pleasure to Evan meant nothing to her—she soon abandoned her new pastime, and the Austin was sent down to the Court for estate work.

"My missis says you were wanting the Austin, madam."

She looked up from her desk, into Pulford's worried face.

"Yes; it's in order, isn't it?"

"It's all right." His reluctance was patent. "Wants a good wash and polish; Mr. Hampden's been mucking it about."

"Then you'd better see to it; I shall want it at three o'clock." She returned to her writing, but was aware of him still shuffling at her side. "What's the matter?" asked Anna crisply.

"The missis has got it into her head you're going off by yourself," he blurted.

"I put it there—I mean, I am going by myself." (There was no

need to sound so jaunty, but a sudden lightening of the heart
robbed her voice, for the moment, of it usual levelness.)

"You never been out by yourself before," grumbled Pulford.

"Considering you taught me to drive, you don't seem to have
much confidence in the results of your teaching," she rallied him.

"Well—I don't know what Mr. Crewe'll say."

"That's not your business, Pulford, but mine. See the road maps
are in the pocket, and that thick book—what is it? A.A., or something—that tells you about hotels."

Hotels? She could see it in his eye. She had a suspicion that,
if she had not been his mistress, Pulford would have growled,
"Here; what's the game?" But, like the rest of the staff, he knew
exactly how far he could go with Anna. She gave him a level look,
that put him in his place, and waited until the door closed behind
him, to continue her writing.

When she had finished the lists she was making, to guide the
household during her absence, she looked round the Green Parlour—the shrine of her private happiness: it was here, said Evan,
that he liked to imagine her, when they were separated, and, ignoring the "finer" rooms, she had lived and even had her meals here
since she was alone. A small table in the window was already laid
for luncheon, in the gold of the midday sun; looking across the
pastures and trees and the rectangles of freshly turned earth which
next year would be the moat garden, she thought how lovely, how
very lovely it all was; how fortunate they were, she and Evan, to
have this for their sunset years; and how pleasant it would be to
return, after what had already, in her mind, become her "holiday."
The faint and guilty sense of running away, which for a little while
—even after giving her orders to the Pulfords—had troubled her,
had changed to anticipation. She already felt better, more like herself, more in command of those around her, and of the situation.

After luncheon she took one of the photographs of Evan from
the top of a cabinet—one of the few smiling ones; his arms folded
across his chest, he was smiling out of the photograph, smiling at

her, where she was sitting, while the photograph was taken. It was an old study—at least fourteen years old—but it remained her favourite; there was a tenderness about the mouth, and in the eyes, which he rarely showed to the camera, and which, perhaps, accounted for his dislike of this particular photograph. She suspected that he did not like to be recorded in a mood of vulnerability. "It makes me look like an actor!" he scoffed—and she had difficulty in rescuing the proof before he destroyed it. He would have no other copies ordered, so this photograph was completely hers. He had always derided it, but latterly she had caught him looking at it, on one occasion at least, with a secret, sly gratification. Why not, indeed? Why should not a man, as well as a woman, feel proud of the record of past beauty? How handsome, how incredibly handsome he was—and remained: although the quality had altered. A painter, she felt, might prefer the present, with its haggard, hawk-like character, and the crackle of fine lines that had appeared—like an old *vernis Martin*—over the skin.

She closed the leather case, and handed it to Mrs. Pulford to put in her dressing bag.

Only when she sat at the wheel, tested—under Pulford's mistrustful eye—the gears and made sure of the relative positions of foot brake and accelerator, did it occur to Anna that she had not the remotest idea of where she was going.

"What about letters?" Mrs. Pulford spoke dismally across her husband's shoulder.

"I'll keep in touch," promised Anna. "There can't be anything important; you know the General's and Sir Roger's writing; at least, Pulford does. I'll tell you where to forward those—when I ring up."

"You'll keep your eye on the petrol, madam?"

She nodded, and lifted her hand in farewell.

"Good-bye, Mrs. Pulford."

"Bye-bye; I only hope we won't get the blame——"

Irritated, she let the clutch in too suddenly, and narrowly missed the stone balustrade. A fine beginning. And all because I let myself be vexed by those two kind creatures, whose only motive is their responsibility to Evan.

She tried to imagine, as she steered carefully into the public lane, how she would feel if she knew she were never to return—then the whole of her concentration passed into the act of controlling this strange piece of machinery, so obedient to her will. Driving slowly and cautiously, fields and hedgerows were curiously unfamiliar. Gradually she became accustomed to the pull and purr of the engine. She was conscious of a forgotten stimulation. She increased speed—but, in obedience to a "Halt!" sign, drew up at the crossroads. North, south, east, west; where in the world, thought Anna, do I go next?

. . . It was almost dark, when she signed her name into a hotel register. Anna Crewe. The name did not seem to belong to her, but to a creature she had left behind. The curious impersonality of a hotel bedroom completed the sense of surrender. A fly crawling on the ceiling could be no less of an individual than Anna Crewe, crawling between the sheets of an unfamiliar bed.

ii

"Chilton Magnates 27?—Long-distance personal call for Mrs. Crewe."

"Mrs. Crewe's away. Who's calling?"

"Hold on, please. . . . Go ahead; you're through."

"General Fitzalan speaking. Who's that?"

"Me, sir—Pulford. Madam's away, sir."

"When did she leave?"

"Thursday, sir, after lunch."

"Has she gone back to town?"

"It's not likely, sir, with the Humbles still away."

"What do you mean—'It's not likely'? You know where they were going."

"Madam went by herself, sir, in the little Austin."

"You mean, she didn't take your wife? Who was driving her?"

"She was driving herself, sir."

"Lord love us," said Pulford, returning to his wife. "It's the first time I've heard the General let rip: it was like being back on the old barrack square! Cor blimey; what a C.S.M. he'd have made."

"Well, so long as we don't get the blame. . . ."

iii

She had cabled the telephone number of the hotel to Evan, and, at the expected hour, his call came through.

"Where on earth are you speaking from?"

"It's called the Rose Without a Thorn; isn't that charming?"

"What the devil are you doing there?"

He had not time—or was not in the mood—for dalliance. Anna blamed herself; had he not trained her, on these long-distance calls, to keep to essentials?—their object being to confirm or to advise her of any alteration in the schedule he gave her by air mail. ("We'll forget all the necessary things if we start cooing to each other like a pair of elderly turtledoves across the Atlantic; keep that for letters." She had grown out of the habit of endearments, except when writing, for his single endearment, to her, was "Anna"; spoken as he spoke it, she wished for no more.)

"I thought I would give myself a little holiday. I had your cable; what a bore. Have you any idea how much longer you'll be away?"

"Several of the people I had planned to see are on holiday; I'll probably end up in Florida."

"Millionaires and private beaches and fabulous estates—don't forget to tell me whether a millionaire looks very different from an ordinary being in a bathing slip! I missed your letters." She had not intended to say it, but the words slipped out before she could stop them. ("Write when you can; don't make a 'thing' of it." Anna, you're a woman in a million.")

"It's been a diabolical week. I'm sick of the sound of my own voice."

"You aren't overdoing things, are you?"—after all he had had to say about the "vitality" in the air, and his own fitness. . . .

"Of course not. It just happens to be unfortunate that there are only twenty-four hours in the day!" She heard his laugh—and felt it was a pity that all those leagues of Atlantic could not blot out the faint echo of irritation in the sound. Or perhaps she was being oversensitive.

"Well—don't bother about letters." What made one say these things, that falsified the whole of one's self? She felt like crying, "For God's sake, write to me; write, write!"—and heard herself say coolly, "You'll be back by the first, of course."

"I'll have to let you know from Philadelphia; I'm flying down this afternoon."

There can't be any uncertainty about it, or he would give me warning. All those friends of his—invited for the shooting: he would not expect me to put them off, at the last minute, or to carry on by myself. I suppose I could get Edward. . . .

"I'm going to turn in for a couple of hours," he was saying. "I haven't seen my bed since yesterday morning!"

"Goodness; what have you been doing?"

"I got let in for a ball. . . ."

She sat on the edge of the bed, willing emptiness, and disappointment, and foolish disquietude away from her.

Incredible as it might be, he had not seen the announcement; if he had, he would at least have called her "Anna." In the pressure of his work, he had only skimmed the papers for the financial and industrial news. She sat there, facing the inevitable: that it devolved on her, to give him the news of Margaret's death. She must cable it; that, at least, would save writing it into a letter.

Probably because she had wanted—and expected—so much, this, of all talks with Evan, seemed the most barren. She was left with the emptiness of someone who, promised a square meal, is fobbed off with a biscuit. The whole of the Atlantic roared suddenly between her and what she suddenly recognized as her life force.

Evan at a ball; she tried to imagine it. He liked dancing (and was a beautiful dancer), and hated it in crowded places. They danced, sometimes, by themselves, in the cool and spacious basement room under Queen's Terrace. At week ends, when there were young people about—Lin and her contemporaries—they danced in the ballroom, with the long windows open on the blue, Berkshire night, and the little frogs croaking in the moat. They danced as much, or as little, as they pleased, and drifted out on the drawbridge, and watched the stars, or the moon. . . . Never in restaurants, or in night clubs.

She tried to visualize Evan, in the whirl of a New York ballroom. . . . She thought, I must wire to the Humbles, and the Pulfords.

iv

"But—do you really mean, Edward, you're going to cut the rest of the trip?"

"I'm frightfully sorry, Sylvia; but I must get back."

"But"—his hostess arched her pretty eyebrows—"isn't Griselda still away?"

"She may be."

She laughed.

"Between friends—do you have to be so awfully cloak-and-dagger?"

"Not at all. It's Anna."

"Oh—that. That miserable announcement. But you don't suppose she's taking it seriously?"

"Evan's away, unfortunately, and—she might want to contact me. It's a bit too difficult, on the yacht. If you'll excuse me—you and Noel—I'll make for the mainland and pick up a plane."

When Edward arrived home, Griselda was waiting, on the porch.

The sight of her grey, stooped figure smote him with compunction. It was so long since he loved her, yet—he might have known he could depend on her. They exchanged kisses—hers colourless, his warmed by gratitude.

"When did you get back?"

"Friday afternoon."

"Anything wrong?"

"No; why?" Her left eyelid had a permanent droop that lent raffishness to her innocent face.

"You were staying to the end of the month."

"I thought you might come home."

"Ah—you saw the papers. Anything from Anna?"

"I looked through your mail; I didn't find anything. I rang the Court on Friday morning; they said she was away."

"So did I; I made them put me ashore." He told her briefly. Griselda took it with calm.

"She wants to be alone."

"It's the damned sort of thing that would happen, with Evan away!"

"When does she expect him back?"

"I haven't the least idea."

They sat, after dinner, in the dark Camelhurst library—with the painting of Edward and Anna, as children, over the fireplace. Edward, in a Court suit, had his elbows on a balcony, on which perched Anna, in a fluff of white muslin; she was offering him a dish of fruit; Reynolds might have painted it. Their favourite animals were about their feet; over Anna's head swung a white cockatoo. It belonged, he felt, to an age that was past; an age of happiness and innocence. . . .

"Have you heard from Evan, since he went away?" Griselda had picked up her knitting.

"No, we've not gone in for letter writing—since our 'Varsity days."

Griselda lifted her grey head.

"You've been a good friend to him."

"What the deuce do you mean? I've always liked 'odd' people," said Edward.

"Oh; so you admit he's 'odd'?"

"He wouldn't be likely to deny it." Edward shrugged his shoulders. "The best thing that happened to Evan was tying up with Anna."

"And was it the best for her?" inquired Griselda mildly.

"I don't know what you're getting at," frowned the General, "but he's made Anna completely happy over—do you know how many years? Because I don't. That marriage of hers was a disaster. You've only got to look at the results—Helen and Roger—to see that!"

"And Lin?" murmured Griselda.

"Oh—she's a throwback—to our side. God knows what her children will be like. . . . I think I'll give the Court another ring."

He returned from the telephone.

"No news. She's taken off, into thin air. I must say, in Evan's place, I'd have climbed on the next plane——"

Griselda smiled faintly.

"One can't judge other people by one's own reactions."

"Reactions be damned. Anna's in a deuce of a disagreeable position. He should come back and get it over—the marriage," he answered, to her questioning look.

"Oh; you think they'll get married?"

"Good God, Griselda!"

Her knitting needles clicked faintly; she lifted the bundle of wool up towards her shortsighted eyes, considered and lowered it.

"After all these years, it seems rather a fuss about nothing."

"It depends on what you call 'nothing.' Even in emancipated circles, there's still a certain amount of old-fashioned prejudice in favour of marriage."

"Aren't they old enough, both of them, to dispense with prejudice?"

"You've been talking to Anna!"

"No; how could I? I've just been thinking; wondering if marriage, in itself, means so much."

He watched her counting stitches; her grey, untidy head, drooped over the needles, was suddenly the head of a stranger. Presently she murmured,

"I think—for so many people, happiness, true happiness, lies altogether outside of marriage. It depends, of course, on the degree of courage——"

Oh God; *Griselda!* He found himself speechless.

"—and on whether there are children."

He stiffened himself.

"Which, in this case, there are. Helen and Roger."

"Oh—*they!*" Griselda's soft laugh; had it ever, within his memory, held irony?

"They'd have a good deal to say, if their mother declined the opportunity to 'make an honest woman of herself'!"

"Poor Anna."

"Griselda; what are you driving at?"

"It's a little hard, if compulsion enters into the picture, at a time like this."

"Compulsion? There's no question of compulsion, in the case of those two!"

"So you say. You may be right. In any case, I suppose it's inevitable."

"You sound as if you were regretting it."

She shook her head slowly. She lifted her head, and gave him her strange, uneven, but candid gaze.

"Why should I?—so long as she's happy. When I was a girl," said Griselda, with apparent inconsequence, "I longed for a black silk gown! Of course, it was out of the question; girls only wore white, or pink, or blue, until they were married. I don't suppose you remember"—her lips twitched into a smile—"the first gown I bought, when we came back from our honeymoon, came from

Doucet; it was a black *moiré*—with a lot of lace. I was ashamed to show you the bill."

"I think I remember——"

"I don't suppose you do." She laughed without bitterness. "I put it on for a dinner party and tore it off after one look in the glass. To realize one's great ambition, and have it turn out such a failure makes one feel extremely foolish!"

"What happened to the dress?" He smiled, not caring, but touched by the artless confession.

"My cousin Elspeth went into mourning and I sold it to her. It was very lucky; one can't usually get rid of one's mistakes so easily."

His brain had followed her simple parable.

"You surely don't think it would be a mistake, for those two to get married?"

"That would be rather a presumption, on my part, wouldn't it?"

"Hang it, Griselda—stop foxing. You know you've got something in the back of your mind." He heard himself saying, "You don't care for Evan, do you?"

"Not very much," she admitted. "But we can't all share the same tastes. I know you're very fond of him. That's enough to prove he has qualities that don't happen to appeal to me."

"You're infernally reasonable, aren't you?" he grumbled. "You're an odd creature; women aren't given, as a whole, to being 'reasonable' about Evan."

"No, so I believe."

"Well, you don't mark that up against him, do you? You can't say he's taken much advantage of it, since Anna had him in hand."

"My dear, I don't know anything about it. I don't take any interest in Evan, apart from his relationship to you and Anna," she protested. "He's not the kind of person I could make a friend of—that's all; and I'm sure he would say the same of me. He's very charming, and I quite see the reason of his popularity with both men and women."

"And children," he persisted, lifting the cat, which had been stropping itself against his ankles, onto his knee. He pressed his irritation into its hard, round head and stiffening spine, and smiled despite himself as it broke into a trumpeting purr. "They're supposed to be the best judges of character, aren't they? Lin and the boys were devoted to him——"

"Yes; it used rather to surprise me. I often thought he was quite ruthless with little Hugh."

"Pooh—boys understand discipline," asserted the General. "Where's Buster?" he broke off to ask, missing the ancient spaniel, who, blind and crippled with rheumatism, had latterly accepted the cat's leadership and was usually to be found by its side.

"Isn't he in his basket?"

"No, he's not." He got up, opened the door and lifted a patient heap of faded yellow hair in his arms. "Poor old boy, poor old boy; had they shut you out then? Griselda, I wonder if you'd mind having his basket in the bedroom, for a while? If he stumbles out in the night, he can never find his way back. . . . What were you going to say?"

She had opened her lips, and closed them again; but her smile was very sweet, as she folded her knitting and pushed it into the bag.

"Nothing. Of course, dear." She stretched her hand to the bell. "Take him up now, and I'll tell them to bring up the basket." It would have sounded foolish to add that Evan had never been known to care, apart from their usefulness, for any of his dogs.

v

She drew to the side of the lane, to let the cows go by for milking; broad curly foreheads, the colour of clotted cream, shining chestnut shoulders, swinging bags of tender pink left behind them a warm scent of summer. She remembered, at Camelhurst, being taught to milk, with her head in a sunbonnet pressed into a soft, sweaty flank. Now all the milking was done mechanically; the milk was pasteurized, graded—goodness knows what. She had a mild longing once more to dip the cup in the pail and drink one more draught of sweet, warm, untampered-with milk; a moment of mild regret that Lin—child of the age of Pasteur—had never known this pleasure.

The terraced slope of the Roman camp was barred with dark green and gold by the setting sun; she recognized, with a little shock of surprise, a spot where she and Evan had halted, on one of their few expeditions. Driving on to a place where the lane widened, she got out, and leaned for a little while on a gate, feeling the sun on her bare neck and arms; then she unlatched the gate and passed through into the roughness of the field—bracken already golden, furze that crumbled at a touch, gold and silver and bronze of heat-dried stalks, pewter-coloured seed pods—but still a scattering of restharrow, campion and celandine, with the sod apple that smells of apple pie and the sweet-scented "boy's-love." All these she had learned to know at Camelhurst, and had tried to share her knowledge with Evan; but she came to realize that he did not care for them: that flowers, to Evan, were the products of gardens and greenhouses: that the enthusiasm he showed for his roses, his liliums and small, precious orchids did not extend to the little flowers of the fields. So she had crushed back her interests, and had forgotten much of the country lore of her childhood.

As she went higher, the sweet, pastoral pattern of the countryside unfolded itself below her: small, winding streams, tree clumps —the leaves already yellowing; a little abbey nestling in a grove of elms; new haystacks clustered about a low range of farm buildings; cloud shadows lengthening and shortening in the hollows of the land; the slow sun lingering in a sky that maintained its pure, blue arch like a tent over the earth.

Of the five days since she left the Court, the first two were lost terrain. All of her thinking self must have gone into the unfamiliar act of driving the car, into the multifarious small problems of gear changing, and braking, and observance of traffic lights and zebra crossings and parking. At the end of the days, she found herself holding a post-mortem on her own achievements, then sleeping like a log. Then came the discovery that she had dominated all that, and that the car was no longer a piece of complicated machinery, to be handled with respect and care, but an extension of herself: as much part of her as a limb. So she had time for thinking, and thinking was no longer blurred with emotions.

. . . For, of course, she thought, as she stretched herself in the grass, the answer is solitude. We don't realize how important it is, in any sort of crisis, to be alone. To choose one's aloneness. That's different, of course, from an imposed solitude, that forces one into all kinds of adjustments: inconvenient, and, possibly, painful.

She let her eyes close, and felt the sun on the lids, and the wind lifting the hair from her temples. Her drowsy brain spun a web of hazy imagination about Evan—wherever he might be; wondering about his reception of her letter—if it deserved the name.

"Your letters, Anna, come as the gentle rain from heaven," he had written, in one of his brief absences.

> Without them, I sometimes think I might go crazy. So, however I may fail, in this spinning wheel, to keep my share of the compact, don't fail me. Tell me the foolish things—about the grass, and the sprouting of that branch we cut on the sycamore outside your window, and the colour of the downs at sunrise—because these are part of yourself; and, little as I may seem to understand, each one is precious to me. More so than ever, when I haven't got you here, at my side.

How I miss you, she thought; and how foolish I have been, not to realize that the answer to "missing" is to be alone. Who was it said that people addicted to loneliness make the faithfullest lovers and friends? Let me learn patience and quietude—like this earth on which I am lying. Just to be still. . . .

She felt the grass-blades stirring under her hands; the minute crepitations of innumerable earth dwellers invisible to the human eye, but communicating through the senses a message of escape from a complicated human world.

Evan and me: two minute grains in eternity. Blown about in the wind. Human contrivance tries to drive us into a pattern, and, up to a point, we submit; but, beyond that point?

One has to live so long, before one knows anything. And however long is only a fraction of a fraction of a second in time itself. Human life: an infinitesimal pause in the magic of the spheres. Just time enough to be still, and wonder; but we thrash about, and agonize, and it's time to go—before we've resolved anything. In all our fuss and fret we've lost our sense of continuity: our "mysterious acquaintance with profundities," on which wise people of all the ages have based their living. If we could recapture that, wouldn't it be the answer to all our griefs? That's the answer; that's the real meaning of this search in which—hardly knowing it—each one of us is engaged.

The wind blew a long stalk of grass across her teeth, she caught it, and tasted the clean, acrid juice that tasted of childhood: of chewing leaves, biting the honey sacs at the base of clover blossoms, of filling one's mouth with the *fraises du bois* that grew on the same bank with the tiny, lilac-coloured violets that bloomed mysteriously all the year round. She felt happy; happier and healthier than she had done for weeks.

What's going on at the Court? she wondered, as she pressed the self-starter. I must ring up Pulford—poor soul! And in London? My poor old Humbles. It isn't fair to leave them to face some spate of kitchen gossip. I must go up to town—I'll wire him. I must go home at once. (Home—what a lovely word: it brings you close to me.) All right, Evan; I'm going up tonight, to put things right at Queen's Terrace, before I go back to the Court.

She laughed, let the clutch in and allowed the shadowed green of evening slowly to slide past her.

CHAPTER XI

*I*s that you, Uncle Edward?"

He felt like retorting, "Who the devil do you suppose it is?" having heard the servant who answered the telephone announce his name.

"We don't often have the pleasure of hearing your voice," said Helen archly.

"I don't spend much time in London, these days. Is Lin about?"

"I think so." A pause, in which he could feel her curiosity worming its way along the line. "Shall I call her—or can I take a message?"

"I'd prefer to speak to her," said the General. Normally he would have taken some mischievous pleasure in thwarting his niece's curiosity, but he was conscious only of impatience before Helen answered, on a note of slight offence.

"Hold the line, will you?" He heard her high heels clicking away across the parquet.

"Uncle Edward?"

It was Lin, sounding as though she had been running.

"I wondered if you could drop round to see me for a minute or two." He was at great pains to make his voice sound casual, for there was no knowing how the child might react to so unexpected a summons. It was after nine o'clock. But he had underestimated Lin's intelligence. She answered, after only the slightest pause,

"Where are you?"

"At the Beaulieu Hotel. Top Secret," he added, to confirm her discretion. He guessed that Helen was within hearing.

"Yes," said Lin, and hung up.

"What on earth did Uncle Edward want?"

"Nothing in particular."

"Oh, don't tell me anything! I'm sure I don't wish to pry into any of your secrets with Uncle Edward!"

"Well," said Lin vaguely—her brain had been working quickly; what a nuisance that, on this night of all others, no one was calling for her—"I think I'll go to bed."

"Of course"—Helen shrugged her shoulders—"it would be too much to expect—that you'd give your parents the pleasure of your company—for once in a while."

"You've been complaining about my late hours," frowned Lin. "I didn't get in until nearly three this morning—so you can't be vexed with me for taking an early night, for once."

"Come here; I want to speak to you." Helen's voice recalled her daughter from the foot of the stairs.

"Does it ever occur to you, what a lot of trouble you've been giving us lately?"

"I don't know what you mean. I didn't mean to upset Daddy—or you."

"I suppose you don't call it 'upsetting'—to oblige us to spend the whole of August in town?"

"What's obliging you?" asked Lin, with candid astonishment.

"You don't imagine we can go away, and leave you alone in the house?"

"Why, Mummy, there are the servants, and I wouldn't mind in the least!" Lin was sincerely taken aback by the suggestion that her parents had been inconveniencing themselves for her benefit. "Why on earth didn't you mention it before? I thought it was Daddy's work—of course I knew you usually went away; but, really, you mustn't give me a thought——"

"Don't be ridiculous," snapped Helen. "You know as well as I do, that a girl of your age can't be left in town by herself."

"Why not? Do you mind telling me why not?" demanded Lin. "What do you think I'm likely to do? Let men bring me home after dances and ask them to spend the night?"

"There's no need to be vulgar!"

"You're being vulgar, not me," accused Lin. She struck the back of the chair by which she was standing with her clenched fist. "Even if you were brought up in the old-fashioned way, and you happened to marry young, and—and anyhow, you aren't the kind of person who cares about careers—you ought to know what having a job means!"

"Perhaps, when you've finished abusing me," said Helen coldly, "you'll tell me what kind of a job yours is. So far as I can gather, it seems to consist in sticking on stamps and making cups of tea for those young women who stare at one when one goes in——"

"Somebody's got to do it. What's the use of pretending, Mummy, that work's some kind of a postwar phenomenon that has nothing to do with people like us? Everybody works today—except the so-called working classes, who're paid not to. Nor would I, in their place! If you'd been exploited for generations and generations——"

"There's no need to drag politics into it—and don't let your Uncle Roger hear you saying things like that!"

"I don't waste my breath on Uncle Roger," muttered Lin.

"Your manners certainly show the kind of people you're mixing with." Helen sighed. "Do try to be sensible, child; plenty of girls of your age are in jobs; I'm perfectly well aware of that. I can't think why you couldn't have chosen something pleasant—in a dress shop, or one of the photographers—where at least you'd have been meeting people of your own class——"

"Oh yes; one of the 'plushy' jobs!"

"If that's what you call them. I admit I can't see anything disgraceful about working short hours, wearing nice clothes and not being addressed by your Christian name in a cockney accent! Most girls would have jumped at the position you were offered by Evan——"

"We've been over all this before, and I've told you I don't want to work for Evan." Lin bit her lip; it was not what she had said, exactly. Out of the corner of her eye, she saw with relief that the discrepancy had escaped Helen.

"Well, whatever you want, or don't"—squaring her shoulders, Helen looked her daughter in the face—"let me remind you it's more than two years before you come of age. Even in these days, parents have some authority, I imagine, over their children!—and your father and I have been talking it over. We don't like the way you are behaving, or the company you keep, and we agree it's not improving you——"

"If I'm old enough to earn a salary, I'm old enough to have a life of my own. Oh God!" groaned Lin, "it's not possible we're saying these things to one another—in 1952! It's the sort of thing parents used to say fifty years ago——"

"And that proves that, basically, there's no change!" brought out Helen triumphantly.

"Oh yes, there is. We're the change. I'm not blaming you, Mummy"—she ignored Helen's sarcastic interpolation. "You couldn't help being born before the first war, and growing up in that revolting period of the 'Bright Young Things,' and 'treasure hunts' and the benzedrine racket. Naturally—being what you are —you went reactionary. I was born before the last war, and there's never been time for what I suppose your lot called 'fun.' Your generation thinks that every girl's instinct is to leap into bed with some young man. Well, Mummy, apart from the fact that three quarters of the men one ever meets are pansies—that sort of thing's too easy. If you really care for a person, you want to make a solid thing of it: marriage, a home, children—and all that. Sleeping together—even living together—'s not good enough; when it comes down to brass tacks, it's ducking responsibility. It's old-fashioned, and sort of—cheap." She gave a gasp as she caught sight of the clock. "Mummy, I must go up—really—if you'll excuse me. Say good night to Daddy for me, will you?—and tell him, as I'm not going to Granny's for the week end, I'll play golf with him on Saturday afternoon, if he likes."

She did not stop to see the suddenly softened and relieved look on Helen's face, as she rushed up the stairs. Like Anna, Helen was thinking how little one knew the young. Of course, characters like hers and Norman's must have put some kind of foundation under that seeming wildness. So Anna, after all, had not won!

"You're looking very cheerful!" observed Norman, as she walked into the drawing room.

ii

"I'm so sorry to have kept you waiting, Uncle Edward," said Lin, appearing suddenly before the General, where he sat sunk in one of the vast armchairs which are part of the furnishing of any reputable hotel. She had thought, mistakenly, he was dozing, and that he looked very much older than the last time she had seen him—which was in some restaurant, months ago. Perhaps, after a certain time, age came on people rapidly. His miniature elegance belonged to a past barely legendary to the majority of the people by whom they were surrounded; before disturbing him, Lin's eye covered comprehensively the adjoining company. Young though she might be, Camelhurst and the Court had taught her some kind of discrimination; what a spiv lot they were! And what would happen to a society of which, since the war, all the dregs seemed to have risen to the surface?

He struggled to his feet, to welcome her.

"This is nice of you, child. I hope it wasn't too—complicated."

"Not a bit. Ostensibly, I'm in bed," said Lin cheerfully. "I came down the back stairs and up through the area—after a slight randan with Mummy; oh, nothing to do with this. Only the periodical, maternal jeremiad on the shortcomings of the rising generation."

Although he was far from a mood for levity, the General could not forbear to smile.

"What will you drink?"

"Some coffee, please."

"Not a dry Martini?" He cocked an eyebrow as he nodded to a waiter.

"No, thanks; I'm on the wagon. I had rather a lot of champagne last night," she told him candidly. There was no point, thought the General, in wondering what his mother would have said if Anna, at Lin's age, had talked of being "on the wagon," and confessed to an overdose of champagne. Lin, he thought, looked a good deal older than at their last meeting; no less pretty—prettier, if anything, in her dark tailor-made, sprinkled on the lapel with little diamond darts—but quieter, more poised and more serious. He told the man "A pot of coffee," and called him back to ask, "Isn't there any place where one can be out of this—rabble?"

"There's the little smoking room, sir—through there; it's generally pretty quiet at this time of the evening." He hurried ahead of them, to switch on the lights. The General stood aside, for Lin to pass him.

"Why anything should be called a 'smoking room,' in these days, when any place is virtually a bar parlour!"

"We could have gone up to your room, I suppose," she said innocently.

The General brushed this aside; in his category, one did not conduct a young woman to one's bedroom. The small room was empty.

"Where's your grandmother?" he shot at her.

Lin blinked.

"Well—well—I don't——" Her eyes fell; no, one could not tell lies to Uncle Edward.

"Cut it out, Lin," he said wearily. "Where's Anna?"

"If—if you want to know"—she stammered—"she's turning up at Queen's Terrace, sometime tonight."

"How on earth do you know?"

"She sent me a long wire. She's been away, you know——"

"I certainly do know! What the devil's it all about?"

"Well, I suppose she felt like taking a little holiday."

"And why, may one ask, did she wire to you?"

"*I* don't know, Uncle Edward!—except she was sorry about putting me off this week end and asked me to come in for lunch tomorrow. Evan's not back yet."

"You know?"

"About that thing in the paper? Yes, I saw it. I told her myself."

He drew a painful breath.

"That's something to be thankful for, at any rate. So you've known about them—all along?"

"About Grandmamma and Evan not being married? No, I didn't know a thing, until she told me."

"That"—he looked at her with his haggard eyes—"must have been a shock."

"No. Not particularly—I wasn't in a frame of mind to be shocked. It was such a filthy trick, to play on Granny—putting that notice in the papers!"

"How did she take it?"

"Can't you imagine? Wonderfully! You know that loftiness of hers, and her habit of thinking about everybody but herself. I stayed a few days, but—oh Uncle Edward! He *ought* to have come back—not left her to face it all by herself!"

"Go on—tell me."

She told him, rapidly, about the incidents at Wantage, and about Helen's descent, and the letters—a few of which, the kinder ones, Anna had shown her.

"I should think there would be plenty of horrid ones, as well—and you know what villages are; the news would be all round—especially after Mother's arrival, and dragging me back to town. Mummy does such stupid things, at times. . . . Of course, that's why she—Granny—went away. I think she was quite right—though I do wish she'd sent for me. It will make everything different, when Evan's there——" She broke off; his face, she thought, looked like a little Chinese carving—one of those yellowed bits deeply pocked with black by the carver's tool. He made a dragging noise of clearing his throat.

"Lin. I believe—I've heard—that there are times when a man can't be of much help."

"Don't you think"—she heard herself appealing to him: against what?—against some indefinable fear, that had slowly taken shape in the course of their conversation. She went on hurriedly, to outrace it: this soft, slow-moving fear—"I think, don't you, that Anna and Evan were different from the majority of people? She seems to draw her life from him—if you know what I mean. That beastly thing in the papers wouldn't have meant anything to her if he'd been here, to give her confidence. I can't understand his not coming home at once—no business could have been as important as this. Even if he didn't see it himself, in the English papers, someone is sure to have told him——"

"He's married."

"You mean," gasped Lin, "he's back—already?" Of course he had said "they're" married, not "he's" married; willing it so, she drove the points of her nails into her palms.

"Try to take it quietly, Lin. He was married yesterday to a girl in Philadelphia."

". . . This isn't true, Uncle Edward," Lin heard herself say pitifully. She watched his hands shaking as he fumbled some papers out of his wallet.

"We were rung up, last night, from New York: an old friend of your grandmother's—and mine. If I had seen tonight's paper, before ringing you up——"

"Do you mean it's in our papers?"

"In the New York column; they'll probably give it a spread tomorrow—it's too late, I'm afraid, to get at any of the editors." He passed the news sheet to her and leaned back, closing his eyes. "I'm astonished your parents haven't seen it."

"Mummy never reads the evening papers, she listens to the wireless; and Daddy only looks at the stop press and the leader page," she murmured, as she stared at the close print, trying—trying to make sense of it.

> Marriage of the President of Crewe & Company. Mr. Evan Everett Crewe, age 63, was married on Sunday to Miss Marie-Angela Weissmann, 22, daughter of Hugo D. Weissmann, of Weissmann Marks, Inc., steel merchants, Philadelphia, Chicago and New York. Mr. Crewe was formerly married to Miss Henrietta Margaret Cotter, from whom he was separated in 1914, and whose death took place earlier in the month.

"Do you suppose Anna's likely to see that?"

"Oh, don't—not if she's somewhere in the country, in the car." One was bound to snatch at hope. "She's not much of a one for newspapers, at any time." She let the sheet slide from her knee to the carpet; she was feeling dizzy, and terribly sick. It would be too frightful, to be sick in front of Uncle Edward. "A dynastic marriage," she heard herself saying drily.

"Well," said the General, "I think I'd better be getting along to Queen's Terrace."

Looking up at him, Lin understood that—in the whole of his military career—no forlorn hope had held, for the General, the horror of his present errand. Her stomach steadied itself, as she sprang to her feet.

"May I come? Please let me come, Uncle Edward."

"Aren't you rather young, to be involved in all this?" But he looked at her kindly; almost, she thought, with a shade of relief.

"Nobody's young, in that stupid way, any longer."

While a page was getting the taxi, she rushed to the toilet, vomited suddenly and copiously and felt better. Giving a hurried glance in the glass, her eye fell on the scatter pins; with a gasp, she tore them out and was about to fling them into the lavatory pan, when she remembered she had no money with her for the attendant.

"Here—have these"—she thrust them on the astonished woman, and fled back to the entrance hall; the Beaulieu Hotel was not one of her haunts—with luck, she would never see them again.

The night was close; standing on the steps, they saw the light glow up behind the grille and Humble's portly figure advancing towards the door. It was all too calm, too quiet, too orderly— thought Lin—to be true.

"Good evening, sir. Good evening, Miss Lin."

"Has Mrs. Crewe arrived?"

"Not yet, sir; she rang up, about two hours ago, from Hungerford, to say she was on her way. She should be in any minute now——"

He's a good servant, thought Lin; his face is like a mask. But I bet he knows. I bet he and Pulford have been on the phone. All right; I'll show him we can play it his way! She stuck her hands in her pockets and grinned in Humble's face.

"Have a good time in Switzerland, Humble?"

"Very agreeable, thank you, Miss Lin. Can I get you anything, sir?"

"No, thanks. We shan't be staying long; we only came in to make sure madam was all right, after her journey."

"How long does it take from Hungerford?" asked the General, as Humble withdrew.

"Not much more than two hours, I think, at this time of night; it depends how fast she drives. . . . I suppose," said Lin, "I ought to ring Mummy. She *might* pick up the evening paper; she might go into my bedroom—and then there'd be hell's bells."

"You're having more than your share of trouble in all this business." He reached up and patted her shoulder kindly.

She crossed the hall into the little telephone room, with its chinoiseries, and its scent, which was Anna's, and all her pretty possessions, arranged in lifeless order on the table. With a sensation of nightmare, of walking in her sleep, Lin lifted the receiver.

"She's expected back from the country. I might—I might be stopping the night."

"Kind of you—to let us know! So this is what you mean, by 'going to bed.' So now you've started to be deceitful——"

"Please don't get steamed up, Mummy. . . . Have you read the evening paper?"

"What?" Helen's voice faltered, flattened and failed. "There's not—something else, is there?" She was almost inaudible.

"Please read the New York column."

"Do stop being mysterious! What is it?"

"Evan's married."

The silence was so long that she wondered whether Helen could —possibly—have fainted. She was aware of the General, coming into the room, as she faltered—"Mummy?"

". . . not . . . possible. . . ."

"I'm afraid it is."

"I'm coming round."

"No; please don't. Uncle Edward's here——"

"Do you mean to say *that's* what he rang you up about? I never heard anything like it! Treating me as if it were no business of mine!"

Before Lin could reply, the receiver was taken out of her hand. She listened to his voice, flattening out all the indignation at the other end of the line.

"Helen?—I gather Lin's told you. Yes, it's a bad show. . . . No, I don't think you and Norman can do anything by coming round. I hope Anna will get to sleep early—I'm going to give her a sleeping draught."

"She's *my* mother!" Helen was whimpering. "Surely, I've got as much right as anybody!"

"Shall we leave 'right' out of the question, until tomorrow?" said the General quietly. "Tomorrow she may be prepared for sympathy, and comfort; tonight—she'll be better left alone."

"Alone? I don't see why Lin—— That *infamous* creature!" burst, with the full force of Helen's lungs, down the telephone.

"Good night," said the General.

He glanced at his watch.

"I'm going along to my chemist; he has a prescription of mine——"

"Don't be long, will you?"

He gave her a look of understanding.

"Come with me, if you like."

"No; one of us must be here, when Anna arrives."

Her lips shook, she crumpled, dropping her head on his shoulder. We'll never know, thought Edward, how it works: this queer combination of weakness and strength, in the young. I shouldn't have allowed her. . . .

"I beg your pardon," said Lin, dabbing her eyes.

"All right now?"

"Of course. And"—she glanced at the clock—"of course you'll be back, before Anna comes in."

With his departure, a quivering silence settled on the house. Somewhere, in the kitchen, or perhaps upstairs, the Humbles were anxiously trying to do their best. But the empty rooms—the drawing room, and the little *salon* through the archway and the telephone room—which were in darkness, though she had switched on two or three of the drawing room lights—were like—were like a death house!

If I hadn't happened to fall in love—in a sort of way—I could never have understood all this. It's the whole of Anna's life.

It's like watching over a corpse! Any moment, the ghost of Anna will walk in—without even knowing it's a ghost—and we, Uncle Edward and I, have got to tell her. I've got to help kill the person I love best in the world. I'm a sort of assassin.

It was too intolerable down there: among the pictures, and the sculpture, and the objects of jade and quartz that Anna cherished—mainly because they belonged to him. All her own things—the portraits, and a few old-fashioned but charming, though valueless, still lifes, left to her by her mother, had gone down to the Court, to be distributed through the guest rooms, where she wandered sometimes, renewing her acquaintance with them. Evan's taste must dominate there, as well as in the London house: Evan's primitives, his abstracts, his drawings, signed Epstein, or John—Lin gave a smothered exclamation, and fled up the stairs, straight into Gertrude, coming out of Anna's bathroom. The old woman's eyes met the girl's, exchanged a flash of feminine complicity, switched away. As always, when she was uneasy, Gertrude looked bad-tempered, forbidding and disobliging. Lin's lips twitched into a mechanical smile.

"Hello, Mrs. Humble. Had a nice holiday?"

"Is madam back?" She disdained frivolities; the flesh sagged anxiously on its ugly framework.

"Not yet. The General and I came in——"

"Mr. Edward's here, is he? I suppose you'll all be wanting some supper. There's nothing but eggs—and some asparagus. The shops was shut, when madam telephoned——"

"Don't bother; we don't want anything—and you know what Granny is!"

"Tearing about by herself in the car at this time of night! Wait till I get at that Pulford!" To Lin's astonished embarrassment, Gertrude's eyes filled with tears. "And Mr. Crewe—changing his plans at the last minute! How's anybody to know where they are?"

She's old and she's very tired, thought Lin, laying—as Anna might have done—her hand on the old woman's shoulder. She's devoted to Anna; she's heard something from the Pulfords—and it's all been too much for her. She felt the shoulder, hard, resistant and resentful, under her hand.

"Don't worry," she said gently. "Go to bed, Gerty"—she had never said "Gerty" before, but it was part, somehow, of being "grown up," of assuming authority—"it's nearly midnight—and I'll look after Granny; I can poach her an egg, or boil her some milk, or whatever she wants, when she comes in."

Gertrude stiffened.

"Me go to bed, before my lady comes in?" She shook Lin's hand off, with a noise between a grunt and a sob. Suddenly she burst out, "It was all in the cards! I'd never have gone away, but Miss Anna made me! I'd never have gone——"

Lin stared after her along the landing. The baize door swung after her with a dull *clok*.

Lin retreated to the drawing room; sat on a couch, under a lamp, pretending to look at an album of reproductions; seeing nothing. A bell whirred faintly. She leapt, to let Edward in. She answered his questioning look.

"No."

iii

For half an hour they had kept up a faithful pretence of reading. The General was a distant dwarf, hunched into the corner of the Knole couch, whose yellow cushions, in some terrifying fashion, matched his flesh.

Anna should have been in, at least an hour ago. Could there have been an accident? Her eyes fixed on the print, Lin tried to think coldly. If there had, would it not be a mercy? If Anna could die, in happy ignorance of Evan's perfidy—who among those who loved and mourned her, and who knew, would not be thankful? But God, thought Lin, with rare bitterness, was not as good as that. An accident did not mean death; it meant, more probably, the addition of physical to spiritual suffering—and neither strong enough to cancel out the other.

". . . to betray her, like that, with a chit . . . !"

The exclamation, bursting from the corner of the couch, jerked Lin's head up.

"But—if he was going to—it would be!" She listened to her own voice, aghast.

Handsome—old—wolf: who said that?

"What do you mean?" He was standing in front of her. "What are you talking about? I thought you were fond of Evan."

It was like an abscess, bursting inside one: something that had grown there, and one had forced oneself to ignore, for years—and years. . . .

"I used to be, when I was little."

"Out with it!"

This, I suppose, thought Lin, is how one feels when one goes to confession. She heard the words coming slowly, like the dripping of water.

"It was when I was about fourteen. It was the holidays. Some of the girls came home with me, to the Court. One night there was dancing. I danced with Evan three or four times. It was hot, and I was thirsty. The drinks were in the anteroom—you know it. But he insisted on taking me into the—I don't think they called it the Green Parlour, then; it was just a nondescript sort of little room, opening out of the ballroom. He made me sit down and went to fetch me some lemonade, or something. He sat down on the arm of the chair, and made jokes while I drank it. Then he put his arm round me. . . ."

"Go on."

"He—we'd often 'cuddled'; I remember going to sleep on his knee, when I was very little. I didn't think anything of it, until. . . ."

"All right; I understand."

"I tried to get away, and he wouldn't let me. Then he began to kiss me. He'd always kissed me—but not like that. I managed to get away. . . . After that," said Lin, in a low voice, "I was always frightened of him. I couldn't show it, for Anna's sake; but I took care never to be alone with him. It wasn't easy, because he was always trying to trap me. It made me—sort of—despise him."

"Anything more?" His voice was flintlike.

"Not so far as I was concerned. But Anna always let me take my school friends home for the holidays. And some of them told me——"

"What?"

"Oh—that he'd 'tried it on.' I'm sorry; I know it's a vulgar expression. Most of them took it as a joke; one idiot—I had positively to scare the life out of her, to prevent her telling Anna."

"You mean to say, Anna never knew any of this?"

"You know how Evan was perfect in her eyes! I've even heard her joke about his 'volcanic effect' on young girls. She trusted him—oh, to the point of lunacy! And I suppose she infected me, up to a point, with her own trustfulness. I made myself think—I suppose, because I wanted to—that his flirtations meant nothing; I persuaded myself that he was only vain, and rather silly, because—Uncle Edward: can you imagine anyone letting down a person like Anna? If she didn't mind, I used to tell myself, why should anyone else?"

"So that's why you wouldn't take the job at Head Office."

"Oh—Granny told you? Of course. The girl whose place I was to take—well, it's just a guess; but I felt pretty sure she'd been Evan's mistress. She was just his type—thin, and mid-blondish, with rather a nice voice. Perhaps she got tiresome, or Evan got bored with her. Oh—one can feel these things: there's no sound reason for suspicion, and you're rather ashamed of yourself, but—you see the red light, and that's enough: unless you're a fool!

"He was terribly careful, after he saw I wasn't playing—but I could feel him tracking me down. He was always giving me presents —through Anna; so that I couldn't refuse, for fear of upsetting her. And the offer of that job was just—an arrow, shot in the air! He knew I was crazy to find a job of some kind, and that Mummy would make it as difficult as possible. He got her thoroughly on his side—and it was sheer murder, getting out of it! If you want to know, that's why I threw myself at Henry Crome and absolutely made him get me into Mynte's—to put an end to the argument. If

I'd waited, I could have got a heavenly job with Phena—Granny's dress man—modelling his autumn collection——"

"Hush."

The bell was purring. Edward and Lin leapt to their feet; he gave her a look that passes, ordinarily, only between men; saw her blanch and brace herself.

"This is *it*." She nodded, her lip caught in her teeth. She heard his crisp footsteps cross the hall, heard him call to Humble—"It's all right; I'm letting madam in"—and——

"Edward!" Anna's gay voice. "How wonderful. I thought you were somewhere off the Hebrides."

"And I thought you were at the Court."

"We seem to have stumbled on each other's hidden lives. Look, darling; do you think I can leave the car outside? It's such a bore, to run it round to the garage."

"I could take it round for you——"

(Oh no, Uncle Edward; oh, for God's sake, please don't!)

"—or you can park it under the street lamp; it will save your battery. Where's your key?—and what about the baggage?"

"Only this little case—and something I bought in Hungerford. Do you think you can manage it?—it's rather heavy. I'm not sure if it's Spanish or Italian—but the most adorable thing; about *this* high"—her voice retreated with their footsteps; Lin, her knees trembling, strained to hear the conclusion—"just what we've been looking for, to fill that niche at the foot of Evan's bed."

Lin uncurled her fingers, and looked at the dints left in her damp, pink palms. This was worse than they had expected; it was shooting down a bird of paradise. . . .

The lights in the hall made a halo about Anna, as she walked in, carrying in her arms—as if it were a baby—a wooden figure, with faint traces of colour and gilt about it. Her cheeks faintly glowing, she had a gay, uplifted look, a look of victory; the hair rolled back like spray from her square, pure brow.

"Isn't it beautiful? Won't he love it?—*Lin!*" She stopped dead.

"My blessed child! Well, you two have prepared a surprise for me." She deposited the wooden angel on a couch, and swept Lin into her arms.

(Please, Uncle Edward, come quick. . . .)

"I'm terribly late." She tossed her gloves on the table. "I'm a fool in the dark, and I hate arterial roads, and I got all knitted up with one-way streets and the traffic streams at Hyde Park Corner. But it's marvellous to be driving again, and I'm going to do all the 'chauff'-ing in the future, except dress-up occasions and theatres, and—darling, you do look rather peaky," she broke off. "What is it? Too many late nights and too long hours in the office? . . . Isn't this room too terrible, without flowers. Where's Gertrude? She'll have all the time she wants, now, to scrub and polish, before Evan gets back."

"Wh-where's Uncle Edward?"

"Putting the car under a street lamp. . . . Isn't that lovely?" She indicated the wooden image; her words, her movements had the fluttering inconsecutiveness of a moth. She dropped on the couch, with one arm round Lin and the other round her treasure. "I'm so sorry about last week end. I thought you'd understand."

"Yes, I did."

"And I'm only up for a couple of nights—to see the Humbles, and get this fixed in Evan's room. It's the wrong period, and nationality, and everything, but won't it look wonderful, with the Chinese carpet?"

The General appeared in the doorway, like a little, withered doll; some such thought appeared to strike Anna, for she said quickly,

"Edward? You look terribly tired."

"Here's your key." He gave it to her.

The excitement of driving in London—all that unaccustomed tension of coping with traffic lights, and avoiding the swoop of the leviathans which, since last she had driven, seemed to have monopolized the highway—began to die down. Her mind cleared. She sat still, looking from one to the other; feeling, with the antennae which had served her since childhood, trouble in the air.

"What's the matter?"

Silence.

She got up. She was aware of Lin's protective movement, as she rose beside her, and slipped her arm quickly round the child's waist; if protection was needed, it was for her to afford it. All her anxiety rushed towards these two—Lin and Edward; in the crystal world that contained her, and Evan, and the wooden angel, there was no space for inquietude.

"Edward? *Not Griselda?*"

He told her. . . .

iv

Somewhere a clock struck three. The light was on, at the bed head; the rose and lilac gauze made a tent about the elegant figure, propped upright against the pillows. Lin faltered in the doorway. Anna's head turned slowly.

"All right, dear; I'm awake."

"I just wondered if you'd like some tea, or—or anything."

Anna smiled and held out her hand; it was cold and steady and firm in Lin's shrinking palm. And the smile was the smile of the crucified.

In a chair at the end of the bed, the carven angel leaned block-ishly. Suddenly, for Lin, it focussed all her pain, on Anna's behalf, all her hatred, all the misery of this intolerable hour; she would have liked to take a hatchet, to splinter its smug face, to lop off its hands, folded in priggish submission, and its silly, flattened wings. As she stared at it, the eyelids—lowered in a false meekness— seemed to stir, to let out a glint of pure malevolence. Lin shivered, and wrapped more closely round her the quilted dressing gown she had found in Anna's wardrobe. Would this night never be over? She had promised to ring Edward at six o'clock; three more inter-minable hours. . . . Her knees felt weak; she pressed them against the mattress, to stop their trembling.

"Poor dear," said Anna, in a gentle, wondering voice. She tilted her lovely head, from which all the flesh seemed to have withdrawn, leaving only the pure bone structure, up towards her grandchild's.

"I do so want to do *something* for you, Anna!" burst from Lin's trembling lips.

"Do you? Then"—her voice gathered a sudden strength—"don't think evil of Evan. Don't let people say bitter things. Don't ever forget—that those who have sinned against honour suffer worse than those who are sinned against; that they need all we can send them, of love and compassion. Don't forget that I depend on you—more than anybody—to help me to remember all the goodness, all the happiness. . . ."

Am I old enough, am I wise enough, thought Lin, as she drew the door quietly behind her, to support all this? If she'd broken down, even for a moment, it wouldn't impose such a strain on one; but one daren't even cry!—not even by oneself.

She stretched herself on the narrow bed in the dressing room, staring at the wall. Presently she thrust out her arm and switched off the light; it was better to lie in the dark than to stare at pictures, ornaments, hangings, all of which, in some way, were associated with Evan. Why could there not be an earthquake, or something, to destroy all this in a night?

The hours and the half-hours sounded silverily from the clock over the fireplace. Five—at last. It would soon be dawn. Lin rose and drew back the curtains, to look at the thinning sky. The first time I've ever been awake all night. I might as well get dressed.

She was chilled to the bone, and wondered whether it would disturb Anna if she ran the water for a bath. Better to go to one of the other bathrooms. She collected her clothes and crept along the landing. While the water gushed from the taps, she thought of the emptiness, for Anna, of another day; strange, that emptiness can weigh so heavy. Hugging her weak and hollow body, she could feel the weight lodged there, permanently, under her breasts.

In four hours' time I ought to be at work. That means ringing up Richard; I can't leave, until somebody else is here. Richard . . . such a darling; but my heart wouldn't break if I were never to see him again. Isn't that funny. I'd be terribly sorry, of course—but it wouldn't be a case of "willow, willow!" Isn't that funny: to imagine you're in love with a person, and then . . . oh, thank God!

When she was dressed, she tiptoed to the door of her grandmother's room and pushed it ajar.

Anna, apparently, had not moved; she still sat, propped against the pillows, a small, coloured effigy under its tent of lilac and rose. The bedside lamp threw its shadows into eye sockets and cheeks—the shadows violet, the flesh like thin silver-gilt, the hair composed like a wig about the brow. The Islip Chapel! flashed into Lin's mind; her heart, leaping into her throat, almost choked her. It was Anna who had taken them—the three children, for this was before Peter was born—into the small chamber where lay those lords and rulers of men, eternally imbedded in crystal, in the overwhelming majesty of death. Lin opened her dry lips—put her hand to her throat.

Then Anna's hand, stretched on the counterpane, moved faintly. Lin gulped and felt her face burning as the blood ran back to her head.

The silent house was withdrawing itself from darkness as she ran downstairs; a thin, watery pallor, seeping through the high windows, drained the surroundings of colour and liquefied woodwork and paint. Lights were still on in the lower rooms, and turned livid as she flung back the curtains. A thin haze of summer rain was wetting the pavements. She went into the telephone room.

"Uncle Edward?"

"Well; what news?"

"She hasn't been to sleep. She's just as she was when you left us."

"I'll send Maxwell in," said the General, after a pause. "He'll probably give her an injection. What about you? Can you stay, for the present?"

"Oh yes; I've got dozens of things to do."

"I've been talking to Griselda; she's coming up on the nine-o'clock. We think the best thing to do will be to take Anna down to Camelhurst."

At noon, or thereabouts, Anna turned her head, and her blank eyes showed vague recognition of the face of Gertrude Humble.

"Gerty. Where've you been?" Her speech was blurred.

"Packing your things, Miss Anna."

Anna's brow knitted confusedly—and cleared.

"You'd—better—read the cards for me—Gerty."

Gertrude's worn face twisted.

"There'll be plenty of time for that—down at Camelhurst," she muttered—as she signed to the uniformed figure behind her to help her to lift her mistress out of bed.

CHAPTER XII

From dark to light, and back to dark again—there was no other way of knowing day from night—Anna's mind floated in cloudy water; foundering a little more each hour, then briefly upborne by a clear bubble of thought that dissolved almost in the moment of its conception.

Who can foresee the crises of the human soul, its mysterious excursions towards the forbidden? How dread was that moment, when you found yourself in the grip of a desire that ran contrary, not only to the whole current of our lives, but to the thing called honour?—that was going to cover you with the blight of universal condemnation, and destroy something that once you valued next to life itself?

Nobody but I will understand the way you did it. I do, of course. When you've made up your mind, there's nothing to be gained by talk: discussion, argument—all the long-drawn-out misery of explanation, which, in the end, explains nothing. . . . As it had to be done, you took, perhaps, the best way out—even though it meant depriving me of the one thing you could have left with me: assurance of your confidence. You couldn't have thought I would weep, or cling, or reproach you! And it never occurred to you, that I might have helped to shield you from the bitterness of those who don't understand.

Not to blame, not to justify. Those are the important things—if one can only rise to them. If one can find strength.

For forty years, consciously or unconsciously, my life has been planned for the pleasure or convenience of one man. For twenty of them, it has been you. I poured myself into you like water, I took my shape from you. I only asked you to contain me.

It's pulling out the plug. It's the water rushing down the pipe. . . .

I wish you could have told me what tremendous thing it was, that made you sacrifice us both. Were you suddenly tired of a sterile fidelity? Did your age and mine stalk suddenly, an ungainly ghost, across the bright panorama of the last few weeks? Did you suddenly doubt my ability to pick up the pace that suited you, and remember the shortness of time, and feel you must, at all costs, make the most of it? Probably you were right; but surely there was never anything between us to prevent your telling me all that, and depending on me to understand? I've always known about the attraction youth held for you, and never grudged those who possessed the gift it wasn't in my power to give you. I trusted you completely, and, even now, nothing will ever convince me you let twenty years *burn* for the sake of young limbs, young flesh, the stimulus of young blood. Why didn't you tell me you wanted a son?

How stupid, how vain I've been—in imagining that I could fulfill all your needs, as you fulfilled mine; one sees these things too late. But you blinded me with your kindness. No woman has the right to impose on her lover the sacrifice I imposed on you. I would have taken your child, by whatever mistress, and brought it up lovingly, as my own. I made my own children the excuse for failing in my duty to you, and perhaps this is my punishment for being dishonest. Perhaps your name and the power it carries could have made up to your son for being born out of wedlock; perhaps I had no right to cut off from the next generation the stream of knowledge and experience he would have inherited from you. If that is so, you have more to forgive than I.

I'd have died for you. Sometimes to die is easier than to live. I shall love you till I die.

ii

Fifty-eight—nearly fifty-nine—years ago, thought Anna—while she waited for me to be born, Mamma lay in this bed, listening to these same sounds: the stable clock, striking the hours and half-hours; the tiny squeak of the weather vane, as it swings from east to west; the clack of the pump handle in the stable yard; the cooing and the scratching of the pigeons' pink feet on the leads; the gurgle of wind in the chimney and the shell-like rustle of the trees, before autumn filled the air with their flying gold and scarlet.

Sometimes she got up, to rest her arms on the sloping window sill, and see the bubble of the early-morning moon floating over the spinney, and the little heads of fallow deer come poking through the mist—making the most of their last hour of proud, exquisite solitude before broad day let loose its tide of industry across the park and pastures. Did she feel it was all worth while, the discomfort and the heaviness—to bring a child into so lovely a world? Did she feel impatient, in a celestial dawn, and cry to the child in her womb, "Come, come!—you mustn't miss this!"—and then grow calm, in the thought of the innumerable dawns that awaited little Anna Fitzalan? "I never doubted you'd be a girl," she, sometime, told her daughter. "I laughed when they suggested boys' names for you: Bertrand, and Basil, and Ralph—names that belonged to your father's family, and mine. So far as I was concerned, you were Anna, from the beginning." Yet Anna knew, instinctively, she had never wanted a girl. Edward was ten when, unexpectedly, she was conceived. Lady Fitzalan resigned herself to the inevitable; since she had to bear another child, it was bound to be a daughter.

One of Anna's earliest memories was lying there, curled into her mother's arm: listening to stories about the man with a falcon and the lady with a greyhound, stitched by some remote ancestress into the tapestries which drew an enthralling privacy round their games of make-believe. She learned words like hennin, gyrfalcon and mangonel: no less magical than the "roly, poly, gammon and spinach" sung by Nanny in the nursery. She grew up in a world conditioned, by tradition, to security. She assumed, from childhood, responsibility to those less privileged than herself. She accepted, in all matters, the lead and the authority of her brother Edward, who, someday, would be the master of Camelhurst.

Apart from a few minor changes—the candlesconces she remembered loaded with wax had been adapted to electricity, and the closet where Orinthia Fitzalan's women powdered her false and fabulous head was transformed, about the beginning of the century, into rather a cramped and old-fashioned little bathroom—nothing had altered. The treetops she watched as a baby were still there, beyond the deep mullion of the window: dark lace in winter, then green haze, then a thick brocade, spired with pink, and finally—as now—shining gold and gilt, with patches of burnt crimson. "I'm sending you a little leaf, to lay over your poor, sore heart!" wrote Mamma, when she was at school in Paris, and terribly homesick. She remembered borrowing a pot of gum, and sticking the Camelhurst leaf, with painful earnestness, over her breast.

How long have I been here? wondered Anna.

Her fingers, weak and clumsy, groped for her diary. The pages slid through them—blank, blank—back to the middle of August. Was it really only nine weeks? She seemed to have been lying there for ever, in an eternity of shameful indolence. Waking, sleeping. "To sleep—perchance to dream." Ah—that, please God, never, never again. Never again, beside her on the pillow, the thin, exclusive face, of which she knew each line, each hollow, each pore: the quizzical eyes, flecked with a golden brown that brought light and life into the cold, basic grey. Never again the strong, exploring hands. Never the laughter, the sharp moods and the soft moods, and the moods when, as lovers can be, they were courteous friends, coolly discussing matters that touched their minds, but not their hearts; or the moods in which he spilt his brilliance over her as carelessly as he spilt it on his friends: when he was witty, or acid, or fiendish . . . !

No more waking to new plans, projects, excitements. No more share in the imponderabilities of a man's life.

What's the answer? Anna asked herself distantly.

Death.

She dismissed it, with an involuntary grimace of distaste: clumsy, unmanageable, melodramatic—ill-mannered!

The immediate problem that presented itself seemed to be the endurance—not of existence, but of the solicitude of friends. Griselda's grey benevolence; her noiseless entrances, her poor, distorted eye, sending its crooked shaft of kindliness across the bed; her endless anxieties—"Are you hot, are you cold, are you thirsty, will you read, can you eat?"

Letters—from those who had recovered from their horrified silence. She opened a few—pitying those who, so painfully, so delicately, offered affection, in place of that for which there is no replacement. A long, long letter—much of it illegible—from Aunt Belinda: with many references to God, all underlined, and blurred with tears. Poor darling old dear; why should you be hurt? But it will pass. You will find your consolation, somewhere, in your eleven-o'clock Communion, and your evensong, and the radio services! For Thy goodness to people like Aunt Belinda, O God, I praise and thank Thee. Continue her in Thy strength . . . and, for what Thou hast done to me, help me to forgive Thee, O Lord.

Lin's flowers, that arrived punctually, twice a week. (The flowers people sent! It was almost like taking part in one's own pompes funèbres!) Could Lin be accepted as a reason for living? No false sentiment! Anna adjured herself. Lin, with the whole of her youth before her, needs me no more than I need her. No clinging; nothing that might make the child conscious of me, as an obligation.

Poor Helen, and poor Roger.

They arrived together, humbly awaiting the doctor's permission, to see their mother: Helen so miserably kind, so utterly at a loss! Anna's heart ached for her; my poor child, can't I spare you this? Roger's deportment was perfect; so might Hugh have behaved at a regimental funeral, involving sentiment as well as respect. Taking his mother's hand, he lifted it to his lips—walleyed, speechless; and hurriedly left the room. She suspected tears in his eyes. Were they for her, or for his blighted prospects? For God's sake, prayed Anna, inwardly, let me be generous! The boy cares about me. . . . Helen remained, wretchedly blowing her nose. Who had warned them— it must have been Edward—not to speak Evan's name? That, at least, must not be!

"I hear they're back—Evan and his wife. I'm so glad she'll see the Court, before the leaves are off."

"*Mother!*" gulped Helen, and dashed from the room. In her confusion, she failed to close the door. Her encounter with Griselda was audible, past the lady with the greyhound and the man with the falcon. "Aunt! Do you think her mind's affected?" "Hush"— and the click of a latch.

How stupid of me, thought Anna; I'd forgotten the Court belongs to me. What a pity. It would have been nice, for their honeymoon—but it might embarrass them. . . .

iii

"The General's just arrived, Mrs. Crewe; he would like to see you, if you feel well enough."

"Do you know," said Anna slowly, "I think I'll get up."

"That's right," said the nurse cheerfully. "I'll get your dressing gown; I was wondering if you'd feel like having your dinner on the little table."

"No. I mean—get up. Dress. Go downstairs."

"Well—isn't that going a bit too far? There's no company, and

I'm sure Lady Fitzalan would understand, if you just slipped something over your nightgown."

"Thank you," said Anna carefully, "I'll get dressed. Please send Gertrude to me. Gerty, I want to put my clothes on," she said, as the old figure trundled into the room.

"What do you want to wear, Miss Anna?"

"Has that pink thing come, they were making me at Phena's? (Nothing that has associations. What am I going to do with my old clothes? Gerty must cope with them.)

"Yes, but you haven't tried it on."

"That doesn't matter."

After living for nine weeks in a nightgown, it was strange to be offered one's ordinary clothes.

"There's something the matter with this corset. Get me another. . . . But what is it? Look, it slides off my hips!"

"You've dropped weight, Miss Anna."

"Well, fix it, can't you? . . . That's better. It feels funny, but I suppose it will hold my stockings up. All right, Gerty; drop the frock over my head. . . . No, no; it can't possibly fasten there—let me sit down. Now get your glasses on. Isn't there another row of hooks, somewhere?"

To feel so light—so light, like a ghost!—it couldn't be natural. She accepted Gertrude's support, to stand before the cheval glass and see herself—a mere sliver of crushed pink velvet, topped with an ungroomed crop of lifeless, silver-gilt hair!

"My collarbones: oh, how ugly. Find me a scarf, or something."

"That pink gives you a bit of colour," encouraged Gertrude.

"Not nearly enough."

She dropped on the stool, and set her elbows, for support, on the table. The old routine was mechanical: foundation, then rouge, then powder. Green, for the eyelids. The eyelashes—bother; a spurt of black. Try again. Oh—worse! She groped for a tissue, and blotted out the disastrous result. Again—but my hand's shaking——

"Gerty: couldn't you do my eyelashes for me?"

"If I was you, I wouldn't bother; it's only the General and her ladyship."

"Do my eyelashes."

Vanity dies last. "A painted death." I look like Grandmamma. ". . . Come, Anna; it's time you went to bed."

"Presently; I feel—lazy!"

"Don't treat her like an invalid." Dear, understanding Griselda! Edward was helping his wife out of her chair, offering her his arm. She bent, to lay her soft, dry lips to Anna's cheek. "Good night, my dear; I'll tell Gertrude you'll be up presently."

Edward and Griselda, going slowly and carefully to the door, with the cat and the dog behind them. These old people—my brother and my sister-in-law. And now I'm in their category.

Edward came back; she watched him, moving about the room, switching off some of the lights. The vast, kind room, lined with family records, narrowed to a small pool of light round the hearth, with its glowing heap of logs. He lit a cigar.

"Now—Edward. What were you wanting to tell me?"

She saw him start.

"To tell you?"

"Come; we don't prevaricate."

His small, tense face bent vexed towards the rosy tip of the cigar. Poor Edward; must I hurt you, too?

"You've heard from Evan," she hazarded.

"From Patcham."

The name of the solicitors startled her.

"Patcham? But what can they——"

"He proposes"—Edward's voice was brittle—"a settlement."

"A—? No; this is a misunderstanding," she heard herself saying.

"Nothing of the kind." The General spoke brusquely. She understood; he was right, over matters like this, to ignore personalities. "The Court belongs to you; that's in the previous agreement. But he realizes that its upkeep is beyond your means. He wants——"

"Don't say it." She checked him, with an upflung hand.

"You don't wish to live there?"

She gave him a look that left no need of words.

"My dear; I know. But have you thought—at all—about the future?"

She shook her head.

"Will you stop with us?"

"Here?"

"You know we want you."

"I think," said Anna slowly, "I can't make plans—just yet. If I might stay—a little longer——"

"Anna. This is your home."

Can I, she thought, be so wanting in dignity as to weep? Recovering her composure, she said,

"You'll write to Patcham; say I'm grateful—very grateful——"

"I've written. Perhaps, if you approve, you'll sign it."

"My glasses, please."

He found and gave them to her; she took the sheet of paper from his hand and read it slowly.

"Thank you. It's very—adequate. I suppose Evan will see this?"

"Probably." He shrugged his shoulders.

"Lend me your pen."

She added, after some hesitation, a line to the rest, and offered it to Edward, like a pupil, hoping for approval.

" 'I shall be much obliged if you will kindly inform Mr. Crewe how much I appreciate his consideration,' " he read, " 'but I could, in no circumstances, accept his offer.' . . . Anna." She felt the pressure of his hand on her shoulder. "My dear. Do you remember when we used to read the philosophers? 'Gentleness is ever victorious in attack, and'—how did it go?—'secure in defence'?"

"Of course; that's Lao Tze."

"And—'When Heaven would preserve a man, it enfolds him in gentleness'?"

"I remember it all."

"Have you no bitterness?"

"Would you have me add that, to all the rest?"

"Sign it." He put the pen back in her hand.

She wrote "Anna"—and paused.

"Is this what they call 'a legal document'?"

"I suppose it amounts to such."

"Then I can't sign myself 'Anna Crewe.' "

"Why not? It's your legal name."

"Only since the deed poll. I can't possibly use it. It's out of the question."

"What do you want to put? Sturges? I suppose there's nothing against it; though I don't know what Patcham will make of it."

"Hugh's name—and Roger's? I've forfeited my right to that as well."

She completed the signature: *Anna Fitzalan.*

When Evan sees this, he will understand that I wish to claim nothing; nothing that belongs by right to someone else.

iv

For the first time for months, the weight of her body was a living tiredness; she was able to locate small, individual areas of pain in the limbs which, after so long, were called upon to support the unaccustomed weight of her body, and to separate small, individual cells of pains in her mind, which had started, at last, to assume control of her actions.

These she marked with some apprehension; for they told her that the time was at hand when she would be required to resume the burden of living. She found herself shrinking back towards the tender oblivion which had shrouded her return to Camelhurst: to the weeks full of childish sounds and thoughts and memories that spread a protective veil over the intervening years. If only, by some act of spiritual surgery, it were possible to cut out all those brain cells that were concerned with the last forty years of life, and go back, bearing for torch and talisman, the name that had belonged to a happy child of eighteen!

> Having emptied yourself of everything, remain where you are.

Strange, that Edward should remember, tonight, their earnest, youthful struggles with the *Tao*.

> This giving over of oneself to the inevitable is called preservation.
> He who knows this preservation is called enlightened.
> He who knows it not continues in misery.
> He who knows it is great in soul.
> He who is great of soul is prevailing.

What an unaccountable memory I have—that mislays so many things of importance and preserves that which we learned, Edward and I, with so much solemn perseverance, just before he went out to France in 1914. I wonder how many soldiers knew the *Tao*? He had just discovered it, and was eager to share it with me.

> Men go forth from Life and enter into Death.
> The Gates of Life are thirteen in number, and the same are the Gates of Death. . . .

We knew nothing about the allegorical meanings, or the mystic content; we took it all very literally.

> One who knows how to safeguard Life . . . may enter into battle without fear of the sword.

He sent that to me on a field postcard just before going into action. I knew, of course, it meant the spiritual life. I must start to read the *Tao* again; perhaps I shall be able to understand more of it now.

Is that all there is left?

What are the answers, the consolations, the ways of preserving dignity, for a woman of my age?

Old-fashioned religionists would say that this is my punishment. I have no sense of being punished, or of having invited punishment.

"To have known a great love makes up for everything"—who wrote that to me? One of the kind, lofty sentiments people invent when they are trying to be kind. You only find out its falsity when you apply the litmus of truth to it.

I have all the usual things to do: duties to perform, people to look after. None of that can stop because of what has happened to Evan and me. But things imposed on one as a duty never carry the impetus of free will.

. . . Suppose all this is a nightmare? Suppose, with an effort, I could wake myself up?

Deliberately, knowing the action to be childish, Anna drew the brooch out of her bed jacket and, with a single, ruthless stab, drove the thick gold pin into her left wrist. She pulled it out and, looking at the dark bead of blood that followed it, felt ashamed of her folly. Probably people who open their veins in baths are ashamed—when it's too late.

She knotted her handkerchief round the tiny wound and, catching a shawl round her shoulders, crept out of bed.

There was no moon, but all Camelhurst spread itself in silence under the stars. Immediately below her lay the faint design of the formal garden, patched here and there with light from the windows. A pale circle, with a spot of darkness in the circle, like an artificial eye, was the sundial, round which she and Edward had played, when he was a sturdy youth and she a tottering baby in flounces of stiffened muslin.

There was that dry rustle in the trees which meant they were prepared, in the first high wind, to shower their leaves across rose garden and lawns, and to stand up in their naked splendour as wardens of the ground they had guarded so long. A vagrant scent was in the air; a scent of autumn.

It's autumn! How quickly it has come, thought Anna. How have I come to miss the changes—the cut lavender, the bulbs with their knots of yellowed leaves, lying out to dry; the falling apples; the hard, waxen buds of dahlia, bursting into rockets of pink and orange? Has the winter green started to push through the furrows? Are the children picking up chestnuts in the lanes, and collecting pennies for the guy? Are all the fields trimmed with russet, and the bulls marching calmly with the cows in the high pastures? Is the morning grass bent with heavy dew, and has the first frost come, to nip the gladioli? Have the swallows gone—oh, have they gone, before I had time to say good-bye?

In a week or two, the lovely trees will spread their dark lace against the sky, and the rookeries will be laid bare, and all the sunsets pure gold. Then, one morning, along the branches, will lie the silver coating of rime. All the small streams will be driven under their skimming of ice. The birds will leave the patterns of their feet on a crust of snow. And then—the melting—!

I could not bear—cried Anna's heart—I could not bear, not to see another spring!

The sudden gush, the conviction, took her by surprise. The vision of pale, singing green, of rushing waters, of green spikes darting through the soil—caught the breath in her throat. The calm largesse of nature, reproducing itself without end. . . . Of the little time one had, to partake of that triumph, who, knowingly, would surrender a moment?

These things outlast human pain.

In them lies the secret of eternal quiet.

Of them I am so little—so little!—a part.

> This going back to one's origins is called peace; it is the giving of oneself over to the inevitable.

> Lao Tze